PROXY WAR

VOLUME ONE

PHANTOM WAR
TRILOGY

VOLUME ONE: PHANTOM WAR TRILOGY

PROXY WAR

VOLUME ONE

PHANTOM WAR TRILOGY

Written by
E.L. Speed

Foreword by
Dr. Angela Browne-Miller

Metaterra® Publications

metaterra®
publications

PROXY WAR
Volume One: Phantom War Trilogy

Published in the United States by Metaterra® Publications.
www.Metaterra.com
Library of Congress Cataloging-in-Publication Data.
Speed, E.L.; Browne-Miller, Angela.
Proxy War/E.L. Speed/Angela Browne-Miller – 1st Edition.
1. Fiction. 2. Adventure. 3. Romance. 4. War. 5. Men.
6. Women. 7. Political. 8. Intrigue. 9. Aviation.
10. Viet Nam.
Title:
Proxy War
Volume One: Phantom War Trilogy
Library of Congress Control Number: (noted on website listed above)
ISBN-13: 978-1-937951-03-0 (Paperback)
ISBN 13: 978-1-937951-04-7 (Kindle eBook)
Published in the United States of America for US and worldwide distribution.
Metaterra® Publications, 1 Blackfield Dr 343, Tiburon, CA 94920, USA.
Cover and content illustrations by and copyright ©Angela Browne-Miller.
Book design by and copyright ©Angela Browne-Miller.
Ordering information and bulk ordering information available through Amazon Books; Amazon Kindle. Also contact:
Info@Metaterra.com

Dedication

This book of historical fiction is dedicated to
the Navy pilots and flight officers
who flew combat during the Viet Nam War,
especially the following:

In Memoriam

CAPT Leonard M. Lee – MIA/KIA
CAPT Robert J. Sweitzer – POW
CDR Michael W. Doyle – POW/KIA
CDR Charlie N. James – MIA/KIA
CDR Vincent D. Monroe – MIA/KIA
LCDR Roger B. Innes – MIA/KIA
LCDR J.D. Peace III – MIA/KIA
LCDR Edward D. Estes – POW/KIA
LCDR R. Saavedra – KIA
LT R.C. Nelson – MIA/KIA
LT G.L. Mitchell – MIA/KIA
LT G.S. Perisho – MIA/KIA
LTJG Ronald L. Roehrich – KIA
LTJG William W. Boles – KIA
LTJG William C. Niedecken - KIA

MIA – Missing in Action
KIA – Killed in Action
POW – Prisoner of War

PUBLISHER'S NOTE

This is a work of historical fiction. With the exception of historical figures such as U.S. Presidents, historical events such as the Viet Nam War, and historically related locations such as the U.S. White House, all names, characters, places, and incidents are either the product of the author's imagination or are used fictionally. Note that reference to the Navy ship, U.S.S. Constellation, is not intended to place the fictional events of this novel as occurring on this particular ship, or on any particular ship. Any direct resemblance to: actual persons living or dead is entirely unintentional. (See also the more detailed author notes and observations at the end of this book.)

Additionally, terms and phrases used on the part of certain characters in this book are used to create the atmosphere and dialog of that time and that war. The author indicates that where these terms may be in any way offensive, these are merely an attempt to replicate the tenor of the actions, times and characteristics depicted herein, not an expression of the author's own attitudes.

•••••••

TABLE OF CONTENTS

VOLUME ONE: PHANTOM WAR TRILOGY

FOREWORD
by
Dr. Angela Browne-Miller

I am honored to introduce to readers around the world this classic of our times, and classic for all times, *Proxy War*, Volume One of the *Phantom War Trilogy*, written by E.L. Speed.

Proxy War immerses us in a fascinating yet chilling, romantic yet troubling story of love, war, heroism, confusion, and intrigue. Against the disturbing backdrop and hidden truth about the Vietnam War, E.L. Speed's fascinating piece of historical fiction, *Proxy War,* tells the tale of two dishonest and strong willed presidents, a young diplomat on the brink of treason, and its star protagonist, a naval aviator and war hero. This hero, living the moral dilemma of the period, is increasingly and dangerously conflicted about his role in the War. Nevertheless, he puts his life on the line daily as he fights a *Proxy War* in the skies over Vietnam. Modern warfare and international affairs teach us that a proxy war is a particular type of war, *a war played out in someone else's backyard in hopes of keeping it away from home.*

This work is, in some ways, a Vietnam era Winds of War (Wouk) with a hint of Catch 22 (Heller). Certain chapters do describe the air war over Vietnam as it truly was, with the intensity that We Were Soldiers Once and Young (Moore) brought to jungle warfare, weaving in overtones of A Year of Living Dangerously (Koch).

This engagingly intelligent novel takes the reader from the time of the Tet Offensive and the related demonstrations here in the U.S.

11

(early 1968) to the brink of the Watergate scandal and the Ellsberg Papers (early 1970s). And, in the tradition of *For Whom the Bell Tolls* (Hemingway) and *From Here to Eternity* (Jones), E.L. Speed masterfully and romantically recreates an era. This work reaches to and beyond the White House and skies over Vietnam to capture -- and to then expand well beyond -- the moral dilemma and introspection of *Platoon* (Stone), and does so while applying the tone of intrigue and technical precision of a Clancy novel.

Proxy War is indeed far, far more than a war story. This is the timeless story of the search for honor, truth, and dignity – all in the context of an intensely controversial war and a perilous global Cold War reality, both landmark predicaments of those times. The reader glimpses death as an acceptable solution but only if it is not meaningless. Duty, a rather complex psychological phenomenon, provides the key to understanding choices made, such as the choice to continue fighting while questioning war's very *raison d'être*.

Novelist E.L. Speed has embedded within the psyche of his lead character the angst, lost innocence and moral confusion inherent in America's coming of age during the Vietnam War. Where the fascinating story of the ground war found in *Up County* (DeMille) leaves off, *Proxy War* picks up, sweeping the reader "up close and personal" into first hand, real time air combat. Again the air war as metaphor reveals itself. There is an implied distance combined with a powerful in-your-face reality found in an air war, so far away from the ground, and yet so close to death every second.

No other fictional treatment of the Vietnam War moves so seamlessly from the White House and halls of power in Washington to the combat theatre in Vietnam. No other novel depicts such "shock and awe" regarding President Johnson's targeting choices as his will is carried out with precision and great destruction. No other Vietnam era novel follows its protagonist and main characters from Vietnam to Park Avenue in New York, to Harvard Yard in Cambridge, to secret trips into China, back to Vietnam, and more. And certainly no other novel presents the moral dilemmas and conflicts that an air warrior has the opportunity to confront and attempt to solve.

From the eyes of the air warrior, we participate in the fast moving action, hear the strangely surrealistic sounds, and feel the press of gravity multiplied by ten. This aviator's role is a tradition shared by well known controversial personages on the political stage at the opening of the 21st century -- such as Senator John McCain, President George Bush Senior, Senator John Glenn, Defense Secretary Donald Rumsfeld – all Navy and Marine Corp aviators who flew combat during World War II, Korea and or Vietnam. Clearly, these men who were war heroes remained important figures in other ways as they moved into their senior years. Perhaps they grew still more important than they had been during the wars they fought.

In a particularly unusual category are Vietnam War heroes who were during that war, sometimes ignored, even shunned and belittled at home in the US. Imagine the cognitive dissonance, the shock of being so disrespected, experienced by a duty bound fighter pilot on the ground at home. These men headed back to war having to integrate the treatment they had received at home. Some of these men are still having to integrate the mixed messages of those times.

During the course of *Proxy War*, our troubled "hero" becomes an airborne samurai warrior, programmed to engage in what he comes to see as a hi-tech duel in its most technically "refined" state. Caught between his patriotism, loyalty, and emerging moral crisis, he experiences a dangerous unraveling of his indoctrination, a serious questioning of American foreign policy, and an urgent survival-based need to suppress all this. All the while, he continues daily to kill, see his colleagues killed, and to risk being killed or, worse, downed, captured and tortured -- fighting for those in peril.

No other piece of literature has taken me on such a journey. Thanks to author E.L. Speed, I am drawn into the agony of concurrent patriotism, duty, and doubt over the morality of war today as well as during the Vietnam era. And, I find that I, a most unlikely candidate for such, am pulled, at moments during reading certain chapters, into a mix of perverse fascination and parallel horror, right into aerial combat, prison camp, and paradoxically, the White House. I am taken to places I would normally never go. I experience the actual sensations of supersonic air-to-air combat, high speed ejection, the pain of torture inflicted upon a prisoner of war, the decision of a crashed pilot to kill himself in lieu of being skinned alive, the discovery of the few remains of a dear friend oozing from a recovered helmet, demonstrations back home, and more.

All of these precisely detailed war time experiences are artfully juxtaposed by the author with the piercing degree of passion, longing, isolation, suppressed fear, political intrigue, social unrest, and unflinching honor that only a hotly disputed war enacted on the verge of largely unrecognized global catastrophe can inspire. Played out against the backdrop of the Cold War of the 1960s that was constantly but secretly on the brink of boiling into deadly global nuclear conflict, the conflicted romance, muddled statesmanship, and suggested double-agent activities of other lead characters are compelling and relentlessly unsettling.

Reading this manuscript and engaging in its haunting paradoxes forever changes me. E.L. Speed knows first hand the tale he tells. He's been there, done that, catapulted from a carrier deck, pulled the ejection seat handles, escaped ending up in prison camp, returned to anti-war demonstrations at home after going down off the coast of Vietnam, wondering all the while what in the hell he was doing there in the US and there in Viet Nam – he's "been there got the T-shirt."

Fortunately, this author has lived to tell a great and important story, and to mature his understanding and vast historical knowledge of what he tells. Sadly, many others have not. I thank you very much for this opportunity to share this valuable work with you. With each passing day, as we race deeper into this brave and crazy new world, we can easily see the *Proxy War* realities we face. Can we make our way through the moral and social dilemmas these present? Can we wage a world without *Proxy Wars*? What are the tradeoffs? Who should decide when one man's pre-emptive *Proxy War* is another's homeland invasion?

VOLUME ONE: PHANTOM WAR TRILOGY

And the end of all our exploration
Will be to arrive where we started
And know the place for the first time.

T. S. Eliot
"Little Gidding"
Four Quartets

VOLUME ONE: PHANTOM WAR TRILOGY

PROLOGUE
October 6, 1969

Nervous and trembling, a naïve young reporter pressed her way through the increasingly violent throng of antiwar protesters. From a relatively tame assembly of concerned citizens, the large crowd had, almost without warning, transformed itself into a roiling sea of collective anger. Moving, screaming, struggling bodies surrounded and almost engulfed her. Somehow, she had to get through to the cathedral or be overwhelmed. She knew she was a negligible entity here, a meaningless, nearly unnoticed media person, there for a story and a chance to get her name into print. No one would care if she were injured or worse. She was not one of them. Around her were men and women wearing blood red armbands, old gas masks, torn army fatigues, and even Black Death robes. Their signs, waving furiously in the air like angry balloons, read: "Hell No We Won't Go," "Stop the War Now," "End the Proxy War in Vietnam," and "Stop the Bombing Now!" Their haunting chants grew in tenor and volume culminating in a deafening roar.

Pushed and shoved in the midst of the antiwar pandemonium, the badly shaken young reporter stumbled to a side entrance of the Washington National Episcopal Cathedral. As frightening as the unruly mob was, she was elated that it had enabled her to slip through the cordon of security guards blocking out the uninvited, including the press. Once inside, she tried to stifle her gasps and meld inconspicuously into the solemn congregation as it pretended en masse to ignore the chaos unfolding just outside the massive bronze doors. The slender reporter's eyes darted from face to face and finally slowed to absorb the somber scene. Elegiac strains of Barber's *Adagio for Strings* filled the enormous nave of the great Cathedral, masking the noise of the near riot outside. The reporter stood awestruck by the magnificent but painful ceremony. Not since Jacqueline Kennedy buried her assassinated husband, President John Fitzgerald Kennedy, almost six years earlier had Washington witnessed such an elegant funeral. And, not since Jacqueline Kennedy had there been such a charismatic and beautiful young widow to publicly mourn her dead husband. The fact that this widow was also a fledgling stateswoman and daughter of an internationally renowned Wall Street attorney greatly enhanced the drama. Finally, the reporter spotted the subject of her report, *the* Dr. Marguerite Collins-Marchand.

This morning of October 6, 1969 witnessed the tall, distinguished Dr. Collins-Marchand wearing widow's black, her long blond hair pulled tightly into a bun, bravely bearing her grief. On the right side of the lovely young widow stood her father, Mitchell Collins III, one of the most powerful lawyers of the day. And, on her left, in formal dress blues, stood Navy Lieutenant Lawrence Wolfe braced crisply at parade rest position. With great effort, "Margo" Collins-Marchand choked back wrenching sobs welling up from deep within. Still, she could not control the tears filling her cobalt blue eyes.

As the Dean of the Cathedral mounted the granite podium to address the somber congregation, the *Adagio* faded and the sounds of the turmoil outside could be heard within the great Gothic structure. The

Dean nevertheless began speaking, determined to maintain proper decorum.

> We are here to pay tribute to a fallen hero and to honor his widow and family. Navy Lieutenant Keith Marchand died in battle in a distant land for a nation that he loved, for our great nation, the United States of America. Our words today will never alleviate the pain experienced by his widow, his family, and all who loved him --

The Dean paused a moment as the chants from the crowd outside caught his attention, and then he continued in somber defiance of the noise.

> -- or by a nation in mourning for this hero -- just as our pain will never bring him back to us. But we can promise that his memory will never be lost nor his sacrifice forgotten.

Margo tried with all her heart to conduct herself with the dignity and bearing that her beloved war hero husband, Keith Marchand, would have wanted of her. In fact, it was this thought that enabled her to endure such terrible grief while standing dead center in this most public forum. She prayed for the strength to continue her charade for another hour after which she could privately give vent to her full emotions.

Margo felt herself being watched from all directions. She cringed as she saw from the corner of her eye the alert young reporter scrutinizing her while furiously scribbling notes. I must hang on now, she warned herself, the eyes of the press are on me. She worried: Do any of them wonder or guess how deeply and secretly I empathize with the antiwar protesters outside the Cathedral? If they only knew that a part of me longs to be out there releasing my anger and anguish with the crowd! Of course, Margo knew that she would not and could not reveal this sentiment to anyone, as she was now an important member of the U. S. State Department. And always and even more importantly, she was a very visible member of the Collins family. Margo swallowed hard and stared straight ahead.

Of even greater importance was a more powerful secret Margo kept, a secret which at that very moment was busy changing her life forever. Dr. Margo Collins-Marchand had learned only recently that she was pregnant with the child of Keith Marchand, the love of her life and captain of her heart. Margo stood straight and tall, her right hand resting gently on her still flat stomach, knowing no one could tell. Not even her father knew.

As Mitchell Collins watched his distraught daughter, he told himself he had done the right thing. He reflected on his recent use of considerable political muscle to pressure the Departments of Defense and Navy into declaring that Lt. Keith Marchand had been "killed in action" as quickly as possible. He wanted more than anything to protect his daughter, her career and the Collins name from the limbo-like status of the wife of a serviceman "missing in action." Collins watched the tears fall from his lovely daughter's cheeks and told himself that he was indeed completely justified in his efforts. She should marry again as soon as possible, he resolved. And why prolong this insufferable pain? He asked himself. "Get it over with right away, like this," he mumbled as he surveyed the congregation once and then again rested his eyes on Margo.

Margo felt her father's intensely intrusive gaze and wished he would look away. Seeking whatever relief she could find, she glanced in the other direction, at the tall Navy Officer flanking her left. Lieutenant Larry Wolfe was not only her husband's closest friend in Fighter Squadron Twenty-One; he was the pilot of the aircraft in which

Marchand was flying when they were shot down. She saw the pain written on his handsome boyish face and sensed the survivor guilt he felt so powerfully. Nevertheless, he stood strong and focused, almost without blinking as a tear tracked his tanned cheeks. Inexplicably, she drew strength from him. She felt comforted by his presence.

The somber Dean of the Cathedral continued his address, obviously ad-libbing a little, apparently determined to find a way to incorporate the clamoring events outside into the ceremony within. He gestured toward the doors as he said, "Although our nation is torn in its anguish over the Vietnam War, its causes, its purposes, and its proper conclusion, we nevertheless come together today in unity to honor the memory of our beloved husbands, fathers, brothers, friends, and neighbors who have given that last full measure of devotion to this nation. In our grief, we are one...."

Margo was not listening. Instead, her anguished mind relived her recent meeting with two Naval Officers who had come without an appointment to her office at the U. S. State Department in Washington. Her secretary had announced the surprise visit in a tone and manner that she found disturbing. But Margo had not associated a visit by Naval Officers with personal disaster. She had winced, momentarily fearing that Naval Intelligence had discovered the dark side of her secret visits deep inside Communist China nearly two years earlier. But she hadn't considered death as the reason for the officers' visit. After all, scores of similar young officers served as Naval attaches to the State Department in Washington and in embassies throughout the world without creating concern.

Feeling desperate for a modicum of privacy, Margo now turned her face to the floor. She tried to hide the heartbreak sweeping her face in waves as she remembered how the Naval Officers had come to deliver the news of Keith's death. Dr. Marguerite Collins swayed gently as she was filled with the memory of the moment a few days later when she learned that she was pregnant with Keith's child. His child, she mourned deep inside, a child he will never have the chance to know and love or even know about. A fresh river of tears flowed uncontrollably from her closed eyes. If only she could have sunk into the floor and disappeared, she wished.

Lt. Larry Wolfe turned his head ever so slightly to watch over Margo, ready to catch her if she wilted, fainted, or needed a supporting arm. He saw something disturbing in her face, something he could not interpret. Margo seemed an enigma to Wolfe but then, Wolfe reminded himself, this entire affair was clouded in secrecy. Even the military orders that had sent him and his closest friend, Keith, on that deadly mission just three weeks ago had been Top Secret. Wolfe turned on himself. After all, he had his own painful secrets. Worst of all, he had returned from that mission and Keith had not. What could he have done, what maneuver, what manipulation of the controls could he have used that might have saved Keith's life?

But another secret tormented Wolfe during the ceremony. Wolfe wondered whether he should have told Margo of his persistent feeling that Keith Marchand might still be alive and should never have been declared killed in action, at least not so soon. Wolfe reminded himself that the situation had been and still was far too politically and emotionally charged for him to speak openly about his doubts and questions. Looking at Margo, he concluded that perhaps some things are better left unsaid. Anyway, he told himself, Keith has to be dead. Keith is dead forever no matter how much we want a different reality.

Margo managed to maintain her composure until the memorial service concluded. Finally, she made her way to the special side exit reserved for her, thereby avoiding the handshaking and hugs of family, friends, community members, and dignitaries, as well as the pressure of the frenzied throngs outside. The fact that there were not even remains to be laid to rest and to give her some measure of closure weighed heavily on her mind. Yet, she kept telling herself that the absence of Keith's body was easier for her than knowing it was there in a coffin. With no physical body to inter, she could always hope that he was still alive. Avoiding both her father and Lt. Wolfe, she chose to walk alone the distance from the Cathedral to the limousine she had insisted on reserving for herself and herself alone.

As she reached the limousine, Margo noticed the cub reporter standing just a few feet away. Startled, Margo wondered how the young woman had penetrated this highly restricted area. For a moment, their gazes met and locked. There was something disturbingly curious in the reporter's eyes, a question, or perhaps some kind of secret that captured Margo's attention. What could this reporter know about me, about the deeply buried, secret life I gave up for Keith, Margo wondered. Hesitating briefly, Margo nodded once at the young woman, opened her mouth to speak, and then abruptly stopped herself from further contact and looked away.

The reporter watched the mysterious widow disappear behind the dark windows of the limousine as it moved slowly away. Inside the muted and muffled limousine, Margo reflected upon the troubled rush of recent history that had brought her here....

VOLUME ONE: PHANTOM WAR TRILOGY

PART ONE

December 18, 1967 – January 1, 1968

VOLUME ONE: PHANTOM WAR TRILOGY

1.

EIGHT ELEPHANTS

With almost military precision, the group arose, came to attention, and greeted the burly Texan as he entered the White House Situation Room. "Good morning, Mr. President," they chanted in unison, straining for enthusiasm. Apprehension tinged each voice and a trace of anxiety clouded every face. The President's mood had become increasingly sour as Christmas day 1967 approached. Every flag-rank officer and cabinet level official waiting in the brightly lit room had experienced the grim-faced Chief Executive's sharp verbal brickbats at least once during the previous ten days. Worse yet, the President's demeanor was deteriorating steadily.

Approaching the head of the massive conference table, the President motioned the senior members of his Cabinet and the nation's highest ranking military officers to take their seats while stating brusquely. "Gentlemen, let's get started. I've got a busy day ahead and no time to waste." President Johnson sat down slowly and deliberately, as if in great pain.

A tall, crew cut Air Force Colonel remained standing and waited for the President to make himself comfortable.

"I said let's get started," the President clipped impatiently.

The Colonel replied crisply, "Yes Sir, Mr. President. Let's begin the meeting with your Daily Intelligence Briefing on military operations during the past twenty-four hours."

The Colonel took the podium at the foot of the great mahogany conference table, raised his pointer to the screen behind him and began to deliver the military statistics of the day. Johnson glanced at his watch and grimaced. It read December 18th, 7:30 a.m. "Goddamn," he muttered only slightly under his breath. "Seven goddamn thirty in the morning and here I am listening to the same ol' military horseshit!" He looked up at the Colonel who droned on. "During the past twenty-four hours, Air Force, Navy and Marine Corps strike aircraft have flown more than twelve hundred-fifty sorties in North and South Vietnam and Laos -- against North Vietnamese and Viet Cong forces. We have destroyed an estimated three hundred sixty munitions-laden trucks, seventy-eight anti-aircraft batteries, and twenty-eight personnel carriers engaged in the movement of men and munitions along route 1-A into South Vietnam."

Johnson had not slept well the previous night and he stifled a yawn. Same ol' bullshit, he was still thinking. "Shit almighty, if these bastards really destroyed even half of what they report each day, it would take all of Ford and half of General Motors to keep the Viet Cong supplied," he grumbled half aloud.

The Air Force Intelligence Colonel continued. "In South Vietnam, we estimate that our air strikes have killed approximately three hundred North Vietnamese Army troops, four hundred ninety Viet Cong, and eight elephants."

Johnson suddenly looked up and stared at the Colonel in disbelief. "What did you say? Did you say eight elephants? We killed eight fuckin' elephants! What in Christ's name did we kill eight elephants for?" he bellowed. "Were they Communist elephants or somethin'? Why are we bombing the Goddamn elephants? This is just the last damn straw," he roared.

Johnson burst menacingly to his feet and shouted on, "Don't you know I got a million rampaging college students raisin' hell 'bout this damned War all from one end of this country to the other and now I gotta go out and defend air strikes that are killin' the bloody elephants! Jesus Christ Almighty! Can't I trust you sons a' bitches to do anything right?"

The Colonel blanched and visibly worked to maintain his composure. "Well Sir, as you probably know, the North Vietnamese Army uses pack elephants to move ammunition south along the Ho Chi Minh Trail and our air forces target them just as they would any other truck or mechanized vehicle heading into South Vietnam."

Johnson's face flushed crimson with indignation. "Well, Colonel, I'm tellin' you right now, I don't want any more of our planes bombin' the Goddamn elephants. Do you understand me?"

"Yes Sir," the Air Force Colonel stammered.

Johnson turned to General Westmoreland, the Commander of American Forces in Vietnam, and now shouted at him. "No more damn elephants, Westmoreland! Do you hear me loud and clear? I don't want some snot-nosed college punk accusin' me of killin' the bloody elephants, Communist or not.

"Every day, I gotta' go on television and explain to Cronkite or some other news man why we're killin' villagers in North Vietnam, peasants in South Vietnam, destroying pagodas, temples and monasteries all over the damn Vietnam countryside. Now, I got to defend droppin' five hundred pound bombs in downtown Hanoi. I got to explain how we happened to drop that damned napalm on little girls of all things. Little girls!!! -- Especially on that one poor burned up, bleedin' little girl whose picture's all over the papers. And now you want me to explain why we're bombin' these fuckin' elephants? There's a limit to everything, Westmoreland. So, I'm tellin' you right now. No more elephants. No more!"

Westmoreland knew better than to argue or try to explain. The entire presentation had suddenly taken on a surreal atmosphere. He simply said solemnly, "Yes Mr. President, I understand. No more elephants. I'll get the order out right away."

The Intelligence Officer had regained some of his composure and tried to continue his report with a semblance of dignity. He detailed the number and type of "search and destroy" missions conducted by joint American and South Vietnamese Army Forces in the South and the number of newly "pacified" villages "rescued" from Viet Cong control. He then launched into an iteration of the number of North Vietnamese and Viet Cong soldiers killed, wounded and captured in South Vietnam.

At that moment, Johnson looked up at the Colonel, raised his hand to stop the presentation, narrowed his bloodshot eyes, and stated quite simply, "Let's get right to the point, Colonel. How many casualties did we sustain? How many of my boys are they shippin' home bloody, burned, shot up, and broken, dead in damn body bags?"

The Colonel cleared his throat as he replied, "Yes, Mr. President. I, I," he paused to clear his throat again. "Excuse me, Sir. I was just coming to that. Yesterday, we lost six strike aircraft in combat action, four in operational accidents, and thirteen helicopters flying combat support in the South. We lost forty-two Americans killed in action on the ground and suffered three hundred seventy wounded. Also, it appears that we had two airmen captured. As for South Vietnamese losses, we understand that --- "

Johnson, a look of intense anguish on his face, cut the Colonel off abruptly. As he sat down again, he exclaimed, "Gentlemen, every day I come here or some other place just like this and listen to these Godawful statistics and every day seems like the day before. It's gettin' so that these numbers are losing their meaning. Body counts, Killed in Action, Missing in Action, wounded; these are nothin' but hard cold numbers. But it all comes down to young, precious American boys comin' home in those Goddamn plastic bags. These numbers just don't mean a thing, not to me, and not to anyone else unless you're related to one of those damned numbers by blood or marriage. And then it's too bad. That's all. Just too damn bad. But lookin' at just one body of one American soldier breaks my heart.

"We blow up some fuckin' trucks, kill some bloody Viet Cong soldiers and some innocent villagers. We lose airplanes and take several hundred casualties. Same thing day after damn day."

Johnson paused, leaned back in his seat, and looked around the room. He stared Westmoreland squarely in the eye and saw an empty uniform rather than a man. He glared at Defense Secretary McNamara sitting ramrod straight, his hair combed straight back and glistening in the bright lights like a professional poker player about to draw to an inside straight. Johnson then fixed his terrible gaze on Dean Rusk, the Secretary of State, who looked embarrassed by the whole affair, embarrassed by LBJ's blue-smoke diatribe, embarrassed for all the killing – men, little girls and elephants alike, embarrassed by the War -- its existence and execution, and just plain embarrassed for being involved in the sad and sorry situation.

Johnson continued his deliberate scan of the entire room and everyone in it after which he stated as dramatically as his thirty years in Congress, three years as President and a lifetime in West Texas had taught him to do, "Let me tell you boys something. The American people are gettin' mighty fed up with all this statistical bullshit and so am I. I let you boys from the Pentagon and all you bright shiny PhD's from Harvard and MIT talk me into this Goddamn War and I've got nothin' to show for it. Not a single solitary damn thing!

"All my work all of these years in the Congress, all of my 'Great Society' programs, the Votin' Rights Act, everything I fought for is goin' up in smoke in some Godforsaken Southeast Asian jungle and for what? My entire presidential legacy is goin' straight to hell, for what? For what, I ask you? So we can kill some pore ol' skinny ass elephants schleppin' bullets down the Ho Chi Minh Trail?

"Well, I'm tellin' each and every one of you sons a' bitches. I don't care if you're from Harvard, Yale, MIT or West Point or wherever. You had best figure out a way to end this fuckin' War and end it soon. 'Cause, boys, if we ain't winnin' this damnable War by this comin' spring, I won't be here come next November. By then, you will have a new Commander in Chief, his name will probably be Richard Nixon, and he will fire each and every one of you bastards come the following January twentieth.

"I got half a mind to fire each and every one of you sons a' bitches right now for talkin' me into this damnable box canyon of a war and hangin' my West Texas ass out to dry! So you'd all better get your bureaucratic butts in a circle and figure out some quick way outta' this mess or we'll all go down in history as the sorriest goddamn administration since Harding or Hoover."

Johnson paused again just long enough to glower personally at each and every member of his audience. "Now that I got your attention, let's finish the targetin' session for tomorrow," he said with a self-satisfied smirk as he watched beads of sweat break out and roll down the faces of the most powerful men in America.

Robert McNamara wiped the perspiration from his large-brained forehead and Secretary Rusk cleared the heat condensation from his glasses. A three-star Admiral took the podium to begin the process of target selection for the next day's bombing strikes in North Vietnam. The Admiral knew that Johnson was extraordinarily and uniquely involved, like no other president had ever been -- hands on, refusing to leave it to the military, involved in the very heart of the North Vietnam target selection process. Johnson even reserved final target approval for himself and himself alone.

The three-star Admiral, resigned to this troubling reality, straightened, cleared his throat, and began. "Mr. President, during the last two days, ten Soviet military cargo ships have entered Haiphong Harbor and ten more are on the way. These ships have begun to offload their cargo as we speak and it's more extensive than anything we've seen yet coming from the Soviet Union. The cargo includes trucks, personnel carriers, artillery, and ammunition of every type in use by the North Vietnamese and Viet Cong. And, for the first time, we're seeing Russian-made main battle tanks. This is clearly the most massive military replenishment our photo-reconnaissance aircraft have photographed yet during the War.

"Mr. President, we would like to commence intense air strikes immediately in and around Haiphong Harbor. We want to destroy those docks and rail lines before all this material starts on its way to South Vietnam. We propose a series of intense air strikes launched from our three aircraft carriers in the Tonkin Gulf, the *Constellation*, the *Enterprise,* and the *Ticonderoga*. These strikes in two or three days would destroy Haiphong as an operating port for good. Guaranteed. Do we have your approval, Sir?"

Johnson stared coldly at McNamara who fidgeted with his

glasses. "This your idea, Bob?"

McNamara stuttered, "Well – well -- Sir, as a matter of fact, it is."

Johnson turned to the Admiral and inquired sternly, "What are the chances that one or more bombs will hit a Russian freighter?"

"Statistically speaking, Mr. President, the probability we have calculated is that at least one of the ships will take a direct hit by two point three Mark 82 general demolition bombs."

Johnson's florid face turned blood red. "Admiral, ignoring for the moment how three tenths of a five hundred pound bomb can hit a ship or anything else for that matter, what will happen if, let's say, just one damn bomb hits just one of those Russian ships?"

The Admiral shifted uneasily on his feet, feeling that the ground beneath him was about to give way. "Sir, if one bomb hits one of those ships as it's unloading the type of munitions we've seen, the ship and everything close to it will most probably be destroyed."

Lyndon Johnson was a large man towering well over six feet in height and weighing at least two hundred sixty pounds. His jowls and ridiculously large ears sometimes gave him the appearance of a bloodhound. This morning they gave him the look of a very tired, very disgruntled and angry bloodhound on the verge of total rabidity. Suddenly, Johnson growled and sprang out of his seat, this time up to his full height, his face flashing warnings. "Gentlemen, if I've told you once, I've told you a dozen times, I am not about to give the Russians an excuse to start World War III over some third rate, backwater country like Vietnam. If we sink a damn Russian ship in Haiphong Harbor, all hell could break loose before our strike aircraft even return to our carriers. No fuckin' way will I let that happen!

"You generals and admirals have damn lousy memories when it

36

comes to the really tough decisions that we politicians have to make, like starting a damned war. But I don't forget so easily. No sir, I don't forget at all. Just five short years ago, I was sittin' right here with President Kennedy – bless his soul --as he sweated blood during the Cuban missile crisis, hopin' and prayin' that some trigger happy Admiral enforcin' the blockade didn't sink a Russian ship, or some hotshot fighter pilot didn't blast a Soviet aircraft outta' the sky and start the nukes flyin' all over the damn world, turnin' this goddamned Cold War hotter than the fires of hell in a few days or even a few hours.

"No sir, I haven't forgotten that awful time. I never been so fuckin' scared in all my life, couldn't sleep at all. Not scared for myself or even my own family, but scared for this whole bloody planet. That's how close it came. Now I'm tellin' you boys for the last damned time that we ain't gonna' do nothin' in Vietnam that might start us down the road to World War III again. Not on my watch, we won't. You understand that, Bob?" Johnson blasted at McNamara.

"Yes, Mr. President, I do clearly understand your comments and directives."

Johnson again took his seat, knowing he had made his point, hopefully for the last time. "All right then, what's the alternative plan?"

The Admiral, still flustered by Johnson's bombastic comments, cleared his throat again and responded. "Mr. President, may I suggest a five minute break so that I can quickly confer with Secretary McNamara and General Westmoreland before presenting our alternate plan?"

Johnson glanced around the conference table, his bushy eyebrows dancing a lively jig. "You boys confer all you want, Admiral, just as long as it doesn't take more than five minutes. I'm gonna relieve myself of a heavy burden while you confer and have your coffee."

"Yes Sir, Mr. President, we'll resume as soon as you return," the

Admiral replied, hoping that Johnson's ill humor might improve after he completed his morning constitutional.

Twenty minutes later, Johnson re-entered the Situation Room, his demeanor and constitution in an improved condition, at least momentarily. "Alright boys," he said narrowing his eyes, "What brilliant backup plan did you come up with during the coffee break, oh – pardon me – last night? How we gonna' deal with all the guns and ammunition our Russian friends have so generously provided to the North Vietnamese?"

Admiral Stephenson, the Operations Officer of the Navy's Seventh Fleet which projected American power throughout the Pacific Basin, continued his interrupted presentation. "Mr. President, Operation Rolling Thunder will concentrate action in the area within a seventy-five mile radius to the south and west of Haiphong. The Air Force will take primary responsibility for roads and traffic heading south, southwest from Haiphong to the vicinity of Than Hoa, and the Navy will cover roads leading south toward Ha Tinh.

"Air Force and Navy air strikes will be targeted to cover nearly every mile of roadway in those areas in order to destroy and bottle up as much of the arms and munitions coming out of Haiphong as possible. It will be crucial to destroy the bulk of this materiel within the described area while it's concentrated there since it will be much more difficult to locate and target these supplies after dispersal along the Ho Chi Minh Trail.

"Of course, the North Vietnamese know that this will be our plan, so we can expect extremely heavy air defenses along each roadway in this sector, especially in the vicinity of Than Hoa and Ha Tinh. Since the North Vietnamese know that we'll be gunning for these supplies, they will most probably move the bulk of these supplies at night by truck convoys, navigating by moonlight. They will make it very tough for us and we will lose a significant number of aircraft before completing this mission. That's why we had hoped to destroy most of their supplies in Haiphong before it left the docks as in the first plan we presented to you."

Johnson's booming voice interrupted the Admiral again. "Admiral, I know why you wanted to hit those damn supplies on the docks, I'm no damn fool, you know. And I do know that it will be much more difficult to destroy this stuff after it leaves Haiphong. It's gonna cost us airplanes and airmen. But I have no damn choice to do it any way but this way. As I said before, we will not sink a single solitary Russian ship in Haiphong Harbor. And just in case any local wing commander or squadron commander tries to second guess me on this issue, I want an order to go out today to every Navy carrier air wing, and every Air Force squadron and wing commander to the effect that any pilot who hits a Russian ship in or around Haiphong Harbor without a damn good excuse will be court martialed along with his commanding officer. Is that clear?"

Admiral Stephenson swallowed hard and rasped his acknowledgment, "Yes Sir, your order will go out along with today's targeting orders."

Johnson wagged his forefinger at Stephenson and said, "See that it does, Admiral, see that it does. Now, I got to see to some other responsibilities I have runnin' this Country. So, you boys finish up targeting these roads leading outta' Haiphong. Alright, I have just one more question."

"Yes, Mr. President," Stephenson answered obediently.

"What percentage of these new supplies can you destroy after they leave Haiphong?"

Secretary McNamara intervened with his best statistical answer to Johnson's question. "Our best estimates would suggest that we can destroy about fifty-five percent of these munitions before they get to South Vietnam. If we're lucky with factors such as weather, we might even destroy upwards of sixty to sixty five percent of these supplies."

Johnson responded belligerently to McNamara's statistics with yet another question. "I suppose that the forty or fifty percent that gets through to South Vietnam will result in some very serious combat on the ground, am I correct?"

McNamara pulled no punches. "Yes Sir, you are quite correct. It would appear that Ho Chi Minh intends the New Year to start with quite a bang."

"So, I'll be damned if I do and damned if I don't. That's what you're tellin' me, isn't it, Bob?" Johnson pressed McNamara for greater clarity.

"Mr. President, with all due respect, it's your decision and yours alone whether we destroy these supplies while they're in the harbor or if we do the best we can once they start moving south. Sir, I quite understand your rationale for not wishing a confrontation with the Soviets. I simply wanted to give you the best scenario for preventing wider conflict on the ground in South Vietnam. There simply are no really good options, Sir."

Johnson shook his massive head as he stood to leave the Situation Room. "Well, I'll be dammed if I just sit around waiting to see what General Giap does with all these weapons arrivin' in Haiphong. I'm gonna stop him one way or another.

"I do wish you boys good huntin' around Than Hoa and Ha Gin."

"Ha Tinh, Sir," Admiral Stephenson corrected the Commander

in Chief gently.

"Right, Ha Tinh." Johnson muttered as he stomped out of the room and the others stood at rigid attention.

VOLUME ONE: PHANTOM WAR TRILOGY

2.

ORDERS TO HA TINH

Keith Marchand slammed his heavy steel-toed boot onto the bench next to his locker. He slowly zipped the legging of his G-suit all the way up the inside of his long right leg. He cinched the straps of his torso harness so tightly he could feel his chest pound. Slowly, carefully, Marchand buckled his nine-millimeter survival pistol around his waist. He struggled valiantly to suppress the mounting uneasiness in his gut.

In less than thirty minutes, Marchand would launch on his first night strike mission into North Vietnam. He told himself that he would never forget this day, December 19, 1967, if he lived to tell about it. He paused and closed his blue eyes for a moment, walling out the world and trying to pray. But all he could think about was the coming mission. Meteorologists aboard the *U.S.S. Constellation,* one of the first and most powerful American super carriers, had predicted a low overcast and rain for both the launch and recovery almost two hours later. And, the flight's intelligence briefing had forecast intense anti-aircraft fire around Ha Tinh, the flight's target.

Marchand's stomach churned. Repressing his angst, the resolute twenty-four year old Navy Flight Officer finally pulled on his survival vest, grabbed his helmet bag, then lumbered over to the steel ladder that led to the flight deck. Naval aviators don't snivel, Marchand reminded himself. He was a naval officer and this was his duty, pure and simple. Anyway, he heard during the air intelligence briefing that these orders came straight from the President and Commander in Chief, Lyndon Baines Johnson.

Marchand emerged from the soft, red-lit, almost womb-like world of his squadron ready room into a foreign and hostile darkness. It was night time during the Southeast Asian winter monsoon season, a lurid combination that was almost suffocating to those unused to the climate. The water around the carrier blended into a murky overcast that hung barely two hundred feet above the ship. Depressed by the complete absence of any horizon to separate sea and sky, Marchand labored for breath against the oppressive heat generated during the long tropical day. Almost panting, Marchand began his preflight inspection of the menacing F-4 Phantom fighter-bomber chained to the metal flight deck.

Before he could complete his pre-flight walk-around, the Air Boss thundered his order, "Pilots start your engines." Immediately, the flight deck came alive. Thirty jet engines spooled up and whined into life, transforming the chained attack bombers and fighters into a herd of lethal mechanical bulls. Collective engine exhausts blended with the humid night air, sending the noxious mixture howling in all directions over the steel flight deck that oozed oil, grease and heat like the griddle of a cheap diner.

Still on edge, and chastising himself for even the faintest trace of fear, Marchand went on to complete his preflight ritual. He was a warrior and trained to his task. Nothing should faze him now. And nothing would, he told himself, nothing would. He stopped last to check the fuses on the warheads protruding slightly from rocket launch pods slung beneath the Phantom's wings. These ten-foot long rockets had to perform as advertised in order to complete the mission ahead. Zuni rockets were accurate but they often failed to fire. When that happened, the unlucky crew were diverted to Da Nang Air Base to disarm and unload the dangerous misfired rockets before they were allowed to return to the aircraft carrier.

Marchand checked the rockets briefly, and walked on toward the cockpit boarding ladder, but then shuddered at the prospect of spending even one night in Da Nang where rocket and mortar attacks were a daily occurrence. The risk of being killed on the ground in Da Nang was much smaller than the danger of flight operations from an aircraft carrier, but at least he knew the dangers associated with carrier aviation. Strange how familiarity with danger makes it more acceptable, Marchand mused. Or, do I have it backward, he wondered.

Still concerned about the possibility of hung up Zuni rockets, Marchand compulsively doubled back to reexamine the electrical connections leading to the rocket pods from the aircraft's wing. He told himself that double-checking this way was all right and not a sign of fear. But before he could sweep the red beam of his flashlight over all of the electrical plugs connecting the rocket pods to the airplane, the exhaust blast from a Skyhawk attack bomber parked nearby singed his face. Choking for breath, he gasped, "Screw it," cut short his reexamination, and scurried up the Phantom's boarding ladder into the rear cockpit to strap into his ejection seat.

"Hurry up, will ya," Marchand roared at the young sailor who was connecting Marchand's ejection seat shoulder harnesses. Marchand hurried to close his canopy before shifting wind channeled foul exhaust gases from the aircraft positioned directly in front of the Phantom into his open cockpit. The plane captain was so nimble that Marchand was

45

able to close his canopy just in time. Marchand quickly buckled the oxygen mask to his helmet, began to inhale cold, pure oxygen deep into his straining lungs and experienced a momentary wave of relief.

In the Phantom's forward cockpit, Kelly "The Bulldog" Drummond had already started the Phantom's Number One engine. Marchand felt the fighter-bomber shudder slightly as one generator reached operational speed allowing the plane to run on internal power. Suddenly, red light from the instrument panel cast an otherworldly glow throughout Marchand's cockpit. A few seconds later, a shaft of bright green phosphorescence erupted from the radarscope between his knees and assaulted his eyes. Blinking rapidly, he methodically began to check the fighter's powerful radar and weapon system. Gradually, Marchand became aware of a dull throb radiating from the pit of his stomach. The cockpit seemed to shrink. Normally, he found the six inches of lateral and forward movement quite adequate for his lanky frame. But suddenly, he felt terribly claustrophobic. Surprised and fighting unexpected nausea, he struggled to suppress unwelcome emotions. For just a moment he could barely refrain from unstrapping himself and bolting from the plane. A brief but morbid panic beat through his veins like thunder. He forced himself to take a few deep breaths. He knew better than to let this last minute apprehension disrupt his routine.

"Hey, you're awfully quiet back there, Keith, anything wrong?" Kelly Drummond's voice sounded over the intercom, breaking the grip of Marchand's secret and increasingly unwieldy anxiety, and just in time.

"Uh – uh – that's a negative. Just finishing my weapons checks," Marchand blurted, perhaps a little too unguardedly. Embarrassed, he thought for an instant then added candidly, "I guess I've got a slight case of the jitters, Kelly."

"Oh yeah? Well, that's normal. This is your first night bombing mission, right?"

Marchand exhaled loudly. "Yeah, but Kelly, I don't mind telling you what a relief it is to fly with you tonight. If I were flying with a nugget pilot on a night like this, neither one of us would make it back," Marchand said feigning humor."

Drummond chuckled, but didn't disregard Marchand's apprehension. He could not afford to take it lightly. Certainly, he recalled his own fear prior to his first night strike, and he knew this was not unusual. Still, he also realized that his own safety might well depend upon the inexperienced young officer in the rear cockpit. "Just remember," Drummond exhorted with a slightly paternal tone, "I'm depending on you to help me get this twenty million dollar piece of shit back on board tonight. You let me down and we'll both swim home. So, just stay focused and everything will be cool."

"I'm O.K., Kelly. We'll need everything going for us tonight -- including me," Marchand replied, straining for enthusiasm.

Abruptly, the conversation ended when the Phantom on the catapult directly in front of them roared to full afterburner. Marchand felt sound waves thumping his chest ferociously like a hammer. The twin blowtorches erupting from the plane's engines split the blackness with Vesuvian intensity. The fighter's white-hot exhaust vaporized bits of the massive steel blast deflector that separated the second aircraft from the inferno. Showers of incandescent metallic snowflakes shot a hundred feet in the air falling harmlessly near the carrier's fantail.

Marchand watched as the powerful fighter strained demon-like at its holdback bridle. Suddenly, the catapult fired, severing the block of machined metal that anchored the massive fighter to the deck. In less than two seconds, the twenty-seven ton Phantom was airborne and traveling more than two hundred miles per hour. Five seconds after launch, Marchand saw clouds swallow the fighter's fifty-foot exhaust plumes. Then, he saw only a dull red glow traversing the darkness. The sight was hypnotic and a strange, self-protective detachment overtook him.

As the first Phantom disappeared, the fifteen-foot high jet blast deflector lowered flush into the deck. Drummond then began a delicate *pas de deux* with the plane director, easing the fighter onto the catapult track with catlike precision. Marchand felt a slight jolt as the Phantom braced against its holdback bridle. He automatically locked his ejection seat harness, stowed his weapons control panels, and turned the command ejection control to the rear cockpit position so that he could quickly launch Kelly Drummond and himself out of the plane in an emergency.

Drummond completed a last minute flight surface control check with the white-jerseyed troubleshooter standing to the right of the cockpit. Then he asked, "Keith, you ready to go?"

Before he answered, Marchand thought coolly of pulling the afterburner circuit breakers to abruptly and immediately down the aircraft even before its take-off. But he knew, of course, that this stupid trick would be completely obvious, not to mention cowardly. Instead, he reached down beneath his ejection seat and retrieved the stuffed Snoopy dog he had hidden in his helmet bag. His seventeen year old sister, Christine, had tearfully pressed the little furry creature, dressed in a leather World War I aviator's helmet, flight jacket and red flying goggles, into Marchand's pocket when she had hugged him goodbye at the North Island Naval Station. San Diego seemed so far away now as Marchand wedged the guardian toy dog between the instrument panel and the canopy.

For the love of God, and the love of my country, he pledged silently, then responded over the intercom. "OK, let's roll, Bulldog." To himself he prayed. Lord. Can you hear me? I'm calling you. Then, Marchand shook his head, laughed at himself and assumed the proper fighter jock attitude composed of equal parts self-assurance and quiet arrogance. Seconds later, he felt the aircraft pitch up as the nose wheel strut was extended to give the Phantom the correct angle of attack before launch.

Drummond pushed the throttles forward, running the Phantom's engines up to full basic-engine power while checking his engine gauges one last time. Then, smoothly, his left hand pushed the throttles all the way forward into the last afterburner detent. The Phantom shuddered with power as if to tear itself apart, straining mightily against the blinding, ear-shattering, white-hot thrust erupting from the engine nozzles. After a final scan of the instruments showed the engines were developing full power, Drummond tightened his grip on the throttles then switched on the wing tip formation lights to signal readiness. Finally, he carefully pulled the control stick back close to his crotch, setting the control surfaces properly for launch. Both Drummond and Marchand braced hard against the back of their ejection seats. They watched from the corner of their eyes as the catapult officer dipped his left knee to the deck in a modified genuflect, his right arm fully extended, and touched a pointed flashlight to the deck. The "Cat" Officer's graceful movement signified total commitment.

At that instant, there was no turning back. From the moment the Cat Officer's dimly lit wand had touched the deck, Marchand knew that nothing could stop the catapult from firing the Phantom off the carrier deck. Nervous yet increasingly controlled thoughts flickered through Marchand's mind. He knew that the moment was critical. There is no time to be more committed than this one right here right now at the start of this mission, he told himself. Right here right now. Right here right now. Right here ….

The power surging in the enormous steam piston beneath the flight deck to which the aircraft was connected could fling a small truck a mile into the air. Marchand knew this and mumbled to himself, "OK then, here I am. Right here right now. Might as well enjoy the fucking ride." Marchand braced himself as the catapult fired. The Phantom hunched down momentarily like a sprinter in starting blocks and then it accelerated to one-hundred and eighty knots before reaching the end of the carrier deck barely two hundred and thirty feet down the catapult track.

The acceleration slammed Marchand against his seat like a battering ram. It was at once a shock and a comfort. Although he had logged more than fifty catapult shots, the involuntary deflation of his lungs stunned him as it always had during those crucial seconds. Nevertheless, he was relieved that the monstrous catapult engine beneath the steel deck had worked again, as advertised. But this time, the catapult was firing him into the darkness of his first night combat strike mission. And into the darkness of his soul, where perhaps there was a limit to his profound and sincere commitment to the United States. He didn't know - couldn't know, what was in there deep inside. And now, duty and survival demanded that he not inquire further.

3.

RISK REWARD

President Johnson picked at his Denver omelet disconcertedly and then shoved his plate away. He was typically quite hungry for his 7:00 a.m. breakfast in the White House dining room. But, on the morning of Wednesday, December 20, 1967, Johnson's normally prodigious appetite was nowhere to be found. The First Lady was not feeling well that morning and had not joined him for breakfast so he was dining alone.

Johnson had slept fitfully and his mood reflected it. While drinking his coffee, he decided to call Secretary of Defense McNamara and invite him to breakfast. Johnson hated eating alone and his mood cried out for company. After the tongue lashing Johnson had administered to the entire senior Defense Department staff two days prior, he thought this might be an opportune moment for some fence mending. In addition, Johnson knew to a near certainty that the extraordinarily diligent and industrious Secretary had already been at work for at least an hour and might have some news for him concerning the previous day's events in Vietnam.

Within five minutes, McNamara had arrived from his office in the West Wing of the White House and was escorted into the Presidential

Dining Room. "Good morning, Mr. President. How are you this morning, Sir?"

"Well, Bob, I've had better mornings but then again, I've had worse. How about you?"

The Defense Secretary hesitated a few moments before replying. "Somehow, Mr. President, the days just seem to blend together in blurring succession. Days don't seem to have an individual significance lately."

Johnson took a long sip of coffee then responded, "You enjoyin' the job that much, huh?"

McNamara laughed in a coldly efficient manner befitting his bow tie and dark suit. "These are difficult days, Mr. President. I'm sure you would agree to that."

Johnson scratched at one of his massive ears before answering, "Yeah, Bob, not a lot of fun to be had these days, and I'm afraid that there won't be many happy days ahead either."

Sensing a need for something else that he could perhaps offer his President, McNamara asked, "Is there anything I can do for you, Sir?"

"First of all, call your office and tell the staff that you and I will be half an hour or so late for our briefing in the Situation Room, then let's go on up to the Oval Office and talk. I got a few things to discuss with you before I leave on this trip to Australia for Prime Minister Holt's Memorial Services. And prior to takeoff, I've got a national television address to deliver. So this is just about the only time I can speak to you privately."

"Yes, Sir, I'll be right up."

"And, for Pete's sake, bring the rest of your muffin with you, you haven't eaten a damn thing."

A few minutes later the President and Secretary McNamara

reconvened in the Oval Office. Johnson sat behind the presidential desk, leaned back, and put his large feet on the highly polished wood. "You got any word on those missions we got goin' into Than Hoa and Ha Tinh yet?"

"Not yet, Mr. President. Those strikes are just getting underway at this moment. We have aircraft from the *Constellation*, the *Enterprise* and the *Oriskany* scheduled into Ha Tinh commencing late this afternoon, our time, and continuing for the next forty-eight hours. We plan to send a hundred fifty strike sorties into those areas during that period. As you know, there's a thirteen-hour time difference so our first night strikes should be briefing as we speak. By this afternoon, we may have some bomb damage assessment from our photo-reconnaissance aircraft. I'll make certain that it's delivered to you as soon as it arrives, even if you're on Air Force One."

"Yeah, Bob, I want that information as soon as possible. Now, if I understand correctly, with a hundred fifty missions and one or two pilots per mission, so we got two hundred to two hundred fifty pilots and flight officers at risk. Am I right, Bob?"

"Well Sir, you're about right. But, technically, a 'mission' refers to the entire strike regardless of the number of aircraft involved. A sortie means one strike flown by one aircraft. So, our hundred fifty sorties means a hundred fifty aircraft will be sent against our targets in the Than Hoa and Ha Tinh areas."

"By God, Bob, when it comes to technical, you got 'em all beat by a mile. But as long as I got the general idea, that's what matters to me. Now, tell me how many of those boys flyin' them 'sooortees' or whatever they're called won't be comin' home?"

"Statistically, we may lose one to three aircraft. But it could be many more. However, we may be able to rescue one or more of the downed aviators. So, it's almost impossible to say how many will die out there or be captured. With a sample that small, statistics are pretty rough."

"But some of those boys won't be comin' home, right?"

"Yes, Sir, it's likely that some will not make it back."

"OK Bob. Now, tell me, do you still think that we'll get only fifty percent of those munitions headin' south from Haiphong?"

McNamara finished a small bite of his English muffin, swallowed hard, then replied, "Frankly, Mr. President, that fifty percent figure is somewhat optimistic. Once those ships are unloaded in Haiphong, the odds are against us. General Giap is an absolute master at disbursing munitions to all manner and types of transportation into South Vietnam. We get pretty good results while the supplies are on trucks or motorized vehicles but once they move onto bicycles and troops carrying heavy backpacks, our success rate decreases substantially."

"So, it's true that Giap uses bicycles to move these munitions?"

"Absolutely, Mr. President. The bicycles seem to be quite effective on the foliage-hidden, narrow jungle trails that make up a large portion of the Ho Chi Minh Trail."

Johnson locked his eyes squarely on his Defense Secretary, "So, bottom line is this, Bob. We'll lose at least ten aircraft and possibly twenty aviators in order to destroy roughly a third of the munitions comin' off those ships tied up in Haiphong Harbor right now. Is that an acceptable cost to us?"

"You've framed the issue perfectly, Mr. President. But, only you can answer that question, Sir. However, one thing is quite clear. Ho Chi Minh is planning something dramatic in South Vietnam in approximately six to eight weeks and these munitions he's moving are instrumental for whatever plan he and Giap have in mind. To whatever extent we can attenuate or even stop that plan, I think we must try. At least, that's my assessment."

Johnson assumed a pained expression and said, "As usual, Bob, your logic is damned hard to argue with. But hell and damnation, I just hate losin' those fliers. Just breaks my heart." Johnson paused a moment then added, "But I guess you can't make an omelet without breakin' a few eggs."

McNamara nearly choked on his coffee but managed to nod affirmatively.

VOLUME ONE: PHANTOM WAR TRILOGY

4.

ROCKETS' RED GLARE

By the time Drummond had retracted the landing gear and flaps, the Phantom had accelerated through three hundred knots. Now Drummond began an easy turn to their assigned climb-out heading. At ten thousand feet, the Phantom broke through the thick overcast into a perfectly clear, moonlit sky.

"Ahhh," Drummond sighed loudly.

"Yeah," Marchand responded.

Here was another world. A world untouched and unsoiled by human politics and war. As they leveled off at rendezvous altitude of eighteen thousand feet, Marchand and even the seasoned Drummond were awestruck by the serenity of the night sky. Heaven. Absolute heaven. The air was as smooth as newly fallen powder snow and the only sound was the steady whine of the engines occasionally broken by a radio transmission. Transfixed by the flood of his own endorphins, Marchand gazed at the three-quarter moon casting a soft, soothing, silver finger of light atop rippled, sterling white clouds. He wanted this pristine and perfect moment to last forever, to freeze in this place of peace, but there was no time. It was so beautiful yet somehow chilling. The refrain of a song he had recently heard about a Proxy War came to him briefly, only briefly as he gazed at the moon's reflected light.

And then, Marchand snapped into fighter jock mode. He studied his radar screen where he picked up the other two Phantoms joining them on the strike. He deftly guided Drummond into rendezvous position. As Drummond maneuvered the fighter into flight leader position, the bright white join-up lights on the wing tips and under-bellies of the two circling Phantoms illuminated their ghostly outlines in a manner befitting their namesake.

After rendezvous, Drummond rolled out of the lazy ten-mile circle they had flown until the last plane in the formation was aboard. Now they were three: three phantoms on a mission, three aluminum birds speeding through the night. Checkmate Flight on its way to Ha Tinh, North Vietnam. Marchand gave Drummond the precise bearing to their target area just north of the city of Ha Tinh. Drummond then banked the aircraft to its target heading almost due west.

Fifteen minutes later, Drummond keyed the transmit button on the throttles and radioed to the rest of the flight. "Checkmate Flight," he addressed his team of Phantoms cruising swiftly through the night. "Tighten up the formation a bit, you're drifting out too far. Listen carefully to our transmissions when we get into the target area; we may have some quick changes depending on the fire we take."

Don Kramer, the pilot of the second Phantom in the Checkmate Flight responded, "Check Two, Roger." Phil Winslow flying backseat in the third aircraft radioed, "Check Three, Roger."

When the flight drew within fifty miles of the North Vietnamese coastline, the four-inch diameter face of the electronics counter measure scope in Marchand's cockpit came alive with spidery fingers of green light. His earphones whistled as a tone generator beeped each time a

North Vietnamese radar beam swept past the plane. "They've picked us up. The site that's painting us is twenty or thirty miles north of our coast-in point," Marchand croaked. He knew that they were already a target for North Vietnamese gunners, the world's most experienced.

Before Drummond could answer, two more radar sites began to paint the flight, one south of their intended entry point over North Vietnamese territory, and one close to the point itself. "Yeah, they see us alright, and one of 'em has locked on to us now," Drummond replied matter-of-factly after a quick glance at his repeater ECM scope.

As the noise and light level in Marchand's cockpit increased, so did his blood pressure. Although the cockpit was quite cool, sweat rolled down his forehead stinging his eyes. Inside his gloves, his hands grew clammy and uncomfortable. His underwear stuck like wet plaster to his skin. Two minutes later, as the flight crossed over the beach below, Marchand keyed his intercom button and said, "We're feet dry, Kelly." Looking down, he could see a faint white surf line at the coast. There was an unreal quality to the scene, as if it had been painted into the night.

Drummond responded again matter-of-factly, "Well, right on time. And now they've all found us; check your ten o'clock, about two miles. Let's go to hot mike."

Marchand switched the plane's intercom so that he and Drummond could hear each other's every word and sound, including breathing, without keying their microphones. Then he looked to the right of the plane's nose at a spot about two miles ahead and saw what appeared to be a dozen red flares arching up from the ground in Fourth of July fashion lacking only the sound effects. While the red specks were still climbing, many others erupted from the same vicinity like red-hot fireflies. Marchand was mesmerized. A silent, surreal firework display, seemingly for his personal benefit, was being staged. Marchand found it fascinating.

Suddenly, the "flares" began to explode with ugly yellow-orange flashes. Marchand shifted into a slightly belated alert. "Kelly, those bastards are really shooting at us!" Marchand bellowed, plainly outraged.

"You noticed! Well, as long as they don't shoot any straighter, we can enjoy the show, don't you think?" Drummond replied half jokingly trying to keep Marchand calm and yet alert.

"Damn, this can't be real," Marchand grumbled, feeling perturbed that people he didn't know and couldn't see were seriously trying to kill him.

"It's real all right, Keith. But don't sweat it too much; they can't hit crap at night with or without radar. Let's find that target though. No point in hanging around just to enjoy the show; the price of admission can get pretty high."

Marchand's navigation indicated target passage and he directed the flight to begin flying a giant racetrack pattern at that point. Their target was a very large truck convoy last sighted near the intersection of two roads and a set of rail tracks northwest of Ha Tinh. Defense Department "Rules of Engagement" required visual contact with the target before the flight could attack in order to minimize collateral damage to civilian areas. To aid in sighting the target, the second Phantom, Checkmate Two, carried flares to be ejected on each pass around the pattern. The magnesium flares generated nearly three million candle power each and were attached to small parachutes that allowed them to remain at altitude for their entire three-minute burn time.

When the first flare ignited, Marchand watched the flat Vietnamese terrain light up as though dawn had broken. The world below looked like a miniscule stage set, complete with artificial lighting.

But this world was no stage. Tracer rounds streaked upward from dozens of points on the ground. Thirty-seven and fifty-seven millimeter shells from every anti-aircraft battery within a five-mile radius of the target filled the night sky. Although the anti-aircraft shells were initially well off target, it wasn't long before a few began to burst uncomfortably close to the three plane formation.

"Damn! It's getting crowded up here. What do you think about making a few more bomb craters and goin' home? Those bastards are beginning to shoot pretty damn straight. Did you see that stream of thirty-seven millimeter at our two o'clock just now?"

"Calm down, Keith. We've got almost fifteen minutes target fuel to use up, and you ain't seen close shootin' yet," Drummond snorted, slightly irritated.

At that moment, Marchand spotted what looked like red-hot pencil leads floating up in slow motion from behind his left shoulder. He watched closely as the cherry-red objects gained altitude and realized that a more powerful weapon was now in use. And it was heading their way.

"Kelly, we're taking hundred five millimeter fire at eight o'clock," he shouted.

Drummond strained to look behind his left shoulder, where, at his seven o'clock position, he saw large shells bursting behind them, staining the darkness with a bright yellow glow. There was no sound save the hiss of static on the radio and the whistle of fast, heavy breathing of two men riding along the fragile cusp between life and death.

"That's the first time I've seen one hundred millimeter fire around Ha Tinh. The village chiefs must be pretty pissed off down there. You're right; those weren't bad shots either. Their radar may be working

61

better too, but not that much better," Drummond said, trying to sound reassuring. He nevertheless continued scanning the rice paddies and fields for the light of the flares or moonlight reflected from the negligently exposed metal of a truck flatbed or the glow of headlights foolishly turned on by an inexperienced driver feeling his way in the dark. Suddenly, Drummond barked at Marchand, "There it is at ten-thirty! Hard to see, but it looks like at least a dozen of them snaking along that road two o'clock position, about two miles!"

Marchand, still stunned by the last anti-aircraft burst, forced himself to look at the area Drummond pointed out. After a quick scan, he focused on the glint of the flares from exposed steel. Drummond snap rolled into a forty degree right banking turn toward the target while Marchand took a navigation fix so that the target could be located again if visual contact were lost. His throat was as dry as parchment as he radioed target acquisition to the rest of Checkmate Flight so they could assume proper positions.

When Drummond passed directly over the target, he added power in order to climb up to thirteen thousand feet. As he pulled the Phantom's nose up, he aligned the track of his intended rocket run to the west for fastest target egress. In seconds, Drummond had turned to the downwind leg of the rocket run, still visually glued to the target. Marchand called off the armament checklist and Drummond set the Zuni rockets to fire in pairs. Drummond still planned to make four rocket runs firing four Zunis on each pass even though ground fire was increasingly intense. He estimated that with four target runs each, the three Phantoms in Checkmate Flight might destroy a good portion of the truck convoy.

As he turned onto the base leg of the pattern, Drummond keyed the transmitter button on his throttles. "Check Two, drop your remaining flares on your downwind leg; by the time I make my second run it'll look like a high noon around here."

"Checkmate Two, roger." Marchand heard just a trace of anxiety in Winslow's voice.

Drummond reached thirteen thousand feet and turned to his final weapons delivery heading. When he reached the proper heading with the target dead ahead, he rolled the Phantom inverted and pulled the nose toward the ground until the aircraft was in a steep dive. While still upside down, he brought the target into the reticule of his gun sight. Although Marchand was quite accustomed to these aerial gymnastics, this was the first time he had done so at night while taking hostile fire.

Marchand glued his vision to his instrument panel and soon called, "Forty degrees, five hundred knots, ten thousand feet."

Instantly, Drummond rolled the plane out of its inverted position and concentrated on his last second target corrections. It was a good dive, and he was about to pull slightly back on the control stick in order to aim his rockets at the center of the convoy, when he saw a flaming burst of thirty-seven millimeter fire spurt up from the ground and speed almost directly at him.

In his peripheral vision, Marchand saw the tracers streaking upwards but said nothing. Three seconds later, he took his eyes off his instruments just long enough to see several tracers flash directly over his canopy. Now, he called to Drummond, "Oh shit, they've got us zeroed in!"

Drummond did not respond.

"They're on us, Kelly!!!"

"Shut up and do your damn job!" Drummond bellowed back at Marchand.

"Forty-two degrees, five-hundred thirty knots, eight thousand feet, ease off on the throttles," Marchand replied as steadily as he could. This wasn't a game or a dream or a practice run. This was reality. You blink, you die; he told himself.

Drummond's eyes bulged as he glared into the gun sight; as a stream of tracers came so close it seemed he could reach out and grab them. Behind that one, it looked as though a swarm of molten angry hornets was heading straight at him. Still, he persevered in his precise forty-degree dive toward the truck convoy.

"Thirty-eight degrees, five hundred fifty knots, seven thousand feet, and pull off some more power," Marchand called. Hurry, he wanted to add, but did not. Damn, he thought, only two thousand feet to go until we fire these bloody rockets -- only five fuckin' seconds. We're gonna' make it. We're gonna' make it. We're gonna' make it.

Drummond knew he had a great dive run pegged and knew that he would seriously damage the North Vietnamese truck convoy. But in the last three seconds before the weapons release point, enemy tracer rounds began to explode in a deadly shower all around the aircraft. He heard the brittle, grating tink and slap of hot shrapnel puncturing the Phantom's aluminum skin and knew that another second's delay could well be fatal. Drummond instantly shifted to his emergency mode. With no time to reset his weapon's panel to fire salvo so that all sixteen rockets would fire simultaneously, he decided to fire all the rockets manually. There was no time to discuss his decision with Marchand or the rest of the flight. Drummond abruptly pushed the control stick still farther forward to deepen his dive by several degrees, then squeezed the trigger, rapidly, as though he was emptying a loaded revolver in an old fashioned pistol duel.

The Phantom shuddered and bucked like a car running over railroad tracks at high speed. Vicious orange flames completely engulfed the fighter-bomber. Marchand bolted into overdrive. "Great fuck, Kelly, we've been hit! Do you still have control? Let's get out of this sonofabitch," Marchand yelled, reaching for the handles to the ejection seat face curtain. As he reached, violent "G" forces pressed him down into the seat as the Phantom roared out of its dive. His g-suit inflated hard, fully squeezing his gut so violently that his bladder couldn't stand both the pressure and death stalking all around him.

Drummond pulled back hard on the control stick while his urgent shouting ripped through the microphone from the front seat. Marchand had to hear it several times to accept it. "Goddamn it, Marchand, those were our rockets firing! We're not hit! Marchand? Marchand! Damn! Marchand! **THOSE WERE OUR ROCKETS FIRING!!!**"

5.

COMIN' HOME

Lyndon Johnson snuggled himself deep into the super-soft, overstuffed, kidskin leather seat, and kicked off the tight unforgiving city shoes that he had worn all day. Entirely drained after a series of eighteen-hour days and a morning press conference, he gazed out the window of Air Force One, the immaculate blue and white Boeing 707 jetliner built especially for the President of the United States. As often as he had flown aboard this luxuriously appointed, state of the art aircraft, Johnson still felt a thrill whenever he boarded "his" airplane. It symbolized American might, power and sophistication anywhere in the world, and his own power and might by implication as well. He sipped Jack Daniel's Tennessee Whiskey from the blue and gold tumbler embossed with the Presidential Seal and felt the smooth, mellow liquid light small, cool fires in his mouth and throat. He sighed deeply with relief.

For the first time in weeks, he was beginning to relax knowing that as soon as this unplanned trip to Australia was completed, he would be on his way to the Johnson Ranch in West Texas. For the moment, he felt the enormous weight of his office and the pressure it put on his heart begin to recede as the four engines of Air Force One spooled up to idle power. He planned to spend all of Christmas week roaming the mesquite and scrub oak-covered hills, mesas and arroyos of his ranch on horseback, breathing the clean, dry West Texas air, and enjoying the company of his beloved wife, Lady Bird. This certain brand of relief Johnson felt in departing Washington and all its attendant stresses coupled with the cheerful bonhomie of the Air Force One crew buoyed his spirits enormously.

An Air Force Master Sergeant entered the President's cabin carrying a freshly poured Jack Daniels and three briefing books on a silver tray. Johnson accepted the whiskey and glanced at the briefing books prepared by the State Department, Central Intelligence Agency and the Department of Defense. He shook his head and told the sergeant that he would read the books later. He didn't want to spoil his increasingly good humor by reviewing grim statistics and inflated battlefield reports. In any event, the order of battle for the next few days, both air war and ground had been thoroughly discussed and meticulously planned. The Ha Tinh and Than Hoa strikes were well underway. Even his own hands-on approach to battle planning the War in Vietnam could spare him for a while.

The Air Force Colonel in command of Air Force One began to taxi to the active runway while the tower ordered all other traffic to hold in place so the President's plane could move without any interference whatever. As the elegant Boeing jetliner inscribed with the Presidential Seal on the vertical tail maneuvered toward the active runway, Johnson reflected upon the sudden tragic death of the Australian Prime Minister during a swimming accident and how quickly and cruelly fate could dispose of the mighty as easily as it could the lowliest peasant. While planning his words of condolence for Prime Minister Holt's memorial service, Johnson wondered what fate held in store for him and his legacy.

As Air Force One taxied smartly toward the approach end of the runway, Johnson stared intensely at the hive-like activity happening all over Andrews Air Force Base. He knew that he was watching only a very small part of the enormous American war machine in action, and yet even that was awesome. "His" beautiful blue, white and silver Presidential jetliner taxied past cargo and troop transports being loaded and unloaded, helicopters lifting off and buzzing away, and menacing Phantom fighter-bombers in camouflage paint being manned by Air Force pilots. As Johnson watched, he mumbled to himself, "How in God's name do those little brown men in black pajamas in that strange land half a world away so successfully resist such massive power and give me, the President of the United States, such dreadful headaches day after day?" Realizing that talk about little brown men in black pajamas was becoming increasingly unpopular to people like his Vice President, Hubert Humphrey, Johnson looked around instinctively to be sure no one had heard him.

A moment later, another sergeant entered the President's cabin to remind him to buckle his seat belt. "Another Black Jack, Sir?" he asked respectfully.

"No thanks, Sergeant, I've got several letters and a speech to write and I'm afraid another Black Jack won't help," Johnson replied with a Texas-sized smile. He opened his pen and wrote a few words but found that he could not concentrate. No, it's not the whiskey, he thought. It's something else that's worrying the hell out of me. He closed his eyes and drifted for a few moments, then suddenly he knew. He knew just what had been lurking at the edge of his consciousness for the past two days.

It was all those ships in Haiphong Harbor unloading all those guns, rockets and ammunition. It was all those trucks, personnel carriers

69

and tanks shipped to North Vietnam's major port from the Soviet Union. It was knowing that at least half of all those munitions would somehow make it all the way from Haiphong to South Vietnam. And then what? Johnson asked himself. What in the hell was Ho Chi Minh planning for January 1968? It ain't gonna be fun and games, that's for damn sure, he thought. And I got a goddamned election coming up in just eleven months. "Hell fire and damnation," he muttered aloud. "I hope to Jesus that those Navy and Air Force pilots are kickin' some ass around Ha Tinh and Than Hoa about now." Noting how this new wave of anxiety affected his heart beat; Johnson decided that a short nap would perhaps shed some of the stress.

Before Johnson closed his eyes, Air Force One had nearly reached the end of the taxiway parallel to Andrews' main runway. Looking out his window as the sleek Boeing jetliner passed a cavernous hanger, he noticed a silver Air Force C-141 Starlifter cargo plane parked on the ramp in front. Blinking wearily, he could see a line of forklifts taking oblong shaped boxes down the Starlifter's tail ramp and into the hanger. He wondered idly what kind of cargo was in the boxes. It was then he noticed what he really would rather have not seen, that a line of similar boxes in the hanger were flag-draped. Immediately, he jerked upright and opened his eyes wide. "Jesus Christ, Father God almighty, those are my boys comin' home in boxes," he said to himself mournfully. No one saw Johnson hang his massive head and cry Texas-sized bitter tears.

6.

ROCKETMAN

The heat of combat burned in his veins as Marchand strained to look back over his shoulder at the blazing supply convoy, loaded only thirty-six hours earlier on the docks of Haiphong Harbor, now burning so furiously. The trucks, heavily burdened with Soviet-made mortar shells, machine gun ammunition and anti-aircraft rounds, cooked off in a series of wicked orange yellow explosions.

At seven hundred miles per hour, six air warriors flying their fierce Phantoms crossed over the beach toward deep water still jinking hard to avoid the diminishing anti-aircraft fire. Hot spears of a newly discovered fulfillment thrust up Marchand's spine as he witnessed the violent fruits of their efforts there on the North Vietnamese coastline. The doomed truck convoy was pinned to a stand still between Kelly Drummond's and Tom Baer's well-aimed rockets while the Zunis fired by Don Kramer, piloting the third Phantom, mercilessly consumed the middle of the convoy.

As the three warplanes sped away from their attack, an all-encompassing sense of relief swept Marchand as his pounding pulse began to slow. He knew that "blind ass luck," the most treasured combat commodity of all, and great airmanship had produced the evening's clear winners. He also knew that for the losers, driving those disintegrating trucks ten thousand feet below, there was only hell to pay and only carnage to salvage from the aftermath. Marchand fully realized that he had just survived his first serious combat experience where both sides had given full measure in their respective attempts to destroy each other. He had been instrumental in the implementation of the orders of the Commander-in-Chief himself. And, this time, the Phantoms had been totally victorious. This time.

Marchand also felt an enormous sense of accomplishment juxtaposed momentarily with a nearly equal measure of sadness as he thought about the North Vietnamese soldiers still dying in the conflagration. But he did not have the luxury of exploring either this pride or this bizarre sense of guilt, as the demands of the flight called him. And, the latter of these, the distant guilt and grief, he did not dare examine in depth.

Surely, Drummond and he had maimed and killed tonight. Surely, they had left carnage in the road. And surely this was not the first time they had done so. But when had he, Keith Marchand, crossed the line? When had he received his combat baptism, his life forever changed, his spirit marked indelibly for eternity? At what moment had he first taken another's life, after which he would never be the same again?

Marchand forced himself out of this fleeting but dangerous reverie as the last anti-aircraft tracer rounds sputtered and died while futilely chasing the fleeing Phantom. Now, he began to feel vaguely uncomfortable in a different way. He wondered why. Suddenly, it dawned on him that his flight suit was rather wet and cold. The moisture was more than sweat.

Marchand flushed with embarrassment as he recalled losing bladder control and his near panic when Drummond fired the Zuni rockets just two seconds sooner than he had expected. Still on hot mike, he mumbled sheepishly, "Kelly, I feel like a dumb ass – losing my cool during our rocket run. I --"

Drummond cut him off, "Look Keith, you didn't know what I was doing up here. I fired a bit early because those thirty-seven millimeter shells were so close I could smell 'em as well as hear 'em blowin' holes in our bird. I had to do it. Another two seconds in that run and you and I wouldn't be talking now. I fired the Zunis when the last tracer looked like it had me between the eyes. I'll be damned if we're going to buy the farm for some lousy, Russian-made trucks. So, I dumped the nose and made the best last second corrections I could, then fired it all at once."

"You mean you fired early?" Marchand queried. Early to save our lives, he went on silently. He wondered whether Drummond was saying that he aborted the run and his orders and wrote his own rules. Marchand wasn't sure he really wanted to know. "Kelly – "

"Look – this is seriously just between you and me, kid. Really, you didn't know what was going on and I didn't have time to tell you. We were taking some serious hits, and those Zunis did look like the end of the world when they fired all at once. So don't sweat it. You were doing your job and you did OK."

Rather than asking Drummond exactly what he meant, Marchand simply replied, "Hey, thanks." Still, this was not quite enough for Marchand to forgive himself for breaching fighter pilot bravado. "It's just that – "

"Have a good stiff scotch when we get back to the ship and forget it. And, don't forget to thank the Lord tonight that none of those hits we took knocked out an engine or ruptured a fuel cell."

"Yeah, but I can't get over blowing my composure like that."

"You're lucky you're not swimming home or worse – so don't worry about your composure for God sakes."

Uncomfortably reassured, Marchand let the matter drop. Drummond's compassion hadn't made his flight suit any drier, but his quick thinking had most likely saved their lives. Marchand keyed his intercom once more and said sincerely, "I'm damned pleased and lucky to be flying with you, Bulldog."

"My pleasure, Keith. Say, by the way, do you have a squadron handle yet?"

"No, not really. Why do you ask?"

"Well, you got one now. You're now 'The Rocketman.' What do you think about that?"

"I don't know, Kelly. There's a part of this flight I'd just as soon not talk about, specifically those rockets that I mistook for a direct hit."

"Hey, we did take some flak damage tonight. I'm still checking engine and system gauges for problems. Anyway, no one but me will ever know how you got your handle. Just like no one will ever know how I got to be 'Bulldog' Drummond."

"How did you get that handle anyway?"

"Not tellin', Rocketman. Not tellin'."

"Roger that," Marchand replied, somewhat mollified.

Both men grew silent as the blackness of the night sky engulfed them and the moon cleansed them in forgiving fingers of a cool soothing light....

Here was a separate world, and a separate peace, for airborne warriors, far above the struggling world below them.

7.

NO CHRISTMAS NO MAS

As Air Force One crossed over the Mississippi River winging west toward San Francisco, early reports of the first Than Hoa and Ha Tinh strikes began trickling into the communications center on board. Air Force pilots returning from early strikes against road traffic coming south from Haiphong to Than Hoa were sanguine in their descriptions of their strikes. Many reported numerous secondary explosions after their bombs and rockets struck. Navy attack and fighter aircrews had only just commenced their missions around Ha Tinh so their reports were not yet available.

Just as McNamara had promised Johnson earlier that morning, debriefing and intelligence reports of these missions were delivered to him on a real time basis and Johnson read each set of communiqués eagerly. He knew that his airmen had only a small window of opportunity to destroy a substantial portion of the arms delivered by Russian ships to Haiphong before they were dispersed along the hundreds of miles of the Ho Chi Minh Trail. All along the Trail, tens of thousands of North Vietnamese Army regulars carried hundred pound backpacks and pushed bicycles laden with hundreds of pounds of these munitions southward along the myriad tributaries of the Trail. But not even massive, non-stop bombing strikes along the length of the Trail could prevent the coming major attack.

Johnson pumped his fist in the air as he read the preliminary strike reports. "Goddamn it, I'm gonna get those bastards before they get us!" he roared. But even as Johnson cheered his airmen on, the situation in the Tonkin Gulf was developing to President Ho's favor, not Johnson's. Less than a quarter of the Air Force and Navy missions against Than Hoa and Ha Tinh had been launched when a massive winter monsoon swept into the Tonkin Gulf from the South China Sea. The three Navy carriers in the Gulf would likely have to cancel more than three quarters of the strike missions scheduled for the Ha Tinh area during the next two to three days. In addition, as the monsoon moved overland to the coastal and flood plain regions of North Vietnam, the Air Force found it nearly impossible to attack their targets around Than Hoa.

As the first Navy strike aircraft returned to their carriers from Ha Tinh, the weather had become increasingly dangerous for flight operations. Wing Commanders aboard the *Constellation* and *Enterprise* anxiously awaited recovery of their strike aircraft as the weather steadily worsened. Getting all their birds back aboard became the test of the day. Offensive operations would be on hold until the weather cleared.

President Johnson's mood aboard Air Force One was still ebullient when the Air Force Intelligence Major asked to speak to him. As the officer described the rapidly deteriorating weather in the Tonkin Gulf, the President's mood plummeted like a jet fighter without an engine. When told that continuation of strikes around Than Hoa and Ha Tinh would be impossible until the weather cleared, Johnson exploded and demanded that the senior Air Force general aboard Air Force One report to him immediately.

General Greyson reported to the Presidential office suite and saluted smartly. Johnson looked up from his desk and immediately demanded to know why no further strike flights could be flown for several days.

"General, I know that we have several types of aircraft like the Navy A-6 and the Air Force F-111 that have all weather strike capability and I want to know why they can't pick up the slack while this goddamn monsoon lasts. We've paid billions of dollars for these planes and it's time for 'em to prove their worth, by God!"

The General, still standing at attention, tried his best to respond. "Mr. President, you're quite right. Both aircraft types can strike in all weather conditions. But the problem we have here is that we don't know where these truck convoys are precisely. The pilots must actually find them visually as they travel south. At night we use parachute flares to light up an area so that the aircrews can see them. It's impossible to send out our all-weather attack aircraft against moving targets simply because we can't fix a specific target location in their inertial navigation systems. It's only the old Mark One, Model A eyeball that can do the job. Bottom line, if we can't see them, we can't hit them."

Johnson stood to his full height and pounded on the desk in front of him. "Well, hell fire and damnation, General, you best get on the radio to McNamara, General Westmoreland, Admiral Cousins and whoever else you need to talk to and find out how we can bottle up those supplies coming out of Haiphong Harbor. We can't and we won't allow those munitions to get into South Vietnam. Is that clear, General?

"Yes Sir, it's perfectly clear. I shall report back to you immediately. Do you wish to take part in the conference call, Sir?"

Johnson thought a moment then concluded that his presence would only make the situation more complicated. "No, General, I don't want to be involved. I got to write a speech and get ready for another impromptu press conference when we arrive in Sidney. I just want some damn answers to this problem. God only knows what President Ho and General Giap have up their sleeves and I can't let them supply their men in the South without opposition. So, come up with a plan and do it damn quick. Am I clear on that point?"

"Absolutely, Mr. President, Absolutely."

8.

CHEATING DEATH AGAIN

The tranquility of the night sky illuminated by a full moon slowed Marchand's pounding heartbeat and cooled his emotions. He relaxed a bit and began to savor Checkmate Flight's success over Ha Tinh when Drummond asked whether he had checked the ship's weather forecast for their recovery. "Negative, Kelly, I'll call now," Marchand replied as he switched frequencies to contact *Constellation's* Approach Control.

The air traffic controller replied in a matter of fact tone, "Checkmate One, Grey Eagle Control forecasts an overcast to ten thousand feet extending all the way down to one hundred with half mile visibility in rain and fog for the next recovery."

"Well, fuck!" Drummond exclaimed over the intercom. "That's well below ship's weather minimums for recovery."

Marchand called the controller again to inquire whether the ship would cancel the recovery and send all aircraft to the enormous air base at Da Nang, South Vietnam. "Grey Eagle Approach, this is Checkmate One, are we bingo to Da Nang?"

"Negative, Checkmate, Da Nang and Chu Lai are under heavy rocket and mortar attack tonight. Both are closed to all traffic except emergencies until further notice. Recovery on board will commence at 2300 hours as scheduled."

"Goddamn, Kelly! We can't land ashore and the ship is probably in a fog bank. What a way to end a bitch of night!"

"Yeah, it's raining cats and dogs at the ship and mortar shells at Da Nang. Bet you thought we were home free after we crossed the beach a few minutes ago. Well, get ready for a an E-Ticket ride, Rocketman."

By the time Checkmate flight arrived at the thirty-mile instrument approach gate to the *U.S.S. Constellation's* landing pattern, Approach Control had already transmitted instrument landing instructions to each Checkmate crew. As Marchand checked in with their assigned controller, Drummond prepared himself for the most demanding aspect of a Navy fighter pilot's mission – landing his aircraft on the carrier's constantly moving, often pitching and rolling deck. Despite years of training and experience, Drummond's pulse rate and blood pressure, like those of most Navy carrier pilots, now began the inevitable increase until both were substantially higher than an astronaut's during a return from orbit.

Night carrier landings required the full range of Drummond's finely honed skills in order to fly an instrument approach to the carrier in foul weather. Drummond often explained to his non-flying friends that such landings were like flying at speeds between a hundred fifty and two hundred fifty miles per hour through a thirty-mile long, pitch black corridor a hundred feet wide and thirty feet high that twisted, turned and looped in racetrack patterns while descending eighteen thousand feet to the approach end of a runway. Then, he'd laugh and say it's not a big deal; commercial airline pilots do it every day, several times a day. But just to make it more fun, Navy pilots can't count on their runway presenting itself so nicely at the end of the instrument corridor because their runway is a carrier deck which itself moves at thirty miles per hour and constantly changes directions to keep the wind moving down the centerline of the deck.

Drummond well knew that staying within that imaginary corridor meant never straying more than a few feet above or below the glide path nor a fraction of a wing width from the flight deck centerline. The penalty for straying more than a few feet outside the invisible corridor could be irksome and tiring at best when the pilot was sent to fly the instrument corridor all over again or fatal should he fly into the water at nearly two hundred miles per hour.

Drummond's ace hold card was his finely tuned ability to adjust constantly to a carrier's frequent course changes during an final instrument approach, as the carrier maneuvered to keep the wind straight down the centerline of the flight deck. Unfortunately, at the end of the mission to Ha Tinh, as Drummond was setting up his final approach to the *Constellation*, the weather deteriorated even further below the carrier's minimums for aircraft recovery. As Drummond turned to his final approach heading, the bottom of the mile-thick cloud cover dropped to a mere one hundred feet above the water and visibility plummeted to a quarter mile.

The *Constellation* was, in fact, moving in and out of a fog bank that it could not steer around. Controllers would normally have terminated Drummond's approach and sent him and Marchand to Da Nang. But the massive rocket and mortar attacks on the alternate air bases at Da Nang and Chu Lai had only intensified, so the Air Boss had absolutely no choice but to try to bring Drummond and his two wingmen aboard the carrier despite the foul weather.

Drummond remained precisely on course, airspeed and altitude as he flew his instruments to the ship. His concentration was focused as intensely as a laser beam. Every nerve and muscle was primed to respond instantly to the constant flow of information from his instruments. Drummond's right arm, wrist and hand moved smoothly in delicate increments right, left, forward and back, keeping the aircraft's heading, pitch and roll precisely on the optimum glide path. His left hand constantly adjusted the throttles, continuously modulating engine power so that the Phantom descended at exactly the desired rate. Drummond's feet danced lightly on the rudder pedals to position the fighter's nose onto the assigned heading.

Drummond's entire body was so involved in the landing sequence that he barely noticed that his flight suit was drenched with perspiration. But the real work took place inside his helmet where he integrated all the information from at least eight flight instruments in order to finely adjust the flight controls. His awareness of spatial orientation, position and movement were so acute that the twenty-ton fighter never varied more than ten feet from its optimum glide path.

Neither Drummond nor Marchand had time to look outside the cockpit. They would have seen nothing if they had. Outside the cockpit, rain clouds were as black as pitch, absolutely impenetrable to the moonlight shining thousands of feet above. Only the soft red light of the instrument panel provided a warm glow inside the cockpit. Only the sound of the engines and an occasional radio transmission interrupted their intense concentration as Drummond drove the Phantom on into the void.

As the aircraft continued its descent toward the ship and the water, Marchand wondered fleetingly whether his trust in Drummond's skill and the aircraft's instruments was well founded. "Christ, if Drummond screws up or the instruments fail, we could descend into the water at two hundred fifty knots and disintegrate in a millisecond, " he mumbled to himself. There wouldn't be much of anything left for the rescue helicopters to recover, he thought. There never is, except maybe a cracked, misshapen helmet floating in the waves, bearing contents it was unable to protect. Marchand shook his head then forced himself to concentrate on the instruments.

To free Drummond's concentration so he could focus on the instruments, Marchand handled all radio communications with the carrier. As Approach Control called for Checkmate One to make corrections to course and altitude, Marchand acknowledged each transmission and monitored Drummond's every move on his own instrument panel. If Drummond were to miss or misinterpret the controller's directions, Marchand would provide corrective information.

When their aircraft reached a critical point in the landing profile, just fifteen miles behind the carrier, Marchand called the controller, "Approach, Checkmate One, at the fifteen mile gate."

"Roger, Checkmate One," the controller responded in a steadied voice, "descend to one point five, maintain heading one six five and two five zero knots." Drummond eased the throttles so that the Phantom began to descend to its newly assigned altitude of fifteen hundred feet. Marchand responded to the controller, "Checkmate One, roger, out of two point five for one point five, heading one six five degrees, airspeed two five zero knots. Say again visibility."

"Gray Eagle Approach, visibility is currently point five in rain and fog."

Marchand and Drummond communicated between the Phantom's two cockpits on their own private hot mike as they flew the landing approach. Over the intercom between deep breaths, Marchand commented, "Looks like we earn our flight pay tonight, Kelly."

"Every fuckin' dime of it," Drummond replied. "Damn this weather!" He exclaimed over the intercom through gritted teeth.

The controller transmitted. "Checkmate One, come port to one five five degrees, slow to final approach speed, descend and maintain twelve hundred feet. Eleven miles from touchdown."

While Drummond increased the flap setting and pushed the landing gear handle down to extend the Phantom's landing gear, Marchand transmitted in a paced monotone, "Checkmate One, roger, coming port to one five five, descending to twelve hundred feet, slowing to one six zero knots. State cloud base, over."

"Gray Eagle Approach, cloud bottoms reported one hundred to one hundred fifty feet."

"This ain't pretty," Marchand muttered to himself as he checked the heading given by Approach Control against his own radar picture. He was not pleased with what he saw. He stiffened and said, "I don't like this heading, Kelly, not at all. The bearing is all fucked up and we haven't intersected the glide path yet. This whole approach is totally fucked up. We should be heading about twenty degrees more to port and be nearly a mile downwind from our position. What the hell is Approach Control doing?"

Drummond tried to come up with a suitable interpretation. "Well, they may plan to turn us again when we're a little closer."

"OK, but they better turn us quick or we definitely won't be able to correct in time."

They flew on for another minute before Approach Control transmitted again, "Checkmate One, descend to eight hundred feet, come port to one four five degrees, say fuel state."

Marchand responded, trying not to sound stressed, "Checkmate One, out of twelve hundred feet for eight hundred, coming port to one four five degrees, fuel state one point five."

"Roger, Checkmate One, copy your fuel state at one point five, you are now seven miles from touchdown."

Just eight hundred feet above the water, flying in absolute darkness and with less than fifteen minutes of fuel remaining, the fighter was only three minutes from the carrier but its line up with the carrier deck was becoming increasingly skewed. Marchand knew that something was wrong, seriously wrong. It became increasingly apparent that Approach Control's line up was well off the flight deck's centerline. And, if Drummond could not land on this approach, their remaining fifteen hundred pounds of fuel would not be sufficient for another attempt. In that event, their last chance to avoid disaster would be a rendezvous with an airborne tanker to refuel before trying another landing.

But joining with a tanker was a near impossibility given the darkness and foul weather. Failing that, Drummond and Marchand would be forced to eject from the aircraft and take their chances in the water. Nighttime water survival skills would then determine their fate. Given all that was going against them, they would be quite lucky to make it back safely.

Marchand became increasingly critical and apprehensive as he watched the carrier drift farther and farther off to the left of his radar. "Damn it, Kelly, this is no good. Approach Control isn't getting us into line up quickly enough, we're going to get a fuckin' wave off for sure! We gotta do something NOW!"

Drummond recognized that Marchand was mentally preparing for ejection for the second time that night. Then he looked at his radar screen, "Oh shit! You're right; and we damn sure don't have enough fuel for another instrument approach or to rendezvous with the tanker."

"Yeah, no way I can steer us to the tanker in this damn weather before we flame out," Marchand said over the intercom before keying his radio transmitter, "Approach, this is Checkmate One, check our line up again, will ya. We're drifting too far right of centerline." Too far from home, he whispered to himself.

"Roger, Checkmate One, come port to one three zero degrees, descend to six hundred feet," the controller said trying to correct his previous errors. "Four miles from touchdown."

Now, less than two minutes from landing, Drummond realized that even this correction was insufficient. It would not stop the aircraft's continuing drift to the to the right of the carrier's centerline. In fact, the new heading would inevitably doom his approach if he followed it. Drummond cursed to himself, then relying on years of finely honed flying skills, he moved his stick to the left as sharply as he dared at such low altitude and airspeed. He knew that he had to make a sweeping "s" turn to have any chance of lining up correctly with the flight deck. Drummond didn't even bother telling the controller what he was doing.

Marchand knew exactly what the self-directed maneuver was designed to do. He transmitted their different approach to the controller, "Checkmate One coming port to zero niner zero degrees, descending to six hundred. Do you copy, Approach Control?"

The controller immediately understood that Drummond had taken control of the instrument landing himself, protocol be damned. The controller knew that he had been unable to provide the corrections that Drummond needed. He also knew that Drummond's fouled up approach was primarily the result of the carrier's attempt to stay in the wind and out of the deepest part of the fog bank. No mistake on Drummond's part had created the crisis.

But soon it wouldn't matter whose errors or what conditions had created the problem because Checkmate One would be either be on the flight deck or in the water in just a few minutes. The controller wondered whether it was too late for Drummond and the waiting Landing Signal Officer to salvage the approach and landing and hoped to God they would. Knowing there was nothing else he could do, he simply transmitted, "Roger, Checkmate, I copy your heading change. Two miles from touchdown, switch to Paddles frequency. God speed, Gentlemen."

Marchand changed the frequency of the aircraft's ultra high frequency radio to the channel used exclusively by the carrier's Landing Signal Officers, affectionately known by the radio call sign "Paddles." As the Phantom continued its descent at six hundred feet per minute, Drummond and Marchand hoped that within seconds they would see one of the precisely focused cones of white light projected aft of the carrier by its optical landing system. Drummond would use these tightly focused light beams, emitted by a series of Fresnel lenses located midway up the flight deck, for his final visual reference just before touchdown. The light beams, which to pilots on final landing approach looked like round white balls, were known simply as "meatballs".

Depending upon the meatball's position relative to a row of green reference lights or datum lights, Drummond would know whether he was on, above or below glide path. But his ability to see the meatball was a function of his having a clear line of sight. This night, the low cloud layer hung like an immensely foreboding blanket that completely obscured Drummond's sight line. He saw only the deep velvet blackness surrounding his canopy.

Lieutenant Commander Sam Jones, the senior Landing Signal Officer on the *Constellation* was on duty. He stood on a platform extending from the edge of the flight deck out over the water some eighty feet below. Jones was known to naval aviators throughout the

Pacific Fleet as the sweetest voice in WestPac. For years, he had talked the greenest pilots out of the darkest skies and brought them safely home.

On this night, Jones well knew that with the weather far below normal minimums, approaching pilots would not see the meatball until they were too close to the carrier to make adjustments and were far too close to the water to safely make heroic corrections. Jones would have little time to give pilots their final corrections, and the pilots would have less time to react.

But Jones had developed an uncanny sense of spatial orientation based almost exclusively on the sounds of an approaching aircraft and the different roars, growls and howling sounds its engines made depending upon the aircraft's attitude, power setting, pitch and roll. Jones raised the microphone and transmitted, "Aircraft in the groove, this is Paddles, check in and call the ball."

Marchand's relief upon hearing Jones' voice was palpable. "Paddles, Checkmate One, negative ball, fuel state one point one." Jones was their lifeline now and everyone listening on Paddles frequency knew it. Everyone listening also knew that Checkmate One would run out of fuel in less than ten minutes if it could not land on this approach.

Jones transmitted, "Roger Checkmate, call the ball when you see it and don't acknowledge further transmissions. You're right of centerline and correcting. Now, you're a little high, just take a skosh power off, not too much now; that's right, that's right, OK, now you're on centerline. Straighten it up now and give me a little power. That's good, that's good. Keep it comin' now; soundin' real good now, Bulldog." Jones said, breaching radio discipline by calling the pilot by his squadron handle. "Come on guys, you can do this," Jones said off mike.

Jones maintained his slow, soft southern-sounding LSO-speak that had calmed a generation of carrier pilots' nerves and Drummond flew only by following Jones' directions. If Jones were to make an error, Drummond would fly the Phantom into the water at nearly two hundred miles per hour without ever knowing that there was a problem.

Drummond continued moving his control stick and throttles and tripping lightly on the rudders to the sound of Jones' voice. Suddenly, he saw a bright white ball of light just where it should be, almost centered on the green datum lights. He simply had to correct for a slight right drift which he did with a tap of the left rudder, then he made a minute adjustment of the throttles to stay on glide path. He was already on hot mike so he only had to report, "Paddles, Checkmate One, Ball, fuel state point niner. We're comin' home, Sam!"

Coming home alive. Jones could now see the approaching fighter. The lonely Phantom looked like a dark angel descending from the heavens. Not quite finished, he smiled and responded, "Roger, Ball, give me a little power now, not too much, OK hold that – hold that – hold that." It seemed to Marchand as if the whole world had been holding its breath waiting to see this landing.

At that moment the twenty-ton fighter slammed to the deck in the normal carrier-landing mode and roared to full power as it caught the number three arresting wire. Drummond and Marchand pitched forward in their shoulder harnesses as the Phantom screamed to a full and final halt. The shock of the landing was the greatest reward the night had to offer. Drummond pulled his throttles back to idle and raised the arresting hook handle. He breathed a long, slow sigh of relief then taxied slowly off the angle deck to park and shut down.

"Well, we cheated death one more time, Rocketman," Drummond said in a voice filled with complete exhaustion. Quietly, as he pulled flight gloves from his sweaty hands, he said to himself, "One more time...." Then he trailed off into reflection.

Marchand checked the fuel gauge and saw that they had only five hundred pounds of fuel remaining – less than five minutes of flight time. He heard his heart scream thank you Lord many times, but he only said, "Thanks for the ride home, Bulldog! You done good; - real good!" He looked at the *Constellation's* deck, the mother ship, loving her steel bosom like never before. Suddenly, just being alive was an extreme experience.

9.

SEVEN PERCENT SOLUTION

The Seventh Fleet Operations Officer on board Air Force One reported to the President's suite following a hastily convened phone conference call between senior Department of Defense officials and senior field grade officers at the Pentagon. The officials included Secretary McNamara, Assistant Secretary Clark Clifford, the Air Force Chief of Staff, the Chief of Naval Operations, General Westmoreland in Washington and the senior military officers aboard the President's plane.

As the Admiral entered the Presidential Suite, Johnson was reading an intelligence report describing a strike by three Navy Phantoms just northwest of Ha Tinh that resulted in the destruction of fifteen to twenty heavily loaded munitions trucks. Johnson was smiling when he quipped, "Well Admiral, looks like one of our first strikes from the carrier *Constellation* has struck pay dirt. Too bad this damnable weather won't permit you boys to continue, wouldn't you say?

"Unquestionably, Mr. President. Our early carrier strikes have done a really outstanding job in spite of some very formidable air defenses."

"Yeah, but that's not what you came here to discuss, is it?"

"No Sir, Mr. President. After an intense but brief consultation, the Operations Staff has developed a solution to the problems caused by the rapidly developing winter monsoon and its effects relative to our battle plan for Than Hoa and Ha Tinh."

President Johnson shot a baleful stare at the three star-admiral and said rather dryly, "Go ahead, Admiral. You've got my attention."

"Sir, let me say at the outset that this revised operational plan is based largely on your previous order that no Soviet ship in Haiphong Harbor is to be exposed to an accidental hit from American aircraft. Every officer and DOD official involved in this plan is quite mindful of your concerns that we not risk more direct Soviet involvement in Vietnam by exposing any Soviet ship or crew to collateral damage from our strike aircraft."

"Well, that's a good start, Admiral, continue." President Johnson said leaning back in his high-backed leather chair.

"Mr. President, the operational plan involves three phases. The first is the immediate commencement of continuing all weather strikes by Navy A-6 Intruders designed to destroy every roadway, railway or other transportation facility from the Haiphong docks and south for a distance of fifty kilometers. As you are well aware, the A-6 is an all-weather precision attack bomber that can strike at any time of night or day without any visual reference whatever."

"Yes, I know, but tell me, just how accurate are these Intruders, Admiral?"

"We can program the computers on board these aircraft to strike as close as one hundred meters to the Soviet ships with less than seven percent probability of error. If we enlarge our safety factor to two hundred meters, the risk to a Soviet ship falls to less that one half of one percent for every Intruder strike.

"That ain't bad, Admiral, but why Navy aircraft only? Why not include Air Force F-111s as well?"

"Well Sir, the F-111s would have to fly from our bases in Thailand across several hundred miles of heavily populated and heavily defended North Vietnamese territory all the way to the coast of Vietnam in order to hit Haiphong. The losses would be great but worse yet, since the distance would be much greater than it would be for the Navy Intruders, the statistical probability of an accidental hit on a Soviet ship would be increased substantially as a result of system error."

"We can't have that, Admiral. So let's hear the rest."

"Second, we will continue to send maximum Air Force and Navy strikes against road traffic coming south from Haiphong through Than Hoa and Ha Tinh whenever the weather permits. And we will give Wing Commanders greater flexibility in determining when to launch strikes even in the most marginal weather."

Johnson rubbed his right ear, frowned and replied, "Isn't that just what we were trying to do until the weather intervened?"

"Yes, it was, Mr. President, but with the addition of maximum round-the-clock A-6 Intruder strikes right up to the edge of the Haiphong docks during all types of weather, we will present a seamless attack to the Vietnamese rather than one controlled by the weather. We'll keep General Giap constantly off guard and hesitant to commit all his new supplies to the roads outside the shipyards, at least not in massive amounts."

"OK, Admiral, what's the third phase?" Johnson replied warily.

"As a complement to our A-6 Intruder missions, we will launch a series of Alpha Strikes against a variety of targets in Haiphong whenever the weather is even marginal."

"Remind me, Admiral, what's an Alpha Strike? And what will it accomplish?"

"An Alpha Strike is composed of twenty to thirty attack bombers and their associated fighter escort and support aircraft designed to destroy major, heavily defended targets, Mr. President. Haiphong is the Navy's priority target area for its Alpha Strikes which will be committed to the destruction of warehouses, storage facilities, railroad spurs and loading docks. This will enable us to take care of any targets that individual A-6 missions fail to destroy but avoid collateral to Soviet ships."

The admiral paused to give President Johnson the opportunity to ask questions and to prepare for whatever mood Johnson happened to have settled in for the moment. Johnson was pensive and still troubled. After a long minute, the President replied, "Is this the best we can come up with, Admiral?"

The tall slender naval officer with three silver stars on his starched white shirt collar and aviator wings on his breast pocket rocked back on his heels and took a long breath before responding. "For the moment, Mr. President, that's our best operational plan. Personally, I wish we had the opportunity to go into Haiphong and blow the hell out of every ship in the harbor, all the docks and everything around them but we obviously can't do that.

"In all honesty, Mr. President, it seems that we're fighting a very wily, very cunning and terribly committed adversary with one hand tied behind our backs. I truly don't wish to be insubordinate and beg your pardon if I have been, Sir. But fighting a war under these restrictions is damned difficult. We will do our best but it's difficult."

Johnson rubbed his chin and let his thoughts run before replying. "Admiral, I appreciate your honesty and candor and I suppose this is about as good as you all can do given the constrictions I've placed on you. It's difficult for me as well. But I'm trapped by political and historical forces, Admiral. I'm damned if I do fight this war all out with no restrictions and risk a wider war, perhaps even the Third World War with the Soviets. And I'm damned if I don't fight it with all guns blazing because there is a real possibility, I'm just coming to realize, that we might lose this War and it will be the first time ever it has happened. And, it will be on my watch.

"But, these are my problems, Admiral, not yours. I suppose you and the other Operations Staff have done a good job under the circumstances. Don't let my comments worry you.

"Let me think about this operational plan for another hour or so until we land in California. I'll talk to McNamara and get back to you when we take off for Australia."

"Yes, Mr. President. And Sir, I truly hope that my unauthorized comments haven't caused you any more problems," the Admiral said, wondering if he had just destroyed the rest of his highly successful naval career.

"No, Admiral, you haven't upset me any more that I am already. You've not said anything I haven't already thought. In fact, I wish your colleagues had risked speaking their thoughts and concerns with me as candidly as you've done. There's far too many 'yes men' around. Sometimes they make you think you have all the answers when, in fact, you don't even have all the questions."

"Thank you, Mr. President," the Admiral said while saluting and preparing to take his leave.

VOLUME ONE: PHANTOM WAR TRILOGY

10.

MILLER'S LAMENT

Marchand was still shaking as he removed his flight gear, whether from the damp flight suit or the residual effects of the flight, he didn't know. Although he didn't know exactly why, he had a strong need to see his friend Rich Miller. Quite anxious to find him, Marchand nevertheless made himself stroll in a leisurely fashion to Miller's stateroom. He had known Miller since Officer Candidate School in Pensacola and considered him almost a brother. Miller, a stocky crew-cut blond whose kind face and friendly voice had won him many friends in the squadron, interrupted his reading of a hunting magazine when Marchand poked his head into the steel gray stateroom.

"How about a few shots of Black Jack in my room as soon as I shower?" Marchand asked.

"Sure, I'll come by when I finish this article. But, for Christ sakes, take a good long shower; you stink like hell. What'd you do, piss yourself?"

Marchand scowled.

"You did! You pissed your pants, didn't you? Come on, 'fess up!"

"Fuck you, Rich. Really, fuck off! And don't take all night to come by; I've got a special occasion to celebrate tonight and an unopened bottle of Jack Daniels to do it with."

"Now you're talking; I'll be there when you finish your shower and not a minute sooner."

After a long, hot shower that finally stopped his shakes, Marchand returned to his room, donned a fresh uniform, and flipped on his tape deck. He needed music, soothing music. He opened the bottle of Tennessee whiskey and began pouring the amber liquid slowly over a glass full of ice. Soon, a Beethoven string quartet began to soothe his nerves.

Miller entered the room and went directly to the bottle before saying a word. After helping himself to a generous portion, he said, "Well, what are we celebrating, Keith?"

"My continued existence, dear friend, continued existence on this marvelous planet."

"You had a bad night, I take it," Miller replied while scrutinizing his friend's appearance.

"Damn, Rich, you have a flair for understatement. I barely got my ass back on this goddamn boat tonight."

"OK, OK, cool your jets, no harm intended."

"Christ, your empathy is overwhelming tonight," Marchand replied, his sensitivity somewhat injured. How could Miller of all people be so insensitive?

"Oh hell, I'm sorry, Keith," Miller said genuinely. He paused a few moments then said, "Actually, I've been somewhat depressed lately, and I suppose a bit sarcastic as a result. I was crude. Rude, I mean. I know you had a rough time tonight. There were some A-4 drivers in the wardroom talking about the fireworks around Ha Tinh. They mentioned that the *Enterprise* lost a Phantom somewhere in that area."

Marchand's hair stood on end. "Hells bells, I got a lot a friends on that boat. Did you find out who was flying?"

"No, I didn't. I think someone mentioned the crew but I didn't follow the conversation."

Marchand felt heartsick. He looked at Miller. There was an ambiguous but definitely anxious tone in his friend's voice. He asked Miller what was troubling him.

Miller sat down. "Well, Keith, for the last few days, I've had a premonition that something really fucked up is about to happen." Miller said as he swallowed a mouthful of whiskey.

"Oh yeah, to whom?"

"To me, Keith, who the hell do you think?"

"Bullshit! "

"Well, I wasn't sure at first, but now I am. I really am," Miller said looking Marchand squarely in the eye without flinching. "I think I'm going to buy the farm … and soon!"

Marchand felt irritation and frustration rising within him. "For Christ's sake, Rich, everybody goes through that crap. Don't take it so seriously."

"Yeah, I know all that -- but still, I'm sure it's going to happen to me … and there ain't a damned thing I can do about it," Miller said with the strangest facial expression Marchand had ever seen. It wasn't fear or even the anxiety he had seen moments earlier. It was more like resignation, the kind one feels when taking a dentist chair for a root canal. But this resignation was a vastly greater, more haunting variety.

Marchand tried to ignore his gut reaction to the emotions he had seen on Miller's face. If he had allowed himself to really feel his response, he would have bolted and run away from whatever this sensation was. He would have left Miller alone with this. Instead, Marchand became even more irritated with his friend.

"Hey, man, I asked you to come down to my room and help me celebrate my survival on my first night mission, the first time I got my ass hosed down royally, and here you are with your silly shit premonitions about busting your ass. Damn it, we may all buy the farm before this cruise is over. So why the hell are you brooding so much?" Marchand demanded sharply.

"Keith, I just know it, that's all. I just know it. You can feel these things. Really, you can." Miller looked down at the deck. "I thought you'd understand. I thought you were a bit more sensitive than the average fighter jock. I guess I was mistaken. I had you wrong. You can be as cold as ice when you have a mind to." Miller's disappointment showed on his sunburned face.

Marchand flinched as Miller's comments struck home. "OK, wait. I'm sorry. Really. So, Rich, if you really mean it, why don't you just turn in your damn wings and have the Skipper send you home?" Marchand gazed into Miller's eyes sincerely.

"Get serious, Keith, you know I can't do that. Besides, if I quit, then you or some other SOB would have to fly my missions. How the hell do you think that would make me feel? Having you or some other bastard fly for me? Maybe get bagged in my place. I feel bad enough already. Like shit if you really want to know."

"I think that's a bunch of bull, that's what I think. Let me tell you, if I felt for one second that I wouldn't make it through this cruise, I'd chuck my wings on the Skipper's desk so hard you'd have to chisel them off. And, as far as some other shitbird getting stuck with your missions or my missions or anybody's missions, that's just the breaks. Not your bloody fault," Marchand said, sounding a lot more certain of himself than he really was.

"No one quits out here and you know it, Keith. You either stick it out or you're branded a goddamn …"

Marchand was getting angrier watching the stress and anxiety build up in his friend's face. He decided to cut Miller off abruptly. "Branded like hell. You're awfully melodramatic tonight. But you're right about one thing. You can't fly out here thinking you're going to bust your butt or you'll bust it for certain. You can die that way. Let me tell you a little story that might straighten you out. Do you remember Mike Condon?"

"Yeah, the lucky bastard came down with asthma just a week before we left the States."

"Rich," Marchand said slowly, "Condon didn't have asthma any more than you or I do. About a month before we left for West Pac, he and I went out drinking one night. We both got wasted, but Condon became increasingly melancholy during the evening. He finally told me that he had a feeling that he would get bagged on this cruise, and he told me this just like you're doing now. Then he said that he had to find a way to get out of it."

"You mean he faked it?"

"A week before we sailed, Condon bought a carton of cigarettes, sat down and smoked damned near the entire carton; when he couldn't stand any more he went jogging until he nearly collapsed - almost ten miles - then he turned himself in to sick bay. The rest you know."

"I don't believe that crap, Keith."

"Look, why would I fabricate a story like that? I swore that I'd keep his confidence. The only reason I've mentioned it is to prove to you that every sonofabitch looks out for his own ass first. But even more important, when you're convinced that you're going to prang your butt in some smoking hole in the ground, you do what you have to do."

"Yeah, right," Miller said, plainly exasperated.

"Bloody hell, Rich, I mean it!" Marchand yelled, his face becoming red.

"Even if you're telling the truth about Condon, Keith, I couldn't pull off a charade like that. I just couldn't do it. Not me."

"You seem to forget something else. You've told me at least a dozen times that you hate flying in Dan Mitchell's back seat because he's a wild man in the air. The only reason you're flying with him now is that Condon couldn't hack it either and bugged out."

Miller shook his head. "So you want me to believe that the only reason Condon pulled the asthma stunt was to avoid flying with Mitchell?"

"Use your head, Rich. Condon quit because he was damn sure he'd buy the farm during this cruise. It might be Mitchell's antics in the air or it might be a lucky anti-aircraft round or a SAM missile tracking true, but he was sure of one thing. He knew that if he left on this cruise, he would not come home. So, he found way out of it. Simple as that."

"Well, I'm not Condon and I just can't flake out like that. I'd sooner die before I'd pull that kind of shit. I do have some honor and dignity you know."

Marchand grabbed Miller's shoulders and said quietly, "But, Rich, you don't have to pull a stunt like Condon. We're already in West Pac; all you need to do is to tell the Skipper that you can't handle flying off the boat any longer and turn in your wings. And, it would be the truth."

"But you know as well as I -- that's chicken shit!" Miller shouted.

"Don't be a fool. This isn't Officer Candidate School. You're not playing for demerits or to find out who will be a fucking five-bar man at commission ceremonies. This game is for keeps. You bust your ass, you don't get to play anymore, not this lifetime. Anyway, we're all learning that this isn't the kind of war that invokes honor, just self-preservation."

"I don't see you rushing into the skipper's stateroom with your wings," Rich replied trying to sound indignant and looking more depressed than ever, his skin taking on a grayish pallor.

"Well, I just don't feel the way you do. I don't have any premonitions, at least not yet."

"Fuck you, Keith -- just drink your damn whiskey and shut up. I'm sorry I ever brought it up," Miller said. "I should have kept all this to myself."

"Look, Rich, I didn't mean to piss you off. I'm just a bit fried, that's all. I nearly busted my ass tonight and I guess I'm a little short on attitude. I don't know what to say about your premonition. It's more than I can deal with. It's all I can do to keep my own emotions in check. Why don't you see Chris Davis, the Flight Surgeon, or maybe the Chaplain about this?"

Now Miller looked at Marchand as if he were crazy. "Are you nuts? That sort of thing won't do a damn bit of good. It's not like they're really here to help a guy do anything but fly his fuckin' missions."

"Of course, that's what they're here for, Rich."

"Yeah right," Miller said scowling at Marchand, and then realizing that his friend was being sincere. "Look, let's just forget it -- O.K.? I'm just talking off the top of my head. Just forget it all, and hurry up with your drink." Miller seemed to shift gears. "You don't want to miss the movie in our ready room. It's a Raquel Welch flick."

Surprised but glad to leave that topic behind, Marchand went with the flow. "Oh yeah, I nearly forgot. Can you imagine, as fuckin' horny as I am, forgetting that Raquel is playing tonight? But, Christ, I don't know, these movies drive me up the bulkhead. I don't know why we torture ourselves watching the damn things."

"Yeah, Keith, how long have we been at sea anyway?"

"Six weeks -- tomorrow. I never dreamed I could get so horny in just six lousy weeks."

"Hurry up will ya. The flick is about to start. By the way, I've got to stop by my room for something. I'll meet you there."

Marchand made it to the ready room in time to claim two of the comfortable steel- framed, red leather armchairs for himself and Miller. He put his seat back into semi-reclining position, placed his feet on the extended footrest and felt really comfortable for the first time since landing. As the credits began to run, Marchand looked around for Miller, but didn't see him. So Marchand reluctantly relinquished the saved seat to another pilot.

When the movie finally ended, Miller had still not arrived in the ready room. Marchand headed for Miller's stateroom. After a moment's thought, Marchand changed his mind and climbed up three levels to the flight deck. It was three in the morning. Flight operations had ended for the day. All aircraft had been spotted and chained in place for the next day's first launch. The three-acre flight deck was still and relatively peaceful. The flock of vicious steel birds were all quiet. A slight breeze cooled the sizzling hot steel deck and all the aircraft lashed to it. Marchand pondered his friend's depression as he strolled forward toward the bow: Miller was simply depressed about spending his first Christmas at sea -- and at war, Marchand told himself. "Damn," he muttered aloud, "Almost Christmas Eve, and here I am twelve thousand miles from home and wondering if I'll be alive come New Year's Day. I suppose that's enough to fuck with anyone."

Marchand reached the bow and descended a few steps to a small catwalk perched eighty feet above the water. All thousand fifty feet and five thousand men of the *Constellation* were behind him now. Suddenly, immense loneliness came over him with such force that he almost cried out. Thoughts of family and friends at home in California flooded his consciousness. He wondered how anyone could feel so alone while surrounded by so many people in such a small place. Marchand wanted to pray but couldn't remember how. He felt like sobbing but no sound would come. Slowly, the warm wind dried the salt water flowing down his cheeks. He spoke softly, "Christmas, damn. It's Christmas time and here I am. Why?"

Like a small steel island, the *Constellation* moved slowly in the darkness, barely making enough speed for steerage. Marchand stood in the catwalk for a long while. Gradually, the sound of small waves slapping against the bow soothed him. Again, he thought of Rich Miller. He wondered if Miller truly felt the presence of his death. Marchand chastised himself. He had not doubted Condon's sincerity when Condon told him of his death premonition, although perhaps he should have. On some level, he had not taken the conversation with Condon entirely seriously.

It was different with Miller. Marchand respected him, admired his honesty and his simplicity. In fact, he was quite fond of Miller. Clearly, Miller's foreboding was serious, and deserved a friend's attention, Marchand thought, cursing his insensitivity. He was puzzled by his abruptness with Miller. This was not the way he treated his friends.

VOLUME ONE: PHANTOM WAR TRILOGY

11.

DEMONSTRATION
OR
REVOLUTION

The year 1967 was climaxing in anything but peace. At home on American soil, anti-war protests were moving rapidly toward an eerily contagious violence. On a bitter cold Boston afternoon, just two days before Christmas, strains of increasingly angry protest resonated throughout the Boston University Plaza. In a disturbing rhythm and angst, a restive crowd divided into two arms of an angry choir and banged in counterpoint: "Hell no, we won't go! Hell no, we won't go! Hell no, we won't go!" and "U.S. Out of 'Nam! U.S. Out of 'Nam! U.S. Out of 'Nam!" and "One, two, three, four, what the hell are we fightin' for?"

Flames spiked at the center of the mass as one by one, protesters dressed in purposefully torn and mutilated army fatigues tossed burning draft cards into refuse cans. The cadence, volume, and absolute passion of the crowd were peaking at a near explosion point when finally the leader, a tall, long-haired, rather scholarly man in his forties, wearing wire-rim glasses and a monk-like robe over a tattered wool blazer, captured its attention at least momentarily so he could return to his speech. He was trying to ward off the near riot that was ready to ignite and to counteract the subversive influence of those in the crowd who would do the igniting.

"People! People! People of America! Your rights to protest must be protected! Look around you. Riot squads are here. They are ready for violence. Do not go there! Let's show them that we are not about violence! Remember that violence in protest of violence is no solution. Passive resistance is our model! Passive resistance is our statement!"

Cheers rose up from several quarters but other segments of the crowd rumbled ominously. The speaker continued, hoping to arm the group with quick knowledge of passive resistance. "Yes, people, we are angry. Yes, we want out of Vietnam. Yes, we want to stop the killing! But we..."

Shouts of "Stop the killing. Stop the killing!" came from various places around the plaza and momentarily drowned out the speaker, but he managed to hold everyone's attention and quell the chanting for a while as he continued.

"But!" the speaker shouted as he pulled a dog-eared three by five card from his pocket and began to read it. "Remember the words of Buddhist Monk Thich Nhat Hanh who teaches us about anger saying that, 'when you have seen your whole country destroyed, millions of people dying, it's only natural that you become angry.' "

"Hell yes!" shouted an angry voice from somewhere nearby.

The speaker continued, "But Hanh teaches us that 'through the practice of looking deeply, you can see things that other people cannot see. Why, you ask, have American soldiers come here? Have they come with intention to kill? To destroy our country?' "

"Yeah! Why!" someone shouted. "Why are we killing innocent Vietnamese peasants?" Waves of energy and anger rippled through the crowd. "U.S. Out of Nam" chants began again, but the speaker waved them down hoping his words would be the antidote to the threatening violence. This was, after all, a nonviolent protest of the violence. Suddenly, an angry protester dressed in military garb climbed onto the stage carrying a sign reading "Gulf of Tonkin Resolution Based on a Lie." The speaker read the sign and for a moment looked confused. A policeman tried to stop the protester but could not. The crowd cheered the sign waver on. Other matching signs popped up from among the crowd, as if they had been cued for this moment.

The speaker looked somewhat anxiously off to the side trying to locate and make eye contact with one of his Harvard graduate students and peace movement sympathizer, Marguerite "Margo" Collins. Collins had come in support of the peace demonstration. Maybe she should leave right now, he said to himself. But once he located her by means of her long blond hair, he saw she was not looking his way. She was studying the crowd.

The speaker tried to continue over the increasing noise. "This monk tells us that, 'If you had talked with the soldiers, you would understand that they were sent to Vietnam as pawns, to kill or be killed.'"

"Yeah!" a voice shouted out.

"The Gulf of Tonkin Incident was a lie!" someone else cried.

"' – you would see that Vietnamese soldiers also don't want to be killed, don't want to kill, but are forced to do so.'" The speaker looked around the rapidly growing crowd before he completed his quotation. "'When you practice looking like that, you see that the deep cause of the war is a policy based on a wrong perception of the situation in Vietnam and in the world and this wrong perception is the real criminal. It is a war based upon an invalid perception, my people!'"

While supportive shouts came from a few, the remainder of the crowd lost interest in this pacifist, intellectual approach to the protest, and returned to its chants, this time with a new level of anger and physical tension. Suddenly, there was a surge of activity and the speaker was swallowed up by rushing people. Fires flared as cans of burning draft cards spilled over and more paper was thrown into the flames. The body of swarming humans, now an animal of one mind, began to move across the plaza and down the street, marching rapidly on the verge of full stampede, toward a nearby Army Draft and Induction Center. The anger had not transformed itself into increased understanding this time. Invalid perceptions were irrelevant now.

Police in full mob control uniforms converged from all over the city. In reaction to the crowd, the police began to behave much like them. But they were heavily armed and ready to break bones and heads.

Margo Collins, who had been observing this transition in the behavior of the mob as if to study it, was suddenly trapped in the movement. She saw nowhere to turn for help. If she did not run with the group, she would be trampled. And, if she ran with the group, she could be assaulted by the riot squad. She tried to find a way out, but seeing nothing she began to panic. For a moment, shock prevented her from taking rational action.

She had only recently returned from six months of doctoral candidate research in Hong Kong where she had secretly traveled into Mainland China. She was familiar with scenes uncomfortably parallel to this one, scenes in which Chinese Communist Red Guards had lost control of themselves while trying to manage mobs of Chinese demonstrators.

Now danger surrounded Margo. She spotted an opening between clusters of running people and rushed toward a building for cover.

Halfway there, she tripped and fell. Trying to stand up, she was kicked and stomped. Just as she was about to fold herself into a ball, sink into the ground, and pray for the best, a hand grabbed her arm and pulled her to her feet. She looked at the person attached to the hand to see an armed, uniformed man trying to protect her as he forced a path of exit for them both. He shouted into her ear, "I'm escorting you to safety, Ma'am, so don't panic. Just stay as close to me as you can."

The policeman, or whoever he was, stood some six foot six and weighed at least two hundred and fifty pounds. He was also wearing full riot gear including a plastic face shield and carrying lethal as well as non-lethal weapons. Quickly, he escorted her to an armored limousine parked behind a police cruiser. "Harry, I got her. Get her out of here now," he shouted at the driver as he handed her off and she was tucked into the massive black vehicle.

Mildly hurt and a little dizzy after being caught between the protesters and the billy-clubbing riot squad, Margo was not quite herself until the car started rolling. She looked at the men in dark suits in the front seat. "Wait a minute," she said. "Thank you for helping me, but who are you? And where are you taking me?" My God, Margo said to herself, what if I'm under arrest for something? Oh God, what will my father say? What will his people do? No one can find out about this. Oh, God. How embarrassing for him.

"Anywhere you would like to go Ma'am. We're here just to bring you to safety."

Margo blinked with surprise. So they weren't arresting her. Could these men be her father's people? Or were they with an agency of some sort? "Who sent you anyway, and how did you find me?"

One of the men laughed. Neither of them answered. But they seemed to mean her no harm. "Well then, just get me to Harvard Square, please," Margo answered feeling a confused sense of relief. Why haven't these men asked me my name? Where did these men come from? Why did they pick me to rescue?

"Harvard Square, Ma'am?"

"Yes, please," Margo answered with urgency. Her father, Mitchell Collins III, expected her at home in Manhattan in just a few hours. She clenched her teeth. Her powerful father whom she loved so dearly and who was so precious to her would not understand her absence at an important political dinner later that evening.

She knew that Mitchell Collins was far too visible to have his daughter caught up in an anti-war demonstration since he was a major player in legal and financial circles throughout the Eastern seaboard. Collins was also a leader in and a major contributor to the Republican Party. He would never approve of Margo's attendance at the wild, uncontrolled demonstration, even to watch, let alone participate.

Nor would Republican campaign managers whom her father was guiding through policy debates be sympathetic. Their sole objective was to unseat the Democrats in next November's presidential election, especially "that damn Texan" as they called President Johnson. A man with a bleeding heart liberal daughter did not fit their wish list for a party leader in the slightest, she thought.

As if Johnson could be any worse than whomever they wanted to replace him with, Margo moaned to herself. "Meet the new guys, same as the old guys," she mumbled. Only, this time, the new guys could be even worse, she thought. If only this whole Vietnam thing just would end now, tomorrow, soon, she wished. It's tearing this country apart.

But Margo was simply too upset and unnerved to leave for New York. She decided to forget the party, remain in Cambridge for Christmas and recover from this dreadful night.

12.

CHECKMATE DOWN

On Christmas Eve, 1967, Marchand flew twice. His first mission was a strike flight into Laos. There he and Kelly Drummond routinely dumped their bombs on a "suspected troop concentration" conjured up by the fertile imagination of an Intelligence Officer in Saigon in order to impress his superior officers in the Pentagon.

Marchand found his second mission dreadfully boring but he appreciated it. It consisted of flying a one hundred fifty-mile long racetrack pattern slightly east of the North Vietnamese coastline to guard the U.S. fleet against theoretical airborne or naval attacks that somehow never materialized. Such flights were dramatically termed "combat air patrol" and Marchand took comfort in the fact that the only real danger other than the night landing was the hard bottom of his ejection seat that grew harder and more uncomfortable as the flight time exceeded three hours.

When Marchand returned from his last flight, he showered and joined the rest of Fighter Squadron Twenty-One's officers already seated in Ready Room Two. After everyone had taken seats, Santa Claus of the South China Sea was introduced. Although he was much too tall and thin, Lieutenant Commander Kenny Price played his role enthusiastically. Repeatedly, Price reached into his oversized parachute bag to retrieve one of the gifts that had been wrapped and stored by the officers' wives and lovers before the carrier left San Diego in November.

With the roaring approval of the entire ready room, Price presented a leather World War I flying helmet and white silk scarf with the monogrammed inscription "Old Blue" to the squadron commanding officer, Commander Jack McGruder, whose Navy traditionalism earned him the handle. The squadron Executive Officer, Joe Garvey, received an old flight boot with the leather worn through the toe down to the steel toecap underneath. Price presented the boot to the Exec commenting, "We've all heard so much about your ensign ass-kicking boot that we asked your wife to donate it to the squadron so we could have it bronzed. However, the boot was returned from the machine shop as is -- they said the damned thing smelled too awful to handle. Besides, they didn't have enough bronze in the shop to do the job."

To everyone's delight, Price handed Marchand a box containing a pair of blue lace panties from a former San Diego girlfriend. The squadron Landing Signal Officer, Ron Hickman, received a well-wrapped bottle of Jack Daniel's Black Label whiskey. When the laughs were over and the officers returned to their rooms, Keith realized that only Rich Miller had not received anything.

On Christmas Day, Marchand again flew two missions, a milk run bombing strike against an oil storage depot in Route Package One, the southern most part of North Vietnam, and a photo escort mission to Laos. Returning to the ship, Marchand and Drummond heard a muffled mayday call go out over guard channel. They were both startled by the next full transmission.

"Mayday, Mayday, this is Checkmate 201. Lost visual and radio contact with wingman, Checkmate 207, twenty miles north of Haiphong,

114

010 radial from Red Crown at 87 miles."

"Oh Christ, Kelly, that's Kenny Price and Roger Davis in 207," Marchand shouted.

"Shut up, Marchand, maybe we'll hear something else," Drummond growled.

But only the communications between the rescue and search aircraft were heard. There were no transmissions from Checkmate 207 and no sighting of the crew or the wreckage.

A few minutes later Marchand keyed his mike button, "I don't understand why Price and Davis were sent up North today. The weather is for shit up there. Even if they could find the target, their bomb runs would have been almost entirely in the damn clouds. And those goddamned karst mountains around Hon Gai just poke straight up out of nowhere. What a stupid-ass mission, a fucking suicide run."

"It's bad weather for Hon Gai alright, but Price could handle it. They must have taken a bad hit or a SAM."

"Bullshit, Kelly, they would have gotten a few transmissions on the air if they had taken fire or were chased by a SAM. They flew into one of those God-forsaken karst mountains and for nothing; there's not one target around Hon Gai that's worth the price of the bombs we drop."

"Calm down, Keith; don't bust your gut over something you can't control. I'm sure Price and Davis made it out anyway."

"Screw it, I just want to get back to the ship and have a scotch," Marchand muttered.

Neither Price nor Davis made it back. They had not ejected from their aircraft before it slammed into one of the peculiarly shaped, nearly vertical mountainsides, known as karst, at an altitude of thirty-eight hundred feet traveling at nearly six hundred miles per hour. Only a black smudge mark on the jagged limestone marked the site of impact.

Through broken clouds they had mistaken a collection of abandoned oil drums for the petroleum storage depot that was their intended target. Consequently, Price rolled into his first bombing run three miles south of the actual target. The base of the broken clouds hovering around three thousand feet had obscured the stony face upon which Checkmate 207 disintegrated. Checkmate 201, which had been flying Price's wing, was in clouds when 207 flew into the mountain, so there were no witnesses.

When Ron Hickman and Larry Gross landed in 201, they reported the weather conditions around the target, the presence of the karst-type mountains, and that they were positive that 207 had flown into one. However, since no one had actually seen the impact or the wreckage, Air Intelligence reported Price and Davis missing in action. The telegrams to Angela Price and Shirley Davis reported their husbands as MIA's. The telegrams were sent on the day after Christmas after all search operations were terminated because of continued foul weather. There was little talk among the flight crews regarding the bad luck that had befallen Price and Davis. What could have been said was not said. The questions that could have been asked were not.

13.

RED CARRIER

Life on the *Constellation* moved with its own peculiar but familiar routine. Grief took a back seat to duty. Death took a back seat to orders. For the preceding two weeks, increasingly dense clouds blanketed the North Vietnamese coastline precluding all but a few strikes north of the Demilitarized Zone. Most of the sorties flown from the *Constellation* were close air support missions for American and South Vietnamese troops fighting south of the DMZ. The carrier suffered no more losses and most of the flight crews settled into a relatively comfortable routine.

But the ship's pleasant schedule changed abruptly when it transitioned to "Red" carrier schedule, shifting flight operations that normally ran from noon until midnight to midnight through noon. During the previous two-week period as "Blue" carrier, only three landing cycles were flown completely in darkness. As "Red" carrier, five aircraft launch and landing cycles would be made at night. Aircrew stress increased accordingly.

The *Constellation* was two days into the Red carrier schedule. Marchand struggled to keep awake during the middle of his watch as squadron duty officer. He had monitored the 0300 launch and recovery, made his written reports, made all required logbook entries and all was well.

The ready room was deserted but for a squadron radar technician with insomnia who was stretched out in one of the leather crew briefing armchairs to read. By 0400 in the morning, Marchand resorted to writing letters to stay awake but with diminishing success.

At 0410 in the morning, the ready room intercom blasted Marchand awake. "READY ROOM TWO, THIS IS AIR OPS. We've lost radar and communications with Checkmate 211; get someone up here on the double. 211 may have gone down."

Marchand snapped to his high alert mode. "Air Ops, Ready One, roger. Do you have any emergency beacons?"

"Negative, 211's wingman is still in the area, but hasn't sighted or heard anything. 211's last known position was fifty-five miles on the three five zero degree radial from Red Crown. We lost radar contact when it descended to identify an unknown surface contact."

"Roger, Air Ops, what was the weather in that area where 211 went down?"

"About a three hundred foot overcast with about two miles visibility."

Marchand shut off the squawk box in a white-hot rage. "Those bastards at Red Crown sent a bird down to the water at night, below a three hundred foot overcast, to check out another damn fishing boat! I just know it!" Marchand barely restrained himself from shouting in the empty ready room. As the official representative of the squadron, he had a job to do and he had to do it without emotion.

But suddenly the crushing and ugly realization hit. Marchand recalled who was flying Checkmate 211. "Oh, Jesus, Rich Miller and Dan Mitchell were in that bird!" he shouted. Miller's Christmas Eve premonition exploded in Marchand's brain: Miller had said, "I think I'm going to buy the farm … and soon."

Miller's words reverberated mercilessly against the walls of Marchand's consciousness. Full of rage and grief, he shouted to the empty ready room, "Damn it, I'll bet anything that Mitchell was screwing around too. I'll bet that son of a bitch took the aircraft down to fifty feet just to scare the hell out of the crew of a dumb fishing boat! Now Mitchell has killed himself and my friend in the bargain."

Marchand looked around. The ready room was still empty, even the sleepy sailor had left. No one had heard him crack. No one had heard him yell out the truth. He composed himself somewhat and called the squadron commander's stateroom on the phone.

Commander Jack McGruder was more than irritated when he answered the phone. "What is it, Marchand? My flight doesn't brief until 0730."

"Skipper, I hate to wake you early, but I think we've lost a bird. Rich Miller and Dan Mitchell in 211 are reported down. Fifty miles north of Red Crown. I just received word from Air Ops. They want you down there right away." Marchand took a very deep breath, as if he hadn't breathed since he heard the news.

"Oh shit! OK, Marchand, you stay in the ready room. I'll go to Flight Ops as soon as I'm dressed. Uh, are there any signs that the crew got out?"

"No, Skipper, nothing yet; but 210 is still in the area, and I imagine the search and rescue helos are on the scene by now."

"Jesus, any word about what happened?"

"Only that they were sent down to get a visual I.D. on a surface contact under a low-lying three hundred foot overcast," Marchand responded, muffling his rage and sarcasm as best he could.

"Christ almighty, Red Crown! When are we going to stop allowing ship drivers to order aviators around? I'll call you from Air Ops, Keith." McGruder paused for a moment, then spoke in a softer tone, "Oh, no ... Miller was a close friend of yours, wasn't he?"

"Yeah, Skipper, we went through flight training together."

"I'm sorry, Keith, very sorry about this."

Marchand hung up the phone then suddenly remembered Mike Condon. Condon must have seen this one coming, just as he said. And I thought he was lying; thought he was just a lying coward with that asthma bullshit. But it looks like he was right all along.

"You bastard, Condon; it should have been you in 211 with Mitchell tonight," Marchand said aloud to no one at all. "That's crap; I'd have done the same damn thing. Condon had the sense not to risk his ass in this goddamn undeclared war. Rich didn't; that's all there is to it. Now he's down or even dead." Marchand hoped desperately that Miller was still alive. But he knew better.

Suddenly, the squawk box crackled, "Marchand, this is Commander McGruder in Air Ops. The SAR helos have sighted the wreckage of 211. There is no sign of survivors but the search hasn't been called off yet. I'll see you after I come back from Air Intelligence."

Marchand cleared his throat. "Roger, uh, Skipper, did you learn anything further about Red Crown's order to 211 to go below the overcast?"

"No. That's why I'm going to Air Intelligence."

14.

THE TONKIN GULF LIE

McGruder was fuming, almost spitting fire, when he reached the Integrated Operations Intelligence Center, known aboard ship at IOIC. It was a large internal space located mid ship immediately below the hanger deck, one of the safest areas on the carrier. Armed Marine guards denied access to this area except to those showing proper identification. McGruder first sought out the IOIC Watch Officer, a sleepy lieutenant who had only been aboard ship two weeks. McGruder demanded to see the Intelligence Commander who was, in fact, asleep. After some loud, harsh words, Commander Duffy was awakened and trudged hesitantly to IOIC to see McGruder. Although they had known each other for years and were rather good friends, neither was in a good mood when they met.

"Duffy, what the hell business do those damn people on that destroyer have telling one of my birds to go below a three hundred foot overcast to check out a damn fishing boat?"

"First of all, Red Crown is a cruiser -- not a destroyer. Secondly, how do you know it was a fishing boat? It could have been a PT boat. And if – "

McGruder cut him off abruptly. "I don't give a flying fuck if Red Crown is a rowboat or a cruiser. But I do know that the contact was a fishing junk, because the boys flying an E-2 tonight tracked the damn thing for nearly two hours doing three fucking knots. Three knots, does that sound like a PT boat to you?"

Duffy tried to be diplomatic. "Look, I know you're upset, but don't take it out on me. Red Crown has orders from Task Force 77 to get a visual identification on every surface contact that comes within thirty miles of the Force – been that way since the Tonkin Gulf Incident; you know that. They were only doing their job."

"Bullshit! You people are supposedly intelligent but I don't see much evidence of it. Any contact that small and slow is always a damn fishing boat. The BARCAP birds should only be ordered to check out a surface contact when there is reasonably good weather or in an emergency. You didn't have either one."

"I'm sure Operations had a good reason to call for the visual."

"Good reason, my ass! One of your intelligence people probably wanted to dress up one of your useless reports. Probably trying to get a lousy medal."

"Now wait a minute, McGruder. You're going a bit too far. If you want to take this up with the Admiral's staff, I'll arrange it for you."

"I'll take it up all right, but I'll get some horsepower behind me first," McGruder said, spinning around and heading for the hatchway. "You'd better hope my boys are still alive."

"McGruder, hold on a minute, will you? I want to talk to you," Duffy nearly shouted.

"I think you and I have said about all we can say and still keep it civil," McGruder replied.

Duffy walked over to McGruder and put his hand out in a

gesture of friendship. When McGruder reluctantly did likewise, Duffy asked, "Do you have a few minutes to come down to my stateroom, Jack? I do want to talk to you but not here."

Sensing that Duffy wished to tell him something important, hopefully about his two young airmen who were just lost, McGruder accepted.

When they entered Duffy's stateroom, Duffy handed McGruder a Chivas Regal on the rocks and waited for him to take a deep draft. After a moment, McGruder said, "Look, Pete, I appreciate your gesture, and I'm sorry about blowing up at you, but if you've got something important to tell me, let's not waste time. I've got to get back to my ready room."

Duffy took a long drink of his scotch before replying. "Well, I do have something important to tell you: Do you remember the night of the so-called Tonkin Gulf Incident about three years ago?"

"Of course, who doesn't? Summer of '64 I think. Gave President Johnson a chance to start bombing up North and expand the War in the South. Made Congress give Johnson all the authorization he needed to really rev up this War."

"Absolutely, but that's not what I mean. Do you know what actually happened that night?"

McGruder looked at Duffy questioningly then replied slowly, "Well, the two destroyers, the *Maddox* and the *Turner Joy,* were attacked by several North Vietnamese PT boats while they were in international waters. That was basically it. But there was some confusion, I recall. Some of the circumstances were never really very clear."

"Jack, here you are, a full commander in the U.S. Navy, the commanding officer of one of the Navy's finest fighter squadrons, and you don't have the foggiest idea what really happened that night. But you couldn't know because you aren't supposed to know. So let me tell you, Jack." Duffy paused, preparing himself to make this revelation. "What really happened was confusion. And the confusion was quickly transformed into deceit. And the deceit eventually yielded up a rich harvest of lies. The real truth has troubled me greatly since I learned what actually happened. And what happened is connected to the events that went down tonight."

McGruder looked increasingly irritated, frustrated, tired, and pained, and said, "Pete, suppose you just tell me what the hell you're talking about. It's too damn late for history lessons and I'm in no mood."

Duffy replenished his drink before speaking. "You will want to hear this, Jack. You see, I had just made commander and was assigned to the staff of a very senior admiral who will go unnamed. After the incident, this admiral was assigned the task of determining just what went down only a few miles from where we are right now. I was very involved in the investigation, until all the facts were discovered. And what I discovered isn't very pretty."

McGruder decided to try to listen to what his old friend thought was so important. "So, what did happen, Pete?"

"First the confusion. Shortly after the incident was reported to the Commander of Task Force 77, the captain of the *Maddox*, the destroyer which was supposedly the target of the North Vietnamese PT boats, called CTF-77 to say that he wasn't certain whether he had been attacked at all. "

Duffy eyed McGruder to see if he was taking this in. "To say that he wasn't certain whether he was attacked at all," Duffy repeated calmly. "Said that he had an inexperienced sonar man on duty that night, a night like tonight, as black as coal with no moon. The captain of the *Maddox* asked that his report be withheld until he could verify whether his man actually heard PT boat screws and torpedoes in the water during the alleged PT boat attacks. The problem was that the report had already been forwarded to Washington, to the Pentagon, to the CIA, and to the White House."

McGruder nodded his head, his eyes narrowed, "So, while the skipper of the *Maddox* tried to figure out what really happened, the gears were already turning in Washington. Is that right?"

"As far as it goes, yeah, you got it, you're right. That's the confusion part." Duffy paused and rubbed his eyes. "But there's more. We discovered that the *Maddox* was actually on an intelligence mission that night that brought her within the territorial waters claimed by North Vietnam and just outside the three-mile limit that the United States recognizes. So, the ship was actually intentionally exposing herself to hostile fire."

"OK, but still, the North Vietnamese were acting mighty damn aggressive by firing torpedoes at the *Maddox* just because she was in disputed waters."

Duffy nodded. "Right, except that there's still more to the story. Much more. Turns out that the CIA was conducting Black Ops that night, and the night before, along the North Vietnamese coastline near Ha Tinh where the *Maddox* was cruising. In fact, the CIA was landing SIOPS crews from unmarked Nasty Class PT boats off the North Vietnamese beach. Once ashore, the CIA boys were blowing up bridges and mining the roadways to slow down the truck traffic heading south from Haiphong."

McGruder was definitely listening now. "Secret Intelligence Operations, huh?"

"Yeah, SIOPS," Duffy continued, "The North Vietnamese were onto the CIA's program, and they were righteously pissed about it. So they had some of their own PT boats out patrolling the area to put a stop to these secret mini-invasions."

McGruder was incredulous. "You mean, we not only knew about the CIA's SIOPS, but we also sent our destroyers in close to shore where we knew North Vietnamese PT boats were trying to stop the covert actions?"

Duffy acknowledged McGruder's statement. "Yep. That's what I meant by deception, Jack. But that's still not all I have to tell you."

"More? Goddamn, Pete. What else was the fuckin' CIA up to?"

"That's the basic story, Jack. We, Americans, created or caused the whole damn Gulf of Tonkin incident. The *Maddox* just happened to stumble into the situation in time to transform a messy secret operation into an international incident. But now, now comes the lies."

McGruder blinked several times. "The lies?"

"Yeah, the lies. Turns out, the Pentagon, read the Secretary of Defense here, plus the CIA Director, and the most senior Navy Brass, as well as the White House, all knew what the hell was going on. But instead of defusing the situation, the powers that be decided to present a fuzzied up rendition of this fiasco to the press, the public, and the whole damn Congress, as an example of North Vietnamese aggression. The President then used this thoroughly fucked up incident, which we were largely responsible for creating, to get a near declaration of war from the Congress, the authority to heat up the War and especially to begin bombing North Vietnam."

McGruder sat up so straight he looked as if he were being electrocuted. "Jesus Christ Almighty! That's a fuckin' awful story, Pete. I've known you a long time so I know you're telling me the truth. But I've got one more question for you. What the hell does all this have to do with my boys I just lost?"

Duffy shook his head then gulped his scotch. Now that he had paved the way for the truth, he almost didn't want to tell it. "Just this, Jack. In order to continue the cover-up of this mess, orders went out that every unknown surface contact that was a potential threat to a Navy ship had to be visually identified. Every such radar contact had to be determined to be either friend or foe."

Duffy looked at McGruder to see if he was putting two and two together here. Uncertain, he went on to explain, "So that's why we still send your boys flying BARCAP down on the water's surface when it's dark and the weather is awful. It's to get a visual on whatever vessel might pose a threat to the fleet so that we can claim we're preventing another Tonkin Gulf Incident."

"Damn it, Pete, these so called threats always turn out to be Vietnamese fishing boats, you and I both know that!"

"Yep, we both know that," Duffy replied. "So do the big boys."

"Do you mean, we send our guys into harm's way just to keep up the charade that started with the *Maddox* bullshit?"

Duffy hung his head and answered, "That's why I brought you down here, Jack. I could see how this crap is eating your heart out and I just thought you ought to know."

McGruder looked as if he had been poisoned. "I guess I owe you an apology, Pete, but this information makes me even madder than I already was. This is just pure bullshit! Tell me, Pete, how can the President of the United States pull a damn awful stunt like that on the whole fuckin' country? Tell me. How?" McGruder stood up to leave Duffy's stateroom in total disgust. "I can't talk about this anymore right now, I can't take it. I can't hear it. I can't."

"Just one more thing, Jack. I never told you anything about the *Maddox* and I'll call you a damn liar if you ever say that I did. You understand. I've risked my ass here tonight telling you what really happened, but I don't want to hear about it again."

15.

ALMOST DEJA VU

At 0630 when the search was discontinued, one of the big HS-3 Sea Knight Search and Rescue helicopters headed for the *Constellation* to deliver pieces of the aircraft wreckage that had been recovered. Just after sunrise, Marchand was filling out the squadron flight operations logbook when one of the crewmen from the helicopter entered the ready room.

"Is this VF-21's Ready Room?"

"Yeah," Marchand grunted. "What can I do for you?"

"I got some stuff we recovered from 211's wreckage; where should I put it?"

"Just dump it on the floor here beside the desk," Marchand replied.

"Well, it's wet and kinda' messy; you sure you want it there?"

"OK, in that case, let me take you to our parachute shop; you can leave it there."

After the helicopter crewmen left the ready room, Marchand walked over to the large, green bag and opened it. Amid the small pieces of honeycombed metal and plastic, he saw a helmet. The helmet carried the familiar VF-21 Black Knight squadron insignia on the side, but it was horribly misshapen and cracked as though it had been crushed in an enormous vise. Marchand picked it up. On the back, Marchand could see the stenciled name "**MILLER**".

The helmet dripped seawater from its cracks as Marchand carefully and gently lifted it. Inside, the torn foam rubber padding looked slimy. In the cracks Marchand saw a grayish white, stringy material that looked like mucous. Suddenly, he realized that the material was brain tissue. It was Marchand's personal and private nightmare come true.

Marchand dropped the helmet and ran outside to the catwalk beneath the flight deck. He puked until he could barely stand.

Marchand half prayed, half cried, as tears streamed down his face and fell away to join the dark water below, "Oh Rich, my friend, my brother, I failed you. I'm so sorry, so sorry this has happened. You came to me for a little understanding, a little compassion, and I failed you. I could have done something to stop this, anything to stop this horrible tragedy. Why didn't I pay attention? Why didn't I do something? Will you forgive me? Please forgive me, Rich. Please forgive me."

Feeling as though he might self-destruct as he stared at the quiet sea flowing past the great ship's massive hull, Marchand willed himself to stop the emotional self-flagellation. He willed himself to draw his feelings deep within and construct a wall around his grief like all good military aviators are trained and required to do. He knew that, in order to continue, in order to survive, he had to proceed with as little emotion or feeling as possible. He could not truly touch this experience, not really. He could not go where it would take him. He had to move on without actually pausing to grieve, not even for his dear friend.

Duty called, duty and service to his beloved nation, Marchand reminded himself. Stifling the conflict emerging deep within, in the place where true honor and absolute duty vie with true guilt and absolute doubt for moral control, Marchand trudged back to his stateroom in hope of a deep, painless sleep.

16.

MACK THE KNIFE

As soon as President Johnson returned to the White House from his Christmas trip to Texas, Secretary of Defense McNamara requested a private meeting with him. It was 9:00 a.m. sharp on New Year's Eve when McNamara entered the Oval Office for his one-on-one with Johnson. "Good morning, Mr. President. And Happy New Year, Sir."

Johnson greeted him in as friendly a tone and manner as he could muster. "Mornin', Bob, how was your Christmas holiday?"

McNamara took a seat and straightened his tie nervously before responding. "Actually, Mr. President, it was a working vacation for me. I had a brief but pleasant Christmas but mostly I worked and read. And that's why I asked to see you in private, Sir."

Johnson studied McNamara for a few moments, noting that McNamara's usually sharp cut, professorial look was somewhat rumpled that morning. Then Johnson said in his slowest Texas drawl, "What's on your mind, Bob?"

McNamara took a deep breath before pushing off, the way a runner would do before starting a fifteen hundred meter race. "Mr. President, both of us have been discouraged, perplexed, and even angered by intelligence reports that never seem to describe the reality of our situation in Southeast Asia. Recently, the disconnect between events on the ground and our ability to understand and analyze them appears even greater. Several months ago, I decided to research the problem personally. I read as many undigested and unanalyzed after-action reports from the field as I possibly could during the past three months. I spent many hours looking at photo intelligence from Navy and Air Force aircraft. In addition, I sat in on the debriefing of a number of Marine Corps and Army company commanders, Navy and Air Force squadron and wing commanders, and Intelligence Officers, who had actually been in the field as opposed to the Pentagon. I read everything I could get my hands on from the State Department, Defense Department, the C.I.A. and from some close colleagues outside of government to get a fresh, unadulterated view of our situation in Vietnam."

McNamara stopped, took a long drink of water from a Presidential glass, then continued. "Mr. President, as a result of my personal research during the past few months, which includes a great deal of source material and interviews that I will not bore you with, I am truly convinced that our situation is far worse than anyone in the Administration has recognized, admitted or even imagined. For a variety of reasons, some complex and some institutional, some mundane and others plainly venal, we have deceived ourselves in the worst possible way. There is no 'light at the end of the tunnel' as certain flag rank officers have stated to the press. What we are seeing, to continue the metaphor, is the headlight of a fast moving freight train roaring through the tunnel directly at us.

"I wrote an extensive memorandum addressed to you alone two months ago describing my findings in great detail. I couldn't have been more exhaustive in my research and I rewrote the memo many times to insure its accuracy, detail and analysis. I hoped that you and I would have discussed the memo extensively by now. I hoped that you might have assigned it to other senior staff for review, analysis and a report back to you. I've been prepared to discuss and defend this memo every day since I delivered it to you. Until this day, no one else has seen or reviewed it. But you haven't said a word to me about it. It's as though you simply ignored everything I wrote. And, Mr. President, not since the Cuban Missile Crisis have I written anything as important as this memo. I am truly perplexed."

Johnson leaned back in his chair and held up his hand to halt the presentation. "Whoa there, Bob, I can see you got a powerful sweat workin'. And, I suppose I do owe you an apology about that memo. I got to admit that it's caused me quite a bit of heartburn and I've put off talkin' to you about it. But, Bob, ain't' there a chance that you're mistaken?"

McNamara rose to his feet while shaking his head. "Mr. President, if I were still managing Ford Motor Company and Mr. Ford himself asked me this same question about the business, I would tell him that he could bet the ranch on my message."

Johnson's face began to flush. "Bob, this ain't the ranch we're bettin', it's the whole goddamn country."

McNamara's anguish was palpable. The man was clearly placing all his chips on the table and betting on black. "Sir, I do know what's at stake here. That's why I have spent twenty hours each day for the past three months conducting the most intense research of my entire professional life in order to ascertain the absolute facts about this War and to bring the clear unvarnished truth to you and you alone. This country that we both love without reservation is in serious trouble. We can talk for hours or even days as to how and why we got here, but, we are here, we are in trouble, and we need to undertake serious action immediately in order not to get in even deeper."

Observing McNamara's absolute sincerity and knowing the power of the man's awesome intellect, Johnson arose, came around the Presidential desk, and placed his large hand on McNamara's shoulder. "S'pose you tell me the facts again, Bob. Sit down and tell me the facts." Johnson took a seat and waved to McNamara to sit as well.

McNamara sat, drew his breath, and began. "Mr. President, our after-action reports contain huge distortions and great discrepancies with regard to the number of enemy forces killed, captured and wounded as well as the number of enemy weapons and equipment destroyed. Moreover, the percentage of land we actually control is far less than what we claim. The insurgent forces or Viet Cong, as we call them, actually control far more land mass, villages, towns, and cities than do American and Republic of Vietnam forces. Our air strikes, although helpful, have been so circumscribed by political considerations that they are only partially effective. Meanwhile enormous quantities of Soviet munitions and supplies, along with tens of thousands of North Vietnamese troops, have traveled into South Vietnam where they are currently organizing with local Viet Cong cadres for a major offensive which I believe will commence in the near future.

"Our ally, the Republic of Vietnam, and its army, although not a complete and total sham, have little depth or fighting power on their own. These ARVN troops still cut and run if they're under serious attack and American GI's are not there to protect them. Over the past ten years, MACV, the CIA and State Departments have constructed a façade of South Vietnamese viability and national identity entirely out of whole cloth. The South Vietnamese government, its army, and the constant stream of puppet presidents, are all of our own making. They have no

136

real legitimacy. In fact, they are not real. They simply exist on paper and in our imaginations. Whenever the North Vietnamese Army or Viet Cong regulars challenge them, these puppet troops simply disappear. It is all one enormous Potemkin Village."

Johnson could not stand to hear any more. As he was prone to do when frustrated to an extreme, he leapt up from his seat and bellowed. "Jesus Christ Almighty, Bob, if this is all true, why hasn't anyone else told me? Why have you waited so long to tell me?" Johnson was quiet for just a moment and then he began to stomp. His stomping grew louder and more forceful as did his bellow. "My God, man, you have been right there with the others tellin' me time after time that everything was gettin' better and that we would win this War if we only sent over another twenty or thirty or fifty thousand troops. I've relied on all of you. I've gone back to the Congress to get additional funding for this War again and again," Johnson said, shouting so loudly the windows rattled.

Johnson stopped again. He stared down at McNamara and narrowed his eyes, focusing them into a piercingly harsh glare. He lowered his voice and changed its tone to match his glare. "Yes, you personally, Bob. You have been the centerpiece of my brain trust, the smartest man in government, like the press always says." Johnson paused another time. The absolute misery of a man feeling absolutely betrayed poured out in the pained words of the emotional President. "So, why the hell have you not told me of your misgivings before now? Why? Here I am just eleven months away from the next election and you give me this news here at the damn eleventh hour. And why hasn't anyone else been willin' to tell me this kind of news?"

McNamara knew that he had Johnson's full attention, perhaps for the last time, so he stood and continued. "Sir, as it's been said, 'Victory has a thousand fathers, defeat is an orphan.' There are an infinite number of reasons why men and governments deceive themselves. I'm certain the historians will eventually tell us why we have done so with regard to Vietnam. I am deeply sorry that I have been among those who have given you incorrect information and advice. But I cannot continue to do so. My conscience will not permit it now that I truly see the nature of things. This War is simply a proxy war that's gone wrong in practically every respect, be it tactical, strategic, logical or moral. At the most fundamental level, this War has been a proxy war designed and intended to prevent a Third World War from breaking out between us and the Soviets. However, Mr. President, the real inquiry for the moment is not how we got here, but what do we do, given the predicament we find ourselves in. How the hell do we get out of this damned box?"

Johnson interrupted, "Yes, Bob, if what you're tellin' me is true and correct, how in the hell do we get out of this incredible mess?"

McNamara waited several long and uncomfortable moments before answering. Then he replied with all the force he could muster. "Mr. President, the way I see it, we have three choices, two that will win the War and one that will end it."

"Alright, Bob, the stage is yours," Johnson replied testily.

McNamara, who had been waiting for this moment, adjusted his glasses, straightened his papers, and assumed his professorial posture as he continued his one-on-one presentation to the leader of the free world. "Sir, if we truly want to win this War and are prepared to pay the costs, we have the following choices:

"First, we double the number of our troops in Vietnam to at least one million men, most of whom must be combat troops, not rear echelon personnel. Then, rather than continuing Westmoreland's 'search and destroy' missions on the ground, we must conquer territory and occupy it, keeping the Viet Cong out permanently, not just momentarily as is the case now. We must guarantee the safety and well being of the peasants and farmers. And most importantly, we must have the resolve to stay in place for years, not months, as we have done in Korea, because that's the kind of commitment that Ho Chi Minh and General Giap and his army have and have had all along. This constant 'are we there yet' type attitude is totally defeatist, unrealistic and counterproductive."

McNamara noticed Johnson fidgeting. As he watched, the President, who would have never behaved this way in public, began to pace about the room and look as if he were a child about to throw a tantrum. McNamara continued. "Alternatively, instead of the first option, we could maintain troop strength at current levels but conduct massive air raids against all of North Vietnam, destroying all their towns, villages and cities. In addition we must bomb the dykes that keep forty percent of the North from flooding during monsoon season and basically reduce North Vietnam to a non-nuclear rubble."

Johnson stood still and looked at McNamara as though this Secretary of State had just gone completely mad. He blasted his reply so loudly that the walls shook: "Goddamn, McNamara, what you're tellin' me is complete and utter hogwash. If I was to seriously consider your first option and try to double the troop commitment to a million men, Congress would revolt, they would never agree to it. The American people, who are just about on the edge right now, would never accept it. And, we just plain couldn't afford it even if I was to table all of my Great Society programs and that I just won't do. I would be plumb crazy to even suggest such a ridiculous thing."

Now Johnson shook his head as if he were scolding a very disappointing, very bad child. "As for your second damned alternative, Bob, sure, we've talked about some of those possibilities for our air war, especially General LeMay. But damn it all, Bob, we would wind up killin' a couple million North Vietnamese civilians. And, if we destroy the dykes, we would create a terrible famine affecting twenty million people. World opinion, to say nothing of American public opinion, would turn against us totally, completely and permanently.

"I would lose next year's election by a landslide even if the Republicans ran Mickey Fuckin' Mouse against me much less a powerful politician like Rockefeller or Nixon. The college students alone would raise enough hell to require a half a million man standing army right here in the U.S. of A. just to keep 'em under control. Christ, we're practically on the verge of that now. And what about the Russians and the Chinese? Do you think that they would just sit there holding their dicks while we pour another half million men into Vietnam?"

Although the decibel level of his voice had dropped somewhat, its force had not been softened. "And, Mr. Secretary, I would go down as the worst president of the twentieth century, if not of all time, thank you. So your ridiculous options are totally hollow, absolutely, absurdly worthless. I don't know why you even bothered me with the mention of them." Realizing he was out of breath, Johnson paused and growled. "So, I might as well hear what your third option is, if indeed, you still want to present it. Can't be any worse than the other two," Johnson snorted as he sat back down and slumped low in his chair.

"Well, Sir," McNamara, who was now at least for this moment looking down at Johnson, said, "the last option is to simply declare that this is not a winnable war in the conventional sense and begin to pull out of Vietnam altogether. I'm sure that we could negotiate some face-saving departure with Ho Chi Minh's government if they truly believed that we would leave."

Flabbergasted beyond reason, Johnson jumped up from his chair yet again and roared like a wounded bull. "Well, that's about the most damn fool thing I've ever heard, Bob. We might as well admit that some third rate, underdeveloped, forlorn little country has just kicked Uncle Sam's ass all to hell and back. What the hell do you think the Soviets and the Chinese Communists would think of that? Hell and damnation, we'd have little Vietnam's poppin' up all over the damn world since we just announced to the entire fuckin' planet that we just ain't got the *cajones* to win a war anymore.

"Bob, I can't believe that you just suggested that. Shit, a damn graduate student in political science could come up with somethin' better than that."

McNamara stayed calm and sat back down. Now he looked up at Johnson. "With all due respect, Mr. President, it just might be that many governments, not to mention people, around the world might just conclude that we have come to our senses, that we understand geopolitics and *realpolitik* much better than we ever have in the past, that we can stop this damn proxy war with Russia and that the United States is finally coming of age," McNamara finished with strained but sincere enthusiasm.

Johnson was truly at the end of his rope, but he managed to ask one final question in a relatively low voice. "Alright, Bob, let's just say that instead of listening to you, I decide to stay the course, to keep the pressure on North Vietnam with our air power, and to continue to pacify the South, a little at a time. What's your analysis then?"

With great sadness in his voice, McNamara sat up straight in his chair and answered slowly. "Sir, if we continue on as we have, I believe that North Vietnam will soon conduct massive attacks throughout the South, and that we may well wind up losing the War outright or eventually selecting one of the first two options I just described or something similar to it."

Johnson replied, now with a fine honed steel edge to his voice. "Bob, this meeting is over. I'm damned sorry we ever had it."

Robert S. McNamara, head of the Kennedy brain trust and original White House Whiz Kid, rose to his feet. He replied with sincere sadness, "Mr. President, I rather thought that this would be your reaction. As you know, I announced my intention to resign my position as Secretary of Defense on November 27th but I've stayed on as a matter of personal loyalty to you, Mr. President. But under the present circumstances I am hereby tendering my resignation as your Secretary of Defense effective February 29th or at such earlier date as you find my replacement."

Johnson simply stared and said, "Well, I'll just be damned! I accept your resignation and ask that you not announce your decision for several weeks while I find your successor. You may go now, Bob."

"I'm terribly sorry it had to end this way, Mr. President," McNamara said as he moved to depart the Oval Office. "And, I wish you the best, Sir."

"You've let me down, Bob. I've really depended upon you and you let me down," Johnson said gravely.

McNamara stood at the door, his tall lean figure still cutting its usual image of precision and intelligence, now hunching in regret. "Mr. President, I gave you my best, my very best, when others around you who already either knew or suspected at least some of what I have discovered have held back. The generals and admirals including Westmoreland, Wheeler and Sharpe, the CIA Director Helms, your advisors, Walt Rostow and many others, even Secretary Rusk have hedged their bets and pulled their punches so as not to disappoint you. And you, Mr. President, have continued to push hard for the War ever since Kennedy's assassination! That's been a large part of the problem. No one has wanted to let you down, to disappoint you, or to press the truth on you. And, all of them have had their own personal reasons for advocating this War. But I couldn't do that to you once I knew what I now know. And now I have told you the simple unvarnished truth. That, Sir, is the best I could give any man, even the President of the United States.

"And, Sir, I must say this before I leave. We, that is, both of us, you as well as I, have dealt in lies and deception regarding this War all along. If you recall, when you went to Congress to ask for the Tonkin Gulf Resolution after the incident involving the *Maddox* and *Turner Joy*, we were surely dealing half-truths, lies, and plain bullshit to the Congress and the citizens of the United States. I have always regretted that and I believe that all of those chickens are now coming home to roost. I am sorry, Sir, extremely sorry, more sorry than you will ever know. But I do believe that you know what I say is true."

With that final comment, McNamara turned slowly and left the Oval Office, his bearing, normally so ramrod straight, was slumped over in agony of personal defeat.

17.

SOMEONE'S WATCHING YOU

Margo Collins sipped her Bloody Mary and took two more aspirin tablets to ease her pounding headache. She had celebrated New Year's Eve a bit too enthusiastically in Cambridge the previous evening and had paid the price all morning. The first class flight attendant who was approximately the same age as Margo was totally sympathetic to her condition, having partied on Beacon Hill a little too vigorously herself the previous night. Several times during the brief, almost empty New Year's Day flight from Boston to New York's La Guardia airport, she had stopped to offer comfort, cheerful conversation and her best hangover remedies.

On her last visit to Margo with a reminder to fasten her seat belt, the attendant was pleased to see that her remedies were taking affect. She bent over to whisper, "You're looking much better; I'm sure that in an hour or so you'll feel better. And, I wish you a great New Year."

"Thanks so much for everything," Margo replied while reaching into her purse to find her card. She gave it to the attendant saying, "You've been so sweet, call me when you have a few days in the City and we'll have lunch."

As the airliner made its final approach to La Guardia, Margo thought of her father and hoped that he would be at the airport to greet her. She had missed Christmas with him for the first time in her life and it felt strange. But given the cuts and bruises she had suffered during the rather violent demonstration in Boston just before Christmas, she knew that her extended stay in Cambridge had insured a pleasant holiday with her father. She missed him and wanted to feel his comfort, strength and affection. But, Margo did not want to experience the anger and disapproval that he would express if he learned of her involvement in the anti-war demonstration.

Upon entering the terminal, Margo was terribly disappointed to see a man holding a small sign reading "Marguerite Collins" which she took to mean that her father had not come but had sent his driver instead. She acknowledged the driver and followed him to the waiting limousine where to her complete surprise she saw her father stepping out to greet her.

"There's my Sweetheart. Goodness knows I've missed you. I didn't have much of a Christmas here without you."

"Dad, I'm sorry I couldn't come home but there was so much to do in Cambridge before I leave again for Hong Kong. I've missed you too. I didn't think that you were here and I was becoming rather depressed."

Mitchell Collins and his daughter hugged each other warmly then entered the limousine for the ride to the Collins mid-Manhattan residence. Once inside, Mitchell Collins said, "Don't you fret, we'll have a great time until you leave for the Far East. I have all sorts of plans for us, not to mention quite a few Christmas presents that I didn't have time to send to you in Cambridge. I still don't know why you couldn't have come home for Christmas, even for a day or two. But daddy loves his girl and all is forgiven," Collins said with a grin. "By the way, when do you leave for Hong Kong?

"We have three whole days and I plan to spend each one with you. That is, if you took the time off like you promised."

"Oh yes, I've even told the Rockefeller people that my time is completely booked while you're here."

"The Rockefeller people? What are you doing with Rockefeller? Do you mean his presidential campaign staff or one of his business interests?"

"Well, Margo, I might as well tell you. Rockefeller is assembling a kitchen cabinet in anticipation of his winning the election. You probably know that his first choice for Secretary of State is Henry Kissinger. However, it appears that I may be his second choice should Kissinger decline. So, I'm in the process of being vetted for background, experience and all that business."

"My goodness, Dad. Secretary of State! That's fantastic! My father, Secretary of State! Oh my God. Who'd have thought it?" Margo exclaimed while leaning over to kiss and hug her handsome, silver haired father.

Collins laughed and returned the affection before saying, "Margo, don't get too excited. Remember Rockefeller has some pretty stiff competition just to win the nomination. Nixon has put together a formidable campaign team and has raised an enormous amount of money already. Then there's a little item called the general election. And while I think we Republicans have a great chance to win the presidency this year, it would be foolhardy to underestimate LBJ, Humphrey or Bobby Kennedy. And, most importantly, Henry Kissinger has right of first refusal with Rockefeller. So I'm a long way from taking over Foggy Bottom."

"Still, Dad, that's some pretty rarified company. But tell me, how did they pick you, anyway?"

Collins paused to insure that the window separating the passenger compartment from the driver was closed. "New driver. Can't be too careful, you know."

"No, but I guess I'd better get accustomed to it."

"Well, anyway, to answer your question, I suppose it's a combination of things including the years that I spent in Shanghai as a Naval attaché just after the War, the international business that I've handled in the Orient over the years, the advice that I've given several administrations concerning international legal issues, my language ability and, of course, connections."

"I suppose that law review article you wrote last year didn't hurt too much either."

"Absolutely. It does appear that the emphasis on current foreign affairs is really on the Far East and China for obvious reasons. The fact that the subject of the article was the Chinese legal system before Mao and the Cultural Revolution was also helpful. Have you read it yet?"

Margo exclaimed, "Of course, I read it. I may not appreciate all the legal nuances but I thought it was a very scholarly article. I'm so proud of you."

Collins paused for a moment and took on a somewhat somber demeanor. He reached inside his coat pocket and retrieved a thick envelope. "There is one issue that wasn't too helpful during my interviews though." Handing the envelope to Margo, he simply said, "Take a look."

Margo opened the envelope to find half dozen color pictures. When she looked at the photographs, she gasped audibly. The pictures had been taken during the anti-war demonstration and near riot in which she had been ensnared barely a week ago in Boston. "Oh my God!" she exclaimed after reviewing the photos of her in the middle of the melee. In fact, she seemed to be the photographer's primary subject. "Where in the world did you get these?"

Collins commented rather coolly, "Margo, you can imagine my surprise when I was shown these on the last day of my vetting process with the Rockefeller staff. I didn't know quite what to say. Recognizing my genuine shock, the background staffer had only a few questions for me regarding the pictures. None of which I could answer. As the interview ended, this chap who was clearly a lawyer, simply said. 'If this were my daughter and I knew that she was working on a doctorate from the Kennedy School of Government at Harvard, I would try my best to dissuade her from participating in demonstrations that have the potential of spinning out of control.'"

Margo was silent and stunned. Who could have been watching her that day?

"Marguerite, I assured him that I would speak to you immediately about this matter and advise you to avoid such unfortunate activities in the future. He responded that no one with college-aged children could be certain where and with whom those children may be these days and that this one incident would probably be of no consequence to Rockefeller. Then he suggested that I advise my family members to avoid situations that might be potentially embarrassing to a presidential candidate."

Margo was severely chagrined. But she was also extremely angry that she had been seemingly set up to embarrass her father at a critical moment in his career. All that she could do was to express her regret about the whole affair and promise that it would not happen again.

The senior Collins had one more question for his daughter, however. "By the way, who are those men in the pictures who seem to have rescued you after you fell?"

Margo looked at her father quizzingly and hesitated nervously before answering. "Quite honestly, I don't know. I thought possibly they might have been working for you."

Well, they most certainly were not. One of them appears to be Chinese. Are you certain that they weren't friends of yours from Harvard or Hong Kong?"

"Chinese?" Margo shuddered, "That makes no sense. I'm sure I've never seen them before or since. And, I'm equally certain that I won't see them again."

"I hope not," Collins replied before reaching rather stiffly for his daughter's hand in a gesture of forgiveness and reconciliation.

Margo whispered, "Sorry." But she remained inwardly furious, and resolute that she would investigate the matter fully. Someone was watching her far too closely and she had to find out who and why.

18.

HAIPHONG BOUND

On New Year's Day, 1968, the *Constellation* stood down from combat operations. The Ship had launched strikes for twenty continuous days. The crew, both air wing and ship's company, was fatigued by uninterrupted eighteen-hour working days. Aircraft, catapults, arresting gear, and ship's engines badly needed major maintenance. The stand-down day allowed most of the crew to rest; for those who couldn't, work was done at a leisurely pace. Of course, a few of the combat aviators had not survived the previous twenty-day period and a few had been shot down and captured. For them, wherever they were, rest took on a different meaning.

Marchand slept most of the day. He finally awakened at 1600, in time to shower and dress in short sleeve khakis for evening meal in the senior officer wardroom. He had tired of the loud conversation and pungent flight suits ever present in the combination junior officer/aviation officer wardroom. Now, he eagerly anticipated the elegant service of the large formal dining room located amidships on the fourth level.

The wardroom symbolized civility, culture and privilege of

another age when great British Men o'War ruled the seas and their officers dined elegantly with their captains, commodores and commanders. It was a tradition graciously handed down from the Royal Navy to the Navy of John Paul Jones in the early nineteenth century and treasured since that time.

Marchand arrived, took a position at the junior end of a long, white, linen-covered table and remained standing until Captain Mackey, the ship's commanding officer, entered and the chaplain said a formal grace. When the Captain took his seat, the less senior officers followed and service began. Filipino stewards served the seated officers from elegant silver trays cradled in their crooked arms. Marchand tasted the lobster and found it surprisingly good, almost fresh, he thought. He actually enjoyed the meal and his conversation with Chris Davis, the most junior of the ship's two flight surgeons. Then, Davis grew serious and asked him, "So, Marchand, how's your squadron holding up under the stress?"

Marchand paused for a moment then replied off-handedly, "Do you mean the squadron or do you mean me, Doc?"

Davis raised his heavy eyebrows, tilted his head slightly and replied, "I'm not playing games, Keith. I mean both."

Marchand affected an air of faux nonchalance. "Well, considering our two totally senseless losses so early in the cruise, morale is remarkably high," he paused then added in an also falsely detached manner, "There's some resentment, of course, concerning the circumstances of our losses. They truly were unnecessary, a damned awful waste."

Davis studied Marchand's boyish face and sad blue eyes before replying. "Rich Miller and you were close friends, weren't you?"

"I miss him," Marchand blurted out without thinking. Somewhat self-conscious of this unexpected display of even the slightest emotion, he continued in a stern voice, "Miller had no business flying out here. He should have been a Marine."

"That could have been just as bad," Davis said.

"He also could have been a ship's company officer or better yet, at home in Arkansas where he belonged," Marchand answered, staring at Davis.

"We would all be better off at home, Keith."

"You know, Chris, I really don't want to start that conversation. The fact is, and we all know this, Miller should not have been sent to identify a damn slow moving surface contact beneath a three hundred foot cloud layer at night. Nor should any of us be sent to lob bombs through vanishing holes in an overcast. The fucking clouds are often made of granite or limestone, if you follow me. The stakes just aren't worth it."

"What stakes? Do you mean the war?" Davis asked, still probing.

"Would you keep your voice down? We're surrounded by senior officers."

"Sorry," Davis replied, "I'm still not accustomed to military thinking."

"You can think anything you want; just don't sound as though you might be criticizing this fucking war while you're dining in the senior officers' mess. Anyway, we can discuss the politics of the war some other time. No, I'm simply referring to the stupid-ass targets the Pentagon selects and the miserable flying conditions during monsoon season. They must think we're expendable."

Davis leaned in toward Marchand. "Now you're the one who'd best watch his volume; you're attracting attention." Davis relaxed and sat back in his chair. "Look, tell you what, why don't you stop by my stateroom later this evening and we'll continue the conversation. I'm having a little party in my room about ten, that is, 2200 hours for you fly boys. Come by and we'll talk."

"2200 hours, damn Chris, you're really improving; you'll be a Naval Officer yet."

"Not if I can help it, Keith."

"Should I bring some booze?"

"Yeah, after two months at sea, my cache is running low."

"I'll bring some scotch and see you in an hour," Marchand said, then finished his strawberry sundae.

After supper, Marchand returned to his stateroom and put Mahler's Fifth on his tape deck. He flopped onto his bunk and was quickly absorbed in a book. He had not read long when his roommate, Phil Winslow, entered the austere but comfortable stateroom, and jumped up onto the top bunk. He looked down at Marchand then said, "You told me that you had read *Man's Fate.*"

Marchand wanted to yell at Winslow and send him away, but he was pleasant instead. "I did, but I enjoy Malraux so I'm reading it again. Anything wrong with that?"

"No, of course not, but he's so damn depressing," Winslow said. "Who needs more depression out here?"

"Maybe you could, you clown."

"You're such a wise ass," Winslow said as he slid off the bunk to grab a beer from their refrigerator.

"Touchy, touchy. By the way, are you coming to Doc Davis' room tonight?"

Winslow slicked back his blond hair which was longer than regulations actually permitted and fiddled with his handlebar mustache.

"No, I'm playing poker, I thought you were, too."

"Not tonight, those poker games have a way of degenerating into crap games and the stakes are too rich for me. I'm saving my chips for Hong Kong, and I don't want to contribute a couple hundred clams to someone else's recreation fund."

"Before I go, I do have some good news for you. You and I are going to Clark Field when we arrive in Subic Bay. I just received a letter from an old girlfriend, Alice Turner, who's teaching high school at the Naval Station at Subic. She has a girlfriend visiting her from the States and wants to introduce her to a 'handsome naval officer'. How about that, Lt. Marchand?"

"Now, that's the best news I've heard in weeks. When do we arrive in port anyway?"

"Just twelve days, Rocketman."

Winslow sauntered over to the refrigerator and removed another bottle of Beck's. He stared at the bottle for a moment before opening it.

"Only three left, Keith. Seems like we're running low on everything -- beer, patience and luck."

"What do you mean -- luck?"

Winslow was the squadron's assistant operations officer and he often had critical information before it became common knowledge. "The word around Air Ops is that the weather will break tomorrow up North. If it does, the *Connie* will launch a couple of big ones."

"You mean an Alpha Strike?"

"I'm not talking about an air show for the Admiral."

"Damn, that means Hanoi or Haiphong!" Marchand paused a moment before continuing, "I don't know if I'm ready for it, Phil. I would at least like to live long enough to see Hong Kong just once. I think I'm feeling a little chickenshit."

"Well, you're doing much better than I am. I know I'm not ready for Hanoi or Haiphong. Goddamn, Alice would never forgive me if I got shot down before I banged her a dozen times."

"Would you be serious for only a few minutes!" Marchand exclaimed.

"Serious, hell, I am serious. This damn War doesn't seem serious. There's nothing serious about this fuckin' War except all the killing. One of these days I might understand what it's all about, then I'll know whether it's serious or not. Maybe I'll even tell you."

"Understand it or not, you and I will probably be dodging SAMs over downtown Hanoi or Haiphong tomorrow. Hell, I can't even get drunk now. The only thing worse than flying over Hanoi or Haiphong is flying over Hanoi or Haiphong with a hangover."

"Why, Mr. Marchand, didn't you know that liquor aboard a ship of the United Sates Navy is strictly forbidden? How could you possibly get drunk?"

"Go to hell, Winslow. I'm going to see Davis; he only stocks quality scotch, you know."

Marchand arrived at Chris Davis' stateroom and was met with a full glass of Chivas Regal and the flight surgeon's usual warmth. "Have a seat anywhere, Keith," Davis said while pointing to the one unoccupied chair in the room.

"Sure, Doc."

They were silent for a moment as they sipped the chilled, mellow whiskey. Davis looked carefully at the tall, muscular flight officer. He seemed bright, well educated and patriotic, a fine young man with a good heart. Scuttlebutt around the squadron was that Marchand did his job well and was well liked. But could he take the stress out here? And his grief over Miller? What was brewing deep in his psyche? Davis asked himself.

Davis studied Marchand's black hair, combed straight back in easy waves so thick that on a woman it would be described as luxuriously rich like a horse's mane. Hair like that had to please the ladies. Yet Marchand never spoke of one. No wife, no fiancée, no girlfriend. Rumors before the cruise had Marchand with lots of dates, and many women pursuing him, but no one woman. Of course, not having attachments could be a plus for mental health out here.

Marchand's normally bright blue eyes were dark this evening. And his easy smile was nowhere in evidence. Davis perceived Marchand's anxiety and said, "The weather up North must be clearing."

"How did you know?"

"I've heard the rumors and your face confirms them."

"Well, all I've heard is talk myself. I suppose it's true, though. We've been on station two months and only launched one Alpha Strike. It's long overdue."

"Did you go on the first one?"

"No, I had a bad cold and an ear block so you grounded me, don't you remember?"

"No, I don't. Do you want me to ground you tomorrow?"

"Of course not, what good could come of that? Are you going to ground me every time the clouds clear for the rest of the cruise? I'm going some day, it might as well be tomorrow."

"Well, at least your targets will be worth going after."

"Great consolation if you bust your ass, Doc."

"Sorry. I don't mean to sound cavalier, but frankly, it's difficult to say anything really encouraging. How can I talk to you about combat in a meaningful way? Is it best to simply remain silent, avoid the subject?"

"Now, you're thinking like one of us, Chris. You're right; we just don't go there most of the time. It's almost written in the rules that we can't so we don't."

Davis nodded. "Here, let me freshen up your scotch." Davis paused for a few moments while he added scotch and ice cubes to Marchand's glass then asked, "Did you go to Annapolis?"

"You can't be serious, Chris. I don't seem like a Boat School grad, do I?"

"No, not really."

"Well, why the question – oh hold on a minute. You want to know how I got here, huh? Well, I finished Harvard College in sixty-five and decided to get my pilot's license during the summer before law school. I enjoyed it so much I postponed law school so I could fly high performance aircraft. Oh yeah, my draft number was really low and I didn't want to run off to Canada, so I volunteered for flight training."

"Harvard undergrad, you say. Were you on your way to Harvard Law School, too?"

Marchand flushed. "Never submitted the application, so we'll have to wait and see."

"So Vietnam caught you playing summer soldier, huh?"

"You might say that. Hell, when I started flight training, there were fewer than twenty-five thousand GIs over here and not much action going on. But by the time I got my wings, Congress had passed the Tonkin Gulf Resolution and presto, we're bombing North Vietnam."

"What did you think of Vietnam when you were just a college boy in Cambridge?"

"My God, I wish I had a day in port for every debate, lecture, discussion, or argument about Vietnam that I heard, participated in or slept through. Essentially, it seemed to me that the South Vietnamese wished to remain a free nation, separate and apart from the Communist North. I felt strongly that we had a legal and moral commitment to assist and protect them in their struggle. I thought Ho Chi Minh was just as committed to imposing a Communist regime on all of Vietnam if not Indochina. I suppose I still agree with our policy of support for an independent South Vietnam." Marchand trailed off with a hint of self-doubt. He sipped at his scotch. Why policy talk right now, he wondered.

"But, Keith, at the wardroom tonight you seemed anything but supportive of the War."

Marchand caught himself and replied. "Doc, don't confuse my disagreement over targeting policy with general support of strategic policy. Although, some of the strings tying this package together are beginning to unravel. That's plain enough for anyone to see."

Davis looked sympathetic. "The War, or the 'Conflict' as the politicians call it back home, seems to defy neat packaging, doesn't it?"

"The corruption of the South Vietnamese government and the incredible tenacity of the North Vietnamese are really difficult to reconcile. Sometimes it's difficult to keep the faith," Marchand replied while asking himself whether Davis was actually conducting an interview, or perhaps a psychological assessment. If he is, he's pretty good. He thinks I don't know what he's up to, though.

The conversation was interrupted by several loud knocks at the door. Davis opened the door to face Frank Warden, the squadron Maintenance Officer who entered carrying his banjo case followed by Wayne Richards, the Operations Officer, with a saxophone, and Terry Gross with another banjo.

"What the hell are you having, Doc, a rehearsal?" Marchand exclaimed.

"Exactly. You're welcome to stay, Keith," Warden said.

"We even brought an extra kazoo for you," Richards added.

"You've got time to practice before the rest of the band arrives," Gross chuckled.

"Thanks, gentlemen, but I was just about to leave. Hope you have a fine rehearsal or whatever. Nice talking to you, Doc," Marchand hooted as he finished his scotch.

Perennially red-faced Warden began to tune his banjo and was puffing on a cigarette in an exaggerated holder that Greta Garbo would have been proud of. "Marchand, the poker game doesn't start for another hour at least; you might as well stay here for the band practice. You ain't afraid of little 'ol kazoo, are you?" Warden said with a wide grin.

"Give me the damned kazoo, Frank," Marchand replied, flopping down on Davis' bunk. "What do you guys call yourselves anyway? Or does this half-ass band have a name?"

"Welcome to the finest ragtime band in West Pac, Keith. Of course, as far as we know, it's the only ragtime band in Western Pacific. We call ourselves the Yankee Air Pirate Marchin', Stompin', Fartin' Ragtime Band. What do you think of that?"

"Well, at least your audience won't have any great expectations. You've set the bar pretty fuckin' low. What instrument do you play, Doc?" Marchand asked.

"First trumpet," Davis said while hauling out a somewhat battered specimen of the instrument." Our washboard and gut bucket players will be arriving soon -- along with our first chair kazoo player."

"Incredible, you idiots belong in a frat house, not an aircraft carrier," Marchand said in feigned disbelief. "Do you musicians have any idea where you're performing tomorrow?"

"No, where?" Warden asked.

"H -- "Marchand caught the word Haiphong before it left his

mouth, deciding not to ruin the party and simply said, "How the hell should I know?"

Warden's eyes twinkled as he instructed the band members about the proper way to start their first number. His ruddy complexion nearly matched his red hair and he looked more the part of an Irish bartender who thoroughly enjoyed his profession. "Gentlemen," he intoned sincerely, "the only way to play ragtime properly is half drunk. From the general appearance of this group I'd say we're just about ready to begin. *Cabaret* is always a good starter. So let's tune up!"

Shortly before 0200, while many air wing officers were still drinking and gambling, squadron yeomen distributed the day's flight schedule to the staterooms of the ship's flight crews. When Marchand returned to his room after Chris Davis' party and band rehearsal, he found his squadron's flight schedule waiting for him. He scanned the schedule and quickly found what he was looking for. Air Operations had scheduled an Alpha Strike at 0900, briefing to begin at 0630; Fighter Squadron Twenty One was scheduled to send six aircraft on the strike and Marchand was on the list in one of his squadron's fighter-bombers.

He had not drunk much at Davis' party because he anticipated an early flight assignment. But, seeing his name on the schedule made him feel lightheaded. His stomach knotted and churned. Christ, he thought, I might as well be drunk. Marchand undressed and climbed into his bunk. But sleep came slowly and fitfully.

VOLUME ONE: PHANTOM WAR TRILOGY

19.

OH LORD, DELIVER US

The Intelligence Center was crowded when Marchand arrived shortly after 0630 hours in the morning. Thirty aircraft would be launched on the strike to Haiphong. Flight crewmembers filled every available seat in the large briefing area and lined the bulkheads. Marchand stood taking notes. He paid little attention to the weather briefing, noting only that the weather forecast for the entire North Vietnamese coastline and for a hundred miles inland was clear for the first time in more than a week. Even though he already expected the worst, Marchand's heart pounded when the Air Intelligence Officer identified the target for the strike.

As he spoke, the Air Intelligence Officer, flashed slides of Haiphong harbor, a railroad siding, and a loading area near the docks. At first, Marchand did not fully understand that the target was the only the siding, noting more; that reality was just too absurd. The AIO described the target ad nauseam - geographically, strategically, militarily, economically, socially, and politically. Snickers and sneers began before he finished. After all, this target was an insignificant railroad siding near the docks. Muttered sarcasm subsided only when the nearby anti-aircraft batteries and surface to air missile sites were identified on the projection screen. The AIO didn't relish his assignment or the quiet derision palpable throughout the Center, so he hurried to finish.

Marchand overheard Wayne Richards' half whispered comment to Commander Jack McGruder, "Skipper, I don't believe it, we're sending twenty-six planes to Haiphong to knock out a goddamn railroad spur and siding. If it weren't so heavily defended, I'd laugh."

"Well, it sure as hell is well defended and there won't be any laughing when it's over," McGruder replied, looking privately troubled. "But look how close the target is to the docks. We could just as easily take out every one of those docks and really accomplish something."

Richards frowned and asked, "Who the hell selects these friggin' targets, Skipper? Is it true that President Johnson himself clears each target up north? If true, Johnson must be smokin' some really bad weed."

"That's the word I hear from some pretty senior people, Wayne. CAG tells me that LBJ himself clears each target after a presentation by the Sec Def McNamara and the Joint Chiefs. Why he'd send us after this stupid rail siding is a complete mystery to me."

Richards spoke barely above a whisper. "Well, it's no goddamn wonder that this war is so fucked up. Score one little railroad siding for the warriors on LBJ's staff to be followed by some more worthless lip service at the Paris Peace Talks. Meanwhile, we just go merrily along, dropping bombs and slip sliding deeper into this morass. I tell you, Skipper, we need to go in there and bomb the fuck out of Haiphong Harbor, bomb those damn Russian ships, Hanoi, and Uncle Ho, then get this war over with. Either that or we should go the hell on home and quit risking our butts just to hit these ridiculous bullshit targets."

McGruder looked away. When he looked back, he had put on his official face. As Marchand strained to listen unobtrusively to the barely audible conversation between McGruder and Richards, the Commander

Errol Lord took the podium. The Air Wing Commander had selected Lord, the commanding officer of one of the Ship's two attack squadrons, to lead this strike into Haiphong.

Lord appeared lean, almost wiry, and stern-faced as he began briefing the strike force on formation procedures. He was prematurely gray around the temples; Marchand guessed him to be nearly forty. His bearing and demeanor bespoke an Annapolis background. Lord instructed the group in precise, carefully chosen words, crisply pronounced and forcefully delivered. He thoroughly described each phase of the intricate mission from navigation, air defense penetration, and weapons delivery, to the evasion tactics to be used in escaping surface to air missiles. "Remember," he emphasized, "it's virtually impossible to avoid a SAM until it's seen. So, it's imperative for the first man who sees a SAM to call its position for the entire flight and, if necessary, to call for the SAM break."

Marchand recalled practicing again and again the SAM break in training. It was a violent high "G" maneuver designed to escape a tracking surface to air missile that could follow its target around the sky as adeptly as the target aircraft could try to evade it.

Each aviator in the Intelligence Center listened attentively, knowing that mission success and personal survival depended heavily on Lord's professionalism in the planning and execution of the strike, not to mention leading the strike force to the target. Marchand gazed intensely at the distinguished senior pilot at the lectern. He'll be an admiral someday, Marchand concluded. Winslow nudged Marchand gently and whispered, "It's a pity there aren't a few officers like Lord back at the Pentagon to plan this damn war."

"If there were, you can bet we wouldn't be on our way to Haiphong to bomb a friggin' railroad siding," Marchand replied.

"Or, perhaps, we wouldn't be on our way to Haiphong at all."

"That's not a healthy way to think right now, Phil."

"No, I suppose, you're right; but this mission doesn't sound too healthy anyway."

Marchand didn't reply but looked again at Lord who was carrying out orders originating in the fertile mind of some general or admiral near the President or perhaps the President himself. Lord stepped from behind the podium in order to deliver his final comments to the strike crews. Lord's pale grey eyes were piercing as lasers as he spoke, "Gentlemen, I don't have to tell you that this is only the second time during this cruise that the weather has cleared sufficiently to schedule an Alpha Strike, nor do I need remind you that Haiphong will be heavily defended. But, for those very reasons, I demand that each one of you perform at a hundred percent efficiency today. You must. We all must. We are at a substantial disadvantage. Our procedures lack the precision we develop with practice; our strike force coordination will be slow; we cannot count on smooth execution.

"The enemy, on the other hand, knows that we're coming. Clear weather is a signal to him and us. His anti-aircraft batteries will be repaired, well supplied, and fully manned. His surface-to air missiles will be replenished and poised. In short, he will be ready and waiting."

Lord stopped and looked around the room to be certain everyone present was listening with every available brain cell. Then he continued in a slightly lower tone, "Don't allow your subjective target evaluation or your disdain for Pentagon targeting procedures to dull your reflexes or impair your effectiveness. Your wingman depends on you. I depend on you. And I want to see each one of you back on this ship this afternoon. That's an order! Good luck, gentlemen."

Marchand and Winslow left the Intelligence Center together and walked to the escalator that ran between the first and fifth levels of the ship. While riding up, Winslow asked Marchand, "What do you think Lord meant by his comment about subjective target evaluation?"

"You know full well what he meant, Phil. He knows everyone is pissed about the target selection for this Haiphong strike."

"Well, it is absurd. Hell, the Vietnamese will have their coolies out to replace the damn tracks in about two days. It will probably cost every bit of a thousand bucks to repair the damage we do with a million dollars worth of bombs."

"Sounds like a bit of subjective target evaluation to me."

"Oh, cut the crap, Marchand. Some poor bastard could well bust his ass on this hop."

"That's exactly what I'm trying not to think about. So, let's just go to the ready-room and finish the briefing. Worrying about the friggin' target won't increase our chances of surviving this mission or any other."

"That's for sure."

Exercising commanding officer's prerogative, Jack McGruder decided to lead his squadron's six-plane contingent on the Alpha Strike. When all of his officers participating in the strike were seated in the squadron ready room, McGruder took the podium to deliver his portion of the brief. He was perhaps the most handsome pilot on the carrier. Tall, tanned and lean with salt and pepper hair that invited a female's touch and pale green eyes that were a trap for the unwary, he could easily have been a film star. He spoke with a deep, command voice that resonated throughout the ready room.

"As flak suppressors for the rest of the strike force, our mission is critically important," he began. "We must accelerate ahead of the force at precisely the right moment. If we move out too soon, our cluster bombs will have lost their effectiveness by the time the attack bombers roll in on the target. The Vietnamese gunners will recover their positions in time to direct their heaviest fire just as the Skyhawks are committed to their dive runs. If that happens, we will have failed our mission and the strike force may well lose one or two birds as a result. On the other hand, if we arrive late on target, the attack aircraft will suffer full exposure to anti-aircraft artillery during their target runs with equally disastrous results."

McGruder ordered the squadron intelligence officer to distribute aerial photographs of the six antiaircraft artillery sites closest to the actual target and assigned each crew the task of neutralizing one specific anti-aircraft emplacement. Then he admonished his officers.

"Upon close inspection of the photographs, you will notice that the gun sites appear to be situated in residential areas. While such location would normally put these sites off limits, we do have permission to hit them in order to protect our strike force. Nevertheless, you must take all precaution to avoid civilian casualties. The Joint Chiefs have carefully selected each target area so as to avoid civilian casualties inasmuch as it's possible.

"As you recall from Commander Lord's brief, the target itself is situated at least one mile from any residential areas. This is still very close. Unfortunately for the civilians, the North Vietnamese don't give a damn and have deliberately established their triple-A and SAM batteries in the midst of populated areas, assuming that we will not strike them. So, the need for absolutely accurate ordnance delivery is obvious.

"There is one final matter that requires your utmost attention. Our target area is less than a quarter-mile from the docks where there are now ten Russian freighters waiting to offload cargo; several may be tied up at the pier when we arrive. If one of you should hit one without a valid excuse, I will personally seek your court martial. An example of a valid excuse would be that your plane is hit, you eject, and your bird falls out of control to hit one of those damned ships. In other words, gentlemen, keep your ordnance in the target area. The ships and docks are strictly off limits. Is that clear to everyone?"

Marchand paused for a moment then said, "The brief is over, let's go suit up. The knot in my gut is getting larger by the minute. I gotta put my torso harness on soon or the SOB won't fit."

"Take care, Rocketman, see ya when the fun is over."

"That a promise?"

"Bet your sweet ass, it is."

VOLUME ONE: PHANTOM WAR TRILOGY

20.

SLIPPIN' INTO DARKNESS

During the course of the sixty-five day combat line period, Marchand had resigned himself and even adapted to a constant state of anxiety. This morning, he knew and even accepted the probability that this Alpha Strike at Haiphong would result in one or more aircraft losses. But this low-lying, nagging apprehension, although well under wraps, exceeded anything he had experienced since the start of the cruise. Marchand surveyed the deck. A tropical, yellow-white furnace burned fiercely in the morning sky as sixty airmen pre-flight inspected their planes.

Waves of heat simmered slowly up from the gray-black flight deck pushing the temperature well past ninety-five degrees. Marchand perspired profusely as he inspected his aircraft and the cluster bomb units attached to it. He sweated even more heavily as the plane captain helped strap him into the cockpit.

The young plane captain smiled as he watched Marchand remove his stuffed Snoopy dog from his helmet bag and wedge the doll carefully in place between canopy and instrument panel. The sailor had seen other pilots and flight officers observe certain rituals, like the placement of a St. Christopher's medal over a rear view mirror, but this was the first time he recalled seeing a ritual based on Charlie Shultz' famous flying beagle.

Marchand's ritual was widely known among the flight deck plane handlers but no one ever said a word about it to him or the other aviators. It was a secret Marchand shared with them and his teenaged sister, Christine, but no one else. The ritual, Marchand's engaging smile, and his easy banter had endeared Marchand to them more than any other officer in the squadron.

Marchand left his canopy open and draped his arms over the sides of the fuselage to cool himself. Feeling an unwelcome sentimentality come over him, he began to inspect the faces of the aviators whose aircraft were parked close by. He strained to see their exact expressions and tried to fix as many of their faces in his memory as possible. It might be one or more of these faces, already half-hidden by helmets and dangling oxygen masks that he would never see again.

Marchand stared out at his friend and roommate, Phil Winslow, and prayed quickly for his safe passage. His eyes moved quickly past Wayne Richards' strong, lean profile for he knew that this thoroughly professional Operations Officer would always survive. For a moment, Marchand thought he had captured Jack McGruder's silent attention when the Skipper's dark eyes focused in his direction. But then it seemed that McGruder was simply staring out to sea. Marchand next looked at Frank Warden, whose friendly, ruddy face was still absorbed in pre-flight checks, and he knew that squadron morale would suffer a terrible blow if anything were to happen to Warden.

As Marchand searched the half hidden faces around him, he felt intense warmth and affection arise within him. He understood how much his squadron mates meant to him. They had become more than friends, more than associates and colleagues, more than individuals sharing a powerful emotional, life-altering experience. Those faces, which he had barely known six months ago, had become the intimate faces of his new family.

For a fleeting, eerie moment, Marchand thought he caught a glimpse of Rich Miller smiling at him from the rear cockpit of a Phantom parked nearby. Marchand shuddered, blinked hard, and realized that it was just his imagination. He knew it was just his imagination.

It took nearly twenty minutes from the launch of the first aircraft for the carrier to complete the intricate task of sending thirty aircraft aloft. Overhead the ship, the gathering strike force wheeled round in a ten-mile circle until the last strike aircraft had joined its formation. Then Commander Lord, using the call sign of the Strike Commander, transmitted to everyone, including the North Vietnamese and Russians who monitored the frequency, "Gray Eagle Ninety-Nine, this is Barbed Wire heading out." The attack aircraft responded immediately by assuming a northwesterly course toward the Vietnamese coastline.

Flying at nearly eight miles per minute, the strike force reached the coast south of Haiphong Harbor in less than twenty minutes. Marchand watched the coastline approach on his radar screen, then looked outside the cockpit as they neared the harbor. One by one the electronic warning devices in his cockpit came alive as the Vietnamese radars scanned and tracked the force. These instruments, designed to indicate the specific location of enemy fire control radars, lost all significance as they all lit up with myriad, multiple and indistinguishable warnings.

Marchand keyed his mike, "Kelly, there are at least a dozen fire control radars tracking us. It's going to get good and hot real soon."

"Our welcoming committee has started festivities already, check your one o'clock," Drummond replied.

Ahead of the aircraft and slightly to the right, Marchand saw the first few grayish puffs of anti-aircraft artillery shells dotting the clear blue sky. Within seconds, the strike force passed over the mouth of Haiphong Harbor and the sky around them erupted violently. The small gray puffs were joined by the larger, darker clouds created by heavy caliber guns that Marchand had rarely seen before. Marchand flinched when he saw the larger shells explode with dull orange bursts and noticed the ugly black scars staining the sky. His mouth became drier and the saliva stopped flowing altogether as every view from the cockpit filled with the violence of exploding steel. He called to Drummond. "This shit looks even worse than those old World War II movies on TV."

"Ain't no movie," Drummond replied tersely. "How much time to target?"

"Forty-five seconds."

Instinctively, Marchand hunkered down in the cockpit trying unconsciously to make his body smaller as crimson shells streamed silently past his canopy. He wondered what sound the exploding shells made outside the aircraft. He heard only the whistle and shriek of the electronics in the cockpit and the dull rush of wind over the fuselage. For a moment, it seemed to him that all forward progress had stopped, that the flight was suspended motionless in the sky over Haiphong harbor and that forty-five seconds had frozen into an eternity.

Marchand's nightmare paused when Commander McGruder called out to his squadron, "Checkmate Flight accelerate now." Drummond shoved his throttles forward into the afterburner detents. The Phantom's powerful engines surged, slamming Marchand back into his seat as the six fighter-bombers roared ahead of the rest of the strike force. The jolt forced Marchand's attention back to his instruments, which were flashing an electronic warning that a surface to air missile was about to launch. He keyed his mike button, "Kelly, we got a SAM about to lift off at our eleven o'clock in about ten seconds."

"Don't waste time telling me. When you see it, call its position on the radio."

"Roger."

Marchand looked hard at the harbor's edge slightly left of the airplane's nose and was utterly fascinated at the spectacle of the SAM taking off. Even from his perch at eight thousand feet above the blue-brown harbor water, the bright orange exhaust from the rocket engine was brilliant. At that instant, the red SAM warning light on his instrument panel began flashing and his headphones emitted a fast, high pitched warbling sound. Drummond and Marchand watched the missile for a moment as it quickly gained altitude then Drummond keyed his transmitter, "Gray Eagle Ninety-Nine, SAM launch, eleven o'clock, three miles, **BREAK PORT**."

Instantly, thirty strike aircraft rolled into steep descending turns to the left in a practiced SAM evasion maneuver. As they dove towards the water, Marchand locked his eyes onto the sleek twenty-two foot missile even as his aircraft banked hard into a gut wrenching six "G" turn. He stared in disbelief at the missile's orange-crimson exhaust as it steered hard toward the flight. The damn thing seems alive, Marchand thought. "My God, it's so beautiful to watch. I can't believe it's trying to kill me," he muttered to himself.

"Keith, I think it's locked onto us," Drummond grunted into the microphone embedded in his oxygen mask.

"Christ, I think you're right. Pull that damn stick harder, will ya."

Drummond rolled the aircraft nearly inverted and pulled the control stick back into his lap. The Phantom shuddered as the acceleration forces reached seven times that of gravity. The fighter plunged sharply toward the dark water of the harbor while Marchand activated all of the radar jamming equipment at his disposal. Marchand saw the missile begin to change course to counter their evasive maneuvers and forced his deflated lungs to gasp, "Kelly, it's tracking us, pull harder."

"Shit! I've lost it in the sun. Where the hell is the sonofabitch?"

"One o'clock, low; pull harder port, hard as you can. It's hot on us." Marchand grunted as he fired round after round of radar deflecting chaff bundles and tuned his jamming equipment to full power output. "This is all we've got," Drummond strained into his mike. Marchand's vision was riveted on the SAM as its guidance system, confused by Drummond's evasive maneuvering and the thousands of small aluminum strips finally broke its electronic lock on the Phantom.

"Goddamn, it broke lock!" Marchand said, straining for his breath.

The lobotomized missile sped beneath the aircraft at nearly two thousand miles per hour just close enough to detonate its proximity fuse. The blast was not close enough to damage the plane but this time Marchand both felt and heard the explosion.

Marchand saw the brilliant orange flash an instant before he felt the shock wave's severe buffet. Marchand growled into the cockpit intercom, "We made it, Kelly."

"Just barely. Get us to the target. Gotta' get this done now. We're taking fire like a sonofabitch -- we've lost so much altitude."

"Steer two eight zero, you should see the target in thirty seconds. Firewall this fucker, will ya!" Come on Bulldog, Marchand mumbled to himself. Let's shoot and get out.

The lone fighter-bomber blasted its way back to the strike

force's altitude and caught up with the other Phantoms just as they climbed to their perch for their dive runs at the selected anti-aircraft batteries surrounding the target. No one had time or inclination to transmit congratulations on their surviving a close call. In quick succession, the six fighter-bombers of Fighter Squadron Twenty-One rolled into steep forty-degree dives and released their deadly cargo on the anti-aircraft-artillery blasting furiously back at their attackers.

From five thousand feet above the ground, the Phantoms released their ordnance payloads. The canisters containing the Cluster Bomb Units split open, releasing hundreds of softball-size bomblets spinning rapidly as they fell. Fifty feet to one hundred feet above ground, fully fused CBU bomblets began to detonate, spraying the artillery sites with red hot, marble-sized pellets that cut through armor plating like cellophane. Marchand strained to look over his shoulder as his aircraft pulled out from its dive. He saw the CBUs explode like strings of Chinese firecrackers and imagined their effect on the Vietnamese gunners.

When the enemy crews manning the anti-aircraft artillery recognized the explosive pattern of CBU bomblets, they fought for any protection available. But violent death rained upon them from all directions and nothing offered real protection from the red hot, supersonic steel pellets.

Just as the enemy gunners began to take cover, Skyhawk attack bombers led by Errol Lord rolled in on the railroad siding. Five hundred pound general demolition bombs destroyed rail tracks, loading docks, and the storage facilities nearby. The accuracy of the attackers' dive runs resulted in nearly all of their ordnance hitting the target area. There were no hits to the Russian ships tied up at the piers, but many North Vietnamese gunners did not survive to fire on the escaping strike force.

Commander Lord did not know, nor did he even suspect, however, that the railroad tracks they had just demolished were rusting from disuse, that the loading docks were rotting, and that those storage sheds had long stood empty. In fact, none of the aviators from the *Constellation* had any reason to suspect that the North Vietnamese Army had carefully and meticulously prepared the railroad siding, complete with dummy rail cars, so that it appeared to be an ideal target. For all intents and purposes, the Americans had just destroyed a stage set. Millions of dollars worth of fuel, ordnance and effort were wasted while thousands of tons of munitions sat in the cargo holds of Russian ships anchored in the harbor and tied up at the nearby piers.

The Phantoms, led by McGruder, were first to leave the target area. Initially, the Skyhawk attack bombers, led by Lord, followed close behind the Phantoms. But then, as a new surge of anti-aircraft fire became more intense, the supersonic Phantoms increased speed, opening a wide gap between the two groups of aircraft. Marchand scanned his true air speed indicator as they passed over the mouth of the harbor. It read more than nine hundred knots, over one thousand miles per hour. Marchand felt increasing relief as the Phantom accelerated and the ground fire diminished. But he was startled when his instruments again warned of another impending SAM launch. Seconds later he heard Errol Lord call for another SAM Break.

Knowing that SAM missiles had a range of seventeen miles, Marchand energized all of his aircraft's electronic jamming equipment while Drummond shoved the throttles into full afterburner, deciding to outrun the SAM rather than out-maneuver it. Their aircraft was traveling more than twelve hundred miles per hour and was passing out of range of the missile when Marchand, straining to sight the SAM over his right shoulder, glimpsed an utterly silent and awesomely bright orange fireball two miles behind.

Then came an anonymous radio transmission, "Mayday, Mayday, Mayday!!!! Gray Eagle Ninety-Nine, Barbed Wire is hit. He's on fire and breaking up. He's ejecting. Tally ho a 'chute. There's a good 'chute."

Shrapnel from the exploding SAM had torn through the Skyhawk's fuselage, shattering the aircraft and fracturing Lord's right arm in two places. His legs were badly burned in the areas where his flight suit was ripped away by the warhead's blast as it spewed hell fire in the cramped cockpit. Lord was able to eject, but he was barely conscious as his parachute drifted toward the murky water of the harbor. The shock of his water entry revived him enough to enable him to inflate his life preserver. Lord was about to lose consciousness entirely when the strong hands of a North Vietnamese Army officer grasped his torso harness and pulled him into a small sampan.

Lord was overcome with blinding pain from his wounds. He slipped into darkness as his captor roughly removed the service pistol Lord always carried and began to search his seemingly lifeless body.

VOLUME ONE: PHANTOM WAR TRILOGY

PART TWO

January 15, 1968 – February 5, 1968

21.

DENIAL IS A RIVER

Marchand struggled with his demons in the heavy, moisture-laden Tonkin Gulf atmosphere. Walking alone on the flight deck, he wondered why no one would talk about the loss of Errol Lord. The attack squadron commander was either missing, captured or dead. One of the finest and most skilled warriors in the air wing was now a combat statistic. Perhaps it was the way Lord's loss had shattered expectations that kept the *Constellation's* aviators so silent about his death or capture. But silence was safer, infinitely more appropriate and honorable. Among warriors, honor rules, and fear has no place. Honor above all else. Honor until the end.

"Hey, do I have some great news for you," Phil Winslow exclaimed as he snuck up behind Marchand.

Marchand froze momentarily, his quiet moment destroyed. "I know, this fucked up War is over, tell me it's true." Marchand said with feigned elation, his precious solitude broken.

"Not that good, wise guy, but good." Winslow laughed uneasily then relaxed. "The *Connie* just received permission to go to Hong Kong during this off-line period instead of next. And, get a load of this: the line period has been cut by a week. Task Force 77 must have decided to give us a break because we've been at sea so damn long."

And taken so many hits, Marchand thought but did not say. "Yeah, sixty days is enough for me. Hell, Noah only had forty days to deal with the friggin' flood! But hold on a minute, Phil, you wouldn't pull my string about something like this, would you?" Marchand asked sincerely then resumed his walking.

Winslow tagged along enthusiastically. "Hell no. Our last day of flight ops is January 24th, then we sail to the Philippines for repairs at Cubi Point. After two days, we depart for Hong Kong. Yep, Hong Kong. We arrive on January 28th.

"In fact, Frank Warden and a couple of lieutenant commanders from Ship's company are flying off tonight to arrange a big ship's party there. Huge invitation list. Warden himself told me about fifteen minutes ago. You know that means women, women, and more women."

"Christ, women, the antidote to all this bullshit; that's great, but what about those school teacher friends of yours that we were supposed to meet at Clark Field?"

"Don't worry. I'll call them when we arrive in Subic Bay and tell them to fly over for an evening. We might even persuade them to meet us in Hong Kong. On second thought, let's not mention Hong Kong. Frank and his crew are going to invite every available British and American nurse, schoolteacher, secretary, and model in Hong Kong. There's no point in taking a date to that."

"For sure," Marchand said and paused a moment. He had been walking at an increasingly fast rate to see if Winslow would tag along. Suddenly, Winslow stopped. Marchand turned and put his hand on Winslow's shoulder. "Phil, we've been at sea so long I started to think I'd never set foot on dry land again -- at least not as a free and healthy man. Maybe in a box, but not free, alive and walking," Marchand chuckled uneasily.

"Man, not more of this, not now. You're letting this business get to you way too much, Keith. Don't. It's not good for you. And it's not good for me either."

"You're goddamn right all this is getting to me. In fact, it's affecting me in ways I don't comprehend. And I don't like it."

"What don't you like? The cuisine, the décor, or the company?" Winslow remarked, trying for humor.

"You know what I mean."

"Not exactly."

"Well, for one thing, no one says a word about Commander Lord. It's like it never happened, like he never existed. And, damn it, I saw the SAM blow his plane out of the sky. I can't get the scene out of my mind and it's really fuckin' with me."

"Keith, don't go there. No one wants to go there."

Repressing a new wave of indignation, Marchand changed the subject somewhat. "Do you ever get the feeling that as much as you want to go ashore, some part of you doesn't? It's like I'm hooked on something but I don't know what." Marchand hoped that it wasn't the intoxication of war that he was becoming addicted to, the alert adrenaline high of survival pressure and constant combat.

Winslow didn't respond. He knew that they were all getting hooked on the high of fighter squadron life, bombing runs and air battles included. Marchand too. But why rub Marchand's nose in it? Phil and Marchand resumed their walk, now at a more moderate pace, in silence until they reached the ship's bow. Finally, Winslow broke the silence. "You know, Keith, it'll probably take years for anyone to understand what's going on here in 'Nam or what goes on in our minds as we just

185

try to deal with it. So, don't try to figure it all out right now."

"I'm not. It's just that there seems to be a lot of pressure to avoid certain issues."

Winslow replied, "Look, we're on a fuckin' floating city full of weapons, including nuclear weapons. And we know that we kill a lot of people and occasionally some of us get killed. That's just the way it is for us. What good does it do to talk about it?"

Marchand stiffened up. "That's pretty cold, Phil."

Winslow snapped back, "Hey, we coldly refuse to think about who we're killing in their own damn country. And it's only natural not to talk much on the guys who ain't coming home."

"Cold isn't the word. It's damn weird, bizarre even."

"Keith, knock it off. You know, if you keep thinking and talking like this, you're going to lose it. You just can't go on like this. You gotta stay in a good mental place."

"You mean in denial? That's a river in Egypt, I hear. Denial's a good place, right?"

"No, damn it. I mean, stay clear and clean of all this metaphysical bullshit and don't let it get to you. I'm learning to live one day at a time. You should too."

"Shit, I know that, Phil, so don't give me a lecture now – or a sermon."

"Come on, you know me, I never talk this way. But right now, I'm talking to you like this because you scare me sometimes. You think too much and you know you do. Go for the one day at a time approach. That's all any of us really have anyway, one day – the day you are living at the moment. Don't anticipate anything too far in the future; don't think about what happened yesterday. Don't think. Just try to appreciate each day, even the really tough ones."

Marchand refrained from telling Winslow what he thought of the simple approach to survival. Winslow clearly needed to think this way for his psychological well being. " Yeah, sure, Phil, you're probably right."

"I probably am ---"

Marchand cut him off. "I know we shouldn't talk like this but I couldn't stop myself tonight. Maybe it's those memorial services scheduled in a few days, I don't know. Maybe it's because one of them is Rich Miller. Maybe it's because Errol Lord is out there dead or captured. Sometimes, I think I feel guilty because I've made it and they didn't. You know what I mean?"

"Yeah, I know what you mean." Phil admitted reluctantly. He winced and then stood tall. "I just can't let myself touch it."

"Don't then, Phil, don't touch it. Sorry I brought all this up. Really. It's just that I feel like I'm losing touch with the world outside the *Constellation*. I feel like we all are."

"It's a weird experience. But we just have to deal with it. It's the job we trained for, the job we swore to do."

"Yeah, you're right, but does anyone really care about what we do out here? Do the folks back in the States give a damn?" Marchand asked rhetorically.

"Probably not, Keith. Let's just hope that they don't despise us for following orders and doing what we're ordered to do."

"Some probably do. Maybe quite a few do. Hell, if you kill a lot a people during a popular war, you're a hero. If it's not that kinda' war, people back home probably assume we're bloodthirsty assholes." Marchand replied sadly. "Christ, who knows, maybe they're right!"

The two men, fancying themselves bloodthirsty assholes for a moment, wandered on down the deck in search of a reprieve from the unyielding night. They both wanted answers to questions that were better left unasked. They both needed sanity somehow amidst the regimen of war.

22.

FOR THOSE IN PERIL
IN THE AIR

At sunrise on the morning of January 23, 1968, the Ship began threading its way through the maze of small islands composing the Philippine Archipelago. Many officers and crewmembers had assembled on the peaceful flight deck for the early morning memorial services in honor of the airmen who were lost during the first line period.

Soft dawn colors silhouetted the dark islands as the chaplain began the brief service. Marchand's eyes clouded when the names of his dead squadron mates were mentioned. The absence of coffins made it even more difficult to accept their deaths. As the Memorial Service was about to end, Marchand joined in the singing of the *Navy Hymn*. He choked back tears as he sang the words every Navy officer and seaman learns:

> *Almighty Father, strong to save*
> *Whose arm doth calm the restless wave*
> *Who bids the mighty ocean deep*
> *Its own appointed limits keep.*
> *Oh hear us as we cry to Thee*
> *For those in peril on the sea.*

Lord guard and guide the men who fly
Through the great spaces in the sky.
Be with them always in the air
In darkening storms or sunlight fair.
Oh, hear us when we lift our prayer
For those in peril in the air.

Listless clouds waited overhead and then moved on slowly, as if purposefully forming their own solemn procession. As they departed, the sunlight poured down in rays as if offering its own blessing. Gulls and other seabirds wheeled low over the ship in a silent salute, and flew on. Fly away brave airmen; fly away to your new home.

Afterward, Marchand wandered slowly toward the bow to find his secret spot of solitude. He descended the steps from the flight deck to the empty catwalk below and sought comfort from the all-knowing sea. The gentle morning wind and the splendid clear, new day breaking over the now sapphire water took him in, soothed him like a mother's hand on her child's fevered brow. Marchand was immersed in a feeling but could not define it. He felt he was being cleansed of something but he was not certain of what. It was some form of transition.

At first, the longing that beswept him was so unbearably intense, he fleetingly contemplated diving into the sea, joining the Ship's dead heroes. His friend Rich was gone and he felt to blame. Suddenly, Marchand knew he had to stop this survivor guilt or it would kill him. His dead comrades were not coming back; just let them go, he told himself, just let them go. This is the way of the warrior and you must follow it. Marchand had carried a small picture of Miller in his wallet since his death. He retrieved the picture and gave it with Miller's memory to the sea.

Marchand stood in desolate but rich reverence for quite some time. There was something good about this new wave of cleaner grief. It was at least a temporary watershed, a short-lived break from the unexpressed subsurface angst of the air warrior who buries his unseen body-less dead in a funeral at sea. The Sea - what better place to return to? After all, it is the place from which we started.

VOLUME ONE: PHANTOM WAR TRILOGY

23.

TERRA FIRMA

The chop of helicopter blades bringing the harbor pilot from Subic Bay interrupted Marchand's reverie so he headed below to prepare for the Ship's arrival. As the land drew closer, the War hid itself deeply in the minds of the crew craving a break from the tight confinement of their warship. Their excitement bubbled like sparkling wine. Many crewmembers had changed to liberty uniforms or mufti by the time the hawsers securely anchored the *Constellation* to the enormous pier at the Cubi Point Naval Air Station in Subic Bay. Although it was only 0830 in the morning, the ships' officers and men streamed down the brows located at the bow and the stern of the aircraft carrier.

Marchand and Winslow approached the head of the officers' brow with no less anticipation than their fellow crewmembers. Marchand came to attention before the Officer of the Deck, a very thin lieutenant in short-sleeved dress white uniform.

"Request permission to go ashore, Sir."

"Permission granted," the O.D. snapped back.

Marchand turned slightly to face the stern of the Ship and briefly came to attention in the direction of the Ship's Ensign, the American

Flag, curling gently in the breeze, declaring American presence and power. Then he and Winslow, dressed in Levi's and sport shirts, descended the long brow to the concrete pier. Marchand felt a powerful surge of exhilaration as he stepped onto land for the first time in two months. Resisting his urge to kneel and kiss the ground, Marchand turned to his friend Winslow and said with a small lump in his throat, "My God, this feels so good."

As they began walking along the pier, they both wobbled a bit, experiencing phantom motion beneath their feet, as all sailors who've been at sea for long periods have felt throughout the ages. "I know. There were so many times I didn't think I would live to do this," Winslow replied. "Times I really thought I wouldn't make it."

"Well, we made it! Phil, there's so much I want to do, I don't know where to start."

"So Keith, do you still feel like your world has shrunk to the confines of the ship?"

"You had to remind me that I said that didn't you? OK, so I'll eat my words."

"OK, what first?"

Craving space after weeks of confinement to the ship and its city of fifty-five hundred men, Marchand hit the brakes. "Well, if you don't mind, first I think I'm just going to wander around a bit, do some walking, do some shopping, listen to the birds sing, smell the sweet earth. I'll catch up with you later. Why don't we meet at the B.O.Q. at noon; we can get a good steak for lunch, then lounge around the pool until dinner and do some serious drinking. And one more thing, don't forget to call your lady friends at Clark Field. Can't forget them. We need some female company in the worst way."

"Tell me about it. But, don't worry; I'll make that call before lunch. See you in a few hours, Rocketman. Enjoy them birdies."

Transitioning from the alien world of war and carrier life to the new experience of land, land everywhere took a while. Working to shake an ambiguous but distinct hesitation which lingered within, Marchand wandered aimlessly a while. Eventually, he located the Base bookstore and browsed for material for the next line period. Surprised to find copies of his favorite novel, *Catch 22*, he bought several for friends who hadn't experienced Heller's supremely sardonic black humor. He gathered up eight of the ten books on the New York Times best fiction list and a copy of *Barry Lyndon* for good measure.

Marchand headed back to the ship, quickly deposited his cache in his stateroom, then took a cab to the Bachelor Officer Quarters. He quickly changed into swimming trunks and joined the crowd of aviators at the pool. He soon spotted Winslow and ambled over to join him. Women, Winslow had promised, women. The antidote to everything in this rotten, masculine-run world, women. "So, what time do your school teacher and her friend arrive, Phil?"

"They don't."

"What? After all that build up for the last three weeks, your friend Alice and her buddy fink out on us just like that!"

"Keith, Alice is not even in the Philippines. She and her roommate thought we were coming next weekend so they flew to Tokyo for a long weekend. If you remember, we're here a week early."

"Great. That settles it. I guess I'll just have to get knee walkin' drunk tonight."

"Well now, Rocketman, we could always go into Olongopo and buy a couple of whores."

"Oh right, and catch some awful tropical venereal disease for which no cure has been found. We could spend the rest of the cruise watching our peckers shrivel and fall off. No thank you, I still plan to get drunk. Besides, in a few days we'll be in Hong Kong where we'll find true love or at least some health-department-certified whores," Marchand snickered.

"Yeah, sure. Dream on. Man, what I wouldn't give to meet a couple American girls! I'm so damn horny I can't believe it but more than anything, I just want to talk to an American girl and hear her laugh."

24.

MARGO

Hong Kong is only a short one-day sail from the Philippine Islands and one of the Seventh Fleet's favorite liberty destinations. Winslow, Davis and Marchand were packed and ready to disembark by the time the Ship dropped anchor far out in the magnificent harbor. Marchand's edgy anticipation greatly increased during the slow ride into Hong Kong from the ship on the walla-walla, a small flat-bottomed boat made for this purpose. Well, I did it; I lived to see Hong Kong, Marchand said to himself. Yeah, at least I did that.

The walla-walla made agonizingly slow progress on the two-mile journey to the dock. Marchand's impatience subsided somewhat as he viewed the breath-taking scene of Hong Kong from midway out in the harbor. This was a city like no other. The early afternoon sun gleamed off of hundreds of dazzling white high-rise office and apartment buildings hugging the shoreline and sprinkled throughout the adjacent hills. The deep harbor produced the same azure hue as the open ocean. Ships, boats and junks of every size and description sailed, motored or cruised one of the most spectacular harbors of the world. Yet, the harbor's enormity seemed to scarcely contain the incredibly dense waterborne traffic. Marchand's impatience to be ashore changed to fascination as the small, crowded boat he rode wallowed its way toward the glamorous and beckoning shore. There was a mystery about this island city. It called to him and Marchand wanted to find it. And, he wanted to submerge himself deep within it.

Marchand, Winslow and Davis spent the rest of the afternoon exploring Hong Kong like all spellbound new arrivals. While much of the crew frequented the countless shops along Queen's Road, the threesome tried to absorb as much of the fascinating island as possible, basking in the easy confluence of Orient and Occident found only on this "Fragrant Island." By early evening they had checked into the Peninsula Hotel on the other side of the harbor, in Kowloon. After the austerity of the aircraft carrier, Marchand found the Peninsula's elegance almost shocking. The old hotel rivaled Europe's finest for opulence and décor but with the added grace and grandeur of old British colonialism.

Marchand dressed quickly and left the hotel so as to arrive early at the party for the Ship's officers. When Marchand arrived, the sight of so many attractive women gathered in one place dazzled him. Beautiful women of every description, European, Asian, Australian, and American, filled the ballroom. Accustomed only to the presence of men, it took a while for Marchand to feel comfortable.

Marchand wore a cream-colored khaki suit with an open neck white shirt. It perfectly complemented his tan and he knew it. He strolled through the crowd, stopping to chat occasionally, looking carefully for a beautiful woman to charm. Many approving glances came his way from a variety of European, Eurasian and Asian women. From time to time, he was tempted to stop searching for the perfect someone and settle for a pretty but not spectacular lady. Suddenly, Marchand spotted the most striking woman he had seen in the ballroom. She was Eurasian, tall, olive-skinned with jet-black hair that cascaded in splendid waves to her shoulders. Her features were sharp and well defined; her figure and clothes strongly suggested the fact that she was a model. Though surrounded by admirers, she smiled demurely at Marchand as he approached. Marchand felt confident that he would search no more that night. At least a half dozen young officers were trying to engage her with polite, lightweight conversation, but Marchand walked straight up to her and asked for a dance.

As he danced, Marchand plied her with questions. Yes, she was Eurasian, Indian and British. And yes, she was also a model and had recently begun to get good work. She was twenty-three and getting a bit tired of Hong Kong. Yes, she wished to go to Europe or America as soon as she could find work there. The dance ended and Marchand left her to get drinks. When he returned, Marchand saw the lovely model arm in arm with a British Naval Officer, obviously more than a friend, heading for the door. The model turned toward Marchand, smiled impishly, and departed with her companion.

"Well, I'll be damned," Marchand fumed, "and I thought I had it made. Women!" He sipped his scotch then looked at his watch. Ten-thirty, it was time for him to get serious or find himself with few choices for the evening. He resumed his casual strolling around the ballroom but it appeared that every attractive woman was already quite occupied with an officer. After several circuits around the ballroom, Marchand glanced at his watch again, it was eleven-fifteen and he began to worry. Couples were beginning to drift off to the nightclubs, bistros and bars located throughout Hong Kong and Kowloon. The available women began to look less and less appealing. Just as he resigned himself to an evening with a very plain Jane or worse, Marchand noticed an extraordinarily attractive blond watching him from a table not far away.

She was seated with a pilot from the Fighter Squadron Twenty-One's sister squadron, the Raging Bulls of Fighter Squadron Two Fourteen. Marchand knew Jerry Spence but did not particularly like him. And, it was obvious that the blond was bored by Spence's conversation. So, Marchand walked slowly toward the seated couple, extended his hand and said, "You don't mind, do you, Jerry?" Before the startled fighter pilot could protest, Marchand and the stunning blond were dancing.

"My name is Keith Marchand, may I ask yours?"

"Marguerite Collins; my friends call me Margo." She paused and said, "I'm assuming that you would like to be my friend."

Good start, thought Marchand, as he studied her closely. She was even lovelier than he had first thought. Her hair was softly waved and honey gold and her features were patrician with high cheekbones and eyes the color of a robin's egg. Her lips were full and slightly pouting, almost too full, Marchand thought, likening them to a ripe, exotic fruit. Her dimples danced when she smiled, highlighting snow-white teeth.

"Oh, that's a certainty, Margo. But let me ask you a quick question. Are you as unimpressed with Jerry as you appear?" Marchand queried.

"My, what an unkind thing to say about your Navy friend."

"Friend? Oh, I'm afraid not."

"Well, come to think of it, he didn't seem to care too much for you either, particularly since he noticed that I was looking at you."

"Well, I'm flattered. But, actually, I don't have much use for Jerry and I can assure you that he is a dreadful bore. In fact, Margo, why don't you and I just leave when this dance is finished?"

"Are you serious? I couldn't do that. Jerry has been talking to me for an hour and a half and -"

"And you're bored stiff," Marchand interrupted.

Ms. Collins laughed and flashed the most beguiling smile Marchand had ever seen. "You're absolutely right but still it would be so cruel to simply walk out as you suggest. Anyway, my purse is sitting on the table next to him."

"Look," Marchand said running his hand through his thick black hair. He was not going to let this one get away. "The music is almost over; so let's not waste more time. Just stay with me and I'll get your purse."

"I don't believe this," Margo said.

"Neither do I," replied Marchand quietly, knowing that Jerry Speed would be absolutely furious when they left.

When the music ended, they walked to the table where Margo's purse sat. She took the initiative. "Jerry, I've enjoyed talking to you, but I must leave now. I do hope that you enjoy Hong Kong."

"What do you mean? Where are you going?" Speed stammered.

Marchand quickly interrupted, "Margo and I are leaving, that's all she meant, and she wishes you well during your stay."

Marchand and Margo turned to leave as the flabbergasted pilot jumped to his feet causing a slight commotion. "You can't do that," Speed said in a flustered tone.

"But we have. Goodnight," Marchand replied as kindly as he could.

After leaving the ballroom, Marchand turned to Margo and said much too quickly, "Let's go to Kowloon," Immediately he thought. God, I just blew the whole thing. What an idiot I am. I could have asked her to go anywhere.

A short ride on the Star Ferry and a short walk brought them to a cozy nightclub with a passable dance band. As soon as they were comfortable, Marchand asked, "Margo, you obviously know what I am and what I do so why don't you tell me a bit about yourself?"

"But I really don't know who you are," she interrupted.

"Well, perhaps, not yet. But are you certain that you want to know?"

"Of course, I do. But to answer your question, I'm a student in Hong Kong doing my doctoral research. I've been working here for about six months now, took one short trip home for the holidays, and I'll be here for perhaps another four months."

"Fascinating. What's the subject of your dissertation?" Marchand queried as he studied the sparkle of her intelligent eyes as she spoke.

"The educational system of the Peoples' Republic of China," Margo replied somewhat tersely, not wanting to become overly technical and risk spoiling the excitement of the evening.

"Impressive. That must mean that you speak Chinese."

"Mandarin and some Cantonese."

"Do you read and write as well?"

"Of course."

"Now, I'm really impressed. What university do you attend?" he inquired not believing his incredible good fortune.

"Harvard," she replied somewhat concerned that the disclosure might discourage the young naval officer who seemed as inquisitive as he was handsome.

"A Cliffie, too?" Marchand pressed, thinking that they might have common acquaintances.

"No, Wellesley." Margo quickly changed the subject. "Are you a pilot or a ship's officer?"

"Neither."

"But you are a Navy officer, aren't you? Are there other types of Naval officers?"

"I'm not a pilot, but I do fly. I'm a flight officer, a weapons officer. I fly F-4 Phantoms."

Margo looked at Marchand and replied, "I don't have the foggiest idea what an F-4 or a Flight Officer is or does but it sounds rather intense."

"I won't bore you with it but suffice it to say that my job is to put whatever weapons we carry onto or into a specific target, whatever that might be."

"Do you find many targets?"

"Enough," Marchand replied bluntly, not wishing to go further into his combat status with a lady that he had just met.

"And you bomb them?" Collins inquired with great intensity.

"Sometimes," Marchand answered with increasing apprehension. Damn, he thought, is she a journalist or some other non-desirable?

"Do you enjoy it?" she asked.

"Enjoy what?"

"Dropping bombs. I've heard that you pilots, or excuse me – flight officers - rather enjoy what you do."

"You can't be serious," Marchand replied, severely wrinkling his brow. "Aviators enjoy flying but few, if any, enjoy dropping bombs, and I assure you that I'm not one of those who do," he said with clear exasperation.

"Do you drop napalm, too?"

"No, I don't. We don't keep it on the ship. It's too dangerous," Marchand replied with a frown. "Nor do we bomb temples, pagodas, hospitals or schoolhouses."

"How ironic, no napalm because it's too dangerous." she repeated then said, "Forgive me, please; I didn't wish to offend you. This really isn't a proper topic for a first evening in any event." She sensed that she had crossed a line into *terra incognita.*

"Agreed," Marchand quickly responded. "You've also neatly changed the topic of conversation. I was attempting to get to know you. I don't know what you truly are or really do. You could be a reporter for the *New York Times* or some other damn paper that would get my goose cooked, but good. So, please tell me you're not a reporter, a government agent, or a spy."

"Well, if I were really a spy, would I tell you?" Margo paused a moment, clearly thinking the better of this question. "But no, wait; I'm really sorry, Keith. I assure you that I'm not a spy or a journalist or anything else that could 'cook your goose'. I really am a graduate student at Harvard's Kennedy School of Government and I'm here completing my research work for a doctorate that seems to have taken forever to finish. So, can we start over again or have we missed our chance?"

Marchand did a double take. He didn't want to let the gorgeous blond doctoral candidate slip away but the conversation seemed to have reached a critical turn that he knew he had to direct carefully. "Please forgive me if I seem a bit defensive. We've all been warned about dangers that might surface during our stay here and your questions just seemed a bit sensitive. You know there's so much concern over Soviet and Chinese intelligence operatives digging into U.S. presence in Southeast Asia. You can imagine we've all been warned about this... But let's start all over, please. Where would you like to begin?"

"Well, let's begin by being very direct, OK?" Margo said,

clearly relieved.

"OK – you first."

"Alright. You see, I've longed for some good company for quite a while. I'm alone here and I'd love to spend days and days talking to you. In fact, I'm actually quite attracted to you. And, well, this will probably shock you, and it surely shocks me to say this, but life is short. So, look, I simply have to tell you that I would very much like, uh...like, to go to bed with you," Margo responded softly while looking directly into Marchand's eyes. "So there, I've said it!"

Sincerely astonished, Marchand stammered slightly but finally replied, "My God, you are certainly full of surprises. I've fantasized that some day a beautiful blond will mysteriously appear and invite me into her bed without all the required gaming. But, of course, it's never happened. Now that it has, I'm stunned, shocked, practically speechless. However, before you change your mind, I graciously and most humbly accept your offer. In fact, I suggest that we not waste another minute here. I'm staying at the Hong Kong Hilton, shall we go there?"

Margo's eyes widened. This man, Lieutenant Marchand, was clearly serious. "Oh my, well then great. Better yet, shall we go to my place?" Margo giggled, somewhat awkwardly.

"Your place it is."

VOLUME ONE: PHANTOM WAR TRILOGY

25.

HANOI HILTON V.I.P.

Orange and violet rays from the rising sun poked through the miniature window high on the east wall of Errol Lord's tiny cell. Lord awoke at daybreak to begin the daily routine that he had followed religiously since his transfer to the infamous Hanoi Hilton Hotel. Wistfully, he scratched another "X" on the cell wall to mark the thirty-first day of his capture. Slowly, Lord began his exercises starting with deep knee bends which he thought would loosen the thickened, scarred skin covering the badly burned areas around his lower thighs and knees.

The burns had healed rather well considering the lack of medical treatment since his ejection over Haiphong Harbor. Lord finished his sit-ups but still couldn't manage a push-up for the knitting of the fractured bone in his right arm was not yet complete as the sharp pain so clearly indicated. He looked at his now deformed right arm and the odd angles it took and chuckled to himself. It's probably good I can't do a push-up; the right arm is so much shorter than the left, I'd probably fall over. He was about to begin the yoga exercises that his wife had taught him before he left San Diego when the cell door was unlocked and swung open.

Lord's stomach constricted immediately in anticipation of what was sure to follow. As he was being manacled and blind folded, sharp recollections of past interrogations paraded painfully through his consciousness. The interrogations had begun shortly after his transfer from Haiphong where he had been plucked, burned and broken, from the Harbor and trucked to the notorious prisoner of war camp in Hanoi. By the time of his transfer, his burns had almost healed, no thanks to the Vietnamese, and his right arm had nearly set in its curious dogleg shape. Upon Lord's arrival in Hanoi, North Vietnamese senior officers in charge of the camp had determined that the time for serious business had arrived. As far as they were concerned, Lord's convalescence had ended. The events of those first interrogations some two weeks ago were still quite fresh in Lord's memory. He recalled that his interrogator, a young Vietnamese Captain, spoke heavily accented but grammatically correct English. "What is your name?" the captain had demanded as the now familiar litany began.

"Erroll Francis Lord, Commander, United States Navy, Serial Number Two One Nine, Seven Nine Four. " Lord had responded as crisply as all the Midshipmen at Annapolis had been taught from the earliest days of officer training.

"To what ship are you assigned, Commander Lord?"

Lord had responded again with his name, rank and serial number, as he had been taught throughout his long naval career. The Vietnamese Captain replied coldly, "Commander Lord, do not play your foolish games with me. I know that your ship is the *U.S.S. Constellation* and that you are the Commanding Officer of Attack Squadron One Twenty One. I also know other matters about you which make such responses totally ridiculous. You will either cooperate with me or you will regret it."

"Now, Commander Lord, let's talk seriously with one another. Why was Haiphong selected as your target?"

Again, Lord responded with the recitation of name, rank and serial number. The Captain, whose back had been toward Lord's bound and seated figure, suddenly whirled about and landed full force an open handed slap to Lord's face. Lord's head snapped sharply with the force of the blow. The shock proved more devastating than the pain which rapidly began to fill Lord's head.

"You will learn that it is not wise to cause me to repeat my questions, Commander Lord. Again, why was Haiphong your target?"

Still Lord's training and dedication to military principles prevailed and he answered as before. Not wishing to exert himself, the Captain administered successive blows by proxy. The sullen faced army regular who had bound Lord to the solid wooden chair began to administer blows. First he applied open hand slaps to Lord's face. As Lord persisted with the same measured response, the Captain's aide began to deliver heavy body blows to Lord's midsection. The first blow to his stomach shocked his entire body. He could neither inhale nor exhale and he began to convulse for lack of oxygen. The Captain allowed him to recover before repeating his question but still Lord persisted with the standard response required by the U.S. Code of Military Justice. The next well-aimed blow delivered just below Lord's diaphragm was so severe that he could not regain his breath and passed out, thereby ending the day's interrogation.

Each day the interrogation continued and each day the results were identical but increasingly brutal. On the third day of questioning, the Captain seemed to lose all control, began screaming in Vietnamese and ended by slamming his fist into Lord's mouth. When Lord awoke in his cell, he discovered, along with the renewed pain, that one tooth was missing and one was badly chipped. His lips were split and too swollen to move and an intense headache seemed to cleave his brain. But remarkably the interrogations stopped for four days. Lord concluded that his show of personal resolve had been successful and gradually he began to relax. However, just as abruptly as the brutal sessions had abated, they had begun anew.

On the eighth day of Lord's ordeal, he was manacled and brought again to the small, stuffy room where the Captain waited. Upon entering the room, Lord stared with all the contempt and hate he could muster upon the slightly built North Vietnamese officer. He was nearly a foot shorter than Lord and his teeth, like those of many Vietnamese, had turned black from the lack of even the most rudimentary dental hygiene. Lord thought that the Captain's mouth looked as though it were a small black pit or entrance to a dark cave or mineshaft. Lord nicknamed the officer Captain Pit.

Captain Pit ordered the two guards escorting Lord to seat him in the accustomed heavy wooden chair but much to Lord's surprise he was not tied to it. The escorting guards remained, however, along with Captain Pit and the enlisted soldier who usually performed the heavy-duty thug work.

Once Lord was seated, Captain Pit began. "You are a very strong man, Commander Lord; you are to be commended for your perseverance and loyalty. But, you see, we Vietnamese are also quite perseverant, as you, Commander Lord, and your fellow Americans will soon learn. We will defeat you, Commander, just as we Vietnamese, under the leadership of our illustrious President, Ho Chi Minh, will defeat you Americans, just as we defeated the French, the Japanese, and the Chinese before you.

"Commander, be reasonable. Save yourself the pain and futility of resisting my questions. You will, I assure you, be much the better for it. We Vietnamese are not brutal people by nature, Commander. But we can rise to the occasion. And, I must convince you, as the glorious People's Republic of Vietnam will convince your President Johnson, continuing this struggle is pointless.

"Now again, Commander, I ask you: why did your ship send its attack against the People's Harbor at Haiphong?"

Lord knew that Captain Pit's abrupt tactical reversal required a different response on his part as well. Yet, notwithstanding the pain of the previously administered beatings, Lord was not willing to break with the strict code of conduct taught him over the years of his naval service. Lord strained to think of some response that would allow him to uphold his code of conduct yet avoid the beating that he knew would follow. He knew instinctively that some new course of action was required, for he also knew that his ability to withstand the beatings was approaching. Suddenly, he focused on a way to end his dilemma.

As violently as possible, Lord wrenched out of the chair and fell to the cement floor clutching his sides with both hands. Simultaneously, he began to moan, then to twitch and finally to convulse. With his hand wedged between the floor and his heaving stomach, Lord managed to pull his penis out of his prisoner pajamas and begin urinating on the prison floor.

At first Captain Pit and the guards recoiled in surprise and shock at the sight of the six-foot American writhing on the cement before them, his moans rising to a loud wail and his urine spurting over the floor. Captain Pit wheeled in utter disgust and left the interrogation room, ordering the guards to return the stinking, wretched Naval Officer to his cell.

After his transfer to the Hanoi Hilton and on his way to his first interrogation session there, Lord recalled his triumph over Captain Pit and nearly smiled, but his reflections were cut short by his arrival at the prison's interrogation room. The Guards thrust him into the room that would have been quite similar to its counterpart in Haiphong but for the naked incandescent bulb hanging from the ceiling and the absence of any windows at all. The guards shoved Lord into another heavy wooden chair but did not tie him to it; then they took up station on either side of him and waited. Lord's left leg began to twitch uncontrollably as he gazed at the door but otherwise his composure was granite.

After what seemed to Lord like the passage of an hour, the door to the interrogation room swung open and a young lieutenant, probably not older than twenty-five, entered the room followed by a more senior officer wearing a well-pressed uniform and a pistol in a gleaming leather hip holster.

"Good morning, Commander Lord, I am Major Tran Van Dung, Army of the People's Republic of Vietnam. You and I will learn to know each other well. Whether our acquaintance is pleasant or otherwise is entirely up to you."

Much to Lord's surprise, Major Dung reached inside his tunic and produced a pack of cigarettes. Cyrillic lettering identified them as Russian. The Vietnamese officer tapped the pack and offered a cigarette to Lord, smiling as he did so. Lord was as much amazed by the even white teeth of the Major as by his proffering of a cigarette. Nevertheless, he accepted and gladly inhaled after the Major produced a lighter and actually lit Lord's cigarette. The smoke went straight to Lord's head and he felt almost inebriated. The Major watched intently, obviously pleased; he did, however, allow Lord to finish nearly half the cigarette before asking his first question.

"Commander Lord, how many aircraft were in your attack

group?"

"Thirty," Lord replied casually.

Major Dung concealed both his surprise and pleasure at Lord's response and continued. "What was your actual target, Commander?"

"The storage depot at Bach Lai."

"Did you know what the depot was used for, Commander?"

"Not really."

"Not really? Surely you must have had some idea, Commander."

"Munitions from your Russian friends, I suppose."

Major Dung paused, quite pleased to learn that the American Strike Force had been tricked by the Vietnamese ruse of placing empty railcars near the docks so that American reconnaissance would order an attack on worthless targets. Delighted with this information and the fact that the American Naval Officer was responding for the first time, Major Dung allowed himself to relax and enjoy his triumph.

"Commander, I'm pleased to tell you that the target which your squadron destroyed at such a terrible personal cost to you, was simply a decoy. Our target was designed to fool you. Your strike force destroyed several empty railcars but we have destroyed you and your airplane. Don't you find that amusing, Commander?" Major Dung ended his message with peals of high-pitched laughter.

Lord's composure visibly withered. His plan was to give his tormentors only such information as he knew they would already possess, pleasing his captors and sparing himself further torture. But Major Dung's revelation injured him more gravely than any beating he had endured. My God, he thought, could I have been shot down trying to bomb a decoy? How many of us have been killed or captured trying to destroy worthless targets? How can our Intelligence Service betray us this way?

"You seem surprised, Commander. Are you upset?" The Major laughed. "I have so enjoyed our conversation, Commander. I shall see you again tomorrow."

Lord's first few hours after returning to his cell were agonizing. He had bravely, if not courageously, taken the worst that his captors could administer. He had coolly led his strike force to its target through sheets of exploding fire and steel. Under his direction, the target had been destroyed; he was sure of that since he had watched his own bombs detonate on target. He had in all respects performed in accordance with the highest traditions of the Naval Service of the United States. For his efforts, he had been ridiculed in the most inglorious manner and been made the fool.

Lord's spirit gamely fought back. He decided that Captain Dung had lied to him about the decoy targets, that the Captain's comments were an elaborate plot designed to weaken his will to resist. For a few moments, Lord felt enormously relieved and his strength renewed. Then Lord recalled several anomalies he had subconsciously noted during the Haiphong mission.

First, he remembered that the loading docks and the piers near the target seemed to have been in a general state of dilapidation and disrepair. He also recalled that the piers adjacent to the rail siding were at least two miles from the piers where all the Russian freighters were tied up. Lord remembered thinking for an instant as he stared through his plane's gun sight at the railroad tracks which were his last target that the tracks didn't glint and gleam in the morning sunlight as they usually did. The tracks were difficult to see and target because they were --- Oh God --- dull and rusty. Seldom used tracks, he knew became rusty, whereas, heavily traveled rails always remained bright from the constant polishing action of railcar wheels. Finally, Lord recalled his surprise as he watched one of his bombs score a direct hit on one of the parked railcars. The car and several others were totally demolished but there were no secondary explosions or intense fires as there would have been if the cars had been loaded with munitions, petroleum products or lubricants.

The evidence yielded but one conclusion: Captain Dung was not lying. Lord's mission was a sham, a farce; Lord's injuries, his capture, were another cruel joke in a cruel war. Despair crept slowly into the strong Commander's soul. Captain Dung's high-pitched laughter echoed in his brain. Hot bitter tears etched lines down his face. He would have killed himself but he could think of no way to take his life in the bare, unfurnished cell.

During the long hours following his last interrogation, Lord determined that he would resist no longer. He could not kill himself, which is what he preferred to do, and would gladly have done if only he could have found a way. But he had no will to accept further punishment. Additional resistance, he had decided, would prove even more futile than his last flight. When Dung sends for me tomorrow, he thought, I'll cooperate with him for the most part. As long as he doesn't ask me about nuclear weapons, I'll tell him what he wants to know.

But for the next several days, Captain Dung did not send for him. Instead, he spent the long, slow hours in solitary confinement. He prayed for the opportunity to even see another POW, but in vain. The isolation must be part of the punishment he concluded.

Three days after his last interrogation with Dung, the door to his cell was unlocked and two guards entered and began to manacle Lord. The isolation had been so intense that Lord was almost pleased to see them. He even looked forward to the next confrontation with Dung since he had decided not to resist Dung's questions. The techniques these bastards have developed must be working, he thought. But just as Lord was being led out of his cell, air raid sirens began to wail fiercely. Lord was quickly ushered back to his cell and chained to an iron ring anchored to the floor of the cell. He heard the staccato pounding of anti-aircraft cannon nearby. Soon he could hear the whistle of falling bombs and the scream of jet engines as the attacking bombers pulled out of their dives. Lord had never heard the sound of five hundred pound bombs detonating since the cockpit of tactical aircraft allowed almost no sound from the outside, not even exploding bombs or anti-aircraft artillery. The ferocity of the explosions shocked him. The walls of the cell, the floor and even the air seemed visibly disturbed. The sound was so deafening as to be felt rather than heard. The explosions made him physically ill.

The thought that he might be killed by American bombs had never occurred to Lord before but as he crouched for cover he recognized just such a possibility. He tried to slide under the wooden bench, which was his bed, but the chain was too short. The best he could do to protect himself was to crouch with his head between his legs. The bastards have chained me here to die, Lord thought, cruel irony for me, poetic justice for them. The sons-of-bitches could have at least given me another three feet of chain, though. They've thought of everything like putting this goddamn prison adjacent to military targets so that our own bombs can kill us. How damn clever!

The walls of Lord's cell shook and the floor rumbled but the only damage he could detect when the three-minute attack ended was to his nerves. God, he thought, when silence returned, I hope you boys did some serious damage to these bastards, damage to a real target not a damn decoy like yours truly did. With that thought, the anger, frustration and futility of his capture again flooded back into Lord's awareness and he began to sob silently.

26.

VICTORIA PEAK

Keith Marchand and Margo Collins exited the tram close to the top of Victoria Peak, walked a hundred yards along a small narrow street then entered a modern high rise apartment building that could as easily have been located in San Francisco as Hong Kong. They took an elevator to the tenth floor where Margo led Marchand a short distance to her flat. She opened the door, hesitated for a moment before motioning him to follow her inside. Marchand entered a beautifully decorated apartment and felt the sweet shock of full and complete reentry into the civilian world for the first time in months.

"Margo, your apartment is charming. Harvard has certainly done well by you. They certainly never treated us this well at The College."

Upon hearing Marchand's reference to The College, Margo paused a moment then said. "So you went to Harvard. Hmmm ... anyway, Harvard had nothing to do with this flat; my father picked it out. He had to find some way to control my Far Eastern adventure so this is how he attempted to do it."

Marchand briefly wondered what kind of man the senior Collins was to spend so lavishly on his daughter. He certainly loves her, Marchand concluded, then said, "In any event, I'm delighted to be here with you. I wonder why I never saw you at Wellesley, I know I visited nearly every weekend."

"I made it a policy not to date undergrads," she teased, but then softened. "Make yourself comfortable and I'll fix you a drink." Suddenly more aware of what she had actually engineered, Margo quickly left the room. "So now, here I am with a Naval Officer, of all people," she murmured to herself, feeling just a little nervous, "who actually drops bombs, of all things."

When Margo emerged from the kitchen with his drink, Marchand sensed her internal tug-of-war and inquired, "Margo, I've got to ask you, why are you doing this? We could slow down, get to know each other better if you'd like."

Margo studied Marchand a moment as she sat on the sofa next to him. Slowing down might be a good idea, but how much time did either of them really have to get to know each other? She wondered. "Since you risked the question and the possibility of my having second thoughts about this truly bizarre evening, I'll risk a reply."

She sat down near Marchand and seemed to relax a bit. "I've been doing research in Hong Kong for six months now. As I said, I've made only one trip back to the States in that entire time. It was very short and while I was there I almost got arrested in a pretty serious antiwar demonstration in Boston." Margo thought to herself about the afternoon near Boston Commons; well, that was not exactly a near arrest, but more of an executive round up. But why try to explain right now? She looked at Marchand. He looked quizzical. Why? Was it the anti-war demonstration? "You look troubled. Don't worry, I wasn't protesting, I was observing the protest, studying the phenomenon." Although I should have been protesting, Margo said to herself. And rioting if need be.

"I didn't say anything about it," Marchand said quickly. What did it matter to him what her views on the War were anyway? He asked himself somewhat uncomfortably.

"So what is it, what crossed your mind as I mentioned it?"

Marchand shrugged.

"Really, I want to know, come on, Keith," Margo pleaded.

"OK, well, its just that I – I – how do I say this? I never imagined myself consorting with a real live antiwar radical." He sipped at his drink and smiled as he waited for her reaction.

Margo giggled briefly and then feigned a serious approach. "Consorting, huh? Is that what you think I am? An antiwar radical? What is an antiwar radical anyway? Just because I went to watch a demonstration that for some reason brought out the riot squad doesn't mean I was involved in it. I am student of authoritarianism, social policy, and international politics, and the Orient, so of course this big war in Southeast Asia might interest me, just as what happens in the U.S. or in China might."

Marchand decided he had to steer them away from certain topics, and quickly. "OK, look, let's just move onto what you were telling me, and I won't second guess you."

"Good idea. So where was I? ... Oh right, so anyway, I admit that I'm a bit homesick. I've tried to stay connected by dating a few businessmen and military officers from the States. I've even dated a few Royal Navy officers and British Embassy staffers who all turned out to be crashing bores, totally taken with themselves. For a few weeks, I even dated an American Navy Commander who was on holiday from his ship and, as it turned out, from his wife. So, I'm tired of stuffed shirts and married men masquerading as bachelors. And, after spending an hour talking to your friend, Jerry, I was quite ready to simply give up, come home and read a book.

"And then I saw you. You seemed different, very different, even from a distance. I liked the way your eyes sparkled when you smiled. And your smile seemed warm and sincere. Right away, I knew that you were special.

Marchand blushed and said, "How special?"

"Pretty special. I waited to catch your eye for the simple reason that I'm attracted to you, very attracted. And, I'll bet a semester's tuition that you're not married. Strangely enough, I feel I can trust you. Instinctively, I know I can."

Marchand reached for this woman that dreams are made of. When she did not resist, he kissed her softly, and drew her closer to him. Her fragrance intoxicated him and her warmth was overwhelming. She stroked his face with long satin fingers and returned his kiss with eager parted lips. He ran his hands through the silken folds of her hair and kissed her neck hungrily. When he stopped to look at her, she traced his lips lightly with her finger. Marchand's mind and pulse raced. "I'm going to wake any minute and find myself in my stateroom on the ship, I just know it. This is all just a dream. It's just too good to be anything but a dream," he sighed.

"No, Keith," Margo whispered in his ear. "You're not on your ship and I'm not a dream. This is as real as it gets. Want me to pinch you to prove it?" she laughed. She excused herself and went to her bedroom where she lit a dozen candles and incense sticks. Moments later, she called for him to join her.

Almost in a trance, Marchand walked into the bedroom, drawn to this woman he had found at another man's table. Drawn, hungry and speechless. She was far more than merely the antidote to the effects of war he had thought he was seeking. He stood quite still before Margo for a moment, hesitating. For some reason unclear to him, waves of pain and grief rushed through him. Not now, not now, Marchand instructed himself, not now, you fool. But he paused a while longer. He realized that he was hurting, really hurting, uncontrollably grieving the loss of his friend, Rich Miller. But why right now?

Margo touched his face softly, and whispered, "What? What is it?"

Marchand shook his head no, repressing the memories, whispered back, "Such a beautiful woman, and I'm here, here and alive and ecstatic to be with you."

"Thank you, my dear Lieutenant Marchand," she whispered in his ear.

He began to unbutton her blouse, each button with great care and deliberation, while kissing her neck again very softly. The veins in his forehead pounded as he undid her brassiere and he gasped audibly as his gaze fell upon her breasts, milk white, delicate pink, and formed as if by an sculptor's hand. It seemed forever since he had seen a woman this way. It might have been lifetimes ago, for all he knew that moment. Marchand trembled as his hungry fingers touched the warm, satin-soft skin of her breasts. Forever, since he had seen such a beautiful woman and touched her.

He pulled her to the bed, slowly kissing erect nipples. He carefully removed her remaining clothes, as if beginning a ceremony. A ceremony of intense lust, but also of something more and greater. The moist warmth of her sex overwhelmed his senses with pleasure and anticipation as he opened his eyes to feast upon her magnificently proportioned and suntanned body. Marchand's eyes consumed the counterpoint of her white breasts against her otherwise bronze skin, the golden down barely visible on her flat stomach, the flair of her hips that tapered into long graceful legs, and the soft blond waves that guarded her most intimate area. He hesitated again, this time gazing without blinking at this exquisite woman.

"You stare so intensely, do I please you or are you disappointed with what you see?"

"Margo, you are absolutely the loveliest woman I've ever seen. I'm sorry for staring; I just can't help it. You're beautiful beyond words."

"You're forgiven; but why am I totally undressed while you're still in your suit?"

Marchand practically ripped off his clothes, his strong, lean body fully aroused and hungry. They sank onto the cool, crisp sheets locked in a deep kiss. Marchand urgently but gently entered her and they made love feverously, intensely, passionately, until they were exhausted. Then they loved each other again and again.

Finally, there was neither urgency nor haste in their lovemaking. Marchand sought to please Margo and she gave sweetly in return. Needing feminine warmth as much or perhaps more than he craved sex, Marchand drank more deeply of Margo's essential self than from the passion she so warmly offered. Margo finally shuddered in complete ecstasy, everything given up to complete passion. Afterward, they stayed locked in embrace for hours, not willing to relinquish the intense pleasure of their union, not wanting to let go of this happenstance meeting.

After a night of intense passion and a peaceful morning of quiet lovemaking, Margo and Marchand left the flat and Margo began a personalized tour of Hong Kong. They began with a tram ride from her flat to the top of Victoria Peak, the highest point of the island of Hong Kong, and a walk along the walkways at the summit. As they walked, Marchand gazed intently at the splendid harbor formed by the deep channel between Hong Kong Island and the Peninsula of Kowloon. Now this is the way to see Hong Kong, he told himself. As he watched, a thoroughly modern hydrofoil glided onto its water-borne wings heading for the Portuguese Colony of Macao. The large white catamaran gracefully threaded its course at fifty miles per hour through ancient fishing junks and ponderous walla-wallas plying their trade on the sapphire waters of the harbor. Marchand estimated that at least a hundred freighters were riding at anchor throughout the splendid channel between the island and Kowloon.

He seemed almost mesmerized by the view until Margo tugged his arm and asked, "Is that your ship out at the end of the harbor?"

Yanked back into reality, Marchand stared at the massive gray steel island in the distance, its motionless flight deck and the four story high numerals "64" that were still visible from Victoria Peak. "Yes, Margo, that's the *Constellation*; ninety thousand tons of steel loaded to the teeth and ready to deal with anything or anyone who wants trouble. That comes to almost eighteen tons of steel and loneliness for each man aboard."

"You sound somewhat melancholy; I'm surprised."

"Why?"

"I don't know; being lonely just doesn't fit the fighter pilot image."

"It's difficult to live up to the image sometimes."

"But what about the grand *esprit de corps* and cavalier manner that one always hears about military aviators?" Margo pressed.

"If you seriously analyzed it, you'd probably discover that much of the bravado, machismo, pomposity and aggressive attitude have only one purpose - to keep us alive and somewhat sane. The bravado keeps the fear at bay. Without it, you have too much time to reflect on the danger. The macho attitude keeps us going, keeps us aggressive. A good

223

method of coping with fear is to taunt it, to jeer at it, even to tempt it. So, we often mock the reaper; cheat him every day if we're lucky. We conquer fear with jest and bravado. You should hear some of the songs we sing at the bar. Unfortunately, it just doesn't work all the time."

Margo was taken aback by Marchand's honest comments. She stared toward the open ocean in silence for almost a minute before turning to Marchand. Gently she reached up and caressed his face with both hands. Marchand kissed Margo softly at first then deeply as he wrapped her into his powerful arms. She shuddered just for a moment, sensing blood on his hands. Fragmented images and haunting cries of bombed Vietnamese flickered through her mind. But, in an instant, the images and sensations passed and she held him tightly.

He was troubled, she knew it, and it touched her deeply. It also frightened her. She was afraid to love a man at war; he could die, lose a limb, or be captured. He could be taken from her for no reason on any given day. No reason but a senseless, virtually irrational war, she thought.

27.

CAT AND MOUSE

Lord lost track of time during the days before his interrogation resumed. He was quite prepared to play the game of cat and mouse with Captain Dung, to feed Dung bits and pieces of information the totality of which would be harmless and previously known by his captors. The game for him, he now knew, was to stay alive by pretending to cooperate. The game was not at all what he had been taught at the Naval Academy, dogged refusal to answer even the most elementary questions. In Vietnam that single-minded resolve would lead only to his death, a difficult and terribly painful death at that. But Lord had not yet begun to comprehend Major Dung's game.

Lord was seated but not bound as Dung entered the interrogation room. Dung immediately walked over to Lord, handed him a typed page and instructed him to read it. Lord could scarcely contain his outrage as he read the page....

> I, Commander Errol Francis Lord, United States Navy, confess that on January 1, 1968, I was the strike Commander of an American attack force composed of fifty bombers which without warning or provocation dropped hundreds of powerful bombs and missiles on a civilian hospital located in the city of Haiphong in the Peoples Republic of Vietnam.

For many weeks, American Intelligence Officers have observed the work of the Bach Lai Hospital from spy planes and determined that grave harm could be perpetrated on the heroic people of Vietnam by destroying the Hospital so that the sick and injured citizens of Haiphong would have to be tended by the doctors and nurses of the courageous Peoples' Army. In this way, the American Navy Admirals concluded that the brave and heroic efforts of our President Ho Chi Minh to reunite our country and drive out the imperialist American aggressors would be hampered.

I have learned that during the cowardly raid on the Bach Lai Hospital, many innocent women, children and sick persons were killed by American bombs. However, the people of Haiphong fought back bravely and my bomber was shot down. Through the courageous efforts of the local militia, I was pulled from the waters of Haiphong Harbor and saved from drowning.

Since my capture, I have been treated with humane kindness and sympathy by the Army and the people of Haiphong and I have received the best treatment for injuries sustained when my bomber was hit by Vietnamese marksmen.

I sincerely regret my criminal actions and I implore President Johnson to stop the bombing of innocent Vietnamese civilians immediately.

Errol Francis Lord
Commander
United States Navy

Lord shoved the paper back to Dung and growled, "This is a pack of lies and you know it, Dung. There's no way in hell that I would ever sign it."

"You should not be so rash, Commander. I have been very lenient with you, as have my comrades in Haiphong. But my patience is very short and if you refuse to sign this confession, I will see that your life will become, shall we say, quite unpleasant, if not altogether brief."

"This confession is all a lie, Dung."

"Perhaps you didn't bomb the hospital, Commander, but one of your comrades has bombed the Hospital. Unfortunately for you, we have captured you, not one of your criminal comrades so you must sign the confession. What difference does it make to you or to anyone if you sign the confession or if some other Yankee Air Pirate signs the confession? Some American pilot will sign it. That, I will assure you.

"Frankly, Commander, it will benefit you greatly if you do sign the confession. We can make your stay in Hanoi as pleasant or unpleasant as is necessary to obtain your cooperation. Make your life easier, Commander, sign the confession now." The Major ended on a most insistent and demanding note.

Lord waited for nearly a minute before he began to respond. During the agonizingly slow passage of seconds, Major Dung could see the anxiety and stress written deeply on Lord's face. Both men knew the consequences of Lord's response. Both were aware of the painful price that Lord would pay for refusing to cooperate. Dung knew the tortures in great detail; Lord recalled the rumors that circulated in squadron ready rooms of exotic Vietnamese techniques designed to exact maximum pain on the unfortunate victim, techniques which were almost always effective unless death mercifully interceded. Nevertheless, Lord felt constrained by codes of conduct deeply etched into his ethical system, codes engrained from his earliest days at Annapolis, written by men who had never faced Major Dung or anyone like him.

With full awareness of the consequences of his reply to Major Dung, Lord looked squarely at his tormentor and said, "Take your carefully prepared confession to hell with you, Major Dung; I shall not sign it."

Dung's thin, flat face remained nearly expressionless but for a slight narrowing of the epicanthic folds of his eyes, giving him an even more menacing look. "We shall see, Commander Lord, we shall see," he said, turned on his heel and left the room motioning to three squat but wiry Army regulars as he left. Lord was bound to the stout chair with heavy rope. His torso, legs and arms were all pulled tightly against the frame of the heavy chair. Lord would have expected another severe beating had it not been for the taping of his right hand to the extended arm of the chair. Lord's fingers were painfully spread apart and taped to a small board inserted between his palm and the arm of the chair. The hand and board were secured to the chair by additional wrappings of surgical tape.

By the time the taping was complete, Lord knew what Major Dung had planned for him. Blood surged around and through his temples, his face was flushed and perspiring and his stomach felt knotted and nauseous. For the first time since the SAM turned his aircraft into a tumbling inferno, Errol Lord felt genuine terror enveloping his being. He tried the meditation exercise that his wife had taught him but to no avail; terror had set too deep for him to reach the threshold of the proper mental state. As his right arm began to quiver, Lord focused the totality of his concentration on his beloved wife and hoped for strength and control.

Major Dung returned to the room and without uttering a word nodded to the most sinister and brutish looking of the three guards. The guard smiled, slightly exposing the blackened and rotten vestiges of his teeth. He turned towards Lord, reached into a small canvas bag and produced the instruments of his specialty. He placed a small wooden mallet on the table situated alongside Lord's chair then laid thin slivers of dried bamboo on the table. The slivers were nearly two inches long and slightly more than one-quarter inch wide. The thickness tapered from an almost knifelike edge at an end to nearly an eighth of an inch at the opposite end.

Slowly, as if to exaggerate his motions, the guard took one bamboo sliver and inserted it between nail and flesh of Lord's middle finger. He raised a wooden mallet, then with a nod to major Dung, he carefully aimed a short, quick blow to the end of the bamboo splinter. The bamboo sliced all the way to the cuticle of Lord's finger and a small jet of blood spurted from the tip.

The shock of the penetration exploded up Lord's arm, spinal cord and into his brain. Lord had never experienced pain like that radiating up from his hand; not even the painful burns and broken arm he had suffered when his plane was hit had prepared him for the exquisite stab of the bamboo. Lord's wrenching scream was an uncontrollable reflex emanating from the core of his body. Waves of pain rolled in quick succession from his hand so severe that Lord could scarcely breathe.

"You have powerful lungs, Commander. But we do not wish to disturb the other American Air Pirates who may be resting quietly now," Dung sneered as he motioned another guard to insert a wadded piece of cloth into Lord's gasping mouth. "And we certainly wouldn't want you to choke on your own tongue while screaming. Perhaps, you would like to avoid the rest of Corporal Minh's manicure, however. Would you care to sign the confession, Commander, or shall we proceed? What do you say, Commander? Would you like to sign?"

Lord didn't know whether the shaking of his head was an involuntary reaction from the searing pain or his act of defiance to his tormentor but he had resolved not to sign.

The black-mouthed Corporal wasted no time in inserting another bamboo, this time in the nail of Lord's index finger. The Corporal's mallet blow became more vicious and sent the silver beyond the cuticle and into the flesh behind the fingernail. Blood spurted with such force that some spattered on the Corporal's uniform causing him to jump backward nearly falling from his stool.

The searing pain boiled up and down Lord's arm in waves of increasing intensity. His arm and the right side of his body quivered violently almost as though his body was convulsing. He could not scream but deep moaning and grunting sounds escaped from the cloth stuffing in his mouth. His head shook violently and he was not certain whether by design or accident he was able to snap his head backward against the masonry wall of the cell against which his chair was positioned. But the blow to the back of Lord's skull was sufficient to render him unconscious and call a halt to Major Dung's vicious work.

28.

NEW YEARS IN
OLD HONG KONG

The door to Margo's flat had barely closed when Marchand scooped her into his arms, embraced her tightly, and began to kiss her hungrily. In moments they had stripped and Marchand entered her slowly. He satisfied her like a soft summer breeze cooling a torrid night. They were worlds away from everything.

After a languid and lusty afternoon in Margo's flat on Victoria Peak, Marchand and Margo rode a small junk from the Hong Kong Ferry Landing toward the largest floating restaurant in Aberdeen. They motored slowly past the thousands of boats of all shapes and sizes on which tens of thousands of Chinese were born, lived and died while Margo described the history and culture of the spectacle to a fascinated Marchand.

Once aboard the *Wah Kong* floating restaurant, Margo and Marchand feasted on an exquisitely prepared eleven-course parade of Mandarin Chinese cuisine at its finest. Dishes of pork, beef, chicken, prawns, bok choi, and several other local vegetables were delivered to their table, all preceding the main course which was a crisp Peking duck. Copious amounts of piping hot tea called *Bo lay tsa* aided digestion.

She leaned slightly forward and asked, "So, tell me how you came to join the Navy anyway? Why didn't you just go to med school or law school or whatever after Harvard? You surely had many options."

Marchand put down his ivory chopsticks and responded, "It's in my blood. My father was a Navy fighter pilot in the Pacific during World War Two. My grandfather was an officer in the French Navy during World War One. And my great grandfather commanded a French frigate at the turn of the century. Believe it or not, my great grandfather six generations ago, Lieutenant Louis Marchand, was the aide de camp to Napoleon who wrote Napoleon's first biography. But that's only part of it. I grew up in La Jolla where it's always been an honor to serve the country as a commissioned officer, particularly a Naval Officer. So, you see, naval service has been a family tradition for generations."

Margo placed a delicate morsel of Peking duck dipped in a sweet red sauce onto Marchand's tongue. "You must be very proud of your family tradition."

"I am indeed and proud to serve in the Navy. Proud to serve my country. It's the pride of belonging to a great military organization with hundreds of years of tradition. And it's pride in being a part of an elite group that fights in the air, almost hand to hand, with the best aircraft ever designed. It's up front and personal combat fought almost as it was nearly a thousand years ago."

Marchand watched Margo lick the sauce from a pot sticker. He was terribly distracted by her mouth. There was something so magnetic about her, he opened up, "But, to tell you the truth, I had no idea when I entered Officers Candidate School that I would receive orders to Vietnam. No idea at all. Still, here I am, ready and willing to serve." Marchand stopped and shook his head. There was more to admit to her. "Truth is, I just don't know what for. But that's a secret I'll tell only

232

you."

Trying to keep it light, but wanting to know more, Margo dipped a prawn in hot sauce. "Try it this way," she said as she placed this new morsel into Marchand's mouth.

He looked at her as he chewed, surprised at how lightly she had responded to his deeply secret admission. Had he said too much or not enough, he wondered. Would she keep it to herself? Could he trust her? Oh, yes, yes, just look at this woman. Of course, you can trust her.

Alert to such details, Margo saw the surprise and confusion flicker across Marchand's face. "Would it have made any difference to you, had you known just how divisive and controversial this War would become?"

He savored the prawn and said, "Hmmm...perhaps not. I've always wanted to serve; old-fashioned patriotism, I suppose. Unfortunately, all that's rather out of fashion right now. As I reflect on it now, Vietnam wasn't a serious concern to me three years ago but I probably would have volunteered anyway.

"But to be quite candid, I'm feeling somewhat betrayed by what I've seen and experienced. There doesn't seem to be any coherent strategy for this War. We have nothing to show for our sacrifices; no cogent plans to conclude the War." Marchand shrugged. "Sometimes, I really don't know who or what we're fighting for. I don't mind telling you that it's damned hard to keep your spirits high under these circumstances."

He pushed his plate away. "Most of my squadron mates just don't seem to notice or care, or perhaps they just keep their thoughts to themselves. But I wonder just how long I can continue to follow orders blindly while everything becomes increasingly incoherent." He took a deep breath, hunched his shoulders and rubbed his forehead. "And, it doesn't help that we deal in death in such huge doses. I can't imagine how many Vietnamese I've killed or helped to kill." Marchand felt the suppressed anxiety he'd hidden away so well surfacing now.

Margo shuddered visibly, wondering just what roiling emotional cauldron she had pried open. "Keith, I think I understand. There's certainly nothing very logical about this War." She pushed his plate back in front of him. "But you should eat. It will help to calm your nerves."

Marchand shook his head at the food. Now that he was revealing himself, he found it difficult to stop. "Margo, none of this makes any damn sense to me these days." He pushed his plate away again and looked around. He lowered his voice to a whisper, "Take a look at that Chinese fellow seated two tables in front of us, the one in the tan suit and blue shirt. I think he's watching us. Haven't we seen him before?"

Margo turned around to look but answered somewhat uncomfortably. "Yeah, I think so. I've been trying to think where I've met him before. I think he's attached to the Beijing embassy staff here in Hong Kong. I've seen him several times in Hong Kong book stores and several seminars sponsored by the British Embassy."

"So, why is he watching us? Do these guys follow you around or something?" Marchand said with a note of concern in his voice. Now he sat a bit taller and wondered whether the nosey onlooker had heard and understood his inappropriate, almost treasonous revelations.

"I don't know, but he may be trying to communicate with me for some reason. I don't think it's anything dangerous though."

At that moment, the well-groomed gentleman stood and left the dining room.

"Well, he's gone, whoever he is," Margo said. "Anyway, you wonder why you're flying missions over Vietnam of all places. Sometimes, it's good to start with a recent history. Secretary of State

John Foster Dulles is as good a starting point as any. Dulles didn't know much about Southeast Asia but he was quite concerned about Communism, particularly, a united Communist Chinese and Soviet threat to the West. When Ho Chi Minh's Communist Viet Minh routed the French Army at Dien Bien Phu in 1954, Dulles became quite alarmed that a monolithic Communist state would extend throughout Asia. At that point, he was only too willing for America to replace the French in Vietnam in order to prevent further Communist advances. It was easy for Dulles to persuade Eisenhower and Congress to adopt his world view and the rest of the story you probably know quite well."

Marchand listened and watched attentively but more from fascination with Margo's soothing voice and stunning blue eyes than her history lesson. "You sure sound like you have it all figured out, Margo," Marchand said a bit too condescendingly.

Neither Margo nor Marchand noticed the Chinese gentleman who had been watching them earlier walk past their window on the narrow deck outside. He stopped for a moment, looked in, then walked away innocuously. Margo decided to press on, notwithstanding Marchand's sardonic comment. "From Ho Chi Minh's perspective, the United States represents the most recent in a long line of colonial powers including China, France and Japan that have invaded his country during the past two thousand years. Ho is a classic nationalist who will stop at nothing to reunite his country and expel all vestiges of its colonial past."

Margo paused and looked around for any signs that anyone else was observing them before continuing, "Tragically, the State Department's real China scholars who truly understood contemporary Chinese history and Mao's 1949 Revolution, who would have warned Dulles and Eisenhower against direct involvement in Vietnam, had largely been purged by Senator Joe McCarthy as 'Communist sympathizers'. As a result, the United States has paid more and more each year to prop up American puppet regimes in Saigon ever since the C.I.A. helped assassinate Diem in 1962. Predictably, the more money and power the U.S. has given those puppet governments, the more corrupt they've become."

Marchand responded, "Yeah, I've heard all that before but I must admit that your delivery is better than anything I've heard since Professor Steinberg at The College. But tell me, whose eyes did you inherit?"

"Have you paid any attention to what I've said, Keith? I'm trying to answer some of your serious questions, not questions about my eyes. And, I got my eyes from my mother, if you must know."

On the dockside, nearly a hundred yards away, small fireworks explosions began to detonate and long strings of firecrackers rippled away at the peaceful night. Marchand glanced in the direction of the noise then looked back at Margo. He could love this woman, but what was this graduate school stuff she was feeding him, he wondered. Yet, Margo's comments did not grate on Marchand's nerves like the simple-minded antiwar rhetoric he often heard or read. He wondered if it was her logic or her beauty that was so compelling. He gazed out the window for a moment before responding.

"Still, Margo, there are millions of Vietnamese south of the demilitarized zone who don't want to become Communists, who want to remain free. If we pull out, they're doomed."

"Doomed to what? South Vietnamese are mostly peasants who simply want to be left alone to tend their rice paddies and raise their families in peace. They could care less whether they're governed by Communists or anyone else as long as their government is ethnically Vietnamese and it protects them from violent invaders."

At that moment, several long strings of powerful Chinese firecrackers exploded noisily in celebration of the Chinese Lunar New Year. Marchand was startled, on edge, maybe a little shell shocked for a moment, but he quickly regained composure. He shook his head and laughed, somewhat embarrassed. He peered out at the dockside at what definitely appeared to be some type of Chinese New Year's parade with thousands of people marching, celebrating, blowing horns, and millions of exploding fireworks. But the commotion did not end his unusual conversation with this fascinating and stunning woman with potentially dangerous opinions, a woman with whom he feared he was falling in love.

They were silent for a while, looking at each other, marveling at the fact that they had somehow met. And then the onlooker returned. Marchand saw him first. "Margo, don't look now but our friend has just returned, this time with a newspaper. He's sitting to our right, just a bit behind you. Am I getting paranoid or is he really watching us?"

Margo was purposefully nonchalant. "I really don't think it's anything to be concerned about. You know, I get around Hong Kong and the New Territories quite a bit. As you might imagine, I tend to stand out somewhat. I think he recognizes me and is just too shy to come over and introduce himself."

"Well, if you're not worried about it, I suppose I shouldn't be. So, look, maybe your explanation for this unholy mess is the only rational explanation, but how should I know?"

"Well, that's encouraging, Keith, at least you're listening to me. You know, everyone seems concerned about possible Chinese intervention in Vietnam," Margo said while turning and giving a nod of recognition to the gentleman who still watched her from behind his newspaper. "But, unlike North Korea, where Chinese armaments are

237

flowing in, there are no Chinese troops in Vietnam, North or South. In fact, the Chinese are much more concerned about Russian rather than American presence in Vietnam.

"The Chinese will allow the United States to waste blood and treasure in Vietnam as long as it wishes to, without too much interference. The Russians, however, trouble them greatly."

Marchand listened pensively. "I suppose you also have a convenient explanation for Russia's interference in Vietnam's affairs."

Before Margo could reply, the well-dressed Chinese gentleman surprised them when he rose from his table and walked over to them. He bowed slightly and introduced himself. "Kindly pardon my interruption," he said in perfect Oxfordian English while looking directly at Margo. "But I believe I have made your acquaintance at a British Embassy reception several weeks ago. My name is Dr. Tsing, Mow-sung Tsing, professor of political science and history at the University of Shanghai.

"You and I had a delightful conversation about the Cultural Revolution and I was most impressed with your Mandarin as well as your knowledge of current affairs in the Peoples Republic. I couldn't allow the evening to end without greeting you and inviting you to visit the University as soon as diplomatic conditions permit."

Dr. Tsing turned towards Marchand and bowed slightly again. "And, Lieutenant, please accept my apologies for intruding in your New Year's celebration. You are a most fortunate young man to enjoy the company of one your country's finest scholars."

Margo was gracious but cool now. "I knew that we met somewhere in Hong Kong. And I certainly accept your invitation to visit your University. Now, I simply have to wait for the United States and China to normalize relations. And that should happen in the near future I hope."

"Perhaps we shall have the opportunity to discuss the issue in greater depth before you leave Hong Kong," Tsing said enthusiastically. Perhaps even in the Peoples Republic of China, he commented to himself.

"I would like that very much," Margo replied without revealing that she understood what Dr. Tsing meant.

"I will be in touch. Well, I should leave now. I certainly don't want to interrupt your evening any longer." Tsing bowed again toward Marchand, "Good evening, Lieutenant."

As Dr. Tsing left the restaurant, Marchand turned toward Margo, a look of utter amazement on his face, and said, "How in the world does he know I'm a lieutenant? And how does he know you're leaving Hong Kong soon? I'll be damned if you haven't made quite an impression here in Hong Kong, even the Communists have taken note. But I have an uncomfortable feeling that we're being watched continuously. And by the way, how does he know how to get in touch with you?"

Margo shrugged. "Oh, I don't know." She chose not to tell him she had indeed already been inside The Peoples' Republic of China. This was a well-kept secret, even from loved ones, especially from loved ones, and this man was becoming a loved one rather quickly. But since there was no official admission of Americans into China, it was not a difficult secret to keep. However, Dr. Tsing or whatever the Chinese gentleman's name was, should contact her some other time, she thought, whatever he really wants.

Marchand, still trying to keep the tension between them at a low level, changed his approach. "Dr. Tsing is certainly right about one thing. I am a very fortunate man indeed. But inviting you to visit Shanghai, given the chaos in China with the Red Guards rampaging all over the place and the United States and China verbally assaulting each other whenever possible - - that's a joke if I ever heard one."

"It's not as humorous as you think, Keith. And I'll wager you that I'll visit Shanghai and Beijing within the next two years. I'll even write you a post card from the Great Wall," Margo replied with a mysterious smile.

Marchand thought for a moment. "But really, tell me, how in the world will Dr. Tsing find you among all the millions in Hong Kong?"

"I suspect that there's not much that goes on in Hong Kong that Tsing does not know, Keith. Finding me will be quite simple for him."

"Well, my father said that I should never tell a woman what she cannot do. And, if there was ever a woman to whom that advice applied, it's you. So, I'm certain that one day you'll indeed visit Shanghai. But, I'll bet my next paycheck it won't be in the next two years."

Margo laughed a little. "Your father sounds like a wise man. But don't risk your paycheck so easily."

"For you, I don't mind."

"And I am sorry if my political banter sounds like a reprogramming campaign."

"No need to apologize for trying to reprogram me. I know it's tempting and I appear to be a ready candidate. Just remember that I am a man of honor and I do love my country. And, just tell me that you'll miss me after the *Constellation* departs Hong Kong."

"I'll miss you more than you know and more than I want. I wish it weren't so but it is. What are you doing to me, Lieutenant Marchand?"

"I'm willing you to fall in love with me, that's all," he replied honestly.

"Oh you are, are you?" To Marchand's surprise she added, "And I think it's working…"

Slightly flustered, she dropped her napkin but as she reached to retrieve it, she deftly picked up a handwritten note on a small scrap of paper dropped by Professor Tsing which she quickly tucked into her shoe.

Marchand, still glowing from Margo's last comment, noticed nothing at all.

VOLUME ONE: PHANTOM WAR TRILOGY

29.

GOTCHA

When Lord regained consciousness, he found that he had been returned to his cell. Not only his fingers but also his hand and arm up to the elbow throbbed with pain only slightly diminished from the time of its infliction. He surmised that he had been unconscious for many hours or would still be facing the Major in the interrogation room. The intensity of the pain made it clear to him, however, that he could not continue to resist the Major's demands for long. Dung would see to it that Lord's head would be restrained so that he could not render himself unconscious during the next session.

Lord looked at his throbbing fingers. The index and middle digits of his right hand were swollen nearly twice their original size; the nail beds were so purple as to seem almost black; in certain places the bamboo had cut completely through the nail and through the slits dark blood still oozed. Flesh behind the cuticle or what remained of the cuticle was inflamed, an angry reddish color resembling the color of a roadside flare. He realized that infection was a likely if not a probable outcome of the Vietnamese barbarity, the consequence of which might be the loss of fingers and possibly his hand. If that happened, he would never fly again.

Should his flying be terminated at this critical juncture in his naval career, he would undoubtedly be promoted to the rank of captain out of sheer recognition of the suffering he had endured. But in all probability, he would not be awarded the broad gold stripes of flag rank that he had sought since his midshipman days eighteen years ago. So the vicious Major Dung threatened not only physical torture and humiliation but also Lord's career and lifelong objectives that were paramount to him. Pain and this bitter recognition caused salt water to fill his eyes and spill down his face.

But Lord did not cry out. The thought of signing Dung's stilted and jargon-filled confession was repugnant in the most profound sense. He knew that the North Vietnamese had become increasingly skillful in using the communications media and that a senior American officer's signed confession, no matter how stilted and unrealistic the wording, would have significant value in what was rapidly becoming a propaganda war as much as a shooting war. There would be some news coverage which would lend credence to the confession that American pilots methodically bombed Vietnamese hospitals, and by logical extension, churches, pagodas, temples and villages.

To many observers, one of two perceptions would be inevitable; either the confession was signed more or less freely by a repentant senior American officer or, alternatively, American officers and pilots must be considered weak and incapable of remaining firm in the face of adversity. Of course, persons reaching such conclusions would have no concept of the physical suffering or the inescapable fact that under such duress any human being would eventually sign anything put before him.

Lord also thought of the mockery that Dung's artlessly written confession would make of the constant briefings, admonitions and often heroic efforts that American pilots routinely made in order to avoid bombing civilians, churches and hospitals. He recalled the times that he had pulled out of dive runs with bombs still attached to his plane because a hamlet or pagoda had appeared in his bombsight instead of the intended truck park, oil storage depot, or gun emplacement. He also remembered how his aircraft and doubtless many others had shuddered and buffeted under the stress of the extra weight of unreleased bombs as the aircraft struggled out of its dive and laboriously gained altitude. Bitterly he remembered the intense antiaircraft fire directed at him during those agonizingly slow pull outs while carrying unexpended ordinance so as not to cause unintended collateral damage. Now Dung wanted to force him to sign the damned confession.

At that moment, Lord accepted the fact that he would indeed sign the confession. Additional resistance would only produce greater agony, greater probability of losing one or both hands and possibly his life. The outcome of the matter was already determined. Major Dung knew this to be so; Lord now accepted it. So Lord began to focus his pain-wracked attention on some method of discrediting the confession, a sign to military intelligence that the confession had been coerced, that it was a terrible sham.

The next day Lord was again tied securely in the heavy wooden chair, which, as he had correctly anticipated, had been placed nearly in the center of the interrogation room. These bastards really mean business this time, he thought. Just as the evil-looking sergeant began to tape Lord's left hand to the wooden chair frame, the door to the interrogation room swung open and Major Dung entered the room.

"I have come to see whether you wish to continue your manicure, Commander, or whether, perhaps, you have reconsidered your decision so rashly made yesterday."

The sergeant stopped his fiendish work while the Major spoke.

"Yes, Major, I have reconsidered. I will sign your damned confession," Lord replied bitterly.

"It's not *my* damned confession, Commander; it's *your* damned confession."

"Yes, of course, Major, my confession; please excuse my lapse of memory."

"You are finally coming to your senses, Commander Lord. You appear to be an intelligent man, Commander. I thought that you would see the wisdom in cooperation. I'm pleased that you are not as obstinate as the stupid Air Force Captain who preceded your arrival here several weeks ago. After just five bamboo treatments he became quite mad. I think we eventually had to shoot him. He actually became a raving madman, can you imagine that, Commander? Yes, you probably can, can't you, Commander?"

"Certainly, Major;" Lord gritted his reply as he stared at his swollen and inflamed right hand.

Seconds after Major Dung barked several orders to one of his attendants, the typewritten confession and a pen were produced for the Major. Dung ordered Lord to be unbound then placed the paper and pen on the small table in front of Lord. "Well, Commander, what are you waiting for?"

"Major Dung, despite your skill at your profession, you must be rather new at it. How do you expect me to sign the confession when I can barely move my hand? Or have you overlooked the results of your handiwork? Perhaps, you could allow me several days to recuperate so that I can properly sign the confession. After all, what good would the confession be to you, if the press were to discover that the signature did not appear voluntary and authentic?"

Dung thought for a moment before responding. "You have a point, Commander. But please do not think yourself too clever. If you intend this maneuver as a delaying tactic, I promise you that the next session you have with my apprentices will not be as pleasant as your previous experience and I shall insure that we will not limit our efforts to your left hand or to the special manicures only. Do you understand me, Commander?"

"Absolutely, Major."

As Lord had anticipated, he was given rudimentary medical treatment to hasten the healing of his right hand. Within four days, the swelling subsided and the inflamed fingers began to grow dark with hemorrhaged tissue. Although the pain was still intense, Lord knew that he would not lose his hand, at least not yet.

Several days later, Dung himself came to Lord's cell to inspect his hand. "I see that the excellent medical treatment which you are receiving from our fine doctors is beginning to heal the injuries to your right hand sustained when you were shot down by the Peoples' Army.

"Well, Commander, just to insure that your injuries are completely healed before you sign your confession, I shall give you another week. But during this week I want you to take very good care of your hand. I don't want anything to spoil the pictures of the document signing ceremony."

"What pictures?" Lord inquired.

"Oh, we shall have lots of pictures, Commander, lots of pictures, still and moving pictures, television too. Don't you want to be a television star, Commander? This is your grand opportunity," Dung fairly giggled.

"Whatever you say, Dung."

"Major Dung, to you Commander Lord, Major Dung. And let

me encourage you to give a good performance or I promise you, it will be your last."

"You've made yourself very clear, Major."

During the following week, Lord strained his imagination to its limits trying to conjure up some method of conveying the coerced nature of the so-called confession, some method that would not result in his immediate torture and death. Whatever signal was used, Lord knew that it must be subtle enough to escape Dung's attention. But Dung's command of English seemed too complete to allow the sign to be passed by slight nuance or innuendo. Moreover, Lord had no way of knowing whether he would be allowed to speak or write anything other than his signature on the confession. The task of communicating the reality of his plight began to appear impossible. Exactly one week from the day of his last session with Major Dung, Lord was blindfolded and led from his cell to the small prison infirmary where his hand had been treated each day. Antibiotics and antiseptic lotions had taken away the gross infection and inflammation of his hand and fingers. The torn and mangled fingernails had been removed and new tissue had formed over the raw, open flesh. Though tender and throbbing, the fingers regained usefulness.

The prison doctor conducted one final inspection of Lord's hand, lightly bandaged the damaged fingers, then sent Lord to his meeting with Major Dung. Lord couldn't tell how many guards accompanied him as he was blindfolded. While being led by the guards, Lord cursed the Vietnamese medical personnel who had carefully tended to the mangled hand but had given no care whatsoever to the burns on his legs or his badly mended broken arm. "It's all for the performance. You bastards," he mumbled under his breath.

When Lord's blindfold was removed, he found himself in a large room seated behind a moderately sized wooden table looking out toward several rows of chairs. Several feet from both sides of the table numerous high-intensity lamps were arranged at varying heights. Lord recognized them as studio Klieg lights. Minutes later, Major Dung entered the room.

Dung strutted to the table where Lord sat flanked by four obnoxious guards. "Commander Lord, we have invited members of the capitalist press to witness your signing of the confession. We want them to see that you have not been coerced and we shall give them an opportunity to ask you about your treatment since your capture. Commander, do not say anything to these news correspondents that you will regret later. Your treatment thus far has been most lenient. Do not force me to demonstrate the fruits of thousands of years of Oriental techniques in the art of inducing exquisite pain; do you understand me, Commander?"

"You have shown me all I care to see, Dung," Lord replied holding up his right hand.

Lord was led out of the room into a small antechamber. Within minutes the room was crammed with news correspondents jockeying for the best vantage for photography and sound recording. When the room was filled with Western newsmen, Lord was ushered into the makeshift pressroom. The glare from the Klieg lights nearly blinded him so that he could not focus on the peering faces behind the lights. Lord was led to the heavy wooden table where Major Dung waited. He was seated behind the table upon which the printed confession and a fountain pen had been placed. The room was hot, humid and thick with anticipation.

When all motion picture and television cameras were whirring, Dung looked at Lord and exclaimed loudly, "The American military prisoner will now identify himself."

"I am Errol Francis Lord, Commander, United States Navy,

Serial Number 219794."

"Commander Lord was shot down and captured by the heroic gunners of the Peoples Army during a shameful air raid on the hospital in Haiphong on January 1, 1968. Commander Lord has been shown the terrible destruction which he and his fellow war criminals have perpetrated upon the helpless sick and wounded civilians of Haiphong. He has been shown the effects of his crimes against the Vietnamese people and all of humanity.

"Commander Lord regrets his cowardly actions and has agreed of his own free will to sign the confession before him as repentance for his crimes. Isn't that correct Commander?"

Lord nodded his head weakly.

"Speak up, Commander. The reporters cannot hear you."

"Yes, that is correct, Major Dung," Lord replied. At that moment, Lord balled his left fist in front of him on the table and extended his middle finger toward Dung. Lord knew that Dung's vision was as obscured as his own by the Klieg lights.

"Kindly sign the confession, Commander."

Lord obediently took pen in his injured right hand and painfully scrawled his signature on the page. When he had signed the document he placed the pen carefully on the table then doubled his right fist, extended his middle finger in the most obscene manner he could manage and placed his hand just beneath his signature on the coerced confession.

"Commander Lord, has your treatment been humane and compassionate?"

"Yes, Major," Lord replied while giving Dung the bird.

"Have you received proper treatment from the heroic doctors of the Peoples Army?"

"I most certainly have, Major," Lord answered giving the "fuck

250

you" sign with a flourish.

"Has this medical treatment resulted in the healing of the injuries to your hand?"

"Yes." Lord's bird nearly squawked.

"And the burns on your legs?"

"Splendid treatment, indeed." Lord said as he waggled the third finger salute at Dung.

"Are you grateful for all that we have done for you?" Major Dung inquired.

"Without question, Major, the doctors of the Peoples' Army have given me the most unforgettable treatment for which I am truly grateful." Lord answered as his vision focused sufficiently to see the barely suppressed snickers of several newsmen.

Major Dung also noticed the pressmen's smiles and immediately knew that something was going awry while reporters from every major network in the world looked on. Dung didn't know what it was but clearly there was something seriously wrong. Nervously, he terminated the conference before events could spiral further out of control.

Commander Lord smiled as the cameras were shut down. He knew that he had won his battle with Major Dung, even if he had to die for it. And, this time Lord was ready to accept all consequences of his actions, including death.

30.

FAREWELL

Marchand knocked on the door to Margo's flat for their now daily date, consisting of splendid sex, fabulous dining and intense conversation. But this time, instead of overwhelming excitation, he felt quite distressed.

Margo opened the door ready for romance and immediately realized something was wrong. "God, Keith, what's happening? World War III?"

Marchand wanted to get it all out quickly, because it hurt so much to say. "Not quite, but it's bad, Margo. I have to leave. North Vietnam has launched what they call the 'Tet Offensive' celebrating the Lunar New Year. They're kicking our butts from Saigon to Hue. The *Constellation* is being recalled as soon as we have most of Ship's Company and the Air Wing back on board. I actually must leave immediately. I'm so sorry, so very sorry, Margo."

Knowing she was powerless to prevent Marchand from leaving, yet feeling very much attached to him, Margo was in instant turmoil. Desperate, she pulled him inside and shut the door. She buried her face against his chest to hide the tears she couldn't hide. She had always been fiercely independent, always in complete control of her emotions, but now it was changing. That she had known Marchand only a week made it all the more frustrating. And the fact that he was an American military officer fighting in Vietnam made a mockery of her own convictions.

Margo's tears soaked through Marchand's white shirt, warming his chest, then burning through his skin to places deep within. All that he could think to say was, "Dearest Margo, I'll be back soon."

She raised her head, blue fire in her eyes, and said, "Will you, will you, Keith? Or will you become another worthy sacrifice to a worthless government? I'm terribly afraid for you, Keith. And I'm angry with myself for allowing this silly, foolish affair to have happened. I simply wanted to become acquainted with you, to understand you. I didn't want to love you or even care about you. I'm really frightened by everything that's happened."

"Do you love me?" he asked.

"Oh my God, I think I do, and I just can't believe it."

"Tell me that you love me, Margo. I swear by all that's holy I'll come back to you. I've fallen completely in love with you. I can't help it. And, I don't want to love you."

"My beautiful Lieutenant," Margo said sobbing, "you're a fool to return to that Ship but I love you dearly. Will you make love to me, before you leave?"

"God, I wish I could. But if I did, I'd never leave. You've touched my heart and my soul and I leave them with you. Kiss me and then I've got to go. If I miss Ship's movement, I'll be court martialed for sure and spend the next five years locked away in Leavenworth."

31.

LAST LAUGH

On the morning of February 5, 1968, as President Johnson sat staring at the yellow pad before him, Lady Bird Johnson quietly entered the Oval Office. The First Lady winced as she observed the intensity of her husband's pain. She sighed deeply, wanting to help him in any way possible. When Johnson looked up from the desk, she moved slowly to the rear of the President's desk, stood behind him, and began to massage the knotted muscles of his massive neck. Johnson allowed his large head to settle slowly back onto her bosom in almost complete exhaustion. It was the first relief he had felt in days.

"This is the first time in my life that I just don't know what to do," he lamented quietly.

"I know, Lyndon. I know how hard it is for you," she replied gently in her soft West Texas accent. "But can't you take a break from all this for just a few hours?"

"My Darlin', nothin' would please me more than to take a break, but now's the time for action. This great Nation is in real danger of sliding into civil war. This damned Tet Offensive has exposed all of our weaknesses in Vietnam, all of the lies and deceptions; it's all coming out.

The shock is tearing the national fabric apart. For me personally, one of the worst results is that my advisors are just as torn and confused as I am. Some want to escalate. Some want to withdraw. Some want the status quo. Now, if I make the wrong decision here, this Republic could slip into the abyss."

"Is it truly that bad, Lyndon?" the First Lady inquired.

"Unfortunately, it is. The advice depends totally on who is giving it and none of the advice is consistent. Hell, Lady Bird, I don't want to be the first American President to lose a goddamned war, but we're in such a mess."

"But, Lyndon, perhaps this isn't a war we are meant to win." Mrs. Johnson replied as diplomatically as she could.

"And just what does that mean?" Johnson answered while swiveling around in his chair.

"Only that some wars are worth winning at all costs and some are not. Maybe this is one that isn't, dear."

"Oh Gawd, Lady," Johnson moaned, "you know that there is no way I could run for reelection if I were to unilaterally withdraw from Vietnam."

"Well now, suppose you were to decide not to run in November. Just think about it, Lyndon. I don't want to say more. So I'll just leave you to think a moment, my Darling." While slipping out the door of the Oval Office, she smiled at him wisely and said, "I'll be back in a few minutes, Sweetheart."

After Lady Bird left the Oval Office, Johnson thought he would give himself a short break. He turned on power to the multi-screen televisions built into a wall cabinet across from his desk, one screen tuned to each major network, thinking that he might find some momentary distraction. As the hour turned, one of the network morning news programs began a segment featuring prisoners of war, an increasingly tender subject as ever greater numbers of American airmen were shot down over North and South Vietnam, and Laos.

The occasion for this particular show was recent film footage of a Navy pilot signing a confession describing his alleged war crimes against North Vietnamese civilians. Thirty seconds into the report, the video broadcast a picture of a recently captured Navy pilot, Commander Errol Francis Lord, sitting in a straight-backed chair, staring straight ahead and looking as though he was practicing Zen meditation. A moment later, the film began showing the early moments of the Lord interview. As Lord spoke his name, rank and service number, Johnson thought he recalled the day Lord was shot down and captured. It was only six weeks ago, Johnson remembered because it was unusual for such a high ranking pilot, in this case a squadron commanding officer, to have been shot down and captured.

Johnson stared at the spectacle of the senior American pilot clad only in black pajamas being interviewed by a North Vietnamese Army Intelligence Officer. Johnson winced as he saw signs of poorly disguised physical abuse as the pale, gaunt Navy pilot answered a few preliminary questions put to him by the interviewing officer. His heart sunk as he watched the Vietnamese interrogator identify a document that he called Lord's confession of war crimes on the table in front of Lord. The interrogator, Major Dung, then asked Commander Lord several questions intended to expose Lord's participation in atrocities against the North Vietnamese people. The American pilot stoically acknowledged his guilt in committing numerous war crimes from the air.

Johnson was so depressed by the sight that he was just about to turn it off. But the President noticed something peculiar. Suddenly, from deep in his gut, Johnson let fly his deep Texas horselaugh that had become increasingly rare around the White House.

As Johnson watched, Commander Lord presented every variation of the "bird" that he could without being perfectly obvious. "Great job, Commander, great job," Johnson bellowed while enjoying the last heartfelt laugh he would have in quite some time.

PART THREE

February 5, 1968 – March 31, 1968

VOLUME ONE: PHANTOM WAR TRILOGY

32.

OFFICIAL DOCUMENTS

UNITED STATES
DEPARTMENT OF STATE

FOREIGN RELATIONS, VOLUME VI:
VIETNAM
JANUARY – AUGUST 1968
(January 30 – February 8)
DOCUMENT #33

Following attacks that took place in parts of I and II Corps on January 30, 1968, a force numbering initially 58,000 and quickly rising to approximately 84,000 Viet Cong (VC) cadre and North Vietnamese Army (NVA) regulars launched an extensive series of coordinated assaults on most of the urban centers of South Vietnam. The Vietnamese Communist leadership in Hanoi had infiltrated forces into these areas over the preceding weeks. The offensive sought to instigate a mass uprising against the Americans and the government in Saigon, generate instability and a loss of security in the South, draw strength away from Khe Sanh, and position North Vietnam favorably in any future peace talks. The insurgents rose up in the capital, the six largest cities of South Vietnam, 36 of 44 provincial capitals, 64 of 242 district centers, and numerous other smaller villages and hamlets. The tactical surprise the NVA/VC achieved was evidenced in the audacious nature of their attacks, which included penetrations by VC sapper teams of the U.S. Embassy compound, the Presidential Palace, and Ton Son Nhut airport in Saigon; damage to ships in Cam Ranh Bay; the seizure of the U.S. military billet in the center of Dalat; and the fall of the ancient imperial capital of Hue to NVA/VC units after an assault lasting only a few hours. A summary of the situation broken down by corps tactical zones in the immediate aftermath of the Tet Offensive is in Intelligence Note No. 89, February 1.

The impact of the Tet Offensive on the American public was immense. Press reports stressed that the NVA/VC forces had achieved a strategic victory. In retrospect, it became clear that they had suffered a devastating tactical defeat, with the eradication of nearly 70 percent of NVA/VC cadres in the South. In the immediate aftermath, however, public opinion polls reflected that the American public turned sharply against supporting a continuation of President Lyndon Johnson's effort in Vietnam.

AUTHOR'S NOTE:

Notwithstanding the grave situation described in detail by this U.S. State Department Official commentary, the Commander of the Military Assistance Command in Vietnam (MACV), General William Westmoreland, was only vaguely aware of the dire circumstances that he and all American forces faced as the Tet Offensive began. Westmoreland's closing comment to his initial report of the Tet Offensive telegraphed to General Earle Wheeler, Chairman of the Joint Chiefs of Staff, was characteristically euphemistic, if not somewhat cavalier. In a statement that captured the myopic naiveté of many American military, intelligence and political leaders of the day, Westmoreland claimed in the final sentence of DOCUMENT 34 (below) that, "All my subordinate commanders report the situation well in hand."

DOCUMENT #34.
Telegram from the
Commander of the Military Assistance Command, Vietnam
(General William Westmoreland)
to the
Commander in Chief, Pacific Forces
(Admiral U. S. Grant Sharp)
and the
Chairman of the Joint Chiefs of Staff
(General Earl Wheeler)
Saigon, January 30, 1968,
1255 Hours Greenwich Mean Time

MAC 01438. The events of the past 18 hours have been replete with enemy attacks against certain of our key installations in the I and II CTZ (Corps Tactical Zones). The heaviest attacks were launched against DaNang, Kontum, Pleiku, Nha Trang, Ban Me Thuot, and Tan Canh in the Dak To area. Lesser attacks were made on Qui Nhon and Tuy Hoa. Although enemy activity in III and IV CTZs was comparatively light during this period, we are alert to attempts by the enemy to attack significant targets in these areas. Repeated attempts can also be expected in the I and II CTZs. While our operations reports to your headquarters have covered these attacks in some detail, I felt it would be helpful to give you a wrap-up on the situation as it stands now.

It is significant that in I CTZ none of these attacks were directed against our installations north of the Ai Van Pass, perhaps because of the thickening of US forces in that area. Danang was the prime target and was attacked beginning at 20 minutes past midnight. The facilities at Marble Mountain and the Danang air base were mortared and rocketed with a number of aircraft receiving damage, to include five jet aircraft destroyed. The rocket site was immediately located and brought under fire with unknown results at this time. Simultaneously, the ARVN Corps Headquarters came under enemy mortar and ground attack by an estimated reinforced enemy company. An attempt was made against the Danang

Bridge by underwater swimmers. It was thwarted with three enemy KIA and one captured. Timely warning of the attacks plus rapid reaction by US/ARVN/ROK forces has brought the situation in the Danang area under control at this time. Casualties so far list 89 enemy KIA (Killed In Action) and 7 friendly KIA. Noteworthy among the counteractions launched in the early morning hours was that of the ROK (Republic of Korea) Marines, who, in response to an enemy ground attack in the Hoi An area, inserted a force by helicopter, engaged the enemy, killing 21 with no friendly casualties.

The II CTZ received the bulk and intensity of the enemy attacks. In the Kontum area, in excess of 500 enemy attacked from the north in the vicinity of the airfield, and were engaged by elements of the 4th U.S. Division and assorted Vietnamese units. The area is now under control with artillery and air strikes being employed against an estimated two enemy battalions. Seven U.S. were killed in this action, with 165 NVA KIA. Vietnamese casualties are unknown. In Tan Canh of Kontum Province, contact is sporadic with elements of the 3/42 ARVN regiment opposing an unknown size enemy force. Four friendly have been killed and five NVA. In Pleiku, contact continues with an enemy of unknown size in the city, with friendly forces attempting to cut off the enemy forces trying to escape. The 4th Inf Div captured 220 enemy in the vicinity of Pleiku....

In III CTZ in Binh Dinh Duong Province, southwest of Ben Cat, units of the 25th U.S. Division made a significant contact with an enemy force, resulting in 66 enemy killed, with eight friendly killed and 14 wounded. IV CTZ had one significant encounter in the Vinh Long area, where gunships and tactical support aircraft engaged a cleared target of sampans in a canal area, killing 80 enemy, destroying 124 sampans, with three secondary explosions.

During the course of the day we had a maximum air effort, which was reported to be extremely effective.

The current outlook depicts a situation similar to my foregoing account.

In summary, the enemy has displayed what appears to be desperation tactics, using NVA troops to terrorize populated areas. He attempted to achieve surprise by attacking during the truce period. The reaction of Vietnamese, US and free world forces to the situation has been generally good. Since the enemy has exposed himself, he has suffered many casualties. As of now, they add up to almost 700. When the dust settles, there will probably be more. **All my subordinate commanders report the situation well in hand.** *(Emphasis added by author.)*

33.
THE GENIUS OF
GENERAL GIAP

Marchand's desperately needed weeklong respite in Hong Kong, including an amorous and perhaps even life-changing adventure, ended abruptly on February 1, 1968. Within four hours after the emergency call to report aboard ship was promulgated throughout Hong Kong and Kowloon, almost all of the entire five thousand five hundred-man crew of the *Constellation* had reported back aboard. Grumbling, cursing and moaning, sailors and officers were pulled out of hundreds of shops, restaurants, hotels, bars and brothels that made Hong Kong every sailor's favorite liberty port in the Far East. Five hours after the recall went out, the *Constellation* steamed at flank speed away from the magnificent harbor toward the war-ridden Tonkin Gulf where Ho Chi Minh and General Giap's carefully planned Tet Offensive was exploding across the depth and breadth of South Vietnam.

The combined effects of high speed and rough seas tossed destroyer escorts accompanying the *Connie* about like bathtub toys. Thirty-foot waves washed over the smaller destroyers where white water crashed and boiled as high as the upper level bridge decks.

Phil Winslow was cold, wet and tired, and it seemed as though the last ten minutes of his twilight flight deck watch would never end. Although the great mass and length of the *Constellation* allowed her to ride out practically any severe weather in relative comfort, her wet, slippery, wind swept decks were extremely hazardous under these conditions. Oil and grease seemed to ooze out of invisible pores in the steel deck plating, making Winslow's inspection of the squadron's aircraft that were chained to the deck even more dangerous.

Eventually, Winslow's relief duty officer appeared and assumed the tedious responsibility of aircraft security. Winslow hurried below to shower and dress before the wardroom closed for the evening. On the way to his stateroom, as he neared the Intelligence Center, he saw his roommate Marchand leaving the guarded entryway. Surprised, Winslow asked him, "Hey, what's happening in Intelligence that's about to cost you dinner?"

Marchand turned to Winslow and replied with a wry and troubled smile, "Well, what do you usually find in the Intelligence Center? The blind leading the ignorant."

"Cut the bullshit. What's the word?"

Marchand looked around. "Wait, let's wait on this 'till we get back to the stateroom."

Once the door had closed, Marchand slumped on his bunk and spoke solemnly, "Well, the shit has hit the proverbial fan. Saigon is under heavy attack by Viet Cong and North Vietnamese Army regulars; the American Embassy appears to have been overrun; Hue has fallen completely to the NVA; Tan San Hut airport in Saigon has been attacked hard and is closed, and it may be lost; Cam Ron Bay and DaNang are taking massive artillery, mortar and suicide satchel charge attacks, and several isolated Army and Marine units up in I Corps that are being overrun. All that crap about the 'light at the end of the tunnel' has just been snuffed out by Uncle Ho and his boys. The brass is calling it the 'Tet Offensive'."

Winslow continued standing, clearly nervous. "Shit almighty, can we hold out?"

"Who knows; the Intelligence Boys say that only massive air support will prevent a total defeat all over South Vietnam. That's why we were pulled out of Hong Kong early."

"You say North Vietnamese Army regulars are fully engaged?" Winslow asked.

"Whole companies of NVA troops along with battle tanks and SAM batteries are operating south of the demilitarized zone. In fact, they're all over South Vietnam."

"Christ, this sounds bad -- damn near disastrous!"

"Yeah. Maybe we should declare that we won the war and pack up and go home," Marchand said sarcastically but then caught himself. "Just kidding." Marchand told himself that this kind of talk was not appropriate and could get him into trouble. Even though he totally trusted Winslow, he had to watch what he said when it came to matters of surrender. "Anyway, Phil, the Skipper told Frank Warden and Wayne Richards that we'll be flying two or three missions a day when we get back on line."

Winslow groaned. "You know what that means. Eighteen hours a day in a goddamned flight suit."

"Well, we're actually lucky. It's better to spend eighteen hours a day in your zoom bag than twenty-four hours a day in a foxhole under constant mortar attack. I just heard about a company of Marines holed up on some goddamn hilltop called Khe Sanh up in I Corp that's been under siege for four days straight - no let-up. Four damn days! The poor fuckers have suffered heavy casualties already. And the worst part is that they are completely surrounded by the North Vietnamese troops. The one road into the area was closed by the NVA so the Marines have no way out!"

Neither Winslow nor Marchand wanted to think further about the fighting conditions those men faced. But Marchand added, "You know, Phil, for the first time since we've been over here, I feel that we have some purpose."

"What in the hell could that be?"

"To save as many American Marines and Army grunts as we can," Marchand said.

"Amen."

34.

THIS ONE'S FOR ME

On the morning of February 14, 1968, six weeks after the start of the Tet Offensive, Kelly Drummond led a two-plane, close air support mission to an area just south of the DMZ near the Laotian border. The North Vietnamese Army was nearly in total control of the sparsely populated area which included the Marine Base at Khe Sanh. The flight was directed to assist a besieged Marine battalion under heavy attack by thousands of NVA troops. The attack had been underway for more than two hours and Marine casualties were mounting rapidly during the ferocious assault.

Five thousand feet above their assigned rendezvous position, Drummond scanned the jungle below for a tiny propeller-driven aircraft, flown by an Air Force Forward Air Controller. Crossing about a mile ahead of their flight path, Drummond quickly spotted the FAC. Skimming just a hundred feet atop the treetops in an O-2, Cessna Sky Master, the FAC pilot looked for any signs of the enemy hidden beneath the dense jungle growth. The O-2, "Slow FAC," was the military version of a four-passenger civilian aircraft that had two engines, one pulling in front and one pushing from behind. Theoretically, a FAC pilot in the slow, low flying aircraft could easily spot enemy troops moving through the jungle while two engines allowed him to safely egress a hot spot even if he took a hit and lost an engine.

Looking down from the Phantom's cockpit, Drummond keyed his transmitter, "Smokey Four Niner, this is Checkmate One, Tally Ho, at your nine o'clock high," Drummond transmitted to the FAC pilot.

The FAC pilot looked high over his left shoulder and saw two Phantoms quickly closing on his position. "That's me, Checkmate. Be advised the NVA have a lot of 37 millimeter and ZPUs around here and they're pretty good shots. I'm taking quite a bit of fire. You guys will too, so watch your ass. You don't want to punch out around here. The NVA are everywhere! Whole fuckin' battalions of NVA! Shit, this might as well be North Vietnam," he mused over the air.

"So, what do you guys have for me today?"

"Roger, Smokey, we have a total of twenty Mark 82's. How do you want 'em delivered?" Marchand asked as Drummond prepared his weapons panel to release their load of ten five hundred pound bombs as directed by the FAC pilot.

"Just twenty bombs, Checkmate? Well, I can use whatever you have. Set up your runs heading west; give me two Mark 82's on each run. Set up on opposite ends of your racetrack to give me maximum time between your runs. Okay, I'm rolling in with a "Willy Pete" now. It should be right in the middle of a NVA mortar unit."

The tiny, odd-looking aircraft climbed quickly, rolled into a tight diving turn and fired a small rocket armed with a white phosphorous warhead, known as a Willy Pete, into a patch of verdant jungle growth that looked just like any other to the Phantom crews orbiting overhead.

"There you go, Checkmate; now you guys give 'em hell," the FAC transmitted. "And, one more thing, Checkmate, you gotta' put your ordinance right on the money. Our friendlies are less than two hundred meters to the north of my smoke. Those Marines don't need nothin' else fallin' on 'em. No goddamn friendly fire, you copy?"

"We'll put these 82's right down the pickle barrel, Smokey," Drummond replied as the white puff of the marker rocket rose above the jungle canopy. He knew that the slightest error in his dive run could kill and injure scores of Marines rather than provide the emergency relief from the relentless NVA attack. Drummond pulled back sharply on the stick climbing quickly to thirteen thousand feet, rolled the Phantom inverted, pulled its nose down sharply into a steep dive, then rolled upright into a forty-degree dive angle. He squinted through his gun sight to precisely line up on the smoke rocket, using only his fingertips to move the control stick. "Call a good dive, Keith. We can't miss even once today," Drummond said over the intercom. "Let's pop a few of those bastards."

"Bet your sweet ass, Bulldog," Marchand replied totally focused on the dive parameters.

After dropping two five hundred pound bombs, Drummond hauled back on the control stick to bring the Phantom out of its dive. Straining against the pull of five G's, Marchand looked over his shoulder to see their bombs detonate, then transmitted, "How was that, Smokey?"

"Give me a few seconds to check it out, Checkmate."

The radio was silent for a moment, then it crackled. "Goddamn, Checkmate, you put it right down the tube. You killed twenty or thirty NVA and it looks like a bunch of 'em are on the run. There's a very grateful Marine captain down there thanking you Yankee Air Pirates. Wooooo shit! I gotta' get outta' here. Your wingman just rolled into his dive."

On their fourth bombing run over the blazing battle site, Marchand looked around his canopy at the streaming tracer rounds and exploding proximity shells and said to Drummond over the intercom, "Goddamn, we're taking a hell of a lot a fire! I can't see where it's all coming from."

"We just nailed a piece of a fuckin' NVA battalion from the looks of it," Drummond replied. "They've got their own AAA with them."

Before Marchand could reply, the FAC pilot transmitted, "Checkmate, you guys stirred up a hornet's nest. There must be three or four NVA battalions down there. I can see massed troops and trucks everywhere there's an opening in the trees. Jesus Christ, am I taking fire. Ooohh dammit! I just took a ZPU round through the cockpit. Well, I'm air conditioned now, just like you guys."

Drummond looked down at the small FAC aircraft and was amazed to see thirty-seven millimeter shells bursting all around the tiny, helpless looking O-2. "Keith, those FACs must have the biggest balls in 'Nam. He's flying through a solid wall of red hot metal down there."

"Yeah right," Marchand muttered looking at the tracer rounds whizzing past his cockpit, "they're throwing a lot of hot lead up here, too!"

"You got that right," Drummond replied as several tracers streaked past his canopy and he felt the shock waves of exploding 37 mm shells pummeling the Phantom.

As Drummond pulled off the blazing target area from his final dive run, the FAC pilot wheeled his small aircraft in a tight "S" turns to inspect the results of their exploding bombs. He keyed his radio, "Checkmate, you guys have done one hell of a job. I see a number of secondary fires; you must have hit an ammunition dump. Confirm at least fifty NVA troops as KIA and there's probably a hundred more I can't see. You gave those Marines a new lease on life. You got any more

Checkmates in the area who shoot as straight as you guys?"

Drummond transmitted, "Glad we could help a little but you deserve the credit, Smokey. I'm going to recommend you for a Silver Star when we get back. I've never seen a little bird take so much fire. We enjoyed working with you. Have a good day."

"Checkmate, thanks but I hope your recommendation won't be wasted. I've got some trouble here. Just took a hit in my number two engine and she's smoking. Gotta' shut it down. Appreciate it if you could stick around 'till I get my ass outta' here. I think you better get out a Mayday call for me, too."

"Roger Smokey, we'll stay overhead at three thousand and escort you back to DaNang."

Marchand switched the plane's radio channel to the emergency frequency, known as the "Guard Channel" which every American aircraft and all ground controllers monitored at all times, and transmitted, "Mayday, Mayday, Mayday. This is Checkmate Leader escorting Smokey Four Niner, on the One Seven Zero radial at three zero miles from Channel One Zero Niner. Smokey is hit, one engine out, bingo to DaNang, out."

"Checkmate Leader, this is DaNang Approach Control, copy your Mayday. Launching two Jolly Greens and three Cobra gunships now. Should rendezvous with your flight in ten minutes or less."

"DaNang Approach, Checkmate copies. Tell the Jolly Green to pour on the coal. Smokey may have to put it down soon."

"Smokey, did you copy DaNang Approach?" Marchand transmitted.

"Affirmative. But, I've got real problems now. I'm losing oil pressure on my good engine. I don't know how long she's gonna' last."

"Hang in there, Smokey; you've only got forty miles to DaNang.

Say your altitude."

"I'm at two thousand, Checkmate, and I can't climb. I'm losing power on Number One."

"Goddamn, Kelly, he's in big trouble; what the hell can we do to help him?" Marchand asked over the intercom.

"Not much. You might try saying a prayer."

Kelly pushed his nose over, rapidly descending to two thousand feet altitude and transmitted, "Smokey, we're down here with you to see if we can draw off some of the ground fire. Stay with her as long as you can. Jolly Green is on the way from DaNang."

The FAC pilot reported, "Checkmate, I'm losing RPM fast. Engine's starting to freeze up on me. I've got to find a place to put her down. Climb up to five thousand and tell me what you see from up there?"

Drummond shoved his throttles forward and yanked back on the control stick. The Phantom climbed almost instantly to five thousand feet. Both he and Marchand scanned the rainforest below for a clearing. They saw nothing but the bright green canopy of dense treetops. The other Phantom, Checkmate Two, meanwhile, had already climbed several thousand feet higher than their flight leader.

"Smokey, this is Checkmate Two at eight thousand feet. There's a ridgeline, twelve o'clock at approximately two miles; looks like a small clearing on top. Can you make it?"

"Got no choice, Checkmate. Hate to chew this engine down to powder but I'll try."

"Smokey, can you restart Number Two?" Marchand transmitted.

"Might start a fire, Checkmate."

Drummond keyed his mike button, "Smokey, it don't matter; you won't make that ridge line if you're losing power on Number One."

The radio was silent for twenty long seconds before the FAC pilot transmitted, "Checkmate, I've got Number Two back and it's a good thing too. Number One just froze up. I don't know how long I'll have power though. This engine is tearing itself apart."

"You've only got about a mile to go, Smokey, you should see the ridge any second now." Drummond transmitted.

"Roger, I see it. I think I can make it. If I can walk away, I'll talk to you soon on my survival radio."

The Phantoms circled over the ridgeline as the O-2 came in for a power-off dead stick landing. Smokey flew a perfect approach to the clearing and there was a small puff of dust when the plane touched down. It rolled for about a hundred feet then its left wing caught a tree, spinning the plane around and shearing the left wing off near the fuselage. The plane spun again before settling to a stop. Miraculously, it did not catch fire.

Drummond banked the Phantom steeply, trying to remain directly overhead the downed aircraft. He watched as the FAC pilot darted from the wreckage and ran toward the closest cover.

"He made it!" Drummond shouted over the air.

Marchand was ready to cheer when he noticed puffs of smoke and dust erupting near the wreckage. Suddenly, the remaining wing and fuselage of the downed plane exploded in flame as mortar shells pounded the area around the flaming wreckage. At that moment, the FAC pilot transmitted over his survival radio. "Checkmate, I'm out but I think I've got a broken arm. Where's the Jolly Green?"

The FAC's voice sounded weak and scratchy with static from the tiny fist-sized survival radio, but each man in the Phantom flight and aboard the rescue helicopter was ecstatic to hear it. The pilot of the heavily armored "Jolly Green Giant" helicopter quickly answered.

"Smokey, this is Jolly Green, we can see the Phantoms' smoke trails, should be in your area in ninety seconds. Just hang in there."

North Vietnamese Army regulars quickly began to converge on the burning aircraft. A hundred yards away, hidden in the brush, the FAC pilot watched anxiously as North Vietnamese troops surrounded the plane, hoping to catch a glimpse of its pilot being incinerated. The pilot hurriedly checked his 9mm survival pistol, confirmed a full thirteen round clip, and then cocked its action. He keyed the transmit button on his survival radio. "Jolly Green, this is Smokey, the bastards think I'm trapped in the plane. I've got about thirty seconds before they discover I got out, then they'll come looking for me."

"You should see us any second, Smokey," the helicopter pilot responded as he realized that he might be too late.

"Jolly Green, you know I can't be captured this close to the DMZ. They'll skin me alive."

"What the hell is he talking about, Kelly?" Marchand asked over the intercom.

"He means it - literally," Drummond replied.

Marchand was shocked. No way would the NVA skin a downed pilot alive, he thought. No way. But the Smokey pilot was clearly serious. Marchand said a quick but fervent prayer for the FAC, a prayer to change his fate.

On the ground, pain from his fractured arm and the shock of his crash landing was beginning to overwhelm the FAC when he noticed one of the NVA soldiers scouring the ground in the direction of his hiding place. "Goddamn it! The sonofabitch has spotted my boot tracks." He nearly despaired, then felt his heart pound with relief when he heard the chop of rescue helicopters.

NVA troops near the wreckage began to scatter, firing automatic weapons at one of the approaching helicopter gunships as they ran. The gunship responded with fire from its heavy fifty caliber machine guns, cutting down ten of the troops quickly. Still, the lone soldier doggedly followed the pilot's tracks, dodging the gunship's fire and yelling furiously.

Within seconds the pilot of one Jolly Green Search and Rescue helicopter sighted the clearing and prepared to touch down for the rescue despite the heavy enemy fire and mortar shells that exploded all over the clearing. He called to the downed pilot, "Smokey, make a break for it. We can't stay long."

The FAC started running to the clearing toward the Jolly Green but as he left his hiding place, he saw the persistent soldier approaching, no more than twenty-five feet away. The pilot took aim with his survival pistol and fired four rapid shots.

The soldier spun and fell but not before yelling to his fellow troops that he had found the American pilot. The pilot ran toward the center of the clearing where the Jolly Green hovered just thirty feet off the ground with its rescue sling near the ground.

The Jolly Green pilot held his hover even though he was taking withering fire from the gathering NVA troops. Bullets pinged against the helicopter's aluminum skin and occasionally thwacked off the rotor blades. Still the pilot held his position as he waited for the FAC to reach the rescue sling.

The FAC was no more than fifty feet from the sling when mortar shells began exploding all around the hovering helicopter. The Jolly Green pilot had absolutely no choice but to add power and climb away before his aircraft was destroyed.

The FAC grabbed for his radio and with his voice full of despair and anger transmitted, "Jolly Green, where the fuck are you going? I was almost there!"

"Sorry, Smokey, we'll set down again as soon as the gunships clear the mortars. Another two seconds and we'd all be down there with you for good."

The FAC ran back into the bush but not before other Vietnamese had spotted him. A dozen troops started running toward the downed pilot's position. As they neared him, the FAC calmly keyed his transmit button. "Jolly Green, you guys made a great try; you nearly had me. Do me a big favor, fellas. Promise to tell Mrs. Peter Daniels that Captain Daniels loved her very much.

"This one's for me."

Marchand heard a loud pop in his earphones, then only static. Seconds later came Vietnamese voices, then more cruel static. "Goddamn it, Kelly. I don't believe what I just heard or did I just imagine that Smokey shot himself?"

Silence.

"Kelly?"

"He didn't have much choice, Keith. The Jolly Green would never have made it back in time. He did the only thing he could. The NVA would have made it bad for him, a really bad death. They don't take prisoners this far south."

Marchand gritted his teeth and fought off a vicious, gut-wrenching wave of disgust. He said another silent prayer for Smokey 49, this time for the safe passage of his soul.

"Keith, you with me, buddy?"

"Yeah, shit, I hear you." Marchand grumbled. "This goddamn shit has really fucked with my nerves. I need a good straight scotch real bad, Bulldog, real bad."

"You gotta let it go, Keith."

"Roger that, Bulldog," Marchand replied without emotion. "Yeah right, let's go home. But you know what?"

"No, what?"

"When we get home, I'm gonna find Mrs. Peter Daniels and tell her."

"Tell her what?"

"That her husband was the bravest sonofabitch in 'Nam and that he loved her dearly."

"That could be a tough one, Rocketman," Drummond replied.

"He asked us to do it and I'll be damned if I let him down."

35.

CHESS MASTERS

Marchand leaned forward in his gray steel ready room chair. The red leather squeaked as he calmly reached to move his queen's bishop into a position that destroyed Commander Jack McGruder's erstwhile attack. Twenty fighter pilots waited impatiently hoping that the next move would be the last. All of the unspoken tension in the squadron, all of the anxiety about the unmentioned deaths, casualties and captured airmen, collected in the ready room. Squadron pilots and weapons officers hungered for relief, even in the form of bad cinema.

But McGruder would make them wait. "Damn it all, Marchand, you've done it again. If I don't capture that bishop, it's mate in three moves and if I do, I might as well resign," he complained.

"Come on, Marchand, get that damn chessboard out of the ready room so we can start the movie," Don Kramer snarled, clearly peeved at the delay of the evening movie.

"Kramer, I'll tell you when you can start the movie. This is still my ready room, Lieutenant," McGruder growled, emphasizing his absolute authority. He looked back at the chessboard, shrugged and said, "That's it; I resign."

"Skipper, if you'd like to play again, why don't we play in my stateroom?" Marchand volunteered.

"Tactful, Marchand, but I'll pass. I have a sheaf of intelligence reports to read tonight so I'll be tied up. Thanks for the offer, though. We'll do it soon. By the way, since I'm on the subject of intelligence, you might be interested to know that my bitching has resulted in that snot-nosed intelligence officer who was on duty when Rich Miller and Dan Mitchell went down being relieved of duty and sent back to the States. "

"Thanks, Skipper. I wish you could have managed to send him to Keflivik, or better yet to Leavenworth." Marchand wanted to say more about this, to fully express his intense rage at whoever it was that had given Miller and Mitchell that senseless yet deadly order, but he kept it to himself. "Asshole," he muttered under his breath.

"I know, Marchand. I know how you feel. It was the best I could do. I just thought you'd want to know."

"I really appreciate your sharing the news with me, Skipper."

Marchand got up and started to leave the ready room. But he was intercepted by Frank Warden, the Squadron's perennially flush-faced senior maintenance officer. "Marchand, if you're not busy, why don't you stop by my stateroom for a few moments. I know you wouldn't mind missing another Clint Eastwood movie, right?"

"Absolutely not. If another one of those miserable spaghetti westerns shows up in this ready room anytime soon, I'll personally drop the film can over the side."

"Come on by about 2200."

"Sure, what 'cha serving by the way?"

"My cache of Blackjack is still holding out pretty well and

there's some damn fine banjo music on my recorder."

"See you then."

Half an hour later, Marchand entered Warden's stateroom and was greeted by the cheerful sound of Lester Flat and Earl Scruggs playing *Foggy Mountain Breakdown.* "So that's how you stay in such good spirits."

"That and good sippin' whiskey. How do you like yours?"

"Over ice. Is there any other way to drink Jack Daniels?"

"Not unless it's straight up, my boy," Warden said as he poured a healthy shot of whiskey over ice and handed it to Marchand.

"Thanks for inviting me for a drink, Frank, what's the occasion?"

"No occasion, I just thought you needed a little levity. You spend too much time playing chess, talking too damn seriously, thinking much too seriously. You think too damn much. That can be unhealthy out here, you know."

"I know, Frank." Marchand paused to sip the smooth and potent liquor. "That's what they all say. But don't you think about it too?" he asked as he plopped down on Warden's bunk.

"Think about what?" Warden asked as he grabbed a chair and pulled it close to Marchand.

"The War, what else?"

"Not if I can help it."

Marchand put his drink down and said, "Come on, Frank. You get shot at every day just like the rest of us. How can you not think about it?"

Warden leaned forward and exhaled blue cigarette smoke toward the overhead. "Because I won't let myself think about it. If I allowed myself to brood over the colossal stupidity of the politicians in Washington or the brass in the Pentagon, I'd have one hell of a time doing my job which is flying my missions, keeping these airplanes in decent condition, and trying to keep you junior officers properly psyched up."

"That's a hell of a big job I grant you. But still, you gotta think about it sometimes."

"You bet your sweet ass it's a big job. It's nothing short of an impossible job. I'm working to keep us all alive, Keith, in every way I can. I try to be the best flight leader, maintenance officer, and morale booster I can. If I let myself start thinking about war strategy, politics or morality, I'd psyche myself out. Just like you would."

"Yeah, I know, I know." Marchand stood and started to pace, impatient with more analysis of him. Had Warden been talking to Davis or something? Or Winslow maybe?

"I mean it Keith, you won't make it home like that. You've got to keep your head clear if you want to stay alive."

Marchand began to pace the small stateroom like a rat trapped in a cage. "OK, I really do understand. I'm all right. I just vent a bit too much, I guess."

"I like you Marchand, always have, since the day you first reported to the squadron. You've got class and no attitude. You are one of the best back seat drivers in any Phantom squadron and one of the most squared away young officers I've met in years. But, Keith, you worry and fret too damn much about things you can't change. You've got to leave all that shit alone if you want to survive this War. You understand me?"

Marchand stood still and took a long sip of his Jack Daniels. "I understand, Frank," he said. "And I appreciate what you're saying and what you're doing for everyone in the squadron. You, Kelly, Wayne, the Skipper, the X.O., and the rest of the senior officers in the squadron, I know you're doing your damnedest to help us all make it through this cruise."

"Thanks, you're damn right about that."

Marchand stopped and looked Warden in the eye. "We both know that but in spite of that, in spite of the great job you're doing, some of us won't make it. A lot of Army and Marine soldiers sitting in those fuckin' awful foxhole and bunkers -- guys who don't have the luxury of a cozy stateroom, a glass of well-aged Tennessee whiskey, or the time to discuss it like we do - won't make it either. So, I can't stop thinking about the goddamn War."

Marchand resumed his pacing. "I can't stop thinking about it while those poor fuckers are crawling around in the jungle knee-deep in mud, dodging bullets and mortar shells and stepping on punji sticks. I can't stop thinking about Rich Miller and Dan Mitchell flying into the water on a black-as-hell night trying to get identification on a fishing junk. I can't forget Ken Price and Roger Davis flying into a mountainside trying to drop bombs through a sucker hole in an overcast sky or that poor FAC pilot shooting himself to avoid being skinned alive."

Warden just listened and watched. Lieutenant Marchand was one of their best, and Warden hoped he could hang in there and handle the stress.

Marchand paused, noticed Warden listening attentively, then continued in a more controlled voice. "And you know what? I can't stop thinking about this goddamn War the way you do. I keep tripping over its problems. Like, the very guys we are fighting with and for, the damn South Vietnamese, the ARVN troops, hauling ass and running off whenever a firefight starts. Like, the ARVN officers selling their guns and rations on the black market, probably to the NVA or the Viet Cong. Like, all the collateral damage we do to civilians, even though we do our best to avoid it. And some of us don't try to avoid it at all.

"Really, I have to ask, what kind of war is this Frank? Shit, I don't mind getting shot at every day and risking my butt if it means something. But seems to me that this War doesn't mean a fuckin' thing. The people we're supposedly trying to save from the Commies just don't give a shit. They just want to be left alone to grow rice and raise kids. The people back home don't give a fuck either. The only people who really care are the North Vietnamese and us. So what kinda' war is this, Frank? Tell me, Frank. Tell me, please."

"Slow down and sit down, Keith. You're getting all worked up and you're spilling your goddamn whiskey. If you're not going to sip that Blackjack instead of slopping it all over the deck, I'm going to pour some cheap shit for you."

"Sorry, Frank." Marchand sat down and looked at Warden's ruddy, friendly face. "Guess I haven't been a very gracious guest."

"Not to worry, kid. Drink up and listen good now. I want you to put this shit out of your mind 'till we get home. Will you try to do that for me, huh?"

Marchand grunted.

"Look, I've got something to show you." Warden stood up and walked over to his stateroom closet, opened it and retrieved a miniature leather holster from the top shelf. A small pearl handle protruded from the top of the holster which Warden handed to Marchand.

"What the hell is this? A Derringer?" Marchand asked.

"Take a look, it's not loaded."

Marchand pulled the small double barreled pistol from its

holster, inspected it, and returned it to Warden. "Thirty-eight caliber. Looks like it could leave a couple of nasty holes in some unsuspecting Viet Cong. How will you carry it?"

"The parachute riggers are making a special pouch in my survival vest for it. Pretty clever, don't you think?"

Marchand laughed and said, "Yeah, but I can't imagine being able to use the damn thing, Frank. Hell, if you're shot down and captured, you'll be surrounded by gooks. What will two shots do for you except to get yourself killed in a particularly unpleasant way? If you can't get away using your nine millimeter, I don't think the Derringer will help much."

"Never underestimate a feisty Irishman, my boy, particularly one with a trick or two up his sleeve."

"Christ Almighty, Frank." Marchand laughed again, "I really think you got that thing to protect yourself from the whores in Cubi Point in case one of them decides to help herself to a heavy tip."

"Damn, what a wise ass you've become, Marchand," Warden shot back.

"Sorry. Way out of line.... Look, it's time for me to head back to my room; I've got some paperwork to do. Thanks for your concern, though. I really appreciate it." As Marchand stood, the squadron's flight schedule for the next day, February 15, 1968, slid beneath the door.

"Let's take a look at the program for tomorrow before I leave."

The two aviators studied the page together for a moment then Warden said, "Well, looks like you and I get a chance to fly together tomorrow. Terry is squadron duty officer so you get the honor of accompanying me on, let's see, a bombing mission."

"Yeah, and that's not all, I get to fly twice tomorrow. Kelly and I have an escort mission on first launch."

"With two hops tomorrow, you should turn in soon. And, Keith, I do think about the War but whenever I catch myself dwelling on it for more than five seconds, I lie down until the feeling passes. You see, it doesn't accomplish anything. You can't change anything even if you were to think it all through brilliantly and come up with all the right answers. You've got just one job to do besides following orders – and that's stayin' alive. Remember that."

"Roger that, Frank."

36.

LETTERS FROM HOME

When Marchand returned to the double stateroom he shared with Phil Winslow, he found that Winslow had gone to play poker in the junior officer's bunkroom. Taking advantage of the opportunity for peace and quiet, Marchand started a tape recording of Brahms *Fourth Symphony* then sat down at his steel gray desk to read a letter from Margo.

Margo had touched the stationery with a few drops of her favorite cologne to scent the paper for him. Nearly intoxicated, Marchand's fingers trembled slightly as he opened it.

February 3, 1968
Dearest Keith,

It's only been one day since your ship left but the hours have passed ever so slowly. You left me so suddenly; I feel as though a part of me has been torn away. I never could have anticipated the intensity of my loneliness since your departure. I can only conclude that I care for you much too much -- certainly too much for my own good and, perhaps, yours as well.

My research in Hong Kong is nearly complete -- much more rapidly than I had expected. There is no reason for me to remain here for more than a few weeks -- no reason save one, that is. I *must see you again. I can't return to the States without holding you once more. God knows I would do anything to take you back with me. I promise that I'll prolong my work until your Ship returns to port, anywhere. Please write and tell me when and where the **Constellation** is due to return to port so that I may rendezvous with you.*

I'm terribly worried about you. There are all sorts of frightening news reports about the "new phase" of the War that the press is calling the "Tet Offensive." Are things really as bad as the reports say? If so, I'm not certain that I want you to confirm it. It's been so long since I've actually said a prayer, I've nearly forgotten how, but I do pray for your safety. The Almighty must know I'm serious because I haven't done anything like this since my mother died.

I love you deeply, my Dearest Lieutenant. Please be careful and write soon.

Love Always,
Margo

Marchand reread the letter several times, inhaled its fragrance, then placed it tenderly in his desk safe. He had taken out a pen and paper and was about to begin a reply to Margo's letter when Winslow opened the stateroom door.

"Whew, smells like a French whorehouse in here; you must have received a letter from your girlfriend."

"Winslow, you sonofabitch, your humor or sarcasm or whatever it is totally unappreciated. If you weren't a friend, I'd put my flight boot up your butt."

"Christ, don' t get so bent out of shape; I didn't mean to piss you off."

"Well, you did."

"Keith, calm down for Pete's sake. This has been a tough line period and we're all a little on edge. I guess I am too or I wouldn't have been so callous about your lady friend. I suppose I might be just a little jealous as well."

Marchand was mollified and the tension lines on his forehead started to fade. "Phil, you look wiped out. You OK?" he asked.

"Hell, these fourteen and sixteen-hour days are killing me. I'm so tired I don't get excited anymore even when I get shot at." Winslow paused a moment, shook his head and began speaking dejectedly. "I just had a drink with one of the attack pilots who just got back from DaNang. He took several hits and went in for an emergency landing. He told me that there was a lot of talk about the way ARVN troops refuse to fight. When they come under fire, they mostly just turn around and run, especially when the North Vietnamese hit them hard."

"Well, the South Vietnamese have never been known for their valor under fire; so what's so shocking about that?"

"The bastards run and leave our guys completely exposed, vulnerable, or outnumbered. But those North Vietnamese regulars are damned good fighters, you know. They just don't quit. So our guys are taking a real ass-kicking trying to protect those ARVN fuckers who run first chance they get. How the hell are we gonna win a war like that? Tell me, how?"

"I can't tell you. Maybe we won' t win it. Did you ever think about that?"

Winslow thought a moment, then replied, "Yeah, I've thought about it and I don't like it. You know what baffles me, Marchand?"

"What?"

"How can the North Vietnamese and ARVN troops be so damn different? The NVA regulars fight like tigers; the only thing that they and the ARVN pussies have in common is their feline ancestry. They're all Vietnamese, why the hell are they so goddamn different?"

"Phil, the North Vietnamese and the Viet Cong are fighting for something they believe in. They have a cause that justifies their sacrifices but our guys, the Army of the Republic of South Vietnam, don't appear to know what the hell they're doing or why."

"Then why the hell are we here?"

"You tell me, Phil, I don't know."

"Well, fuck it. I can't worry about that shit anymore or I may jump ship," Winslow said with a little more bravado than he truly felt. "I'm outta' here, Buddy. The poker game in the junior officer bunkroom is red hot. I just came down to get some money out of my safe. See ya'."

Alone again, Marchand poured a scotch and water then began a letter to Margo.

February 20, 1968
Dear Margo,

Today is our twentieth day at sea but it seems like twenty years. The days pass with a monotonous progression like a maddening purgatory. Whatever else the Tet Offensive may have accomplished for the North Vietnamese, it has certainly succeeded in exhausting the crew of this Ship. We have launched strikes every day for nearly three weeks straight and everywhere there are signs that the aircraft, Ship and its machinery as well as the crew will soon need a break.

I assume that you have read about the siege at Khe Sanh. It is truly a tragic situation that has become a major set piece in the War to date. The Connie has launched air strikes in support of the firebase continuously during this line period. I have flown more than twenty missions around Khe Sanh personally and I can tell you that it just gets worse each day. The North Vietnamese have definitely targeted the base for destruction. I don't know how those godforsaken, brave Marines can take the punishment the North Vietnamese are handing out day after day.

As difficult as it has been for us engaged in the air war, I feel so badly for those Marines at Khe Sanh. By comparison, our discomfort is trivial. Those guys live in an absolute hell 24 hours a day, every day. I can only hope that the tactical air support we provide has helped them survive.

Fortunately, there are rumors (confirmed by our Intelligence officer, for whatever that's worth) that we may be relieved by the Enterprise by the end of March. If so, the Connie will require at least ten days in port to make repairs and complete maintenance on our aircraft. I plan to take leave for the entire period and want to meet you somewhere that's as faraway as possible from this Ship. Bangkok sounds like an exotic and romantic place. What sayest thou? Can you make it? Please let me know in your next letter.

I miss you terribly, Margo. God only knows how I miss you. You have become my source of strength and sanity in my otherwise insane world. I could even listen to your political lectures for hours and love each minute (smile). How did you do this to me so quickly and completely?

So you are nearly finished with your research in Hong Kong. I hope you can find a way to extend your stay for a bit longer. Write soon, Margo. Your letters are my sustenance. Don't deny a starving man, my love.

Always,
Keith

Margo received Marchand's letter on March 1st, the day her father called from his Wall Street law office. She had reread it three times when the phone rang. Mitchell Whitehead Collins III was nervous and slightly irritated because of the multiple delays involved in his daughter's return to Cambridge. His worry sounded clearly in his otherwise calm voice.

"I don't understand why it has taken you so long to complete your research, Margo. You've already been in Hong Kong too long. You can't like it there that much. Now you tell me you want to stay until May. What is it that's keeping you? Have you met someone?"

Margo handled her father quite diplomatically. In her sweetest most dutiful daughter voice she told him, "Father, I still have work to complete, that's all. You're just upset because I'm spending more money than you hoped I would."

"Don't be so difficult, Margo," Collins replied as he launched into a combination lecture and entreaty. "It's not the money. I'll send all the money you want or need, you know that. And, you know how dearly I miss you. I'm worried about you. I know that you're fiddling about there at the Chinese border and that makes me nervous. I know you want to find a way into China. Margo, just let it go. You can't go there. And you wouldn't like it anyway. Even the bookstores you like to hang around are dangerous. There are agents and spies everywhere and those damned Red Guards have the whole world on edge. You must remember that you are all that I have since your mother died." He sounded sincerely hurt, truly worried, and Margo quickly apologized.

"Oh please don't sound like that. And don't worry so much. I'm an adult and I'm careful, really I am. I'm sorry I've upset you. Look, I promise to be home by the first of May. I truly promise. Don't be angry with me, Father, please." She implored him like an obedient daughter who sounds most compelling while planning a secret rendezvous. And she indeed had a secret or two of her own.

Collins waited a moment before he answered. "Margo, I'm not angry with you. I'm simply a very worried father, and I miss you. Won't you come home soon and tend to your poor old Dad?"

"I miss you, too. And I will be home on May 1st, just as I

promised."

Somewhat mollified, Collins continued tentatively, "By the way, Margo, I may need your help this summer. Some of Nixon's advisors have been sounding me out for a possible cabinet post should he win the nomination and election. I'm not certain I would want it but just in case, I should do a little entertaining before the campaign enters its final phase."

"Oh no, Dad, you know how I feel about Nixon," Margo interrupted, "How could you possibly consider serving on his cabinet, anyway? You always said he has the morals of a snake oil salesman."

Mitch Collins paused for a moment, a little uncertain about his daughter's transition to informality, wondering why she suddenly felt he was Dad instead of Father. "Yes, but the man understands international politics far better than any Democrat. He'll get us out of Vietnam just as he predicts, Margo, you'll see. He does have a plan to win in Vietnam. I'm sure of it. Just watch what happens now. Johnson will announce that he won't run again because of this Tet Offensive fiasco, the Democrats don't have a chance. And, of course, Humphrey has been fatally contaminated by his association with Johnson; the stink won't come off by election time. And, don't forget, Margo, Professor Kissinger will undoubtedly become Nixon's chief foreign policy advisor or perhaps his Secretary of State."

"Dad, I might agree to be your hostess this summer, but only because I love you and mother is gone. Still, there's nothing you can say to change my impression of Nixon and those Nazis that surround him. Thank God he's not President yet, or he'd probably be taping this conversation."

"Your sarcasm knows no bounds, Margo."

"I got it from you, Dad. I love you and I'm really sorry that the

Rockefeller campaign seems to have come undone. You would have made a great Secretary of State. Goodbye, Dad." As she hung up the phone, she began planning her rendezvous with Marchand in Bangkok.

37.

HANGIN' UP THE SPURS

Mid morning on March 29th, President Johnson sat alone in the Oval Office reflecting upon the events of the previous five weeks. Throughout the month of March 1968, news from Vietnam had grown worse daily. Every city in South Vietnam was under attack by North Vietnamese Army troops and indigenous Viet Cong forces. In Saigon, mayhem ruled as NVA troops killed civilians and South Vietnamese soldiers alike with ruthless abandon.

Even the United States Embassy in Saigon was under siege and was nearly lost to NVA soldiers who invaded the compound before being driven off by Marines and heroic CIA agents. The ancient and lovely city of Hue had completely fallen and was still partially under North Vietnamese control. Despite ample warnings, nearly all of which had been ignored or disregarded, the North Vietnamese Tet Offensive had come as a complete surprise to American and South Vietnamese forces. But for the President of the United States, the Tet Offensive was more than shocking, more than deadly, for it clearly spelled the end of his presidency.

Johnson had difficulty believing that the largest American Army and Air Force bases at Cam Ranh Bay in the south and Da Nang in the north were so besieged that only massive close air support kept them from being completely overrun. He learned that fully fifty percent of all South Vietnamese villages had fallen to the masterful military offensive planned and executed by North Vietnamese General Giap, Ho Chi Minh's most senior and brilliant military tactician. Johnson thought of the enormous areas of South Vietnamese countryside now under North Vietnamese control and the realization nearly made him sick. "Good Lord," he muttered to himself, "damn near the only safe places for American forces these days are the Navy ships in the Tonkin Gulf."

Worse yet, the set piece of the Tet Offensive proved to be an ignominious ugly lump of a hill in the northern most part of South Vietnam known by the American military as "I" Corps. The hill was called Khe Sanh. Just the name of the hill and the painfully long and deadly battle fought there brought the precarious situation of Allied forces into sharp focus for him. The Battle for Khe Sanh epitomized just about everything regarding the status of the War.

Day after day during the month of February and now March, President Johnson joined senior military planners in the Situation Room as they strategized over the grave situation on that dreadful hill. U.S. Marines had constructed the small base and airfield on the Khe Sanh hilltop as a forward base camp designed to stop the infiltration of North Vietnamese troops and munitions from the nearby Demilitarized Zone into the South. Unfortunately, resupply of the Marine companies stationed at Khe Sanh was only possible by air since the single access road, Route 9, had been completely overrun by the North Vietnamese.

Moreover, senior Marine Corps commanders had not reckoned on the difficulty of supporting Khe Sanh if it came under heavy and sustained attack. Lacking ground access, the Base at Khe Sanh had become outrageously exposed and vulnerable, a point not lost on North Vietnamese General Giap who decided to teach the Americans a painful lesson there, just as he had taught the French a horribly painful lesson at Dien Bien Phu just fourteen years earlier.

For seven weeks after the start of the Tet Offensive, the completely surrounded Marines fought as valiantly as any American soldiers had ever fought. Even the great battles of the Pacific during World War Two, including Iwo Jima, Guadalcanal and Okinawa, were no bloodier or more savagely fought. The Marines at Khe Sanh fought day and night without interruption. They fought with machine guns, rifles and mortars. And they fought hand to hand with bayonets when the NVA troops periodically overran the perimeter of the Base. The North Vietnamese were so close the Marines could hear NVA buglers sounding battle charges.

Khe Sanh Marines were supported by American air power supplied by Air Force, Navy and Marine fighter-bombers providing close air support. Often the surrounded and beleaguered Marines called in bombing strikes and long-range artillery right on top of their own positions in order to avoid being overrun. Without these air strikes, the Americans would have perished.

It was the most heroic stand by American forces of the entire Vietnamese War, save perhaps the disastrous Battle of Ia Drang Valley fought a year earlier. Johnson knew that if the Marines at Khe Sanh were lost (and it was by no means certain that they would not be lost), the defeat would be the equivalent of the French loss of Dien Bien Phu that precipitated their defeat.

The Marines of Khe Sanh fought like ferocious but beleaguered tigers. Yet, it was the intensity of the protracted battle, and the American inability to come to the rescue of their own Marines after nearly six weeks of terrible and bloody effort that spoke volumes to President Johnson. For him, Khe Sanh and the Tet Offensive trumpeted the message loudly that America was not winning the War. So after nearly five years of denial and deception during which he had been the chief participant and promulgator, that sad fact was now breaking Johnson's heart. And he truly had no one but himself to blame for the tragic debacle unfolding in the Southeast Asian jungle each day.

As Johnson's former Secretary of Defense McNamara had warned him, each and every lie and misleading commentary, each exaggeration and every misstatement made by senior American generals and admirals, Central Intelligence officers, and Defense Department and State Department officials, as well as the American President himself during the preceding five years was laid bare. During the month of March 1968, President Johnson, the Secretaries of Defense and State watched the intense, bright light of reality finally shine on the awful truth in Vietnam. The truth, as is always the case when great effort has been expended to avoid or obfuscate it, was finally and painfully clear for everyone to see.

And the truth was very simple. South Vietnam had proven to be little more than a fiction, a political construct virtually lacking in substance of any kind, a monstrous Potemkim Village. In fact, Vietnam symbolized the continuing proxy war between America and the Soviet Union played out in the steaming jungles of Southeast Asia. The exaggerated enemy body counts conjured up by field commanders, touted by the Defense Department and duly reported by the American press were now brought to light by the hundreds of body bags and coffins coming home to America each day.

And, Johnson reflected, no matter how many NVA troops were killed or wounded by American forces, many more seemed ready to take their place. Johnson finally realized that the Government and people of North Vietnam were willing to sacrifice everything to drive the Americans from their land and to liberate and reunify their country. Nothing else mattered to them, and for them no sacrifice was too great.

But for President Lyndon Johnson, weeks of reviewing the dreadful battlefield and casualty reports and Intelligence briefings had overwhelmed him with fatigue and grief. He was besieged by the press, and could rarely go anywhere in public. The news was full of the Tet Offensive and the awful surprise of the attacks. Johnson had become a virtual prisoner in the White House. He could look nowhere for relief.

During the awful two months of February and March of 1968, President Johnson talked at length to every Department head, to every senior official of State, and the CIA, even to advisors not in government positions, in a fruitless attempt at finding a solution to the Tet Offensive. One of the few men in Johnson's Cabinet with sufficient intelligence and honesty to venture the truth of the situation had just resigned. In refusing Robert McNamara's advice, Johnson had killed the messenger. And now he had to face the awful truth alone.

And so it was on the early afternoon of March 29, 1968 that President Johnson sat alone in the White House Oval Office. He had to act and he knew it. But the painful and awesome choices at his disposal seemed just too much to bear. As McNamara had so succinctly explained, Johnson could double American troop strength to a million men in order to protect South Vietnam from Tet Offensive type attacks and perhaps even launch an American ground offensive into North Vietnam. Or, Johnson could order all-out bombing strikes in North Vietnam to destroy all significant cities and the critically important Red River dike system that prevented massive flooding of the North each monsoon season. Or, he could mine the port of Haiphong as many of his military entourage suggested in order to prevent Russian supply ships from unloading there.

Alternatively, Johnson could simply order American forces to withdraw, thus tacitly accepting the first American military defeat in the Country's nearly two hundred-year existence. It was a step Johnson could easily have taken as late as July 1964, before he rammed the Tonkin Gulf Resolution, with all its attendant lies and mistruths, down the throat of a gullible Congress and an ignorant American populace. At that time, the world and America would have taken little notice had Johnson pulled up stakes and let Vietnam determine its own fate.

As his beloved Lady Bird Johnson entered the Oval Office to comfort him, the President had finally determined what course of action to take. "Lyndon, I have some hot tea and honey to warm you a bit. This is a such a cold and bitter March we're having," she said with great tenderness and compassion in her voice.

As she poured his tea, President Johnson slowly began to write the words of one of the most important speeches he would ever give the American public and certainly the most difficult. Johnson wrote the words that would soon be televised to the Nation telling of his decision not to seek re-election in November of 1968 and declaring a partial bombing halt in North Vietnam. Johnson had concluded that the only right and just decision he could make was to leave the choice about Vietnam up to the American people themselves as they chose their new president. Eliminating himself as a candidate ran afoul of everything Johnson stood for but he did just that.

Given the wide range of political candidates seeking the Presidency, from Democratic Senators Gene McCarthy and Robert Kennedy on the left who vowed to stop the War completely if elected, to the centrist Hubert Humphrey, Johnson's loyal vice president, to hard-line Republican Richard Nixon on the right who touted his secret plan that would win the War, the American public would be free to make its will known. Just as Johnson knew that he was making the only right decision, he knew that his decision marked the end of his long and illustrious political career. As he wrote the historic words that he "... would not seek nor, if nominated, ... accept the Democratic nomination for President," a few Texas size tears fell onto the pages of his last Presidential speech.

VOLUME ONE: PHANTOM WAR TRILOGY

38.

ROLLING THUNDER

Marchand wasn't listed on the March 30th squadron flight schedule, so he took the occasion to sleep for eight hours straight. He had just awakened to shower and dress for the evening meal when his roommate, Phil Winslow, returned to the stateroom.

"Hey Keith, it's dinner time. You finally getting out of the sack?"

"You got anything better to do than sleep?"

"Not really, I've only been up for an hour myself."

As they were talking, the next day's flight schedule appeared under the stateroom door. Phil Winslow walked over to pick it up and read the order of the following day's events.

"Well, look a' here boy. We've got a mini Alpha Strike to Vinh City tomorrow."

"Who's on it?" Marchand asked.

"Four birds, two flying bomber and two flying MIG patrol. Let's see, you and Kelly, Don Kramer and Steve Grant are flying fighter. Ron Hickman and Larry Gross, Frank Warden and I are flying bomber. We're leading a flight of four Skyhawks."

"You and Frank tomorrow, huh?"

"Yep, Terry is Squadron Duty Officer tomorrow so I'm taking his place with Frank." Winslow said.

"Well, enjoy it; Frank's a lot of fun to fly with and Vinh should be a milk run."

The eight plane strike on Vinh began routinely. The flight arrived on target, an ammunition storage facility two miles west of Vinh, exactly on schedule. Vinh is a small city with a population of approximately twenty five thousand that serves as a transportation and agricultural hub in the southern part of Vietnam. They encountered only light anti-aircraft fire during two planned dive runs each. Secondary explosions followed the detonation of the five-hundred pound bombs that blanketed the target site. Leaving the ammo dump in smoking, exploding ruin, each crewmember felt a sense of satisfaction knowing that as a result of their strike, a few more GI's would return to the States alive and well rather than in body bags or wheelchairs.

Kelly Drummond flew tight "S" turns and figure eights several thousand feet above the Phantoms and Skyhawks as they completed their bombing runs and began to climb back to altitude for rendezvous and flight home. Don Kramer flew a loose combat formation slightly below and fifteen hundred feet to the right of Drummond's aircraft. Winslow and Marchand probed the sky with radar beams in search of marauding MIG Fighters that had attacked American fighter-bombers with increasing frequency in the Vinh region since Johnson's partial bombing halt had gone into effect.

Nothing appeared on the radarscopes. It seemed that Marchand's prediction of a "milk run" flight would be accurate. But suddenly, without warning, the electronic countermeasures equipment in each aircraft simultaneously hummed a warning of impending surface to air missile activity. There had been no reports of SAM activity around Vinh for nearly a month after the previously active SAM batteries were destroyed by a twenty plane Alpha Strike from the *Constellation's* sister ship, the *U.S.S. Kitty Hawk*. Usually, the Soviet-made "track while scan" radar would sweep a large area for ninety seconds or longer before selecting a target aircraft. But this time the operators remained in a tracking mode for only fifteen seconds before locking the radar onto one plane and switching to firing mode.

Phil Winslow flying in the strike force lead plane called for evasive maneuvers over the air. "Checkmate Flight, **SAM LAUNCH, BREAK PORT; say again, BREAK PORT!**"

Frank Warden sighted the bright exhaust plume of the rocket off his left wing tip in the ten o'clock position as it climbed rapidly up to the flight's altitude. He slammed his stick hard over to the left and, as the plane rolled inverted, he pulled back sharply. All eight aircraft followed Frank's screaming split "S" dive in an attempt to evade not one but two SAMs hurtling toward them at two thousand miles per hour. Still inverted, Frank watched the first SAM begin a looping turn toward his aircraft. "Hot damn, that bastard looks like it's got our name on it, Phil," he grunted over the intercom.

"Oooohhh shit, you're right." Winslow strained a response as he fired a dozen bundles of radar deflecting aluminum chaff into the air stream.

Warden pulled out of his dive at five thousand feet and rolled into a tight, high "G" barrel roll in a further attempt to evade the stalking missile. He abruptly eased stick pressure when he saw the missile break radar lock and fly over his plane on a purely ballistic flight path. "That was a close one. Let's get the hell out of here."

"We're not out of the woods yet, Frank. We've got 37mm tracking right up our six o'clock. Jink starboard, hard!"

Without hesitation, Warden pulled the stick hard to the right and back toward his crotch. Both he and Winslow could see gray puffs of exploded anti-aircraft shells all around their cockpits. Soon, Warden couldn't see much daylight between gray and black puffs. Pulling out the heavy stuff now, he thought, as he shoved his throttles to the last afterburner detent in the throttle guides all the way forward to maximum power. As he added full power he pulled back hard on the control stick and sent the Phantom zooming upward at 20,000 feet per minute. "Man, this place is hot; I can't find any clear areas," Warden grunted over the intercom's hot mike.

"There are no clear areas, just climb!" Winslow roared into his facemask as shock waves from exploding AAA shells buffeted the Phantom from every direction.

All eight aircraft banked hard to right and left, attempting to evade deadly AAA fire while climbing to gain enough altitude to out-maneuver additional SAMs that might be fired at the flight. Marchand's altimeter spun through eighteen thousand feet when his SAM launch light flashed red and the high-pitched warning warble sounded in his helmet earphones. The electronic countermeasure scope told him to look back toward the plane's tail to locate the next missile lifting off. He strained to turn around in his cockpit and saw two missiles streaking toward the flights' rear quarter. He keyed his transmit button, "Checkmate Flight, SAM launch, two missiles, seven o'clock low; BREAK STARBOARD!"

Each aircraft again rolled inverted and pulled into a nearly vertical dive. The sharp diving maneuvers caused both missiles to break guidance on the target aircraft but the ten to twelve thousand feet of altitude loss during the SAM Break again placed the flight into a region of intense anti-aircraft fire. When Drummond pulled out of his dive, his altimeter showed only six thousand feet but he looked down at Warden's plane which appeared at least fifteen hundred feet lower. As he pushed the throttles to combat power and yanked the stick back in order to climb, he saw the coastline less than two miles away. "We're almost feet wet, Keith; any more SAMs?"

"Negative, their radar's back in a search mode."

"Ten seconds and we're home free."

"Can't be soon enough," Marchand grunted as rivulets of sweat stung his eyes.

Warden was also in a maximum climb and headed toward the coastline when he felt a sharp jolt beneath the aircraft and heard a loud thump. The combination SAM and triple A ambush proved deadly. The plane rolled hard to the left and as Warden struggled to regain control, his peripheral vision drew his attention to his left wing. "Goddamn it, we've lost eight feet of the port wing," Warden bellowed over the intercom.

"No shit, we got smoke in the cockpit, too," Winslow said anxiously.

"Goddamn it, see any flames?" Warden bellowed.

"Negative but a lot of smoke and heat back here. Do you have control?"

"Just barely, I'm using rudder to keep it level; ailerons aren't responding. Now I've got a fire warning light."

"Can you make feet wet?"

"Not sure; just lost all oil pressure on number two engine, I'm shutting it down."

"I can really feel the heat, Frank, behind my cockpit and on the deck. We're gonna have to get out pretty quick."

Warden keyed his transmitter, "Checkmate Flight, this is Checkmate Leader; Mayday, Mayday! We're hit, on fire, trying to make feet wet."

Drummond rolled his plane and looked below at Warden's aircraft which trailed heavy black smoke and flames from its tail section. He quickly joined the stricken Phantom in a loose formation but close enough to see the extensive damage done to it. In addition to the fire that came from the afterburner section of the engine bay, much of the left wing had been shot away along with a portion of the aileron. White fuel vapor streamed from the damaged wing. Suddenly, flames erupted from the wing's underside. The plane would disintegrate any moment.

"Checkmate Leader, you've got a massive fire going. Eject, eject!" Drummond shouted over the radio.

Warden keyed the intercom, "OK Phil, get out; I'll be right behind you."

"Yeah Frank, see ya when I see ya." Phil Winslow sat as straight as possible in his ejection seat, checked his harness lock then reached up over his helmet to grasp the two yellow and black handles of his ejection seat face curtain. He pulled the curtain down sharply over his helmet and felt an enormous jolt as the explosive charges beneath his seat fired. The seat blasted upward a millisecond after the Plexiglas canopy blew away from Winslow's cockpit. As soon as the seat was free of the cockpit, rocket engines fixed to the seat bottom ignited sending Winslow two hundred feet above the blazing Phantom. Within another fraction of a second a small explosive charge fired to pull Winslow's parachute out of its pack and separate him from the metal seat bucket.

Winslow blacked out as soon as the initial explosive charges fired under his seat, powerful G forces having drained most of the blood from his brain. He was aware of a tumbling sensation after the rockets ceased burning and he felt another jolt as his parachute opened. When his vision returned, he was extraordinarily relieved to look down and see water, not land. His only concern was a peculiar burnt odor that he found somewhat nauseating.

When Warden heard Winslow's ejection seat fire and felt the blast of air enter the cockpit, he immediately positioned himself and pulled his ejection seat face curtain. Within two seconds he was hanging in his chute and watching the burning Phantom begin to tumble out of control. Moments later, the aircraft exploded and disintegrated. He looked down and felt enormous relief to see water beneath him. Warden was shocked, however, to feel wetness from his left knee down to his boot and his boot seemed to be filled with water although he hadn't splashed down yet.

Kelly Drummond flew tight 360 degree turns around the two descending parachutes providing a constant escort to the downed fliers. He noticed that the late afternoon sea breeze was blowing Warden and Winslow's parachutes back toward the shoreline. He assumed command of the flight. "Checkmate Flight, this is Check Three; I've got the lead and I'm the SAR commander. Check Two, stay with me. Check Four, join up with Cowboy Three and Four and head home.

"Cowboy Flight Leader, you and Cowboy Two stay with me for search and rescue."

After the odd Phantom jet joined the two A-4 Skyhawks to return to the *Constellation,* Marchand transmitted another Mayday call and a request for search and rescue helicopters to pick up Warden and Winslow who had just splashed down roughly a half mile offshore.

Drummond continued flying tight circles one thousand feet over the downed airmen while dodging AAA fire from 37mm shore batteries. The two Skyhawks flew protective cover five hundred feet higher. Drummond felt confident that both Warden and Winslow would be picked up since he saw two good parachutes enter the water. But moments later, he saw an enemy patrol boat and several motorized sampans heading toward the swimming fliers.

39.

SMALL PACKAGE,
BIG SURPRISE

Before Winslow hit the water, he saw that the legs of his flight suit were practically shredded. As adrenalin shock dissipated, Winslow began to feel an intense pain in his calves. He realized that the unpleasant odor he detected moments earlier was the smell of burnt flesh from his legs. The fire on the floor of his cockpit had done far greater damage than he had known. When he splashed down, the extent of his injury became evident as the salt water simultaneously cooled and inflamed the raw flesh between his knees and boot tops. Winslow was able to release his parachute and inflate his floatation vest before the shock of the ejection and the pain from his legs caused him to lose consciousness.

Warden splashed down several hundred yards from Winslow. They were out of each other's sight. Warden wasted little time getting out of his parachute, inflating his life vest and small one-man life raft. After he climbed in, he was stunned to see the water in the bottom of the raft turning crimson. Warden slowly rolled up his left flight suit leg, dreading what he might find. A wave of nausea swept over him when he looked at the ragged hole the size of a dime in his calf muscle and a larger more serious looking exit wound on the other side. He leaned over the side and heaved until nothing else would come up.

When Warden regained his breath and stomach control, he looked up with relief to see two Phantoms and two Skyhawks circling overhead. Warden used his survival knife to cut a section of repelling line carried in a pocket of his G suit legging and make a tourniquet to staunch the heavy blood flow from his leg. The repelling line could be used by a downed aviator to lower himself to the jungle floor should his parachute hang up in the high branches of a thick rain forest canopy. Warden laughed to himself as he recalled all of the potential uses of the line described by his survival instructor. This is one he missed, Warden thought. He noted that he was not anywhere close to panicking and was thankful for his rigorous survival training. Anyway, he'd survived. So far, he'd survived.

Having rigged a tourniquet and made himself as secure as possible in the raft, Warden pulled his emergency radio out of his survival vest, turned it on, and shouted for joy when he heard Kelly Drummond's voice.

"Checkmate One, this is Checkmate Leader; do you read? Over."

"Check Leader, this is Check One; read you loud and clear."

"Check One, roger. RESCAP is on the way. Just hang in there. Say your condition. Over."

"Check Leader, I've got a leg wound. Doesn't look too bad though. Any contact with my back seat man? Over."

"Negative, Check Leader. Good chute but negative visual and negative radio contact."

Warden was about to respond when three shells from the nearby shore batteries exploded within one hundred feet sending large columns of water skyward. He couldn't determine whether the gunners were aiming at him or the circling aircraft but it made little difference since the presence of the rescue aircraft would draw fire his way in any event. "Checkmate Leader, fly your pattern, north or south of me, fire's is too close for comfort." Warden transmitted.

"Roger that; we'll keep you in sight."

"Roger, Check Leader. Where is Big Motha?"

"We got one coming from North SAR, one from Red Crown and one from South SAR, fifteen minutes till the first one arrives."

"Roger, any sign of my W.O. yet?"

"Negative, Check One, stay off the air for a few minutes; we got a little problem to handle." Drummond keyed his intercom button, "Keith, how far is that patrol boat?"

"About a mile." Where in the hell is Winslow? Marchand thought aloud.

"Sampans, how many?" Drummond asked.

"At least ten, a couple of big junks, too. All headed toward Warden."

"Cowboy Leader, this is Checkmate Leader, take care of as many sampans and junks as you can. I'm going after the patrol boat. Checkmate Four, fly this pattern; keep a visual on Checkmate One."

"Cowboy Leader, roger." The two Skyhawks immediately roared off toward the coastline and the small flotilla that was headed out to snatch the two downed fliers out of the water.

"Checkmate Four, roger. Good hunting, guys."

The Skyhawk pilots armed their 20mm cannons and aligned their gun sights for low altitude strafing runs at the fleet of motorized fishing boats headed for the downed fliers. The Skyhawk flight leader could see small spits of fire from machine guns on the first sampan just as he squeezed the trigger on his control stick. The small attack bomber

317

rumbled and bucked as his cannons barked red-hot explosive charges at the first three sampans. His wingman put the pipper of his gun sight on two motorized junks fifty yards to the right.

The lead sampan disintegrated as two 20mm cannon shells hit it. It sank immediately in a crimson swell. Another shell exploded within four feet of the second boat killing two militiamen instantly, causing the boat to capsize and dumping six soldiers into the water. The occupants of the third boat having witnessed the destruction of their comrades dove overboard and abandoned their boat. Shells from the wingman's Skyhawk ripped into the largest motorized junk shearing off its mast and setting it aflame. Shrapnel killed the helmsman and the boat swung around toward shore. Seconds later it exploded as fire reached its fuel tank.

Six sampans, one junk, and the patrol boat still bore down on the two fliers in the water. The militiamen knew the value of captured American pilots full well and were not about to abandon their efforts to capture them, even at great cost. Drummond added power and quickly climbed to five thousand feet in order to stay out of machine gun range of the patrol boat. He turned, flew two miles out to sea pulled his stick hard over to the right putting the Phantom into a tight turn. "Lock him up on your weapon, Keith. I'm going to blow that bastard to kingdom come with a Sparrow."

Marchand located the PT boat on his radar screen and locked his weapon guidance system onto it. He keyed his intercom button. "I'm locked on. Arm your Sparrows. In range light on. Fox One, Fox One."

Drummond squeezed his trigger twice in rapid succession sending two ten foot long, radar guided missiles flashing toward the patrol boat. Drummond kept his hand rock steady on the stick as he watched the missiles guide flawlessly toward the boat. He could even see the reflection of their white hot rocket exhaust on the water's surface just before impact. Suddenly, the patrol boat vanished in a ball of orange flame as both missiles struck home. Drummond pulled back on his stick and climbed back to fifteen hundred feet, to survey the situation. Only bits and pieces of the patrol boat remained on the surface smoldering, a burning oil slick marked the spot where the boat had sunk.

The two Skyhawks had now lined up for their second run at the remaining boats. Shells from the Flight leader's cannon kicked up waterspouts as they walked a line twenty feet abeam the last motorized junk. The helmsman managed to swing the boat hard over as the firing run commenced. Still, hot shrapnel started two fires on the deck of the junk and killed one of the militiamen who had been firing a machine gun at the aircraft. The second Skyhawk's cannon sunk two more sampans, one with a direct hit, another with close misses that riddled the boat with silver dollar-sized holes.

The Skyhawks wheeled again in loose formation preparing for another firing run. The Flight leader keyed his mike. "Cowboy Two, this is Cowboy Leader, fall back in a tight trailing position for this run. Go after the junk!"

"Cowboy Two, Roger. This junk won't go fishin' again for mackerel or pilots."

The Skyhawks bore down on the junk but when the Flight leader squeezed his trigger, nothing happened. "Cowboy Two, I'm off target. Go get the bastard." the Lead pilot bellowed over the radio while pulling his stick back to climb. His wingman pressed the attack spraying the junk with explosive 20 mm shells. The boat was hit three times, once in the engine compartment. Within seconds it disintegrated when its fuel tank exploded.

Four sampans still headed full throttle for Warden and Winslow in the water. Drummond surveyed the Skyhawk's attack from two thousand feet and transmitted, "Cowboy Leader, you're doing a hell of a job. You shouldn't have any problems with the last boats."

"Check One, this is Cowboy Leader; my guns are jammed. Cowboy Two, they're all yours."

"Cowboy Two, Roger. I'll take care of 'em." The single Skyhawk turned once again and set up its strafing run, this time abeam of the boats. The young pilot made a nearly perfect run. His cannon scored direct hits on two boats both of which promptly burned and sank.

Only two boats remained but they were less than five hundred yards from Warden and closing rapidly. As the lone Skyhawk returned for one more run, two boats maneuvered wildly, escaping damage. Still they pressed on, determined to get to the downed American pilots.

"Cowboy Leader, this is Cowboy Two; I've got ammo for one more run."

Drummond keyed his transmitter. "Give it all you can, Cowboy. Closest Big Motha is still three minutes out."

The Skyhawk's final run was right on the money. The pilot's hand was deft as a surgeon's on the stick as he gave delicate final corrections with rudder pedals only. When he squeezed the trigger, cannon shells erupted all around the first sampan, one scoring a direct hit; two others were close enough to have destroyed the boat as well. But as the gun sight's pipper passed over the last sampan, the Skyhawk's cannons went silent; the ammunition was gone. The pilot yanked back on his stick in frustration and climbed to join his leader. "Check Leader, this is Cowboy Two; I guess we're gonna have to throw rocks at the last one. My well just ran dry."

"Cowboy Two, Checkmate Leader, you did a fine job. We're lookin' for some goddamn rocks now." Drummond keyed his intercom button. "Keith, can you get a weapons lock on that sampan for another Sparrow shot?"

"There's not enough radar reflectivity, Kelly. Even if I lock onto it, the missile would probably misguide. It could go wide and hit Frank." Or Phil, wherever he is, Marchand thought.

"Yeah, you're right. There's not much more we can do but pray that the Big Mother gets here in time."

Warden stared at the twenty-foot sampan as it raced toward his tiny yellow raft. It was no more than one hundred yards away from him now. He keyed his emergency radio. "You boys did a bang-up job but I think you forgot one of 'em. Cowboys, see what you can do before these bastards nail me."

Drummond answered, "This is Checkmate Leader, we've got nothing else to throw at 'em Frank. Big Motha's gonna be here any minute now."

"Don't think it's gonna help much now. Charlie is here; they're motioning me to put my hands up. I'll see ya, boys, when the War's over. I'll leave my transmitter on until Charlie finds it. So long."

That was Warden's final goodbye Marchand thought and it made him furious.

The sampan drew alongside Warden's raft. Three militiamen grabbed Warden's torso harness roughly and pulled him into the sampan. They stripped him of his pistol, survival knives and radio immediately. The helmsman quickly swung the boat around and headed for shore with their newly captured prize. Warden sat glumly between two Vietnamese visualizing the Hanoi Hilton, the notorious North Vietnamese POW camp.

The four aircraft circled overhead like angry birds that had lost a fledgling. Gloom in the respective cockpits was partially broken when the lead Skyhawk pilot reported spotting Winslow in the water a quarter mile from the spot where Warden had just been captured. "Can you tell if he's alive?" Drummond inquired.

"Affirmative, he's waiving his arms," the Skyhawk pilot transmitted.

As if on queue, the shore batteries began firing again at both the circling aircraft and the second flier that the gunners had sighted. The commander of the remaining enemy boat radioed to shore that he had captured one pilot and was returning to shore. The militiamen determined that since they could not capture the remaining downed flier, they would do their best to kill him.

Now, Winslow had been targeted to die. Shells exploded around Winslow as he struggled with his survival radio that did not seem to transmit although he could hear garbled transmissions from the low flying aircraft. He heard pieces of shrapnel whizzing past him after each ear-shattering explosion. Metal shards and seawater rained down upon him and he shook with fear and pain. Now all I need is for some damn sharks to come cruising by, he thought. I might as well bend over and kiss my ass goodbye.

Winslow heard the familiar beat of helicopter rotors approaching. "Oh my God," he shouted aloud. "I didn't think you guys would make it on time. I love you Big Motha; I love you."

The pilot of the First Sea Stallion helicopter keyed his transmitter. "Checkmate Leader, do you still have a visual on the guy in the water?"

"That's affirmative, Mother One. I'll fly over him and rock my wings as I pass overhead," Drummond responded.

"This is Mother One, confirm another pilot captured in the sampan headed for shore."

"Affirmative, Mother One. There's a boatload of militiamen with guns on him."

"Checkmate Leader, this is Mother One. It's gonna be tough to get him. We could take the boat but they'd probably shoot our guy before giving him up. Might be better to let them capture him."

"Mother Two, pick up the guy in the water. I'll figure a way to get our guy back."

"Mother Two, Roger, we have the other pilot in sight."

"Mother Two, this is Checkmate Leader, watch your ass! They're really hosing us down. They're trying to get our downed man as well as us."

"Mother One, Checkmate Leader, give me a minute or two before you take over as SAR Commander. I want to get our man back," Drummond transmitted.

"Checkmate Leader, you got it for sixty seconds but send the Cowboys home now. The last thing we need out here is a midair. I understand they're out of bullets anyway."

"Mother One, this is Checkmate Leader; thanks for the time. Cowboys, head for home and thanks again for your marksmanship."

"Check Leader, this is Cowboy One; glad we could help. Good luck with your buddy."

As the two Skyhawks roared away from the rescue scene and climbed out toward the *Constellation*, the second Big Mother helicopter began to hover over Winslow, dropping a diver into the water alongside Winslow. As the helicopter hovered, the shelling became more intense. Plumes of water erupted like noisy geysers. The diver quickly swam to Winslow. "You injured?" he yelled.

"Burns on my legs, nothing broken though," Winslow gasped.

"I'll put the collar around you. Don't move or try to help. I've

323

got you from here."

"You bet," Winslow acknowledged gratefully, smothering his pain.

A helicopter crewman lowered what looked like a large, horse collar attached to a high-speed electric winch suspended above the open helicopter doors. When the collar hit the water, the diver expertly placed it under Winslow's arms and signaled the chopper crew to hoist Winslow thirty feet from surface to the helicopter. As the winch took up slack in the line, a shell exploded not more than twenty feet in front of the cockpit. The pilot, feeling the blast and hearing shrapnel rip holes in the skin of the helicopter, added power, shifted the craft sideways and started to climb. Another shell detonated nearby and Winslow felt a hot, stinging sensation in his left arm. He was now skipping across the water like a stone as the helicopter skewed away from the area leaving the diver still in the water.

The pilot knew he would have to go back for the diver immediately or he would be killed in the water by the bombardment. He keyed his intercom to his crewmembers. "We're going back for him now. Get on the bullhorn, tell the pilot in the sling."

The helicopter pilot skillfully maneuvered his ungainly flying machine on a straight line back to the diver, skimming Winslow along the surface. Just as the diver reached out for the collar, the wind shifted and it looked as though he would miss a handhold. Winslow painfully braced himself in the collar with his left arm, stretched his right hand as far as he could toward the diver. The diver's powerful hands grasped Winslow's arm as the collar dragged him away. He pulled hand over hand along Winslow's arm and grabbed a hold on the collar, gave a thumbs-up signal to the winch operator.

With two men still dangling on the rescue collar, the pilot veered away from the shoreline, accelerating as Winslow and the diver came out of the water. The helicopter had moved no more than a hundred yards when several shells exploded within ten feet of the spot where the diver had been swimming. His cargo safely aboard, the helicopter pilot climbed and headed toward the Navy frigate that served as the northern search and rescue picket ship, known as North SAR.

In the lead Phantom, Drummond keyed his intercom, "Think of something quick Marchand. Mother One's gonna take over as SAR Commander any second and order us outta here and Frank's a goner."

"I'm thinking, Kelly, I'm thinking but there's not a damn thing we can do that might not kill Frank as well as the Vietnamese. Wait a minute, wait a minute; there's the derringer! He's got the derringer!" Marchand exclaimed.

"The what?"

"No time to explain, Kelly. Can you hold the bird steady fifteen feet off the deck?"

"I can hold it at ten if I have to, why?"

"Just take it down to fifteen feet and head straight for the boat. Hit afterburner just before we pass over it, then pull up sharply."

"Got the picture. Hang on," Drummond said as he wrapped the Phantom into a tight turn and eased it down toward the water's surface while flying at four hundred miles per hour.

"What the hell are you doing, Checkmate? Your time's up. Wrap it up and get outta here!" The lead helicopter pilot called, clearly assuming command of the rescue operation and unwilling to risk any more lives for what seemed a lost cause.

Marchand keyed his transmitter, "We got one more card to play, Mother One. So just stand by till we finish this hand."

The Big Mother pilot looked at his co-pilot and said

exasperatedly, "What the hell are the damn fighter jocks up to now?"

"I don't know but it looks like he's about to ram the fuckin' fishing boat. He couldn't be more than twenty feet off the deck," the co-pilot replied.

Drummond gripped his stick like a vice, breathing as softly as possible while riveting his vision on the water surface and the rapidly approaching sampan. He dared not move any muscle in his body save his arm for even one slightly miscalibrated movement on the controls would put the Phantom into the water where it would explode like a bomb. Just before the fighter passed over the sampan at three hundred fifty knots, Drummond hauled back on the control stick and shoved his throttles into first stage afterburner. The Phantom's nose reared up and the massive fighter roared skyward.

Warden stared at the lone Phantom as it descended out of a tight turn and headed straight for him. Good God, he wondered, what's he doing, he's practically laying it on the water. Warden noticed the incredulous faces of his captors who were puzzled by Drummond's low altitude flight. As the Phantom swiftly approached, Warden saw panic spread among the boat crew who all thought that the crazy American pilot was about to strafe or bomb them at an incredibly low altitude, the downed pilot included. Suddenly, Warden knew just what to do.

The sound of the big fighter hit the small boat like a bomb. Warden could feel compression waves thumping hard against his chest. The shock waves and jet blast hit the small boat nearly capsizing it. As the Phantom's afterburners lit off, another explosive blast rocked the sampan with sound and heat. The militiamen, thinking they had been strafed and hit by some type of ordnance, jumped overboard and began swimming for their lives, or so they thought. Only one crewman remained on the boat. Paralyzed with fear, he curled into a tight fetal position on the bottom of the boat. He looked up to see Warden aiming a derringer in his face. "Surprise, Charlie," Warden said with a grin.

Suddenly another crewman who had hung onto the side of the boat heaved himself over the side and lunged for an AK-47 lying in the bilge. Warden heard the commotion, turned and fired. The Vietnamese screamed with pain, grabbed his left side, and spun overboard. Warden grabbed the automatic rifle and placed his derringer in his boot top. Warden motioned for the other Vietnamese to jump overboard and the crewman quickly complied.

Warden retrieved his survival pistol and fired several tracer rounds into the air. He found his survival radio and transmitted, "Big Motha, come and get me; I'm tired and I want to go home for a good stiff scotch."

"This is Big Motha One, we'll have you on board ASAP. Checkmate One. And, there will be a bottle of Chivas waiting for you when you get home."

Drummond retarded his throttles and flew over Warden rocking his wings slowly. He could see Warden waving at him. Marchand transmitted and hoped Warden would hear him, "It's good to have you back, Frank."

Drummond added power and climbed slowly as they headed toward deep water.

VOLUME ONE: PHANTOM WAR TRILOGY

PART FOUR

March 31, 1968 – April 10, 1968

VOLUME ONE: PHANTOM WAR TRILOGY

40.

JUST FRIENDS

Sunday, March 31, 1968 had broken cold and clear in the nation's Capital. Frigid air had settled over the grounds and great Gothic nave of the National Episcopal Cathedral like a frigid pall. Despite the intense cold, rich melodic strains of a Bach chorale, sung by full choir accompanied by the Church's majestic organ, filled the immense Cathedral with almost other-worldly beauty. Slowly, the Dean of the Cathedral ascended the steps of the granite pulpit to address the standing room only congregation attending the eleven o'clock solemn high Mass.

But it was not the Cathedral's Dean, eloquent though he was, who had drawn such a large number of guests and parishioners on that bitter cold, late winter morning. In fact, the guest speaker had himself requested permission from the Episcopal Bishop to give his address at the Cathedral in order to attract the widest possible audience. The Bishop, who was in attendance for this special service, had been pleased to grant the request of the recent Nobel Peace Prize laureate and provide the most appropriate forum for a most important sermon.

Almost two years had passed since the Reverend Doctor Martin Luther King, Jr. had made his politically difficult and ethically critical decision to unite the civil rights struggle with the aims and goals of the American Peace Movement. Now, Dr. King was poised to give his most important speech about that decision, detailing his thoughts and message against the War in Vietnam. King felt it particularly important to deliver this speech which he captioned "Remaining Awake Through a Great Revolution" in Washington, D.C.

As Dr. King waited for the Dean Sayre to complete his homily and introductory comments, he reflected upon the tremendous controversy that his ministry had generated throughout the country. King knew that no one had been more affected by his controversial decisions than his erstwhile friend, supporter and benefactor, Lyndon Baines Johnson. Until King's decision to join the anti-war movement, President Johnson had staunchly and enthusiastically supported King and the Negro struggle for Civil Rights. For most of Johnson's presidency, King had even enjoyed rather easy access by phone or in person to the Oval Office. All that had ended eighteen months ago following King's first anti-Vietnam War speech after which President Johnson felt personally betrayed by his erstwhile friend. After King's speech, Johnson no longer personally accepted King's phone calls nor did he extend the White House welcome to King.

Notwithstanding President Johnson's aloofness, Dr. King felt increasingly confident in the correctness of his position. This morning he intended to tell the nation in great detail why, in his judgment, the Vietnam War was morally and ethically wrong as well as inimical to the cause and prosecution of the civil rights movement itself. In fact, King felt that the shock effect of the Tet Offensive and the dramatic increase in American casualties during the previous month made it imperative for him to maximize his efforts towards ending the War.

While Dr. King waited to take the pulpit, President Johnson was at the opposite end of Washington, completing the details of the speech that he would televise to the Nation later that evening. The phone suddenly rang, interrupting Johnson's concentration. Irritation filled his voice as he answered the call. His secretary greeted him and announced the caller. "Director Hoover is on the line for you, Mr. President." It was one of the last calls that Johnson wanted to hear at that moment. But he took the call anyway wondering what additional disaster Hoover could be calling him about on Sunday morning.

"Mr. President, I'm sorry to disturb you, Sir, but I just wanted to remind you that Dr. King is giving another anti-War speech this morning down at the Episcopal Cathedral. Although we don't expect any trouble or violence, certainly not at the Cathedral, you never know how these things can get out of hand after he has left the Church. I'll keep an eye on everything; and, just in case, the Bureau has coordinated with the District of Columbia police should any problems start. But I also wanted to give you a heads up about Dr. King, Mr. President."

Johnson listened carefully before responding. "What about Martin?"

"Well, Mr. President, I know that you have always considered King a friend, or perhaps I should say, you did consider him a friend. So, another purpose for this call is to warn you that King's alliance with the peace movement has created even more powerful enemies for him than he already had."

"Damn, I didn't think poor ol' Martin could have many more enemies than he's already got," Johnson replied, "though I guess I'm getting' to know how he must feel."

"Well Sir, he's now in considerable danger. In addition to the standard racist crackpots and Ku Klux Klan types, King has stirred up a nest of pro-Vietnam, pro-War fanatics, would-be soldiers and other malcontents who have vowed to bring him down for good. Here at the Bureau, I've assigned an excellent crew of under-cover men to keep an eye on him for his own good. But, Mr. President, it might be a good idea if you were to give him a personal warning for his own safety. King really needs to take a lower profile if he wants to enjoy that Peace Prize he just got."

"Thank you, Edgar. I appreciate your efforts and I know that you will keep me apprised of the situation with King. But why don't you or one of your men warn King personally?"

"Mr. President, with all due respect, Sir, I think that you know that I don't particularly like the man. And, for what it's worth, he has no lost love for me either. So, I think it would be better coming from you or your office. King might take it more seriously, that is. If one of my men were to warn him, he might think that we're trying to harass him –" Hoover caught himself before he ended the sentence with the word "again".

"All right Edgar, I'll take care of it," Johnson said wearily.

"Good luck with your speech tonight, Sir."

"Thanks again, Edgar. Be sure to listen tonight. You might be in for a surprise."

President Johnson paused before returning to the final draft of his speech. "Damn it, I shoulda' listened to Martin more closely about this damn War. Looks like he had it right all along," Johnson muttered aloud. "Guess I better have someone talk to the Reverend pretty soon. But it will have to wait a few days until the firestorm over this speech dies down a bit."

It was then that Dr. King began to climb the steps to the pulpit at the other end of town. He thought briefly of President Johnson whom he still considered a friend, although an estranged one. He vowed to call the

President the next day to compliment him, no matter what he might say, on his nationally televised speech to be delivered at eight o'clock that evening. I must somehow explain to him that there has been nothing personal in my decisions about the War, he thought. I'll ask the Good Lord for the right words to say to him and perhaps give the poor man some peace. He surely hasn't had much lately.

Reverend Doctor Martin Luther King, Jr. began his own extraordinary sermon designed to explain and justify his radical departure from the strict confines of civil rights and civil disobedience. King's rich baritone voice resonated throughout the great Cathedral. "I need not pause to say how very delighted I am to be here this morning, to have the opportunity of standing in this very great and significant pulpit. And I do want to express my deep personal appreciation to Dean Sayre and all of the Cathedral clergy for extending the invitation...."

When King finished his sermon, he had effectively aligned the Civil Rights movement in the United States with the anti-War movement for good and in doing so sealed his own fate.

VOLUME ONE: PHANTOM WAR TRILOGY

41.

EAST AND WEST

Having a little business of her own in Bangkok, Margo arranged to meet Marchand there while he was on his week's leave during the first week of April. It was a special time out of time, a week away from the War and the politics of a troubled world on the brink of World War Three, for the second time in only a decade. It was a special time for the newly minted lovers to bond deeply and joyfully before returning to their own demanding routines.

After coming together and enjoying a first sleepless night of high passion, the lovers slept in the next morning – Marchand until well after noon and Margo until nine a.m. when she let herself out of the hotel room quietly, so as not to wake Keith. She left a note reading, "Back soon, needed a little walk. Love M." Once on the street, Margo found a cab and followed the directions she had received in Hong Kong for a ten o'clock meeting at a nearby restaurant. There, she was to receive documents smuggled out of Communist China and deliver them to the CIA station chief in Bangkok. From what Margo understood, the documents would be instrumental in averting a major diplomatic crisis.

Somehow, Margo had been identified and primed as the proper

"citizen operative" for the highly sensitive mission. Her Mandarin Chinese was excellent, she was well connected in the United States and Hong Kong, and she had excellent cover. Marguerite "Margo" Collins was not nervous but she was distinctly aware of the importance attached to these documents.

"Rick's Number One" the cab driver said as he pulled in front of a two-story British Colonial style building just before noon. Margo paid him and hopped out, looking every bit the professional American diplomat. She went into the bar area of the restaurant and waited for nearly an hour but her contact failed to show. Eventually, a waiter called the owner and soon Rick Sero, the proprietor, himself appeared. "May I help you?" he queried.

Needing to avoid any attention, Margo replied, "Oh no, thank you. I was just waiting for a friend, but I think he must have taken down the wrong time or address. I'll return later."

Margo returned to their hotel suite just as Marchand finished his shower and told him that she had found a great restaurant for dinner. At eight that evening, the couple arrived at Rick's which turned out to be an internationally renowned dining establishment, well-known for both excellent cuisine and Rick's world-famous guests. For years, Rick Sero, a wealthy and aristocratic expatriate Hungarian, had owned and operated this most popular European-style restaurant in the heart of Bangkok. Toward the conclusion of a long and fabulously rich dinner, Sero joined Margo and Marchand to introduce himself and join their animated conversation.

Uncertain as to how this young woman wanted to explain her presence at the restaurant earlier that day, Sero followed her lead. When she said she had heard about Rick's and checked it out while Marchand slept, that was the end of the story. Sero apparently enjoyed conversation with the couple so much that he invited them to join him for lunch two days later.

On April 5th, Keith and Margo arrived at Rick's Number One at noon; this time Sero joined them for lunch. After much prompting from Rick, Margo described her doctoral research in Hong Kong and to her surprise and delight, she discovered that Sero spoke passable Cantonese, superb Shanghainese, and excellent Mandarin Chinese. She was also impressed by Sero's extensive knowledge of Chinese culture and contemporary history, most of which he had gained through personal experience during the previous twenty-five years. Marchand listened attentively to their conversation and wondered who was this amazing woman he had met at a ship's party in Hong Kong. Intellectually and culturally, she matched Sero step for step throughout the long lunch during which Sero and Margo often spoke in fluent Mandarin.

The lunch was a breathtaking culinary *tour de force* orchestrated by Sero himself. As the meal ended and coffee was served, Margo excused herself for a moment but was gone far longer. Seeing an opening, Sero wasted little time before shifting conversation to the subject he was determined to discuss. "Tell me, Mr.. Marchand, are the American bombing missions in Vietnam really effective?" Followed by, "How badly has the Tet Offensive hurt American forces?" Sero's questions were smoothly injected into a conversation well lubricated with fine wine.

Before Marchand could answer, Sero quickly interjected, "Kindly forgive my curiosity, Lieutenant. Please understand that here in Thailand we are desperate for information regarding the Vietnam War. For, if you Americans fail in Vietnam and you are correct in assuming that Cambodia and Laos will be next to fall to Communist insurgency, certainly Thailand cannot be far behind. We have, you might say, a vested interest in your success or failure."

Marchand suspected that there was more to Sero's interest in America's War in Vietnam but Sero did not explain further. Marchand vaguely anticipated Sero's questions and carefully phrased his responses since much of the subject matter was militarily classified. The question whether Sero might be a very clever Soviet or Communist Chinese agent had not escaped him.

Nevertheless, something in the older gentleman's mannerisms and speech belied a certain sincerity and personal thirst for information. Marchand concluded, perhaps too naively, that Sero was a concerned Thai citizen, and perhaps a politically active businessman but definitely not a sophisticated Soviet KGB officer, so he tried to answer Sero's questions without divulging classified information. "I will say that our intelligence isn't the best when it comes to selection of worthwhile targets. Quite often, our most effective missions are often those that allow us to seek targets of opportunity or to work with forward air controllers who are actually in visual contact with the Viet Cong or North Vietnamese Army regulars."

Marchand paused, but Sero did not comment, so he continued. "Perhaps, our most ineffective strikes are those directed at urban targets in North Vietnam. The Vietnamese are no fools. They locate almost everything of value in the middle of the most densely populated civilian areas. They're confident that American rules of engagement won't allow us to go after such targets. We know that this is their strategy and we do the best we can under the circumstances. The Defense Secretary, the Joint Chiefs, or perhaps Johnson himself, think that the psychological pressure from the constant bombing, regardless of the target's value, will eventually pay off. I hope they're right because the real cost of this war is rising dramatically."

"Might I conclude that American aircraft losses are perhaps more substantial than the news reports suggest?" Sero inquired.

Not wishing to talk numbers, Marchand replied only that, "Our losses are substantial. Soon, we must determine whether the game is worth the price of admission." He quickly chastised himself for overstepping prudent limits to his comments. Criticizing American policy in front of a complete stranger was way out of line and he knew it.

"Well my young friend, there are, as you Americans would say, so many strikes against you," Sero intoned.

"Meaning what?"

"To begin with," Sero said sadly, "America has little understanding of its Vietnamese enemy. Ho Chi Minh is much more tenacious than you suspect. He wages war for the long term. Five or ten years are nothing to Ho and General Giap. But, I don't think you can say the same for President Johnson or General Westmoreland. Worst of all, neither your politicians nor your generals have the slightest idea what the North Vietnamese are really fighting about. You don't seem to know what their objectives are or what historical forces drive them. I'm afraid that America is ill-prepared to defeat such a cunning and dedicated adversary.

"While you Americans are certainly capable of defeating the North Vietnamese militarily, America is not willing to pay the price, to spill enough blood, your own or even Vietnamese, to win this War. Johnson even refuses to declare war. He calls it a 'conflict' so as to minimize its true meaning or political impact. So, while your enemy is willing to sacrifice everything for victory, to wait years for victory, to bleed and to die, to die a million times if necessary to secure its objectives, America desperately wants and needs to win the War quickly and go home."

Marchand interrupted, "Well, I see you've given a lot of thought to these matters, Rick. I can only hope Johnson, McNamara and Westmoreland have done likewise."

Catching himself, Sero said quickly. "Ah, enough of this old man's prattle. You didn't come to Rick's to discuss war and politics but to enjoy a fine food and excellent wine. You must forgive me. My hunger for information has perhaps exceeded my manners."

After trying unsuccessfully to make several international phone calls, Margo returned to the table and excused her long absence by claiming that she had to contact her father in New York and her faculty advisor in Cambridge.

Marchand nodded but seemed a bit perplexed. Sero said nothing but noted Margo's less than convincing excuse as possibly useful in subsequent conversations with her.

After lunch, Sero led the couple outside to a driveway where instead of saying goodbye, he shocked them by inviting them on a personalized tour of Bangkok in the white Mercedes limousine that awaited Sero's summons, engine and air conditioner running.

The limousine stopped at several particularly elaborate Buddhist Temples so that his guests could appreciate their ornate construction and fine detail. Marchand had never seen such intricate artwork in a place of worship, nor so much gold and precious jewelry as was used to decorate the temples and especially the statues of the Buddha. After an hour of sightseeing, the limousine pulled into the courtyard of the Thai Royal Palace where they were also given a private guided tour. The royal reception for Sero and guests amazed Margo and Marchand. Sero was obviously well-known and respected by guards as well as government functionaries.

Sero was clearly accustomed to the corridors of power all around Bangkok. To Marchand, the most surprising aspect of the Palace reception was the sincere affection shown Sero by even ranking government officials they encountered. After the Palace tour, Palace Guards escorted them back to the limousine where Sero apologized for the absence of a special treat; "I regret that none of the Royal Family was available for an audience today. I had intended to present you and Margo."

"I'm speechless, Rick, I could never have imagined how generous you have been to us," Margo replied. Before entering the limousine, she hugged Sero warmly and said, "This has been such a fabulous day. How can we ever thank you for your time and hospitality?"

But there was more to come. As the gleaming white Benz continued its way through the City towards the Chao Phrya River, Sero, at Margo's prompting, recounted portions of his life story beginning with his birth into an aristocratic Hungarian family shortly after the turn of the century in a castle north of the Pest River near Budapest.

Sero studied at Oxford and the Sorbonne, preparing to eventually take control of the Sero family business and financial empire. But the rapid rise to power of the Nazi regime derailed the gradual process that Count Miklos Gyula Sero had envisioned for his son Ricart. In early 1939, as Hitler prepared to invade Czechoslovakia, Count Sero, having anticipated a long and destructive European war, transferred control of the family's extensive financial and shipping affairs to his son, this very "Rick" Sero, much sooner than he had expected. The Count immediately sent his son to the Far East to manage the family's maritime and banking interests there and hopefully move him out of harm's way before the next Great War began.

343

"How large was your shipping fleet?" Marchand asked.

"Before the War, Sero Maritime Enterprises owned and operated over a hundred fifty ships of a thousand tons or more." Sero replied, his dark eyes twinkling. "But the family's financial holdings in Zurich, Paris and London had far greater value and fortunately, my father had wisely begun to liquidate them before England and France declared war on Germany. With the proceeds of our liquidation plan deposited safely in Switzerland, my father, Count Sero, felt comfortable sending me to China to sell our maritime interests."

"That was an incredibly dangerous period in China. Did you actually travel to Shanghai to close the sale?" Marchand queried.

"I began negotiations for the sale of most of our fleet in Shanghai just as Hitler invaded Czechoslovakia, and by the time the transaction closed, the Nazis had invaded Poland and World War Two had begun in earnest."

"What an amazing story! When did you return to Europe after all that?" Margo asked.

"It was impossible to travel internationally so I spent the remainder of the War years as a refugee in various parts of the Orient. When the War ended with Europe in shambles and the Russians entrenched in Eastern Europe, including my home, Hungary, I felt that my duty was to remain in Shanghai to consolidate the remainder of our business interests throughout Southeast Asia.

"But it was a terribly difficult time for me. The Nazis had executed all of my immediate family during the War. Then, the Soviets finished off the remaining Sero family members after the Iron Curtain fell across Eastern Europe.

"Ironically, my father and I successfully protected most of the five hundred year old Sero estate but at the terrible cost of our family members themselves." Sero said as he dabbed his eyes with a handkerchief.

"Kindly forgive an old man and his memories," Sero said in a melancholy voice.

"No apologies please, Rick. Those memories must be as painful today as they ever were. I know only too well how you feel," Marchand replied while looking deeply into Sero's eyes where Marchand saw the same sense of loss touched with sadness and guilt that had become so familiar to him. It was the "it should have been me" feeling that Sero and he shared.

Sero returned Marchand's gaze and knew that Marchand was a kindred spirit. "Ah yes, Keith, I see that you too have lost loved ones to war's ravages. But we must not linger in this place too long. It is quite dangerous as I'm sure you know. So, let's change the subject before we embark on the final part of our day's journey," Sero said through a sad smile.

Marchand quickly asked, "Rick, why did you remain in Thailand after the War? You could have returned to Europe. You could live elegantly anywhere in the world. Why Thailand?"

"Do you really want me to continue the Sero saga?"

"I wouldn't miss the most interesting part of your story for anything," Margo replied.

Sero nodded and began to describe the final consolidation of the Sero financial empire and his decision to liquidate everything except the remaining ships of Sero Maritime Enterprises, the only part of the family business he had really enjoyed.

"Did you lose many of your ships during the War?" Marchand inquired.

"No, most of our deep water vessels survived the War. But in early 1949, Chaing Kai-shek confiscated most of our larger ships to transport the remnants of his army that had escaped Mao's forces to Taiwan as Mao surrounded Shanghai in 1949. I was so outraged by Chaing's outright theft of my ships in Shanghai that I offered to lease my remaining ships to the fledgling Peoples Republic of China for a pittance."

Margo was stunned to hear about this episode. "Weren't you afraid that Mao would simply confiscate your ships and have you killed?" She asked

"I thought about that possibility but recognized that at some point, every revolution needs a friendly hand. So, I offered mine and Mao's great subaltern, Chou En-lai, accepted my help."

"So, you have been welcome in the People's Republic ever since?" Margo asked.

Avoiding a direct reply, Sero simply said, "My dear friends, you must be bored with Rick Sero's biography by now, not so?"

"Not at all Rick, it's rare to meet a person whose life has been so fascinating. You must finish your story and tell us how you came to live in Bangkok." Margo said sincerely.

Sero hesitated a moment before beginning, "It was Christmas of 1950 and I found myself alone and very depressed in San Francisco. And if one can be blue in San Francisco, one is truly in trouble. So, I decided to continue west after New Year's and complete a trip around the globe, something I had never done before. So, I boarded one of our last ships bound for Hong Kong.

"Once there, I decided to visit French Indochina, especially Vietnam. I was curious to learn whether the French could re-establish their pre-war colonial empire. You see, for years Sero Maritime ships had carried a significant amount of rubber from the Michelin plantations out of the ports of Haiphong, Hue, Manila and Singapore. I wanted to know whether I could recover that business. So I also visited Hanoi, Haiphong and Saigon where I concluded that Ho Chi Minh's Viet Minh guerrillas would soon expel the French from Vietnam making it very risky to resume doing business in Indochina. I continued on to Bangkok before making a final decision.

"I was a house guest of a Thai prince whom I had met and done business with in Shanghai. Prince Bhomibol introduced me to his daughter, Selapha, who has been my wife for almost eighteen years now. She has been the greatest blessing of my life and the reason I have decided to make this peaceful, beautiful land with its warm and handsome people my home."

"Oh, that's so romantic, Rick. I would love to meet Selapha," Margo exclaimed.

Sero winked at Margo as he told her, "You shall meet her quite soon. I see we have arrived at the dock." Sero pointed at a large covered boathouse sandwiched between small shops and restaurants on the Chao Prya River.

VOLUME ONE: PHANTOM WAR TRILOGY

42.

TOO LITTLE,
TOO LATE

As the uproar over President Johnson's announced retirement from politics began to wane, he attempted to bring some order back to the White House. One of the details he suddenly remembered was his recent conversation with FBI Director J. Edgar Hoover. Arriving at the Oval Office early in the morning of April 4, 1968, Johnson was quite upset with himself for not following Hoover's suggestions regarding King's safety. *Here it is damn near a week later and I haven't contacted Martin yet,* he thought. *There's just too damn much to do, too much to worry about. Who in his right mind would want this damn job?* he complained to himself. *This damn War is killin' me and now it threatens my friends.*

Johnson picked up the phone to call his chief of staff with instructions to get Dr. King on the phone. In the six days since Johnson's conversation with Hoover, Johnson had decided to offer King Secret Service protection. Although Johnson disliked Hoover intensely, as had every president since Roosevelt, he did take Hoover's warning seriously and wanted to do whatever he could to protect King, whether or not it was legally appropriate.

Given the personal rejection that Johnson felt as a result of

King's recent anti-war speeches, his concern over King's safety was ironic, if not altogether paradoxical. Johnson frequently wondered why King had taken such a clear stand against the Vietnam War, against *his* war. Now that Johnson had, in effect, tendered his resignation of the Presidency, he understood King's motives and reasons. He realized that King's decisions were morally and ethically justified. And now, Johnson finally recognized that the Vietnamese War should never have been fought. And he, Lyndon B. Johnson, had been the chief architect of the great tragedy. Martin had the courage to speak out, but I lacked the courage to listen.

A few minutes later, Johnson was advised that Dr. King had left Washington for Memphis and could not be reached. "Well, get a message to him as soon as possible that I want to speak to him and that it's quite important. What's he going to Memphis for anyway, do you know?"

"Yes Sir, there's a big civil rights march scheduled in Memphis for April 7th and King intends to lead it."

"In that case, it's urgent that we reach him, so keep trying."

"Yes, Mr. President, we will contact Dr. King with all due haste."

Johnson roared, "No, damn it, not in all due haste. Find him, find Martin NOW. Do you understand me?"

"Yes, Mr. President. I do understand."

Although Johnson was consumed by a thousand vastly important issues, he became increasingly concerned with King's safety. He cursed to himself silently, hell fire, I really should have called Martin while he was here in Washington. Memphis could be damned dangerous if he goes down there to lead a big march and runs into another Bull Connor.

Unfortunately, the White House staff did not have an accurate schedule for Dr. King's movements in Memphis. The White House was still trying to contact King late in the afternoon of April 4th, by which time it was too late.

43.

ROLLIN' ON THE RIVER

On the other side of the world, Marchand and Margo Collins, were enjoying greater Bangkok through the eyes and hospitality of the beguiling Ricart Sero.

Margo and Marchand were escorted to a very large boathouse and then led aboard a luxuriously outfitted motor yacht, sixty feet in length. Sero guided them on a quick tour of the boat and when they returned to the boat's main saloon, a petite, shapely lady wearing a close-fitting, silk sheath dress met them.

The lady's shining black hair was elegantly coifed and she wore a strand of the largest pearls Margo had ever seen. She was perhaps fifteen or twenty years younger than Sero and though in her early to mid-forties, she had lost none of the beauty of her youth. Her features were well-defined, if not almost European, with an almost full mouth and dark eyes. Marchand found her stunningly beautiful.

"Selapha, I'd like you to meet my American friends, Miss Marguerite Collins and Lt. Keith Marchand."

Selapha Sero extended her hand and welcomed her guests. "It is a pleasure to meet you both. Welcome to my country and I hope you shall have a most memorable and pleasant stay."

"Madame Sero, this has been one of the most exciting and romantic trips I have ever taken, thanks in no small part to your gracious husband," Marchand said with a slight bow.

"Yes, he has certainly learned our ways, hasn't he? But then again, I think that Ricart has always been a gracious man," Selapha replied.

Minutes later, the master of the boat gently maneuvered the *Princess Selapha* out of its berth and into the wide Chao Phrya River which ran through the heart of Bangkok south to the Gulf of Thailand. Along the banks of the Chao Phrya and the dozens of minor tributaries and canals that branched from it, thousands of shops, markets and homes protruded into the opaque water, transforming Bangkok into the Venice of the Far East. Shops and homes were raised on pilings a comfortable distance above high tide. Ladders lead to small docks floating at water level. Marchand was astonished by the amount of commerce and activity transacted along the waterways of the magnificent city, as well as the dazzling sights and sounds of life along Bangkok's canals. Sero left them alone to observe river life for nearly an hour before he and Madame Sero joined them on the spacious after deck.

As the Seros were seated, Marchand noticed that the River was widening and becoming more sparsely populated. The boat increased its speed to a comfortable ten knots. "I thought you and Margo might enjoy an afternoon cruise to the mouth of the Chao Phrya on the Gulf of Siam. It's only twenty kilometers or so and the beauty of the river will delight you," Rick offered in his most gracious manner.

"But, Rick, we've already taken so much of your time, you really shouldn't," Margo answered.

"Margo is quite right. We really shouldn't impose upon your

hospitality any further, but how can we decline?" Marchand interrupted having noticed that the cruise was well under way.

"Splendid, we still have so much to talk about," Sero smiled as he spoke.

Given the opportunity, Marchand inquired, "Might I ask you just one more question?"

"Certainly, but try not to make your question too shocking," Sero replied with a laugh.

Marchand paused, determined to phrase his question as diplomatically as possible. "Madame Sero is reason enough for your decision to stay in Bangkok. But why did you cease managing the extensive Sero family holdings and become a restaurateur here in Bangkok?"

"That's a fair question to which there is a long answer. But I will spare you the details. Suffice it to say that I eventually decided to sell all that remained of family business. Running it was a burden that I hadn't asked for nor wanted. It was simply a centuries-old family obligation. And since no other Sero family members survived the War, it was an obligation that no longer existed and the decision that was entirely mine.

"The restaurant is primarily a hobby that allows me to meet and entertain as many international guests as I wish. And I have entertained many fascinating people from Prince of Wales to the Prince of Monaco and Princess Grace. I've served dinner to Clark Gable, John Wayne, Marilyn Monroe and Liz Taylor. I've entertained the Kennedy brothers, the Rockefeller brothers, and even a Pope, and many others too numerous to mention. As a result, I get to dabble in politics, theater and even sports from time to time. What more could a bon vivant and Epicurean like Rick Sero want?"

"Those people have actually dined with you?" Margo asked, her eyes wide and blinking.

"Yes, and a very favorite few have joined Selapha and me on this boat for a leisurely cruise. In fact, Margo, I must tell you this. Your father, Mitchell Collins, has cruised with me several times on this river. Mitchell has been a dear friend and my personal attorney for years. It was he that negotiated and closed the transactions involving the sale of my maritime interests some years ago."

Margo's face blanched and her eyes widened with surprise. "What did you say? My father and you know each other? Why in the world has he not spoken of you? My God, this is unbelievable!"

"I know you're surprised, Margo. I didn't mean to shock you, but I thought that you should know that Mitchell and I have known each other for years. Mitchell called me several days ago to tell me that you were coming to Bangkok. He asked me to extend my hospitality to you and your gentleman friend during your stay. And for reasons of his own, he preferred to remain in the background. But after thinking it over, I concluded that you should know of the relationship and history that your father and I share. It would not be fair to you to do otherwise."

Margo was completely flustered by this news. She thought she had met Sero by chance, while she waited for the contact that never showed up. What was going on here? How could she explain her consternation to Keith?

Although Mitchell Collins had kept close watch over Margo for years, especially since her mother's death, Margo had grown quite resentful of his constant meddling in her life.. She was frequently angered by her father's ever watchful eye. In fact, Mitch Collins' intrusion into his daughter's life had become almost a constant irritant between them. Upon hearing Sero's comments, all those issues came to a boiling point again. Margo stood and walked to the boat railing, then turned. She expressed her exasperation vigorously to all within earshot.

"Rick, I am quite tired of my father's intrusion into my private life and affairs. I truly don't want to ruin this lovely trip and it's obvious that you have gone quite out of your way to be a gracious host. But I'm really angry that my father would interfere like this. Would you kindly excuse me, I'd like to go below to the powder room for a few minutes."

Sero had anticipated Margo's reaction but not her intensity. He attempted to ameliorate the impact of his disclosure. "Dear Margo," Sero intoned most empathetically. "Please forgive your father for loving you too much. And, forgive me for my lack of sensitivity in bringing all this up."

Margo suddenly suspected that her father knew the people who were watching her. As she stood to leave the main deck, Margo seemed ready to cry but she would not allow herself to display such emotion. She simply replied, "No forgiveness required, Rick, you are a perfect gentleman in every respect. Please, let's enjoy this wonderful afternoon and this lovely boat trip. I'll be back in a moment."

Marchand asked whether he should join her below. As she descended the stairwell, she politely declined.

A few moments later, Sero left the main deck, ostensibly to check something on the bridge. Instead he waited in the main saloon for Margo to reappear. He motioned for her to join him on one of the luxurious leather settees. "Margo, I want to talk to you before you leave Bangkok, talk to you alone. Is that possible?"

Margo had regained her composure but Sero's question again took her off balance. "Rick, I'll certainly meet you if you wish but why, and most of all, why alone?"

Sero looked into her eyes with a penetrating, almost frightening stare. "Margo," he paused and took a deep breath. "I know that you've been into China, all the way to Shanghai, in fact. I also know the officials who have helped you make both trips past the border.

"Both you and I know just how dangerous these trips have been and we both know why you made them. I haven't shared this information with your father and for obvious reasons I wouldn't inform your young Navy friend. But, there are some issues that we must discuss before you attempt to go into China again, or to carry any information from them anywhere in the world, both for reasons of your personal safety -- and even more importantly -- for the success of your efforts inside the People's Republic."

For the second time that afternoon, Margo was shocked to the core.

"Rick, I thought we were getting to know you after you shared your beautiful and tragic family history with us today. But now I must ask you: Who are the hell are you and what do you want with me? Or perhaps I should say, with Keith and me?"

"Everything I told you and Keith both yesterday and today is true, Margo. As you suspect, there is more to the story. There always is. But you must remember several things. First, I'm on your side. Second, I know everything that you're attempting to do in the People's Republic of China and in Hong Kong. I know all about the people you are working with. I will protect you and your activities from everyone who has no need or right to know and that includes your father and Keith. But, Margo, you must trust me for you are swimming in very deep water, deeper than you know. Am I very clear?"

"Rick, I do understand and accept your assistance. But your comments are shocking. It's terribly confusing and disturbing that you know so much about me and what I'm doing. I need some time to think all of this over. Frankly, it's not clear to me that I should trust you."

"I know, Margo. Take time to think about our conversation, then call me to schedule a rendezvous before you return to the States."

After he and Margo returned to the main deck, Sero used all his charms to recreate the bonhomie of the afternoon for his guests and after a time he seemed to have succeeded. Then, he went below to ensure that all was well with the boat and its crew. When he returned to the afterdeck fifteen minutes later, Sero's face had clouded over noticeably.

Noticing the change, Marchand inquired whether anything was amiss.

"I have some important news to share with you." Sero said with a somewhat solemn look.

"What's that, Rick?" Marchand asked.

"A few minutes ago, I went below to check the radio telephone for messages. My business manager told me that Dr. Martin Luther King was assassinated just a few hours ago. Black ghettos of the major cities all over the United States have erupted in rioting and violence. America, it would appear, is beginning to come apart at its very seams."

Marchand stared at Sero and then Margo before exclaiming, "What the hell are we fighting for half way around the globe while America seems to be on the verge of a revolution?"

Margo looked at Rick who clearly had no answer for Marchand. The three sat in virtual silence as the sleek white yacht motored quietly past the green mansions bordering the Chao Phrya River.

On the morning of April 7th at Bangkok International Airport, Marchand watched silently at the departure gate as the Pan Am 707 taxied slowly toward the runway. Margo's fragrance lingered with him.

He could still feel her embrace and taste the salt of her tears that he had kissed away as they parted only moments ago.

"Remember," she had whispered as she kissed him goodbye, "I promise to meet your ship when it returns to San Diego."

"Yes, and I promise to visit you in New York and meet your father," he replied.

"Have a safe flight back to your ship," she said, knowing that safety for them was just an illusion.

"You bet," he promised.

"Oh, Keith, I'm trying so hard not to cry but I can't help it. This week with you has been so intensely beautiful and now it will be months until I see you again. I feel my heart is breaking. Please be careful, please," she begged. "Please, please please."

"Of course, I will, Margo. Just keep writing me. Your letters are all I have of the world outside the Ship."

"And, please, at least consider what we talked about," Margo said, referring to her suggestion that Keith resign from the Naval Aviation.

"I'll think about it, Margo, but you know how I feel."

"I won't pressure you. Just think about it, that's all," she pleaded gently as she tearfully kissed him goodbye.

Now, standing at the departure gate, Marchand remembered his shock at Margo's question to him during their last evening together. "Isn't there any way you could stop flying, Keith? Couldn't you just turn in your wings or request a reassignment or something, anything to get out of this stupid War before you're killed?" Her words remained in his mind as if they had just been spoken. So did his reply.

"There's no way I could do that, Margo. I've sworn to follow orders, like them or not, and that includes flying in Vietnam. Besides, everyone will think that I've lost my nerve, that I'm a coward. There's just no way I could do that."

She had answered slowly and deliberately, "But, Keith, ... isn't that what you told me ... that your friend Rich Miller said to you just before he was killed?"

Marchand had nearly choked. Margo had hit home far too hard. When he could respond, he said, "Margo, there's just no way I would ever turn in my wings. And, remember that President Johnson has now declared a partial bombing halt in North Vietnam. That should increase the odds of my coming home quite substantially. So, don't worry. Really. I'll be O.K. I promise you."

Margo had taken his hand and looked him squarely in the eye. "I've fallen in love with you, Keith. Don't break my heart."

VOLUME ONE: PHANTOM WAR TRILOGY

44.

STEEL TIGER

April weather in Southeast Asia was dominated by late monsoon rains that transform the landmass to muddy quagmire and fill the skies from the ground to forty thousand feet with an enormous cumulo-nimbus cloud cover. On such days, Air Force and Navy fighter-bombers were generally restricted to high level, radar-guided, bomb runs in Laos and northern South Vietnam. Air Strikes into North Vietnam were authorized only in the southern-most sector after March 31, 1968 when Johnson announced a halt to all American bombing north of the 19th parallel.

Tactical bombing strikes in Laos, known under Defense of Department code name "Operation Steel Tiger" were intended to disrupt the heavy and continuous flow of men and munitions along Route 1A from North Vietnam through central Laos and into South Vietnam. Steel Tiger rained thousands of five-hundred and one-thousand pound bombs along the myriad trails, muddy roads and footpaths that the North Vietnamese used to infiltrate the South. All these roads and trails were known collectively as the "Ho Chi Minh Trail".

Steel Tiger's big brother was Operation "Arc Light" flown by Air Force B-52 bombers staged out of Kadena Air Force Base in

Okinawa. Whereas a flight of two to four Air Force or Navy Phantoms could deliver five to ten tons of bombs on target, one Arc Light B-52 mission could rain twenty tons of high explosive, general demolition bombs, or ten times that much if the number of bombers was increased proportionately.

The combined effect of Operations Steel Tiger and Arc Light, especially on the North Vietnamese Army, was devastating. Only the incredible tenacity of the North Vietnamese foot soldier and the unwavering will of Ho Chi Minh kept the movement of men and supplies going. When the grim statistics of the War were finally compiled, they clearly showed that Steel Tiger and Arc Light had been extraordinarily deadly and effective. Of the more than two million North Vietnamese killed during the War, at least half were killed along Ho Chi Minh Trail on their way from North to South Vietnam. Only God truly knows how many Vietnamese were maimed and wounded while making the bloody trek and how many were driven mad by the incessant pounding of bombs dropped along their route by American bombers.

Oddly enough, Steel Tiger was, for the pilots and crewmembers, rather boring. Dropping bombs from thirty thousand feet was about as exciting to a fighter pilot as flying instrument approaches on a sunny afternoon at Naval Air Station Miramar in San Diego. Radar guided computers directed flight crews to make single-digit heading corrections and ten-foot altitude changes. Any United Air Lines pilot could have easily performed the same mission. It was no job for a fighter pilot.

Now, boring was just fine for Marchand whose personal mission was to return to California safe and sound when the *Constellation's* combat cruise ended. If some North Vietnamese Army regulars were killed in the interim, so much the better. But even during monsoon season, the skies over Laos or Vietnam would occasionally clear so that heavily armed fighter and attack bombers could launch from the *Constellation* to fly dangerous close air support missions. These flights would rendezvous with an Air Force forward air control aircraft to conduct low altitude strikes against trucks, tanks, bicycles, men and munitions snaking their way through the jungle. North Vietnamese troops frequently used water buffalo or elephants to carry rockets, mortars and small arms to the South. These beasts also became casualties of War.

Working with forward air controllers on low altitude strikes near Khe Sanh was definitely not of the boring variety missions. Often the flights encountered heavy anti-aircraft fire from thirty-seven millimeter radar controlled canons and deadly twenty-three millimeter rapid-fire artillery, known as ZPUs. On April 10, 1968, Marchand and Drummond flew the last daylight strike flight of the day from the *Constellation*. It was a Steel Tiger mission into intensely active part of the Ho Chi Minh trail in Laos. The flight leader was the squadron's new Operations Officer, Lieutenant Commander Mark "the Deacon" Tanner and his weapons officer, Bart "the Greek" Andros.

Each aircraft carried ten Mark 82, five hundred pound, general demolition bombs. The flight arrived in the target area late in the afternoon and quickly joined up with their Forward Air Controller flying an F-100D Super Saber, the Air Force's first supersonic fighter. The Air Force had replaced most of the propeller-driven aircraft used for FAC missions with F-100s to give the FAC pilots greater range, speed and, most of all, survivability. FAC pilots flying the small prop driven O-1s and O-2s suffered an extremely high mortality rate.

As Andros guided the flight to its rendezvous with the FAC, Marchand surveyed the area and saw only the jungle canopy stretching toward the horizon and towering more than a hundred feet above the ground. He keyed his intercom, "There ain't nothin' but trees down there, Kelly. I guess we're here to make toothpicks again."

"Just because we don't see 'em, doesn't mean they aren't there, Rocketman," Drummond replied.

"Yeah, I suppose you're right. Still, I don't get no satisfaction from destroying a stand of virgin timber."

"Some of those trees aren't trees. Take my word for it."

While orbiting twenty-five hundred feet above the FAC aircraft, the Phantom pilots set their weapons panels for the number of desired bombing runs and waited for the FAC pilot to mark a target with a white phosphorus rocket. Shortly after rendezvous, the F-100 fired a marker rocket into an area of unbroken forest canopy that looked just like any other amorphous parcel of jungle real estate. When Marchand saw the dense cloud of white smoke, he keyed the intercom, "So, what did I tell ya, we're gonna make more toothpicks in the jungle?"

"We'll see, Rocketman."

What neither Drummond nor anyone else in the Checkmate flight knew was that nearly an entire division of North Vietnamese Army regulars were moving along the hidden, muddy roads below. They drove trucks and pushed bicycles laden with mortar rounds, one hundred twenty-millimeter rockets and thousands of machine guns, AK-47s and millions of rounds of ammunition, all of it meant for the siege of the U.S. Marines at Khe Sanh. They also carried tens of thousands of rounds for the three ZPU-23 rapid firing anti-aircraft artillery pieces that accompanied them.

The NVA regulars felt relatively safe from low level attacks since they were almost completely hidden from airborne surveillance. They continued moving slowly, almost imperceptibly through the dense jungle growth with little concern for the fighter-bombers circling overhead. As a precaution, however, the NVA major who commanded the division, had stationed three, heavily camouflaged ZPUs in partial clearings with orders to open fire only if the passing column was seriously attacked.

Only the F-100 pilot and co-pilot knew the entire score of the unfolding scenario referred to in Top Secret communications as "Operation Dump Truck". Their aircraft was equipped with sensitive, super-secret radio receivers tuned to a special frequency used by small transmitters dropped days earlier by U.S. reconnaissance aircraft. These transmitters, roughly the size and shape of artificial fireplace logs, had been attached to small parachutes that released them as they struck the jungle canopy.

Stuck in the ground or hanging in the tree canopy, the secret radios transmitted the sounds of troop movements through the undergrowth. Occasionally, human voices could also be heard over the discrete radio frequencies monitored by Air Force and Central Intelligence Agency aircraft. FAC pilots could pinpoint these transmitters with special receivers and mark enemy activity with their white phosphorus rockets.

Marchand perked up when the Air Force FAC pilot transmitted, "Checkmate Flight, this is Misty Two-Zero, I'm rolling in with a second Willie Pete. Align your runs along the axis between the two marker rockets and drop in pairs. Say again number and type of ordnance."

Tanner answered, "Misty Two-Zero, this is Checkmate Leader, we have ten Mark 82s on each aircraft."

"Roger, Checkmate, how much play time can you give me?"

Tanner replied, "We can give you twenty minutes on target, five runs for each aircraft plus ten minutes loiter time."

"Roger, Checkmate, give me a few seconds to scoot out of the way and you are cleared in hot. Give me two runs each, then hold in your pattern for further directions. How copy, over."

"Misty Two-Zero, Checkmate copies loud and clear. We'll give you thirty seconds before commencing our runs." Tanner carefully aligned his aircraft's heading along the line bisecting the two marker rockets after a quick climb to eight thousand feet. On the home stretch of a racetrack pattern, he snapped his control stick hard to the left, rolling the Phantom inverted, then hauled the stick back into his lap. Inverted, he watched the horizon slide from view and the jungle fill his field of vision. When his dive angle reached forty degrees, Bart Andros called him to hold the angle and roll upright.

The Misty pilot, flying at treetop level about a kilometer from the target area, watched Tanner's Phantom as it climbed, rolled upside down and entered a steep dive. Sunlight glistened from the Phantom's aluminum wings as it streaked down toward the unbroken jungle. Midway in the dive, the Misty pilot keyed his intercom and said to his co-pilot, "I like workin' with these Navy guys, they really know how to put their bombs down the ol' pickle barrel."

"Yeah, these guys aren't afraid to get down here in the trees with us. He sure looks pretty in that dive with the sunlight comin' off his wings," the co-pilot said.

Finessing the run with small movements of stick and rudder tweaked by minute power adjustments, Tanner placed the pipper of his gun sight precisely on the spot marked by the first white phosphorus rocket. When the Greek called "Mark" from the back seat, Tanner squeezed the trigger on the control stick, releasing two five-hundred pound bombs at exactly five thousand feet above ground level. As soon as he felt the thump of the explosive charges kick the bombs away from the aircraft, Tanner pulled the stick sharply back, bringing the Phantom out of its steep dive.

Tanner and Andros strained against the force of five Gs that drove them down into their ejection seats as the Phantom strained against five times gravity's pull to come out of its dive. G-suits inflated, squeezing their legs, thighs and abdomens hard, forcing blood back toward their brains to prevent a black out. The Phantom bottomed its dive at three thousand feet above the jungle floor and began to climb back to altitude.

Two bombs sped down to the jungle then disappeared in a burst of flame, smoke and debris. One of the bombs exploded less than twenty feet from a truck laden with mortar rounds and anti-personnel mines causing the cargo to erupt in a continuing miasma of fire and steel. The truck's secondary explosions decimated thirty army troops pushing bicycles laden with rocket-propelled grenades; these, too, began to explode causing further casualties.

The gunners manning the ZPU opened fire immediately at the attacking aircraft. Tracer rounds from the twenty-three millimeter anti-aircraft artillery canon streamed up from three different locations on the jungle floor in a furious attempt to exact revenge for the deadly bombing raid. The Misty pilot transmitted, "Oh boy, you guys have stirred up a real hornets nest down there. We got secondary explosions galore! Those NVA must have been carrying a real arsenal. I guess you can see the ZPU fire. Hot damn, are they are pissed! Keep jinking on your climb out."

Tanner replied, "Yeah, Misty, we got their attention and here comes my wingman."

Drummond decided to take out the ZPU that was directing the heaviest and most accurate fire at Checkmate One as it climbed back to altitude. He rolled into his dive and placed the source of the AAA muzzle flashes directly in his gun sight. "Make this a good one, Keith. I want to nail this goddamn ZPU."

"Roger, we'll get this SOB before he gets one of us. You're shallow, push it over about five degrees," Marchand replied. Seconds later he called over the intercom's hot mike, "We're slow, give it some more power. OK, standby... standby... Mark, Mark."

Drummond squeezed his trigger and felt the bombs release as he hauled back on the stick. The Phantom began to pull out of its dive as the ZPU directed its fire closer and closer to the lead fighter. The FAC pilot called over the radio, "Checkmate Leader, you're taking some serious fire at your six. Better put some heavy jinking in your flight plan about now."

Tanner wasted no time after hearing the warning. He pushed his throttles to military power and wrapped the stick hard to his left, then quickly back to the right and back left again in an effort to throw the NVA gunner off target. Still the gunner kept the Phantom close in his sights as the tracers from the four gun barrels streaked out toward their target. But suddenly Drummond's two bombs detonated less than fifty feet from the menacing ZPU. The entire gun carriage flew twenty feet in the air sending its crew flying into the trees in pieces. NVA troops pushing bicycles dropped them along the roadway and ran for the closest tunnel entrances they could find to escape the exploding bombs and secondary fires from the rockets and mortars they carried. Troops driving trucks that were still running jumped from the cabs to join their comrades heading for the safety of the tunnels dug all along the roadway.

"Nice run, Checkmate Two, scratch one ZPU. I like working with you guys," The Misty pilot called over his radio.

"Roger, Misty, thanks but we still got two of those mothers hosing us down," Drummond transmitted.

At that moment, Tanner was setting up for his second dive run. He reached down to adjust his weapons panel so that it would release his remaining eight bombs on his next run. He keyed his radio transmitter button, "Checkmate Two, we got good secondaries so let's give 'em the whole enchilada this time. Drop everything on your next run. I'm going after one of the ZPUs that's still active.

"Checkmate Two, roger, this will be our last run. Misty, you're picking up some heavy fire, you might want to move down range a bit."

Tanner looked through his gun sight and fixed the source of the tracers right under the sight's pipper. He actually saw muzzle flashes as the ZPU sprayed red-hot, high-explosive shells at the Misty F-100, flying only two hundred feet above the tree tops. Tanner couldn't see his bombs fall but knew that they were well placed as he pulled out of the dive run. Climbing out, he heard the FAC report. "Check Leader, I think you got another ZPU. There's no more fire from the area where your bombs hit and it looks like there's some secondary fires from your run. I'll take a closer look as soon as your wingman comes off target."

Drummond decided to place his bombs toward the end of the target area, hoping to destroy any straggling trucks that couldn't pass the burning convoy. The bombs from his aircraft walked up the trail to the last four trucks of the convoy setting off a series of explosions from the load of twenty-three millimeter ammunition and mortar shells they carried. The convoy commander jumped from the truck he was driving and watched the ammunition his men had so laboriously carried hundreds of miles down the Ho Chi Minh trail explode, killing many of his own men. The NVA major ran to the remaining undamaged ZPU and took command of it himself. He knew that the low flying aircraft had somehow spotted his convoy and all but destroyed it, but he was determined to make the spotter pilot pay. He directed the ZPUs fire with the skill he had learned during five years as an anti-aircraft gunner before taking his present command. He carefully calculated the lead required to bracket the F-100 in the ZPU's deadly two thousand round per minute fire and he kept the barrels going long after he should have stopped firing, knowing that the barrels would probably melt. But he did not care. He wanted to kill the damn Yankee pilot.

On Misty's next pass over the ZPU, the NVA major directed deadly fire that tore through the F-100's engine bay, cutting hydraulic lines and an oil supply line. Shrapnel also sliced through the rear cockpit, hitting the co-pilot in both legs, chest and right arm. Blood splattered from multiple wounds nearly painting the aircraft's canopy crimson. The Misty pilot roared over the radio, "Mayday, mayday, mayday; this is Misty Two Zero. I'm hit, co-pilot unconscious. Need your help, Checkmate."

Tanner immediately aborted his dive run and jettisoned his bombs. He answered the distress call. "Misty, this is Checkmate Leader, I'll join up on your port wing. Once I'm aboard, slide back to a loose right echelon and I'll lead us back to Da Nang. We'll give you a damage report as soon as possible."

Tanner transmitted again, "Checkmate Two, abort your last run, jettison remaining ordnance and join up as a loose number three. Give Misty the best damage report you can."

"Check Leader, Misty copies your last. Give me a steer to home plate."

"Steer zero one two zero, Misty. I'll be aboard in ten seconds. Checkmate Two, where are you?"

"Check Two in a two mile trail, closing fast," Drummond replied.

"Check Leader, Misty is steering to home plate. I'm losing fuel from my port wing tank. Are you aboard yet?"

"Misty, Check Leader is aboard on your port wing. Are you hit, too?"

"Negative, but I think my co-pilot is in bad shape."

When the FAC's radio transmission ended, Air Traffic Control Center at Da Nang came on the air. "Misty Two Zero, Da Nang Center copies your mayday. State your position and squawk mode seven, seven, zero, zero, over."

"Da Nang Center, Misty Two Zero is on three zero zero radial from Channel One Zero Niner, climbing through eight thousand, squawking seven seven zero zero. Center, I'm busy trying to keep this machine in the air. I'm on Checkmate Leader's wing. He's got the lead. I'll talk to you when I have to, over."

"Misty Two Zero, copy your last, we have you on radar; Jolly Green has been launched and is on intercept heading.

"Checkmate One this is Da Nang Center, understand you have the lead. How do you copy, over?"

Tanner answered, "Da Nang Center, Checkmate One, copies your last, give us a steer to Da Nang, over."

"Checkmate One, your heading to Da Nang is one two five zero degrees at one three five miles. Jolly Green is niner five miles from you and on an intercept heading. Climb and maintain Angels one three, if you can. Do not acknowledge further transmissions unless requested."

The Misty pilot struggled to maintain control of his crippled aircraft, the left wing of which was badly damaged. He trimmed his rudder full right and still had to use almost full right rudder pedal to maintain straight and level flight. With his engine at full military power setting, the F-100 could only climb a thousand feet per minute as a result of damage to the wing and flight controls. He dared not use his engine's afterburner for fear of starting a disastrous fire from the raw fuel and vapor streaming from its left wing. With one hydraulic system out of commission, the control stick became mushy and non-responsive. Despite all these problems, the highly skilled Air Force pilot managed to climb to thirteen thousand feet and maintain his heading.

As the Misty pilot leveled off at his cruising altitude for the short flight to Da Nang Air Base, Da Nang Air Traffic Control Center radio reported. "Checkmate Flight, you are seven zero miles out, maintain heading and altitude. Jolly Green is three miles from rendezvous."

Tanner keyed his transmitter, "Roger, Da Nang Center, Jolly Green is three miles out. Misty, this is Checkmate Leader, you're still streaming fuel, can you make home plate?"

"Checkmate, this is Misty; my left wing tank is almost empty, wing transfer pumps are inoperable, but I've got enough gas to get home if the leak doesn't get worse. My PC-1 hydraulics are gone, PC-2 fluctuating slightly, stick is mushy. Give me a close up inspection, Checkmate Two. I need to know just how bad I'm shot up."

"Misty, this is Check Two; hold it as steady as you can and I'll get in real close." Drummond answered then moved as near to the F-100 as he dared. He called Marchand over the intercom's hot mike, "Keith, look him over. I want to concentrate on his movement. He seems a little shaky. Don't want no fuckin' midair."

"I got him covered, Kelly, you just keep us out of harm's way."

Drummond pulled within ten feet of the damaged fighter and began to maneuver around it. His eyes focused intensely on the relative motion between the two aircraft and the movement of the F-100's flight control surfaces. Marchand inspected the Super Saber for battle damage, holes, loose or torn metal, hotspots, blackened aluminum and streaming fluids or vapors. As Drummond slowly eased their Phantom beneath the

FAC aircraft, Marchand observed substantial battle damage to the left wing and fuselage of the crippled fighter, complete with torn and jagged metal and gaping holes. Then he spotted the really serious trouble, a pencil-thin line of red fluid trailing from the bottom of the engine bay. He keyed his radio, "Misty, this is Checkmate Two, you got a lot of battle damage to your left wing and area around the engine bay and you have hydraulic fluid leaking; it's coming from some shrapnel holes near the engine."

"Roger, Check Two, that's consistent with my gauges and stick feel. I just need this baby to hold together another six or seven minutes. I don't know if she will, though."

Marchand's report was interrupted by a call from the U.S. Air controller for the area, "Checkmate Leader, this is Da Nang Center, you are four six miles from home plate. Come starboard three degrees to heading one two eight, maintain Angels thirteen, continue squawking seven seven zero zero. You should have Jolly Green Four Two in sight within one minute. Switch to Da Nang Approach Control on frequency two two five point niner. And – good luck, gentlemen."

"Checkmate Leader, copy. Switching to Da Nang Approach," Tanner transmitted in reply. Bart Andros then reported radar contact with the lumbering CH-46 rescue helicopter, call sign "Jolly Green Giant"

"Deacon, I've got the Jolly Green, two o'clock low at four miles; he's down on the deck."

"Thank God we don't need him yet, but we sure as hell can't slow down for him either. I'll have him follow us in."

Tanner then called the rescue helicopter, "Jolly Green Four Two, this is Checkmate Leader, on Guard, we have you on radar at four miles, do a quick one eighty and follow us to Home Plate. We may need your help."

The helicopter pilot looked up and to the left of his windscreen and saw the exhaust smoke trails from the Phantom's engines, "Checkmate, this is Jolly Green Four Two, Tally ho. We see your smoke. Turning back to Home Plate in trail. We'll stay down here at Angels three and monitor you on Da Nang Approach. Just holler if you need us."

When the flight was twenty miles from Da Nang, Tanner reduced power and began a three thousand foot per minute descent to remain out of small arms fire for as long as possible. He noticed that the F-100 pilot was having increasingly difficulty maintaining control of his aircraft so he called and asked, "Misty, are you losing pressure on your good Control System?"

"Affirmative, Checkmate, I'm showing about fifty percent pressure on PC-1; my PC-2 is dead. Control stick is really mushy now. Utility hydraulic system pressure is down, too. I hope I won't have problems dropping my gear and flaps."

"Roger, Misty, how's your back seat man?"

"He's still unconscious but alive. I hear him groan on hot mike now and then."

"Misty, do you have a command ejection system?"

"Negative, there is no command ejection on this model F-100."

"Copy, Misty, you'll make it home OK," Tanner transmitted.

Three miles from the approach end of Da Nang's active runway, the two Phantoms escorting the damaged F-100 prepared for landing, slowing to approach speed of one hundred fifty knots. The FAC pilot had just enough hydraulic fluid in his utility system to lower flaps and landing gear. Two miles from touchdown, Tanner called the FAC pilot, "Misty, I'll stay with you until we have the numbers in sight. Jolly Green is about five miles behind us and the tower will launch additional SAR helos, if necessary.

"God be with you, Misty." Then Tanner transmitted, "Checkmate Two, break off and make a separate approach. See you on the Marine Corps line."

Drummond answered, "Checkmate Two, roger, switching to tower frequency." At the midway point of the active runway, he banked hard left, pulled his throttles back and pushed the landing gear handle down, executing a perfect Navy entry into the Da Nang airbase landing pattern. On the intercom, he said, "Misty's got his hands full; I wonder if he has enough hydraulic power to land that sucker. Think he should punch out?"

"He can't; his co-pilot is still alive and can't eject himself. Pilot's gotta stay with him."

"Damn, with all the trouble Misty's having, I forgot that his co-pilot is out of commission."

Just then the Tower Controller called, "Phantom in the break, climb back to two thousand feet and do a three sixty while we handle the F-100 on emergency final." Now, Drummond and Marchand were in a perfect position to watch the heroic Misty pilot on his final approach. Both said silent prayers for him and his co-pilot.

Inside the F-100 cockpit, the pilot fought mightily with his increasingly unresponsive control stick and rudder pedals. He alternately cursed and prayed as he nursed the crippled fighter home. He was barely able to maintain directional control with his rudders but the ailerons that controlled the aircraft's rolling motion seemed nearly ineffective. He used every ounce of skill accumulated during five thousand hours of flight time to keep the aircraft level and lined up with the runway's centerline. As his aircraft passed over the runway numbers, the pilot still had the plane under control with less than two seconds to touchdown.

Suddenly, a gust of wind on the fighter's left side caused it to roll to the right and veer towards the right of the runway. Normally, an experienced pilot would instinctively correct for the wind gust by quickly moving the stick to the left and adding pressure to the right rudder pedal. But the Misty pilot had unfortunately used every bit of aileron and trim control to maintain straight and level flight. The power control hydraulic system had lost so much fluid that the ailerons and spoilers on the left side of the aircraft failed to respond to the pilot's control input and the aircraft continued to roll to the right.

Marchand and Drummond watched helplessly from two thousand feet as the Super Saber's right wing dropped and struck the runway creating a shower of sparks. Immediately, the aircraft began to cartwheel down the runway. It traveled no more than three hundred feet before exploding in an enormous ball of orange white flame. The pilot had no time to eject. The co-pilot never regained consciousness.

Marchand and Drummond choked back the bitter taste of anger and sadness and blinked fast to clear their eyes. The North Vietnamese Army Major somewhere in the endless jungles of Laos had done his part to even the battle score.

45.

DISTINGUISHED
FLYING CROSS

On April 22, 1968, all of Fighter Squadron Twenty One's officers and most of its enlisted men were on the flight deck of the *Constellation* when Lieutenant Commander Frank Warden and Lieutenant junior grade Phillip Winslow were carried up to the deck on stretchers from the ship's hospital. The wounds they had received at the end of the previous line period had healed sufficiently to allow their transfer back to San Diego where they could undergo extensive reconstructive surgery and physical therapy. Commander Jack McGruder, squadron commanding officer, shook hands with the injured fliers then saluted them both. The officers and men cheered as Warden and Winslow were carried to a waiting C-2 Greyhound cargo aircraft to be flown to the naval hospital at Yokusuka, Japan for more intensive medical treatment than was available on board the *Connie*. After several weeks in Yokusuka, they would be flown back to the States for convalescence and rehabilitation.

Just as the two airmen were being loaded aboard the C-2, the Air Boss, Commander Bill Scott roared over the flight deck bullhorn. "We're going to miss you guys, on behalf of all the men of the *Connie*, we wish you Godspeed going home and a quick recovery once you've arrived."

Scott's voice carried the good will and powerful emotion of the entire five thousand man crew of the *U.S.S. Constellation,* CVA-64.

Unexpectedly, Captain David Townsend, Commanding Officer of the *Constellation,* walked onto the flight deck and over to the C-2. He stopped the stretchers, spoke in a low, barely audible voice to Warden and Winslow then saluted both of them. A wave of intense pathos washed over those standing on the flight deck; its warm salty spray could be seen in more than a few eyes and sunburned cheeks.

When the gathered crew had dissipated, Marchand climbed aboard the plane. He approached Warden and Winslow slowly then embraced them both gently. He didn't try to hide the moisture that kept filling his eyes. "Pretty dumb ass way for you two bastards to get out of the rest of the cruise," he said, voice cracking.

"Yeah, especially dumb when you think that the cruise is almost over," Winslow said.

"You guys take care of yourselves, will ya? You're both so damn accident prone."

"Hey, Marchand, we're going home a little worse for the wear but we're going home. You be careful and bring your tall butt home, too," Warden said with as much humor as he could muster.

"You bet, guys. See you when I see you," Marchand said as he turned to leave the plane.

Warden stopped him. "Marchand, thanks. I owe you one," he said.

"Who told you that?"

"The Skipper told me all that you and Warden did to get my butt out of that sampan. Thanks again."

"No sweat, Frank. Can I use your derringer 'til you get back?"

"It's all yours, Rocketman. Take good care of it."

The same cargo aircraft that departed with Warden and Winslow on board had earlier brought the ship's mail. Marchand received a letter from Margo that he waited to open until he reached the privacy of his stateroom. Now that Winslow was on his way to Japan, Marchand's privacy was assured. His pulse raced as he eagerly read the letter.

My Dearest Keith,

I'm leaving Hong Kong today. My research here is complete so I really can't delay any longer. But frankly, my Darling, if there were the slightest chance for me to see you again here in the Orient, I would stay and everyone else be damned.

Guess what, Sweetheart? Yesterday I managed to deliver a letter to representatives of the Chinese government here in Hong Kong who promised to relay it to Vice Premier Chou-En-lai. (Don't ask me how I did it and I won't fib to you.) I've asked for a visa to visit Peking and an interview with government officials concerning educational and cultural affairs. I hinted that I'd like to inquire about the possibility of normalizing relations between the U.S. and the Peoples Republic and that I have important State Department connections in that regard. So much of what I've learned here convinces me that Premier Chou and possibly even Chairman Mao are seriously considering a rapprochement with the U.S. I want to be there when it happens. In fact, I want to be part of the process, if at all possible.

I know you think this all sounds absolutely preposterous. Do you remember how you laughed when I told you that I would visit China within the next two years? Well, Mr. Marchand, I may well get the last laugh -- and sooner rather than later! In the meantime, not a word of this to anyone, please.

Father wants to meet you when you return. He's even suggested that you visit us in New York this summer. I was shocked. He must suspect something. Actually, he didn't approve of you at all when I mentioned that you flew fighters. I forgot the expletive he used. But since he was a Navy officer during World War II, he couldn't be too harsh with you. However, he did say that aviators, particularly ones that fly fighters, tend to be irresponsible and excessive womanizers. (I didn't tell him how I met you.)

Dear Old Dad has been full of surprises lately. Upon recovering his composure after I scolded him about interfering with our rendezvous in Bangkok, he confessed that he's actually known Rick Sero for years. He apologized for not telling me in advance and asking Rick to keep an eye on us. He admitted to closing a number of major transactions for Rick shortly after he made partner at his law firm. He thinks the world of Rick and said that he would call to thank him for being so gracious to his daughter. What a strange situation.

My Dear One, need I tell you how I miss you? Yes, of course, I do. I miss your sweet, soft lips and your strong arms. I miss your smile and your hard flat tummy. I miss your laugh and the taste of salt on your skin after we've made love. I miss looking at your beautiful face while you sleep and running my fingers through your tousled hair as you awake.

I miss you so much I ache all over. I love you. Dear God in heaven, please watch over my beloved man. Hurry home soon.

Yours always,
Margo

Marchand finished reading the letter for the third time and inhaling its fragrance when his phone rang. It was Commander McGruder.

"Yes, Skipper, I'll be down to your stateroom on the double, Sir." Marchand hung up the phone somewhat puzzled, left his room and headed down the long passageway to senior officer country. I wonder if he wants to play chess, Marchand mused. He rapped on the door and waited. McGruder was smiling when he welcomed him in. "Make yourself comfortable, Marchand. Would you like a cold beer?" McGruder said as he opened his refrigerator and took out a bottle of Heineken for himself.

Marchand suppressed his surprise at seeing the squadron commanding officer drink openly aboard ship. "No thank you, Sir. I just finished one."

McGruder chuckled, "That's one reason I like you, Marchand. You think quickly. You've got a first-rate mind. You're a good officer - conscientious, responsible, disciplined - a good aviator too. You did a damned fine job in that search and rescue of Warden and Winslow. Your quick thinking probably saved Warden from being captured and you zapped that PT boat. A damned fine job all the way."

"Thank you very much, Skipper," Marchand said somewhat self-consciously.

"But you know, Marchand, there's one thing you're going to have to watch."

"What's that, Sir?"

"It's no secret what you think about the War. I know you think that it's ill conceived and poorly executed. You probably think it's irrational and unjustified as well. Of course, you're entitled to think all that if you wish. Hell, I'm not too pleased about a lot of it myself, like the insignificant targets we're assigned and the losses we sustain in taking them out. It's not like Korea where we had really substantial targets that would allow us to justify a lost pilot. We've all got our gripes, Marchand. Every soldier and every sailor from time immemorial has had his gripes. We may have a few more than usual with Vietnam.

"But, Marchand, you'll have to keep your thoughts and gripes more private. It's not doing squadron morale any good to have my officers bogged down with discussions about the wisdom of this war. You can't do anything about it anyway. You can only become depressed and disconcerted. And that I won't have. A depressed aviator quickly becomes a dead aviator. One of my responsibilities is to get as many of you home alive as possible. Your attitude is not helping me carry out that responsibility.

"This Squadron has had a bad cruise so far. Four men killed, two listed MIA and two seriously injured and we still have fifty days to go. I don't want any more losses. I want everything going for each one of you as you strap twenty-five tons of airplane to your butts each day -- including attitude. I can't stop you from thinking what you want, Marchand, but I can order you to keep your comments about the War to yourself. Do I make myself clear?"

"Yes Sir, very clear, indeed. I hope you don't think that anything I've said has ---"

McGruder cut Marchand off abruptly. "Of course not, nothing you've said has had a damn thing to do with our losses. But I can't take the chance, no matter how remote, that it might have in the future. I think you're a fine young officer and a damn good aviator and I mean it."

"I understand, Skipper. Is that all, Sir?"

"Just one more thing, Marchand. I've recommended Drummond and you for a DFC for your part in Warden and Winslow's rescue ten days ago."

"A Distinguished Flying Cross?"

"Affirmative. I just finished writing the letter of recommendation. You both deserve it."

"Thank you very much, Skipper. I'm overwhelmed. I really don't know what to say."

"You don't have to say anything. Just remember what we talked about."

"I will, Sir. And, I really appreciate your concern."

"Very well, Marchand. Go have another beer."

"Aye, aye, Sir."

46.

WHAT'S A BARCAP?

After evening meal, Marchand joined Flight Surgeon Chris Davis ostensibly for a drink but actually for companionship. Davis handed him a large scotch over ice and asked, "Jesus Christ, Marchand, what the hell is wrong with you? You look like you just lost your best friend."

"Winslow was my roommate, Doc. I thought you knew that."

"Oh damn, I'm sorry. You know it's a good thing I'm a surgeon and not a shrink. I seem to have a knack for malapropisms....Anyway, he's alive, that's a blessing."

"That's for sure, Doc," Marchand said, "and I hear that you're a pretty damn good surgeon, that you did a super job on Phil's legs and shoulder. I want to thank you."

"Thanks back at you. Phil will be fine in a few months. In fact, he seemed much improved this morning before I prepared him and Warden to fly off the Ship. Winslow's burns were mostly second degree and his shoulder wound didn't involve tendons or nerve tissue. By the time we get back to the States, he should be out of the hospital.

"I'm much more concerned about Frank. That piece of shrapnel did some tendon damage and some nerve destruction as well. I know I did a good job on the severed tendons but it's going to take an experienced neurosurgeon to work on the nerve damage."

"Will he be able to fly? That's his whole life, you know."

"We have a good neurosurgeon in Yokusuka. There's better than an even chance that he can repair most of the nerve damage. We'll just have to wait and see."

"By the way, I heard about you and Drummond during that rescue. Congratulations on your DFC."

"Hell, the Skyhawk pilots deserve most of the credit. That was some of the straightest shooting since Wyatt Earp cleaned out the O.K. Corral."

"Yeah, but don't sell yourself short. It took a lot of good flying and headwork to get Warden and Winslow back."

"Just a lotta' luck, that's all."

"Anyway, perk up, fella. The cruise is almost over. There's less than two months left."

"But there's another cruise to think about, assuming the next thirty days turn out well. And frankly, I don't know whether I can make another cruise, Doc. I'm seriously thinking about turning in my wings when the cruise ends."

"You're what?"

"You heard me. I'm thinking about turning in my wings. I've agonized over this stinking war for almost eight months now, trying to justify all the killing and destruction. And, it's becoming increasingly difficult to do. There's not one bit of logic to explain any of this bullshit. I'm certain that we've been fed a boatload of lies and bullshit from Washington, that there really is no justification or rationale for this War. Worst of all, now that Johnson, McNamara, Westmoreland and God knows who else have managed to get us into this morass, they don't have the foggiest idea how to get us out.

"I just can't participate in this bullshit War any longer, I can't continue killing Vietnamese by the score or the hundred, and I can't watch my squadron mates disappear or be blown to bits day after day. Doc, I just can't do it any longer now that I really know the awful truth of it all."

The sympathetic flight surgeon listed attentively and tried his best to offer support. "I know how you must feel, Keith. Would it help to talk it out? I'm a pretty good listener."

"You mean that, Doc? Really mean that? Not just offering some psycho drama bullshit you learned in med school?"

Davis nodded sincerely, "I'm serious, if you are, Keith. Go ahead try me."

"OK, I'll take you up on the offer, Doc. Let me share a little war story with you.

"A few weeks ago, Frank Warden and I spent an evening in Da Nang because of a hung-up bomb on the left wing that wouldn't come off. After landing, we went to the Air Force officers' Club and joined some Air Force pilots for a one hundred mission party. But the base came under a heavy mortar and rocket attack before the party ended. So guess how we spent the rest of the night, Doc? Go ahead, guess."

"I don't have the foggiest."

"We sat on the roof and watched the Base go up in flames. Think about it. There we were at an Air Force O Club situated on the largest American air base in the world, surrounded by hundreds of millions of dollars of the most sophisticated aircraft and military equipment in the world, which thirty or forty fearless Viet Cong proceeded to attack at will, and very successfully too. Next thing I know the fuckin' base is blowing itself to smithereens, ammunition cookin' off everywhere, fuel farms exploding like the Fourth of July, aircraft blown to atoms. I'm sitting there on the roof, drinking beer and watching this incredible surrealistic scene. I couldn't believe it. I felt like Gulliver watching the Lilliputians soundly kickin' American butt that night."

"So tell me, Chris, what kind of job are we doing in protecting the people of South Vietnam when we can't protect our own military bases?"

"Well Christ, Keith, you can't cite one situation as representative of our entire war effort."

"Can't I, Chris. Can't I? These attacks occur every other day or so. We're being hacked to pieces by ferocious North Vietnamese who stop at nothing to kill us.

"And what are we protecting? South Vietnamese who prize Western democratic ideals and free enterprise? Hell no. We're protecting black marketeers and dope smugglers, prostitutes and thieves. And the glorious ARVN army, Doc, what about them? I'll tell you about them. They're gutless wonders who would rather switch than fight, who head in the opposite direction whenever they are called into a battle, who sell their weapons to the Viet Cong and who would just as soon shoot their GI advisors in the back as look at them.

"I'm fed up with this crap, Doc. When we waste good men like Phil and Frank for this garbage, I just can't hack much more of it. If we weren't involved in this goddamn war, the North Vietnamese Army and Viet Cong would destroy the South Vietnamese regime within a month. I think we should let them do it, the sooner the better. I, for one, don't want to protect this army of thieves and con artists any longer," Marchand said and slammed his drink down.

Davis hid his surprise at Marchand's outburst. "So, do you think your quitting will accomplish anything?" Davis asked.

"I don't know and I don't give a shit any more."

"You don't know, but I don't believe you don't care. No matter how fouled up the war is, it won't stop just because you turn in your wings. All you'll do is cause yourself a lot of trouble, maybe a court martial. Forget that crap, Keith. You're just upset about your roommate."

"I'm pissed off about a lot. Hell, even the Skipper told me to shut the hell up."

"So what do you think he would do if you turned your wings in?"

"He'd have my ass."

"Damn right he would. He'd request a court martial for your young ass before you left the ship. He'd have to make an example of you."

"I know."

"So what do you gain? Nothing, except the chance to spend a few years in Leavenworth penitentiary. And what about your plans to go to law school? You could forget that, too."

"You talk a strange line for a doctor, Chris. Have you considered that I may be getting a little anxious about busting my ass? A lot of good law school will do me if I end up as hamburger in a Vietnamese rice paddy or vaporized in a smoking hole in the ground. What about that, huh?"

"Don't give me that. Whatever you are - a moralist, a crusader or fool - you're not a chickenshit. Christ, you'll have a hundred missions and four rows of combat ribbons before the cruise ends. So don't give me that bullshit. Here, let me pour you another scotch. That's the least I can do for you," Davis replied, mildly offended.

"Chris, excuse my piss ant attitude, will you? I've lost my best friend and now my roommate and it's not over yet. Meanwhile, nothing makes sense.

"We've got less than thirty days to go until it's time to go home and I'm nervous as hell because for the first time I think I might make it. Just cut me a little slack," Marchand said.

"Hey, not to worry. I've noticed a lot of stress around the squadrons. When you need to blow off some steam, come on down to see me. It's safe and I'll be straight with you. In fact, if you're serious about turning your wings in when we get back to the States, we'll talk about it then. I can get you a medical disqualification for flight operations. I don't want to see you ruin your life. You've got too much to live for. You're under a lot of pressure, that's all. Why don't you get a good night's sleep and we'll talk about it later."

"Yeah, I think I'll hit the sack early," Marchand replied as he stooped to retrieve the next day's flight schedule that had just slid under the door. "Well, I've got an easy day tomorrow, an afternoon BARCAP. Daytime launch and recovery -- really boring, a piece of cake. I love it."

"What's a BARCAP?" the flight surgeon asked.

"Christ, Doc, the cruise is almost over and you don't know what a BARCAP is. Well, we fly a big racetrack pattern about a hundred miles long and fifteen to twenty miles wide just parallel to the North Vietnamese coastline. It's an acronym for Barrier Combat Air Patrol. Airborne fighters that provide a protective buffer between the fleet and any incoming enemy aircraft."

"So, why is a BARCAP so boring? Sounds to me that a BARCAP could be pretty damn exciting sometimes."

"Nothing ever comes out of North Vietnam to attack the fleet, Doc. MIG pilots know they'd get their asses shot off before they crossed over the shoreline. Vietnamese patrol boats would be blown away in short order if they even looked like they were threatening the fleet. So there's never an airborne or surface attack.

"And forget the Tonkin Gulf Incident. It probably never happened. It was most likely just an erroneous radar sighting by an inexperienced radar man. The rest was probably political bullshit or CIA. propaganda.

"Flying a real BARCAP mission amounts to little more than boring holes in the sky for two hours then coming home. So Doc, thanks for the booze and moral support. I'll see you later. And, Doc, one more thing."

"What's that?"

"I really appreciate the super job you did on Phil and Frank."

"Well, that's my job. I'd even do the same for you," Davis laughed.

"Thanks a million but if it's all the same to you, I'd rather observe your professional skills on another subject."

VOLUME ONE: PHANTOM WAR TRILOGY

47.

MANO A MANO

Kelly Drummond marveled at the incredible clarity of the late April sky as he scanned the horizon from his cramped cockpit twenty-five thousand feet over the Gulf of Tonkin. On this magnificent Easter Sunday afternoon, he felt comfortable and strangely secure as he banked the Phantom into a gentle thirty degree left turn toward the Vietnamese coastline. Drummond could easily discern the verdant Vietnamese landscape meeting the cobalt sea almost thirty-five miles off the plane's left wing tip.

"I must have been in this damn plane too long, Marchand, it's beginning to feel more like home than home," Drummond said keying his intercom.

"It's always like that for you lifers," Marchand replied. "They'll probably bury you with a control stick in one hand and a pair of throttles in the other."

"You damn junior officers just don't have any respect for authority anymore. If I said something like that when I was a lieutenant junior grade I would have been in hack for a month."

"Hell, Kelly, as old as you are, I think the Navy was still keelhauling its fuck-ups. They didn't know what restricting to quarters even meant."

"Aw, shut up and look out at this gorgeous afternoon. How much visibility do you think we have?"

"At least a hundred miles. I saw the Chinese coastline before the turn and it shows up a hundred ten miles away on radar."

"Too bad we can't go sightseeing," Drummond replied.

Being so close, Marchand couldn't help but wonder if Margo had somehow managed to sneak into China. Fat chance, he told himself and chuckled.

While Marchand and Drummond enjoyed the beauty and serenity of their quiet flight, a bespectacled Navy Lieutenant closely observed their progress on his large radarscope situated in the Combat Information Center of the nuclear powered guided missile frigate, *U.S.S. Long Beach.* The C.I.C. space was large, dark and very cool. Phosphorescent green light from more than a dozen radar screens bathed the C.I.C. and muted, red-lit overhead lamps provided the only functional light for the twenty officers and men who manned the combat nerve center of the ship. They served as the eyes for the eighty ships that constituted Task Force Seventy-Seven, including the *Constellation.*

Lieutenant John Cooper was one of the best combat air controllers on the *Long Beach.* He had completed six months of flight training before vision problems caused his dismissal from the Naval Aviation Training Command. But Cooper's limited cockpit experience gave him an appreciation for the abilities and limitations of pilots and aircraft that few of his surface-bound shipmates shared. Cooper had been somewhat tense since receiving his pre-watch briefing. Consequently, he called the Phantom flight from the *Constellation* to warn them of possible MIG activity in their region.

As usual, neither Marchand nor Drummond in the lead aircraft nor Steve Grant or Don Kramer who were flying wing paid much attention to the advice from ship-borne air controllers whose call sign was "Red Crown". Rarely had they or any of the Phantom crews received advice or information from Red Crown controllers that they deemed useful. For them the relationship between aircrews and controllers was characterized by strained tolerance and thinly disguised indifference. To most of Lt. Cooper's fellow controllers, the pilots and flight officers who flew BARCAP seemed extraordinarily arrogant and difficult to manage. Cooper, however, understood aviators much better than most C.I.C. watch officers. Consequently, he didn't have the same problems with the flight crews.

Cooper stared intensely at his screen and the two ghost-like green blips that appeared and disappeared fleetingly over Than Hoa, North Vietnam heading due east toward the coast. The blips were moving fast; Cooper estimated more than six hundred knots. They were difficult to image because they were at very low altitude, probably less than a thousand feet, he thought. Then Cooper tracked three more targets on his screen also heading east about twenty-five miles from the North Vietnamese coastline. These he recognized as a flight of three Skyhawks from the carrier *U.S.S. Ranger*. They had just completed a bombing strike five miles east of the Than Hoa Bridge and were returning to their ship.

The distance between the unidentified low flying aircraft and the Navy Skyhawks was only thirty miles and steadily decreasing. Cooper knew that there were no Air Force or Navy aircraft other than the Skyhawks that had been scheduled into the Than Hoa region at that time. Cooper called the Assistant C.I.C. watch officer to confirm the presence of any other American aircraft in the vicinity.

"Negative, Lieutenant, only the Sundowner Flight," came the

reply.

Cooper tried to electronically interrogate the in-flight identification transponders that all American aircraft carried but his interrogation yielded no response. His analysis of the situation firmed and he decided to warn the flight of Navy A-4 Skyhawks of nearby danger. He keyed the ship's powerful ultra high frequency transmitter and broadcast over the emergency radio channel monitored by all American military aircraft. "Sundowner Leader, Sundowner Leader, this is Red Crown, over."

"Red Crown, this is Sundowner. Read you loud and clear."

"Sundowner, Red Crown paints two bogeys at your six o'clock, twenty-eight miles, down the deck, possible bandits."

"Red Crown, this is Sundowner. Roger two possible bandits at my six o'clock at two eight miles. Are they closing?"

"Affirmative, Sundowner. Bogeys closing on you at approximately one hundred sixty knots."

"You got any other friendlies scheduled for this area, Red Crown?"

"Red Crown, negative. Recommend you go feet wet as soon as possible."

"Red Crown, this is Sundowner. One of my wingman has four Mark 82s hung up on his racks. We can't get out any faster. Send me some fighter cover, will you?"

Cooper's mind raced. He could order the Checkmate Flight to Than Hoa to provide the Sundowner aircraft with fighter protection, but ordering the BARCAP aircraft off station was not a step to be taken lightly. Two replacement BARCAP aircraft would have to be scrambled from one of the other three carriers stationed in the Tonkin Gulf. There would be a great deal of explaining to do and reports to write if the emergency launch proved unnecessary. Cooper had no time to ponder the decision for, if the BARCAP fighters were to provide any assistance to the vulnerable Skyhawks, he must order the BARCAP to intercept the bogeys immediately. As senior C.I.C. watch officer, Cooper had the authority to do so. More importantly, he had the responsibility. He could hesitate no longer.

"Checkmate Leader, this is Red Crown, over."

"Roger, Red Crown," Marchand responded. Vacation's over, he told himself.

"Checkmate Flight, we have two bogeys to identify immediately. Steer two six zero and descend to Angels three zero. Bogeys bearing twelve o'clock at six five miles; Angels approximately one point five."

"Roger, Red Crown, Checkmate Flight steering two six zero, descending to Angels three zero. You got any description of the bogeys?" Kelly Drummond transmitted as he began a sharp right turn to the west.

"Two high-speed bogeys, possible bandits. There's a flight of three A-4s between you and the bogeys heading zero nine zero at Angels one three, Red Crown, over." Cooper studied the situation on his radar screen closely. The BARCAP Phantoms had completed their turn, putting the unidentified aircraft sixty-five miles directly ahead and the Skyhawks in between.

"Say distance to the Skyhawks, Red Crown," Marchand inquired.

"Five five miles, Checkmate. Can you accelerate? If the bogeys are bandits, the Skyhawks need help A.S.A.P."

"We're at six hundred knots, Red Crown," Drummond replied.

"Copy you at six hundred knots, Checkmate, but the bogeys are closing on the Skyhawks fast. They look a hell of lot like bandits. Go buster now!"

"Roger, Red Crown. Checkmate Flight is going buster," Drummond answered. Then he called his wingman, "Checkmate Two, Check Leader, jettison centerline tanks. Looks like the real thing. Go to first stage afterburner. Let's get up to combat speed."

"Check Two, roger. Jettison centerline tanks. Going to combat power," Don Kramer transmitted as he pushed the red emergency jettison button on his fuel control panel instantly blowing the empty centerline fuel tank away from the aircraft. When Kramer felt the thump of the tank tearing away from the fully streamlined aircraft, he moved his throttles smoothly into the first afterburner detent.

Even though the two Phantoms had been flying at almost seven hundred miles per hour, Marchand felt a sudden jolt of acceleration as the engines surged to combat thrust. He glanced at his true airspeed indicator. It read eight hundred fifty knots. Almost one thousand miles per hour, he thought as he scanned his radar screen for some sign of the Skyhawk flight and the possible enemy aircraft behind.

"Say distance to Skyhawks, Red Crown," Marchand transmitted.

"Four three miles, Checkmate," Lieutenant Cooper answered, giving distance and bearing information as though he were sitting in the cockpit of one of the Phantoms now streaking toward the Vietnamese coast. "Bogeys now at your twelve o'clock at five one miles from you and still closing on the Skyhawks." Cooper gave the position of unidentified aircraft then ordered the captain of the *Long Beach* to be awakened and quickly briefed. The unidentified planes were only twelve miles behind the Skyhawks and closing rapidly.

"Roger, Red Crown, this is Checkmate One, I have the Sundowner Flight on my weapon at four zero miles," Marchand said, reporting radar contact with the Skyhawks. He calculated the closure rate between the Phantoms and the unidentified aircraft to be in excess of fifteen hundred knots or more than twenty-five miles per minute. He knew everything from this point on would happen incredibly fast. Still, he couldn't locate the unidentified aircraft on his radar. "Say again bogeys' altitude, Red Crown," Marchand inquired.

"Bogeys still at Angels one point five, Checkmate," Cooper answered.

"Damn, Kelly, I can't find the fucking bogeys. They're too damn low and lost in the ground return clutter," Marchand cursed into his oxygen mask microphone.

"Just keep looking, Keith. Just keep looking. I want to bag a damn MIG today."

Marchand swept his powerful radar beam again and again over the hilly terrain where the unidentified aircraft should have been. He delicately adjusted the radar's controls to distinguish the unknown aircraft from the radar ground clutter. Steve Grant in the other Phantom searched just as intensely with the pencil-thin beam of his radar but without success.

"Checkmate, this is Red Crown. Bogeys now bearing two five zero at four zero miles, come port to two eight zero degrees, bogeys still at Angels one point five." Lt. Cooper was perspiring heavily. The unidentified aircraft would overtake the Navy attack bombers in less than two minutes. But the Phantoms would not intercept the converging aircraft until twenty seconds later. If the unidentified planes were enemy fighters, the twenty-second delay could prove fatal to one or more of the Skyhawks which were not equipped for air-to-air combat against what Cooper highly suspected to be MIG-21s, the most sophisticated fighter aircraft in the Soviet arsenal.

Lt. Cooper pressed his transmitter button. "Checkmate Leader,

401

bogeys will overtake friendlies in approximately nine zero seconds. Can you accelerate?"

Drummond moved his throttles to second stage afterburner as he responded. "Roger, Red Crown. Checkmate Flight is accelerating." Simultaneously, he adjusted the gun sight located on the top of his instrument panel to project the proper lead angle for air combat.

Marchand glanced at his airspeed indicator that read one thousand knots, almost twelve hundred miles per hour. Then he saw two faint radar images on his screen not more than five miles behind the Skyhawks but the radar targets were not hugging the ground at fifteen hundred feet as Red Crown reported; they were at five thousand feet and climbing fast. Marchand notified their wingman and the ship-borne controller that he had located the targets. "Red Crown, I've got contact with two bogeys bearing two four zero at three zero miles, Angels five and climbing."

"Roger Checkmate, this is Red Crown. Those are your bogeys. Your friendlies are bearing two five zero at two four miles, Angels fifteen. Bogeys are accelerating, Checkmate. Do you copy?"

Marchand answered, "We copy, Red Crown. This is a Judy, Judy, Judy. Checkmate is assuming control of the intercept Red Crown. Are these aircraft bandits? Are we cleared to fire?"

"Negative, Checkmate. Bogeys not confirmed as bandits at this time," Lt. Cooper responded as beads of sweat rolled down his forehead. "Checkmate Flight is not cleared to fire. Do you copy?"

Marchand scowled as he keyed his mike button and transmitted angrily, "Goddamn it, get off your ass and start confirming, Red Crown. Those damn MIGs are less than twenty-five miles away and I'm almost in range. Do you need one of these 'bogeys' to shoot down a friendly before you clear us to fire?" Marchand's adrenaline was pumping and he was furious with the air controller for the delay in clearance to fire his Sparrow radar-guided air-to-air missiles at what he increasingly knew to be North Vietnamese fighters.

Cooper looked up from his radar screen to see the Captain of the *Long Beach* enter the Combat Information Center. He practically screamed, "Captain, the BARCAP fighters are almost in range, can I give them permission to fire?"

"Have you confirmed the aircraft as MIGs?" Captain Barnes asked.

"Everything but a visual identification, Sir." Cooper answered.

"Have you gotten clearance from Task Force Seventy-Seven?"

"Negative, Sir."

"Well call CTF-77 again. We can't take the risk that those are friendly aircraft."

"Captain, those bogeys are definitely bandits. I'm absolutely sure of it, Sir."

The red in-range light began to glow on Marchand's radarscope as the target aircraft closed within fourteen miles of the Navy Phantoms. Marchand could tell that they were climbing rapidly to the Skyhawks' altitude. "Red Crown," he roared, "the bandits are in range. Am I cleared to fire?" Off mike, he bellowed, "Damn it! We're gonna lose a Skyhawk any minute!"

"Negative, Checkmate, stand by," Cooper replied, clearly exasperated.

"Fuck it, Red Crown," Drummond bellowed. "We'll be engaged in less than fifteen seconds. Thanks for all the goddamn help." Then Drummond thundered over the Phantom's intercom, "Lock on the closest bandit, Keith, in case we get clearance to fire."

Marchand placed his weapon in fire control mode and squeezed the trigger on his control stick to lock the system's deadly radar beam on the nearest MIG. Drummond quickly scanned the weapons panel switches that would arm the warheads of the aircraft's missiles and prepare them to fire, then said, "Marchand, forget the intercept, we'll never get clearance to fire in time. This is going to be a good old-fashioned dogfight. Mano a mano, Baby. Where are the Skyhawks?"

Marchand immediately disengaged the weapons system from fire control mode back into search. "One o'clock, low at three miles. Bandits are one point five miles astern. The MIGs will make a firing pass any second now," Marchand replied, his breathing coming heavy over the intercom which he had switched to hot mike in order to facilitate communication between the two cockpits during combat.

Drummond did not wait another moment to key his transmitter. "Sundowner Flight, this is Checkmate, make a hard three sixty. You've got MIGs at your six o'clock in firing range."

The flight leader of the three Skyhawks acknowledged the warning and commenced an abrupt turn to the left. As the three A-4 pilots began their evasive turn, two MIG-21 fighters pulled within one mile of the Skyhawks in a climbing attack. Both MIGs fired two heat-seeking missiles at their rapidly turning targets.

Two of the Soviet heat-seeking missiles sped toward the lead A-4 and turned sharply to the left to follow the pilot's evasive maneuver. But the Navy attack bomber's turn was too sharp so the missiles continued their flight without guidance. The third missile guided on the second Skyhawk and it too went into ballistic flight after its guidance system broke lock.

The last heat-seeking missile locked onto the third and trailing Skyhawk that still carried four five hundred pound bombs hung on its weapon racks. The A-4 pilot turned his aircraft as hard as he could without stalling. But the weight of the unexpended bombs greatly reduced the Skyhawk's performance, including its rate of turn and turning radius. As a result, the heat-seeking missile remained locked onto the Skyhawk until it flew within fifteen feet of the burdened attack bomber. When the missile passed its closest point of approach, it exploded in a ball of white-hot flame and red-hot shrapnel. The Skyhawk became an instant fireball and disintegrated. No parachute erupted from the burning wreckage.

Kelly Drummond saw the explosion three miles in front of his aircraft. "Great fuck, one of the A-4's just got zapped. Where the hell are the bandits?" He bellowed over the intercom.

"Eleven o'clock, four miles, slightly high and climbing," Marchand answered. Right here, right now, he told himself. Right here right now.

"Are we still in range?" Drummond shouted.

"Affirmative, my weapon is locked on the lead bandit. Hard port and climb. Fire when ready."

Drummond yanked his control stick hard to the left and back into his lap. The change in aircraft attitude placed the Phantom in a steep, climbing three-G turn to the left, three miles ahead of the lead MIG-21. Drummond checked his repeater radarscope, and, seeing that he was in range and locked on the MIG, he squeezed the trigger on the control stick twice, calling "Fox one, Fox one" on the radio. Two Sparrow radar-guided missiles fired from under the Phantom's fuselage missile stations, accelerating in a burst of orange flame and white exhaust. Drummond strained to see his target as the Sparrows zoomed upward and to the left, leaving white vapor trails behind. Four seconds after the missiles were fired, Drummond saw the missile's fireball consume the MIG fighter.

"Holy shit, we got the bastard!" Drummond shouted. "We gotta' kill the other SOB now!"

"Where the fuck is the other MIG?" Marchand shouted into his oxygen mask.

"Kramer's on him. He's fired two Sparrows but they're not guiding. They went ballistic. Can you find the bandit on your scope?"

"Negative, I've got nothing," Marchand answered. Then he called over the air. "Check Two, do you have a visual on the bandit?"

"Negative, Check One, we fired inside minimum range, my weapon has broken lock on the bandit," Steve Grant answered over the radio.

Lieutenant Cooper followed the air battle intently on his radar screen and over the radio. Now he saw on his radarscope the vital information that neither Phantom crew had. The MIG had climbed straight up into the afternoon sun, entered a high-speed loop and was closing in on the Phantoms from behind on a high perch. "Checkmate Flight, your bandit is at your seven o'clock bearing two two zero degrees at three miles, Angels three five. I say again, Angels three five and closing on you fast," Cooper warned.

"Hot damn, the son of a bitch is at our six o'clock high, Keith. He's ready to attack." Drummond yelled as he yanked the stick hard left and back into his crotch. The Phantom began a sharp climbing turn to the left with Don Kramer following a half-mile off to the right. All four Phantom crewmembers searched the sky in vain for the threatening enemy fighter.

A radio call added even more urgency to the deadly dogfight, "Checkmate Flight, this is Red Crown. I have two additional bandits in your area bearing three five zero at five miles, Angels unknown."

"Oh shit, it's red hot now," Marchand shouted over the intercom.

"Check Two, this is Check Leader, break it off and go after the two bandits to the north, I'll keep this sonofabitch behind us busy."

"Check Two, roger. Good hunting."

Drummond's wingman roared off to the left leaving the lead Phantom still in a climbing left turn. Lt. Cooper called again, this time with great urgency in his voice. "Check Leader, bandit is still at your six o'clock high, less than two miles. Watch your ass, Checkmate!" Cooper transmitted as calmly as he could.

Marchand strained to look over his shoulder to scan the area behind his aircraft. Drummond wrapped the Phantom in a tighter turn and the G forces mounted steadily. Marchand caught sight of a tiny silver speck above and to the left of the Phantom's tail. It was diving and closing fast. Marchand yelled, "Kelly, he's on our seven o'clock, high and diving on us. High G barrel roll now!"

Although Drummond couldn't see the MIG-21 on his tail, he knew the situation was absolutely critical. A call for a high G barrel roll when an enemy aircraft is behind meant that there would be time for only one "last ditch maneuver". If this failed, their remaining lifetime would be measured in mere seconds. Instinctively, Drummond rolled the aircraft violently to the right and pulled the nose high, putting the fighter into the high-acceleration maneuver most likely to throw the MIG pilot off his attack. Acceleration forces seven and a half times the force of gravity drove him and Marchand down hard into their seats like a piledriver. Marchand's vision began to black out just as he spotted two air-to-air missiles streak from under the MIG's wings toward them. "Missiles away, Kelly. Give it all you got."

Drummond pulled back harder on his stick. At eight and a half Gs, he too blacked out as blood drained from his head under the enormously powerful acceleration forces. "That's everything, Keith.

407

Pray, Baby," Kelly grunted, now flying blind.

"I am praying," Marchand grunted into his facemask and into the darkness.

The two heat-seeking missiles looped tightly in an attempt to follow the desperately rolling and turning Phantom. A quarter mile astern of their intended victim, both missiles broke lock, flying straight ahead in simple ballistic flight. Neither Drummond nor Marchand could see the missiles or anything else as they flashed perilously close by their Phantom but not close enough to detonate.

Drummond's vision just returned when he saw the two missiles flash overhead. "He missed us! Holy Jesus, we're still alive!" He shouted.

"I still can't see yet," Marchand grunted into the intercom.

Drummond released a little back pressure on the control stick and Marchand's vision returned in time for him to see the MIG streaking overhead and climbing sharply. "Twelve o'clock high, Kelly," he bellowed.

"Tally ho!" Drummond roared as he followed the MIG straight up in a vertical rolling scissors. Having overshot the Phantoms, it was now the MIG pilot's turn to evade the Phantom. The tables had turned in an instant. The two crisscrossing fighters were so close, Drummond could almost make out aircraft numbers on the MIG's sleek silver fuselage as the planes weaved in and out while in a nearly vertical climb. As the two combatants passed through thirty-five thousand feet, airspeed began to fall off rapidly.

Drummond sensed the deceleration but could not take his vision inside the cockpit to read the instruments. His eyes remained riveted on the MIG. "Call my airspeed, Keith," he roared into his facemask microphone.

"Two hundred fifty knots. We're inside minimum range. Two hundred knots now."

The two aircraft were so close to each other, Drummond could see the MIG pilot's helmet. He pushed his throttles further into the afterburner detents to prolong his climb a few seconds longer as he shot past the MIG. A moment later the Phantom began to shudder and buffet as it approached stalling speed.

"Only a few more seconds, Baby," Drummond mumbled, urging his powerful steed to hold out a little longer, "just a couple seconds."

Suddenly, the MIG pilot ran out of airspeed necessary for flight, pushed his nose over and began to dive in order to gain speed before stalling and spinning out of control.

Marchand shouted, "one hundred fifty knots, we're stalling."

The Phantom began to shake violently. "I know," Drummond answered as he added the last bit of afterburner power. When he felt the plane enter a stall and fall off and begin to spin to the right, Drummond pushed hard on his left rudder pedal, yawing the Phantom's nose sharply toward the ground and away from the developing spin. Then in a steep dive as airspeed built up rapidly, Drummond searched for the MIG below him.

Drummond spotted the bright silver, delta winged MIG-21 just as Marchand called, "he's at your ten o'clock, low, a half mile. In range for a Sidewinder."

Drummond pulled his throttles back sharply, activated his speed brakes and waited several seconds as the distance between the two fighters increased, then as the MIG pilot added power and lit his afterburner, Drummond fired two heat-seeking Sidewinder missiles. "Fox Two, Fox Two," he called over the radio. The extra engine heat from the MIG's afterburner provided an excellent target for the missiles, one of which flew right up the MIG's tailpipe and exploded. Less than three thousand feet separated the two aircraft so that Drummond had to bank the Phantom violently to avoid debris from the disintegrating fighter.

Drummond keyed his transmitter and said triumphantly, "Red Crown, Check Leader, splash another MIG."

"Roger, Check Leader, splash another MIG.

"That's two MIGs today, Rocketman. Not a bad day's work," Drummond shouted.

"Fuckin' A," Marchand rasped into the hot mike as he watched flaming pieces of the MIG fall earthward. Then he whispered to himself... "There but for the grace of God...."

Drummond suddenly remembered his wingman and called over the air, "Check Two this is Check Leader. Where are you?"

"This is Check Two. We're ten miles feet wet and heading home. We splashed one MIG with a Sparrow; the other gave up and headed for home. That makes two kills for the day, Check One. We got some celebrating to do."

"Negative, Check Two. Make that three kills for the day. Break out the single malt good stuff; Check Leader is buying."

"Hot shit, you guys," Steve Grant transmitted over the air then added, "Did you copy that, Red Crown? Three bandits splashed!"

"Red Crown copies, three bandits splashed! Checkmate Flight, congratulations are in order. The Task Force Commander wants to see you guys when you get home."

"Sounds great, Red Crown," Marchand answered, his heart still thumping wildly. "By the way, Red Crown, Happy Easter."

PART FIVE

April 27, 1968 – November 25, 1968

48.

GRACE NOTES

Mitchell W. Collins III looked up from the April 27, 1968 Sunday edition of the New York Times to savor a sip of rich Indonesian coffee and his panoramic Fifth Avenue view of Central Park and mid-town Manhattan. A gentle breeze ruffled the pages of the newspaper as he watched morning joggers chugging along park paths twenty-three stories below his penthouse patio. Grace notes from Vivaldi's *L'Estro Armanico* played luxuriously on a MacIntosh stereo system and matched speakers. Collins stole a loving glance at his only daughter, only child, and only family, while she spread marmalade on a morsel of croissant. He thought how very important she had become to him since his wife's tragic death three years ago. She reminds me so much of Elizabeth, he mused; I wonder whether I could have survived the trauma of her loss without Margo. After a deep and silent sigh, he returned to the Times.

Maxine, Collins' housekeeper of twenty years, was refilling his coffee cup when he abruptly straightened up, almost tipping the cup and saucer. "Well, I'll be damned," he exclaimed.

"What is it, Dad?" Margo asked coolly. She was still somewhat hurt by her father's intrusions into her personal life.

"It seems that your young gentleman, Lt. Marchand, has become something of a hero. That is his name, isn't it?"

"He's become what?"

"This article states that fighters from the aircraft carrier *Constellation* shot down three MIGs over Vietnam yesterday. Lt. Keith Michael Marchand is one of the Navy officers whose names are given."

"Oh my God, is he all right?" Margo asked, plainly startled.

"The article says that both Navy Fighters returned safely to their carrier after an intense air-to-air battle lasting nearly ten minutes. Senior Navy officers admitted that one American Skyhawk attack bomber was lost in the dogfight. They also credit the crews of the F-4 Phantoms with saving the pilots of two Skyhawks whose flight was attacked just seconds before the Navy fighters arrived on the scene.

"The Pentagon reports that communications between the MIG-21 pilots and their ground controllers were in the Russian language confirming long held suspicions that many sophisticated ground control radar installations as well as the late model Soviet-made MIG fighters are frequently manned and piloted by Soviet personnel. A high-ranking Naval Officer claimed that on many occasions when American aircraft have been engaged in aerial combat other than single hit-and-run attacks from the rear, the MIG pilots were thought to be Soviets. He went on to state that the victorious fighter crews would receive the Navy Cross, the Navy's second highest military award, for valor in combat.

"Goodness, child, you look like you're about to faint dead away," Maxine said with motherly concern. She seemed to forget that Margo had long ago grown up.

"I'm all right Maxine, maybe you could get me a glass of water, please."

"Yes Ma'am, just don't fret so about that dreadful pilot," Maxine said as she hurried off.

"What have you been telling Maxine about Keith?" Margo's irritation began to show.

"Nothing, you know Maxine has been aware of everything you've done since you were two years old.... You really care for him, don't you?"

"Well, yes, I do. Please, let me see the paper."

"When is he coming home?"

"I got a letter yesterday. He said he has only six weeks of his cruise remaining. He must have written it a day or so before this combat happened." Margo was quiet for a moment, trying to hide her concern for Keith, but then she blurted out. "Oh my God, Keith might have been killed in that dogfight, or whatever it's called, just a few weeks before he was to come home," Margo said in an anguished tone.

"Relax, Marguerite, the War is over for him at this point. I'm certain the Navy won't let anything happen to him. There are far too few heroes in this War," Collins said as he studied his daughter curiously. "Frankly, I'm far more worried about you. You've always been so independent. I've rarely seen you so nervous. Do you love him?" Collins' queried anxiously.

"Oh, Dad, stop it," Margo said, clearly upset.

"Well, do you?" Collins persisted.

"Yes I do, if you just must know."

"You wouldn't do anything foolish now, would you?"

"Look, this is my life, in case you hadn't noticed. I have at least six months before my dissertation is finished and Keith has another damn combat tour. What is the something foolish you're talking about, anyway?" Margo said harshly, her face becoming flush.

"Nothing, dear Girl, nothing. I just want to see you join the faculty at Harvard next year. Nothing should interfere with that, you know."

"Well, what if I don't want to teach at Harvard? What if I want to do something else?"

"Something else? Like what?"

"Like the State Department."

"Good gracious, no. Not in its present condition. What a waste of talent that would be."

"You know, Dad, these decisions aren't up to you. Anyway, you're sounding terribly hypocritical. You would have liked nothing better than an appointment as Secretary of State if Rockefeller's campaign hadn't disintegrated."

Collins reflected a moment and realized his daughter had a point. "I suppose your joining the State Department wouldn't be so awful. It's certainly a damn sight better than your doing something with that Marchand fellow."

"Doing what, Father?"

"Marrying him, that's what."

"Well, now you've finally said it, haven't you? I'm very angry with you about this and a few other things as well, so I should just let you fret, but today I don't have the heart for it. So let me put you at ease. First of all, Keith doesn't want to get married until he's finished with the Navy and out of law school. Most importantly, Mr. Collins, your daughter has no intention of getting married anytime soon -- to anyone. I have a few things on my own agenda, you know."

"Well, that's a relief."

"We have talked about sharing an apartment in Cambridge the following year if he gets into The Law School and I take a teaching position, though."

Now Mitchell Collins III was upset. "My God, don't tell me. I don't want to know about it. If you share an apartment with him or any man, just please don't tell me about it."

"Remember you said that when my life becomes a closed book to you, which it should, after what you've done."

"What I've done? What do you mean, what I've done?"

"You know exactly what I mean."

"What's that you said about his going to Harvard Law School?" Mitchell Collins replied, eager to avoid the confrontation.

"I told you that before and I also told you that he finished the College *summa cum laude*."

"He'll probably be admitted, then."

"If he lives long enough," Margo replied sadly.

VOLUME ONE: PHANTOM WAR TRILOGY

49.

HIGH ENERGY PHYSICS

In no mood to continue work on her doctoral dissertation, Margo sorted the morning mail delivered on May 2, 1968, took several pieces addressed to her, left her father's penthouse apartment and walked to a cozy sidewalk cafe on Lexington Avenue for lunch. She was seated at a small, sunny table near but not too close to the sidewalk. A large red and white Cinzano umbrella shaded her table. She perused the menu then ordered a *salade nicoise* and a small carafe of chablis. While waiting for her salad, Margo opened a letter with a Kowloon return address that she vaguely recognized.

April 22, 1968
Dear Miss Collins:

Your message has been delivered to appropriate authorities and analyzed carefully. Your suggestions appear to have possible merit and deserve further consideration and discussion. In order to explore the potential of your ideas, your introduction to certain officials of our United Nations delegation would be desirable in the near future.

Prior to your introduction, however, it will be necessary for you to contact a friend of the People's Republic of China who will further examine your qualifications and credentials for presentation to our governmental officials. At the earliest possible moment, you should contact Professor Li Chou-ping, Department of High Energy Physics, Massachusetts Institute of Technology.

You are instructed to tell no one of the contents of this letter which is to be destroyed immediately after it is read. You have my best wishes for success.

Very truly yours,
Ying Soon-ling

Margo read the brief letter several times, then with trembling fingers folded it carefully and placed it in her purse. She resolved to destroy the letter as directed but not before she could read it again in the privacy of her father's walnut-paneled study to assure herself that it was indeed real. By the time the waiter brought her salad, she was too excited to eat it. She only managed to sip the cool white wine while her thoughts raced.

My God, she mused, can it be that my proposal has really been presented to a responsible level within the Politburo, perhaps to Premier Chou En-lai himself? It's too much to hope for, she concluded; this can't be happening. Yet, the invitation, or the potential invitation to meet with the Chinese United Nations delegation seemed real enough. Clearly, it must have been discussed at a fairly senior level. And there was the certainty of meeting the Physics Professor from M.I.T. whose function she understood would be to scrutinize her closely. But, she told herself, she would scrutinize him as well.

While walking back toward Fifth Avenue, Margo tried to determine whether and how much to tell her father about the letter from

Hong Kong. Mitchell Collins had always been quite supportive of her Far Eastern studies, particularly as they involved the real China. As a young naval attaché in Shanghai before World War II, he had acquired a lasting interest in Chinese history and culture.

Moreover, Mitch Collins had developed an early and enduring dislike of Chaing Kai-shek during and after World War Two. He had often and emphatically described to Margo the events culminating in America's ties with Chaing's regime and the alienation of Mao Tse-tung, Chou En-lai and the popular Revolutionary Forces, and she recalled listening to her father's denouncement of John Foster Dulles' confrontational and xenophobic policies. Collins had long predicted that those policies would eventually lead to American military involvement in Asia.

Yet, Margo knew that her father would react quite negatively to her involvement with a foreign government that was so feared and despised by most American officials and the public as well. Such contact could put her at jeopardy with governmental agencies from the State Department, the Central Intelligence Agency, to the Federal Bureau of Investigation. She also knew that communications with agents of the People's Republic of China, if discovered prematurely, could threaten, if not destroy her academic career, her potential future at State, and possibly result in legal action against her.

But what concerned her most were the possible effects of her actions on her father's professional and personal reputation. Ballentine, Swaine and Gates had been one of the more conservative and prestigious Wall Street law firms for generations. Even though Collins had been a senior partner there for years, his daughter's involvement with Chinese Communists might prove troublesome for him. Then, of course, Collins' long suppressed desire to hold a cabinet position with what he considered a suitably conservative but progressive thinking administration would also be jeopardized. All Dad's dreams could be destroyed in an instant if I'm not careful, she told herself. "He may well deserve it but I can't bring myself to risk all that he's achieved and hoped for."

Then, Margo recalled her secret meeting with the mysterious Rick Sero in Hong Kong, just before she left to return home to New York. She and Sero had met in a private room at the Jockey Club in Hong Kong, the oldest and most exclusive private club in the British Crown Colony where Sero had been a senior member for many years. After an exquisite lunch worthy of Sero's Epicurean tastes, he confirmed that from the earliest days of Mao's People's Republic of China, he had been considered a special friend, with special privileges and recognition.

Sero's great antipathy, if not outright hatred, of Chaing Kai-shek and his decision to charter a large number of his coastal freighters to Mao's new Republic at almost no cost, coupled with his family's long term investment in Chinese trade and shipping had made him an early ally of the revolutionary Chinese government. Sero's fluency with three Chinese dialects enabled him to communicate effectively with senior officials of Mao's entourage without interpreters or other interlopers. Most importantly, Sero had been instrumental in the establishment of many international financial arrangements for the fledgling socialist government.

Margo concluded that although Sero would not admit it, he was an unofficial, undisclosed agent of the People's Republic of China. He probably wasn't a spy in a literal sense, but he operated secretly and at very high levels with Mao's regime. Given the current precarious balance of power among the United States, the Soviet Union and the P.R.C., Sero's connections within the Chinese Politburo had become invaluable. He could accomplish things that few other non-Chinese could even dream about, and he could communicate with senior Chinese officials with ease. When Sero told her that he had been asked to investigate her background and report his findings, Margo knew that he did not exaggerate. The last thing that Sero told her was that she would be contacted after her return to the United States and given further instructions.

Sero would not tell her more and he ordered her to observe absolute secrecy with regard to her endeavors and their meeting. But Sero did promise to assist her somewhat naïve efforts in effecting a rapprochement between the United States and the P.R.C. Eventually, Margo decided to trust Sero, but she was uneasy and not at all satisfied with her limited knowledge about this extraordinarily sophisticated and urbane gentleman. Still, as she thought of Sero, she remembered her exotic trip with Marchand, Sero and his wife along the green mansions of Siam.

Margo passed a newspaper vendor and noticed a headline that read "Nixon Expected to Win in Miami" which reminded her that the Republican convention in Miami Beach would be held in a little more than three months. With that reminder, she reached in her purse, took out the tissue-thin letter, and stopped in an alcove to read and memorize the important names and addresses. Then, Margo shredded the letter and dropped the pieces into a public litter can. Feeling slightly relieved, she resolved not to mention anything to her father until she had met Professor Li and the Republican convention had ended.

After returning to the Collins residence, Margo dialed the number she had memorized, then leaned back in the dark leather desk chair of her father's study to wait for an answer. After eight rings, she was about to hang up the receiver when a male voice with a British accent and clipped diction answered. "Dr. Li speaking."

"Dr. Li, this is Marguerite Collins calling from New York, I received instructions to call you in a letter that was delivered today from …"

"Yes, I know who you are, Miss Collins, and I also know by whom you were told to call," Li cut in abruptly.

"I see; well, in that case, you know that I am to make arrangements to see you soon," Margo replied.

"Of course, but there has been a minor change of plans. I will be leaving the country for a brief trip and will meet you upon my return." Li then began speaking Mandarin. "I will return to the United States on August 10th. The following day you are to meet me at the Brattle Street Restaurant near Harvard Square, take a table for lunch at noon. I will join you there."

"Certainly," Margo answered, "but why don't I simply meet you at your office at M.I.T.?"

"I'm sure that you know the answer to that question, Miss Collins. Please do not speak of this meeting to anyone."

"Should I bring anything with me?"

"No, that is unnecessary. And, of course, please come alone."

"I will, but how will you recognize me?"

"That is no problem. I have seen you many times. Good day, Miss Collins," Li answered in English then abruptly hung up.

Margo hung up the receiver staring at it while her thoughts came in waves. "I wonder if I'm being set up," she mused. This could ruin Dad. What the hell, it could ruin me if it all backfires.

She recalled her many long discussions with the proprietor of the small art shop in Kowloon during her doctoral research in Hong Kong, the same art shop whose return address appeared on the letter from Ying

Soon-ling. The art shop was known by a few students to be owned and operated by the People's Republic of China. In fact, it had been rumored that the owner and many of the salespeople were Chinese agents. The proprietor, Ying Soon-ling, often traveled to Mainland China ostensibly to purchase fine Ming vases and scrolled artwork. Gradually, he had let it be known to Margo that his contacts extended to certain influential levels of the Communist Party.

But prior to giving such information or any other to Margo, Ying had queried her intensely about her background, lifestyle, education and family position, and always in the Mandarin dialect. In return for this extensive information, he had provided her with extraordinarily valuable information related to her doctoral research.

Margo had always enjoyed these conversations, even though she found them an exhausting test of her linguistic ability. Yet Ying Soon-ling's interrogations concerning her father's political connections had always left her wary and suspicious. One afternoon shortly before she left Hong Kong to return to New York, Ying had shocked her by asking her whether her father would become Nixon or Rockefeller's Secretary of State after the election.

"How would you expect me to know?" she had replied. "I don't know how well he's connected to the Nixon staff. In fact, I don't even know how well or if he knows Nixon personally. And, if Rockefeller is elected, he is more likely to appoint Kissinger than my father. Besides, you're assuming that a Republican will win the election even though the nominations are still months away."

"But, Miss Collins, your father's Wall Street law firm has associated with Mr. Nixon for years and your father is a senior partner of the firm, is he not? Mitchell Collins has also represented the Rockefeller interests, not so?"

"From that you assume that Father will be in Nixon or Rockefeller's cabinet?" Margo had replied warily. She wondered how extensively they had studied Mitchell Collins and why?

"Of course not," Ying had replied. "But our sources tell us that both Nixon and Rockefeller are seeking influential individuals with knowledge of recent Chinese history to become powerful advisors and ministers in their regimes. Your father is such a person, and we are aware that your Government has sought his counsel on many international issues. Unfortunately, his advice has not been heeded on Chinese issues, at least, not until recently."

Margo wondered what advice her father had given and exactly to whom but did not ask.

"We do believe that President Johnson's announced decision to retire from the presidency, because of the incredibly stupid Vietnamese War, will result in the Republican Party winning the upcoming election. Presumably, there will be a role for him in the new Administration."

50.

THE PRICE OF FREEDOM

Errol Lord tried in vain to find a position on the narrow concrete bed that would relieve the intense pain, an insidious pain that permeated his cramped cell at Hoa Lo Prison, the infamous Hanoi Hilton. After the realization that Lord's news conference had produced little more than ridicule, his Vietnamese captors had transferred Lord to the instructional cell and given him the worst beating of his imprisonment.

Two teeth were broken, several ribs were bruised and one rib had been fractured during the ferocious beating. Each breath came like a fresh stab wound between his ribs. His arms had been bound so tightly behind him for so long that his left arm had been pulled from its socket. He had also been hung by his arms until his fractured arm threatened to come apart. Lord's entire body throbbed and he was dizzy and completely disoriented. Small lights flashed in the periphery of his vision. Vaguely, he knew he had suffered at least a concussion, perhaps worse, when the enraged Major Dung had slammed his head against the concrete floor. Lord feared that he was near death and had actually begun to welcome the prospect.

It seemed like the beating lasted for hours but in truth Lord had passed out after only twenty minutes of extraordinary brutality. Unlike other beatings when the jailors had revived him with cold water, this time his chief interrogator, Major Dung, was unable to bring him back to consciousness. Not wishing him to die just yet the guards dragged Lord back to his cell and dumped him on the stone floor. As his mind began to clear, he knew that his head injury probably saved him from even more damage to his already weak body, perhaps it had even saved him from death.

"Fucking Dung must have been really pissed off when someone explained the 'bird' to him," Lord muttered aloud, almost laughing. But he dared not laugh; the pain would have knocked him off the bench. "I can only hope," he continued quietly, "that the 'ugly bird' showed the Navy Department and the press back in the States know that we POWs haven't given up, haven't sold out. Maybe, even a civilian or two might appreciate the cost of our defiance." With that comforting thought, Lord drifted back into the void.

Little did Commander Lord and his interrogator, Major Dung, know, Lord's bravery had resulted in not only his severest beating but also his impending release. When General Giap, the supreme North Vietnamese Military Commander, saw the news release and recognized the significance of Lord's silent salute, he called for a meeting with the senior members of Ho Chi Minh's staff. Giap explained that the only face-saving action that could be taken in view of Lord's reckless bravado was Lord's release.

Ministers Le Duan and Le Doc Tho and Ho Chi Minh himself agreed. Having spent nearly twenty years in Paris before World War Two, Ho understood Western values. He knew it would surprise and confuse the Western press and the American public if he simply released Lord to return home rather than to continue his imprisonment. Lord's release was scheduled to take place just after the Republicans nominated

Richard Nixon and just before the Democrats began their convention in Chicago.

The morning after Lord's nearly fatal beating, Captain Pit's men dragged Lord from his cell and delivered him to the prison infirmary. There he was deloused, bathed thoroughly and given a clean set of prison pajamas. Lord was taken to a physician who bandaged his ribs, then administered some foul tasting medication which Lord suspected contained a powerful analgesic, probably morphine. After a brief physical examination, Lord received medication which began to relieve the intense throbbing in his head. But Lord remained confused about his circumstances. Why are they cleaning me up again? He wondered. Surely, they don't plan another press conference. Dung could not possibly be so stupid.

The combined effects of medication and the prison staff's perplexing actions, caused Lord to fall into a deep and fitful sleep with dreams alternating between nightmarish beatings and images of his wife and two sons at their last Thanksgiving dinner.

51.

HOMECOMING

Marchand walked quickly through the main Los Angeles International Airport terminal toward the boarding gates on a hot day in late July 1968. Anxious to board his flight to New York, his pace quickened as he neared the boarding gate. Many admiring heads turned as the tall, heavily decorated Naval Officer passed by. Marchand's short-sleeved, dazzling white uniform contrasted handsomely with his deep tan. On his left breast Navy wings of gold topped four rows of combat citations. The resplendent white uniform and Marchand's athletic bearing complemented his pride in the Naval Service and himself.

As he stood in line for a seat assignment, several scruffy looking young men with long unkempt hair, unkempt beards and rumpled blue jeans stood nearby and watched him closely. Just as the ticketing agent marked Marchand's seat assignment and returned his ticket to him, the largest of the bearded men yelled at him, "Hey, Navy officer pig, how many hospitals did you bomb in 'Nam?"

Marchand spun around to locate the source of the epithet. When he sighted the three hecklers, his face clearly reflected his revulsion. He cursed under his breath regretting his decision to travel in his summer whites even though the airlines offered fifty percent fare discounts to servicemen traveling in uniform. He reproached himself for failure to appreciate the depth of anti-Vietnam sentiment but decided to ignore the insult. Marchand turned to walk away.

"Didn't you hear me, Navy pig? How many hospitals did you bomb?" The tall bearded man continued his taunts but Marchand kept walking without giving a reply. Just as he was about to pass abreast of the three antagonists, one called out loudly. "You Navy pigs must be hard of hearing. What's a' matter, too many bombs going off too close to your little piggy ears? Take this and swab yourself down with it." He then spit directly at Marchand.

Marchand flinched as the glob of spittle flew at him landing on his arm instead of his uniform. He stared at his arm for an instant, then instinctively drew back his right arm, cocked it for power and threw a vicious right cross at the laughing thug. His fist crashed solidly into the man's face between mouth and nose. Marchand felt cartilage and teeth giving way beneath his fist. The force of the punch lifted its victim off his feet and sent him sliding to the floor.

Several bystanders began to scream while the unconscious man's friends yelled for police. Out of the quickly forming crowd stepped a beefy red-faced policeman who firmly took hold of Machand's shoulder to lead him away. One of the two hecklers still standing yelled, "That's him, officer; arrest him. He attacked us for no reason. The sailor has gone berserk."

The policeman ignored the hecklers and parted the crowd brusquely. "All right, all right, let us through here," he barked as he took hold of Marchand's arm and directed him quickly down a corridor and into a locked office. He pulled out a handkerchief, grabbed Marchand's right hand and wrapped the cloth around the bleeding knuckles. "Just sit

432

there a moment, calm down and we'll get you outta' here in a few minutes."

"You gotta' take me in, huh?" Marchand asked.

"No, son, I don't. Or I should say I won't. I saw what happened and I just hope you broke that fuckin' hippie's nose as well as his two front teeth. I have a boy about your age who was a Marine at Khe Sanh. He lost a leg in a mortar barrage. If you hadn't bashed that SOB's face in, I might have done it myself.

"Look, there's a washroom just down the corridor. Let's get your hand cleaned up so you don't get blood on your uniform, then I'll take you through the flight crew lounge up to the boarding walkway to your plane."

"I don't know how to thank you, officer. I really lost my head back there. I shouldn't have decked that guy like that."

"Don't worry, son. You boys are catching hell in 'Nam. Nobody's got a right to give you more when you finally get home, least of all, some dirty, draft-dodging hippie bastard who probably spends all his time lying around smokin' pot. Don't you worry one damn bit. Just get on your plane and go home to see your folks and your girlfriend."

"Thanks again, officer."

"Sure. Just one more thing, son."

"What's that?"

"Don't wear your uniform if you don't have to. There are a lot of crazies around who might do more than spit at you. You've been through too much to risk that; I can tell by all those combat ribbons on your chest. Don't give these punks a chance to hurt you or what that uniform stands for, son. It represents honor and discipline, something they don't know a damn thing about."

"I guess they're just frustrated about the War, officer."

"Hell, son, you didn't start the damn War."

Margo caught sight of Marchand's white bridge cap as he walked down the crowded walkway from the plane. When he emerged, she hurried to him with open arms. He saw Margo a moment before she reached him, dropped his garment bag, and scooped her into his arms. The world stopped for them as they embraced. Marchand felt his heart beat wildly. Tears streaked Margo's cheeks as she kissed him. Passersby vicariously enjoyed their unabashed tenderness.

"Keith, I've missed you so much," Margo whispered.

"I love you, Margo, more than I could ever tell you."

Suddenly, Margo stopped and exclaimed, "Keith, what happened to your hand?"

"It's nothing. Just part of my homecoming; I'll tell you about it later."

Marchand settled into the soft leather upholstery of the chauffeur-driven Mercedes and drew Margo as close to him as possible. He shut his eyes for a moment and wondered whether he had been shot down and killed during the dogfight and that he was now in heaven or at least as close to it as would ever get. His throbbing knuckles quickly convinced him otherwise.

"I haven't been in New York since senior year; it feels good to be back," Marchand said.

"I'm delighted to have you here, Darling, and planned so many things for us to do."

"Margo, there's only one thing I want to do and it doesn't involve theatres, museums, nightclubs, restaurants or any other of

Manhattan's wonders."

"What on earth could that be?" Margo asked coyly.

"It involves barricading you in my hotel room, putting out the DO NOT DISTURB sign, turning down the lights, opening a bottle of *Veuve Cliquot*, then making passionate love to you."

"Oh," Margo purred, "I thought that's what you might mean. There's only one problem with that."

"And what could that be?" Marchand replied sitting straighter.

"You, Lt. Marchand, are my house guest. Dad wouldn't approve of your scenario."

"Oh no!" Marchand exclaimed. "I mean I'm flattered to have been invited to your home but, Margo, I just want to be alone with you. Would your father consider it an insult if I graciously declined or decided to stay with relatives or anything like that?"

"Keith, don't fret. Dad leaves for Miami tomorrow for the Republican Convention. We have the entire place to ourselves --- and Maxine."

"Jesus, that's great. But who's Maxine?"

"She's our housekeeper. I know you'll like her; she's been with us as long as I can remember."

"I'm sure I will like her too, but…."

"Not to worry; I'm going to give her the week off as soon as Dad leaves."

"But when he learns of your maid's sudden vacation, he'll explode. Look, Margo, I've got a reservation at the St. Moritz. Why don't you have the chauffeur drop me off there and I'll meet you and your father later this evening. I'll explain that…."

"You're doing nothing of the sort." Margo cut him off. "My father is expecting you and I want to care for you. Your stay will be good for all of us and Maxine will do anything for me. She's practically been a second mother to me. Trust me," Margo whispered as she kissed Marchand softly.

52.

THE CONVENTION

Mitchell Collins hunkered down in his study. He was deeply absorbed in a set of position papers he was drafting for the Republican National Convention being held in Miami in less than a week.

Collins was slightly startled when Margo led Marchand into the study.

"Dad, I'd like you to meet Lieutenant Keith Marchand."

Collins stood and in a brief moment his penetrating gaze took in the whole of Marchand's physical presence. A subtle smile indicated that he approved. He extended his hand. "Welcome to our home, Lieutenant. My daughter has spoken a great deal about you."

"Thank you, Sir. It's a pleasure to meet you, an honor to be your guest," Marchand replied while shaking Collins' hand.

"The honor is mine. It's not often that one has a genuine war hero for a houseguest. Please, sit down, both of you. Let me pour you a drink. Lieutenant, what's your pleasure?"

"Scotch over, Mr. Collins. And, please call me, Keith."

"Fine, Keith. Compari and Soda for you, Margo?"

Margo nodded.

Collins walked to the liquor cabinet and began preparing the requests. "You wear the uniform well, Keith. How is it that you joined?"

"My father and grandfather were naval officers. I suppose it's a bit of a family tradition that goes back several generations. But that's always been true of the Navy, wouldn't you say?"

"Quite so. I served for a time myself, you know."

"Destroyers, Western Pacific, World War II, wasn't it?" Marchand asked.

"Right you are. I see Margo has told you a bit about me, also," Collins replied while offering drinks on a silver serving tray.

"I thought it only fair since I've talked about Keith so often," Margo said.

"That you have, my Dear. I understand that you finished The College, Class of '65, Keith."

"Class of '66, Mr. Collins. And you were in the Class of '40, I believe. Class of '49 at The Law School."

"Right again. It appears you've done your homework well. Tell me, Lieutenant, what are your plans after the Navy?"

"Well Sir, I planned to attend law school but lately I've started to think about going to divinity school," Marchand replied, an sly grin spreading across his face.

"Don't you think Keith would make a fine preacher, Father? He has such a fine tenor voice and he's so sincere when he talks about religion," Margo said with a wink and a laugh.

Collins joined the laughter. "If you do become a parson, would you kindly say a few prayers for my wayward daughter; she seems to have developed a recent problem --- falling for handsome young men in uniform."

"Mr. Collins, I'll do even better than that. I'll keep a close watch over her to make sure she stays out of trouble."

"Both of you are blatant male chauvinists, and if you don't stop your sexist remarks, I'll leave you in this musty study by yourselves," Margo replied with feigned injured dignity.

Collins stood up to leave. "I think I'll take the hint and let the two of you have a bit of privacy. I'd take you to dinner this evening, but I suppose you'd rather have the evening by yourselves.

"Keith, you've brought a little laughter back into this household after a lengthy absence. I hope you feel welcome in our home and visit often. It' s a shame that I have to leave this afternoon for the Convention in Miami. I would really enjoy taking you two to dinner and some Broadway plays or perhaps a symphony or two. But I'm sure that you both know your way around this town and how to have some fun."

"Dad, Keith and I have so much to do and people to see. Don't worry about us. We'll be fine."

"I'm sure you will. At least let me take you to dinner once after I come back. We have so much to talk about."

"That's a deal, Mr. Collins," Marchand replied.

The next morning Marchand gently pulled Margo's silken body on top of him and kissed her partly opened lips. She drew his tongue into her mouth as he entered her. Their lovemaking was full of tenderness; not like the night before when they strained against each other with passion and ferocity.

After their release, they remained coupled. Margo nestled closely against Marchand and spread her golden mane across his chest just the way he liked. She had never felt so content, he never so peaceful.

"Let's stay in bed all week, " Margo whispered.

"Don't you think we should get up at least a few hours before your father is due to return?"

"Right now, my father is the farthest thing from my mind."

"What about food?"

"All I need to sustain me is you."

"What about the Republican Convention tomorrow? Don't you want to watch it?"

"Nixon can win perfectly well without my watching him, dear. Kiss me," Margo purred as she touched Marchand's cheek.

"I never knew you were so decadent."

"I didn't either until we met. I'd never asked a man to make love to me before you."

"I'm delighted to hear that," Marchand said with mock relief.

"What's the matter? Not used to liberated women?"

"Uh oh. What's a liberated woman?"

"One who will stay in bed with you all week."

"Oh, I see. Well then kiss me, my liberated beauty."

The ringing phone prevented Margo and Marchand from making love again. Marchand swore as Margo fumbled for the phone and picked up the receiver.

"Good morning, Dad."

Marchand giggled as he pinched Margo's derriere.

"You sound like you've just awakened. Are you still in bed at noon?"

"I was out late last night, Dad. How's the Convention going?"

"Not so well, it looks like Nixon has it just about wrapped up; he'll probably win on the first ballot."

"You're not surprised, are you?"

"No, just disappointed. But that's not what I called to tell you. It

440

appears that I've had some success that will interest you…. Nixon will include a statement of conciliation toward China in his acceptance speech."

"That's wonderful, how did you do it?"

"I'll tell you when I get back to New York. It's a long story. "

"Is Kissinger making a move toward the Nixon camp now that Rockefeller's star is waning?"

"You know the answer to that as well as I do. Look, Margo, I want you to forget meeting me in Miami. There's not likely to be much celebrating in the Rockefeller headquarters so I'm taking the opportunity to do some foreign policy coaching with the Nixon entourage. I think it will be time well spent since he appears to be genuinely interested in *rapprochement with China.*

"Anyway, I know that you and Keith would enjoy Manhattan much more than this muggy place. How are you two getting along?"

"Oh, we're having a marvelous time, Dad. We're both exhausted from all the activity though. I think Keith slept in also," Margo said with a blush.

Marchand grimaced then put a pillow over his head to muffle his laughter.

"I'd feel much better if he were sleeping someplace else," Collins groused over the phone.

"Dad, don't be such a bore. Keith's a perfect gentleman."

"I'm sure he is…. All the same, I'd feel much better if he were staying at a hotel."

Margo remained silent, hoping to avoid a confrontation.

Alright then. I'll call you tomorrow…. Tell Marchand I said hello or perhaps he can hear me."

Margo stifled a laugh then replied, "What did you say, Dad?"

"Never mind, just have a good time."

"Goodbye, Dad. I love you."

53.

HARVARD SQUARE

Margo and Marchand stepped off the gleaming subway car at Harvard Square Station and walked up the worn stone steps to the sprawling newspaper stand located in the middle of the Square. Both had appointments in Cambridge during the afternoon of August 7, 1968. Margo walked with Marchand to the Massachusetts Avenue Gate to Harvard Yard, kissed him and watched as he strolled toward University Hall.

Margo then crossed the Square and headed for the Brattle Street Grill and her secret rendezvous with Dr. Li Wah-tong. There, she asked for a table near the rear of the dimly lit restaurant where she could easily watch the entrance and ordered tea. She looked at her watch; it was precisely half past noon. There were no Asian looking men in sight. Margo pretended to read a copy of *The New Yorker* as she sipped her tea and scanned the wood-paneled room for signs of Dr. Li.

At twelve forty-five, a slender Chinese man wearing a tan summer suit entered the restaurant, spoke to the maitre d', then walked over to Margo's table. He bowed slightly. "Good afternoon, Miss Collins, kindly pardon my tardiness; I had to be certain that you were not being followed," Li spoke Mandarin.

Margo studied him closely before responding. Quite tall and very fair skinned with delicate facial structure - he's clearly an aristocratic Northerner, she thought. "I assure you that I was not followed, Dr. Li. Please sit down," she replied in also speaking perfect Mandarin. "I do understand your desire to be cautious."

"Yes, there is risk for us both in this meeting."

"Well, tell me, Doctor, what more do you wish to know about me?" Margo asked after the waiter had taken an order for more tea and scones.

"Frankly, I already know all that is important to know about you."

"Then why this meeting?"

"You remember Ying Soon-ling, do you not?"

"Yes, he's the proprietor of an art gallery in Kowloon, I believe," Margo said suppressing a smile since she knew Ying quite well indeed.

"Ying has made favorable reports about you. These reports have been confirmed at another level. You might say that I'm the third level."

"So what is it you wish to know?"

"At whose prompting did you write the letter that you delivered to Ying before you left Hong Kong?"

"No one, the letter was my idea. "

"But whose ideas were in the letter?"

"They too are mine. Why would you think otherwise?" she asked.

"Who knows about the letter and its contents?"

Margo studied Dr. Li closely as she replied, "To the best of my knowledge only you, Mr. Ying, probably Dr. Tsing and those to whom you have shown it."

"No Americans?"

"No one whatsoever, not even my father," Margo replied as she sipped her tea.

Li paused for a moment, watching her, then said. "Will your father join Nixon's cabinet?"

"No, he worked diligently for Rockefeller's nomination not Nixon's. But father has good communications with people who are likely to be members of Nixon's cabinet, if he wins."

"Nixon won the Republican nomination easily; he will just as easily win the election. The question is whether your father will be able to communicate with high echelons of the Nixon Administration after the November election?"

Margo set her teacup down rather loudly, her suspicions and anxiety racing. "What's my father got to do with any of this?"

Dr. Li and Margo Collins gazed at each other coldly for a moment, then Li spoke. "Miss Collins, you are an exceptionally talented young woman; in time, you may reach a position of great authority. But for now, all of your intelligent, even brilliant, suggestions will be worth little without the means to deliver them to those in power."

"And my father is that means?" Margo narrowed her eyes, trying to read Li more clearly.

"He may be. There is, of course, another question."

"And that is?"

"Are you to be trusted?"

Margo's posture straightened significantly as she replied proudly, "Dr. Li, my family traces its lineage back to the Revolution, my father is a third generation Harvard lawyer, senior partner in one of the oldest law firms on Wall Street, and a former Naval officer. I am less than a year from my Ph.D. at the Kennedy School of Government at Harvard. I have employment offers from the State Department and Harvard to name a few. I speak three Chinese dialects probably better than any non-Chinese in the United States."

Margo paused a moment, then continued....

"I don't need money, nor position nor power. Neither does my father. I have pursued this matter because China is the oldest and one of the most developed cultures in the world, because I have great respect and admiration for China, and because I sincerely wish to see my country recognize China rather than continue its relationship with Chaing Kai-shek and Taiwan.

"If you cannot trust my father or me, you cannot trust anyone in the United States," Margo concluded, only then realizing Dr. Li had played her pride like a finely tuned instrument in order to hear her true feelings. What in the world is he really after, she asked herself.

Dr. Li studied Margo for several moments before answering. "As a man who traces his ancestry back seven centuries, I appreciate your lineage as well as your candor. What you say rings true, Miss Collins. I shall report that you are a rather naïve person but one of great intelligence and integrity, notwithstanding your somewhat convoluted political entanglements. I do have one final question, however. Will your father help you in your endeavors?"

"He will, if he deems this a good idea, help us in any way that is lawful and honorable," Margo said with a resolve that concealed most of her anxiety.

"Very well. You do understand that, should you fail to elicit your esteemed father's cooperation, the consequences for you and your father might prove rather serious?"

Margo's pulse soared and her eyes narrowed again, this time

only slightly. "Excuse me, is it possible that you are threatening me?"

Dr. Li was quiet for a moment, as if savoring his power. "…Only, Ms. Collins, if you feel that news of your recent travels inside China might be threatening to you or your father."

Margo reeled with the realization that she had possibly been set-up.

"Now it's my turn to ask a few questions, Doctor," she said as calmly as possible.

Li shook his head no. "I know you have many questions, Miss Collins. But I am not in a position to answer them for you at this time. I will contact you again in the near future. I must ask you to be patient in the meantime. You know how we Chinese are."

Sensing a linguistic and cultural trap, Margo replied only, "Yes, I believe I do, Dr. Li."

Li cleared his throat unnecessarily before responding. "Yes, well, I have enjoyed talking to you, Miss Collins. Just one more item, though. Your naval officer friend must know nothing about this. It would not be good for him to know of our discussions. Not good for him or you."

This is becoming worse by the moment, Margo thought. "Of course not, but how do you know about him?" She asked, feigning charm.

"As I said, we have observed you for some time therefore we know about him, and your feelings for him, Miss Collins. That is all I have to say on this matter. So, I bid you a good day."

"Good day, Dr. Li," Margo nodded, rattled yet relieved that this conversation was over.

Li rose and left without touching his tea or looking back at Margo's lotus white face.

VOLUME ONE: PHANTOM WAR TRILOGY

54.

RETURN TO THE YARD

Marchand walked slowly around Harvard Yard savoring the familiar sights and comforting feeling of three hundred year-old brick and ivy bathed in the dappled sunshine of late August. The Yard was quiet since summer session had ended and students had not yet arrived for fall semester. Only a few tourists strolled the intersecting walkways. He climbed the steps of Widener Library and gazed out at the Yard picturing himself hurrying along to class as he had only three years earlier, three lifetimes it seemed, since he had become a warrior. Feeling nostalgic, he headed toward University Hall and his three o'clock appointment with Dr. Carl Steinhardt, Professor of History, Master of Elliot House, and Marchand's senior year faculty advisor.

Steinhardt was a thin, wiry man in his late fifties with thick black hair and enormous bushy eyebrows which could be either menacing or comical depending upon his mood. He was standing at his lectern writing furiously when Marchand opened the door to his office. Marchand recognized Brahms' Third Symphony as he poked his head into the office that had not changed since he had last seen it. "Mind if I join you? This is one of my favorite symphonies."

Steinhardt looked up from his notes. "Ah, Marchand, there you are. How good it is to see you. Come in; come in. Let me turn the music down a bit."

"It's good to see you, Professor. I was pleased and surprised to hear that you'd be in town since you're between sessions."

"Normally, you would have missed me but last semester was such a disaster around this University, I decided to stay here during the summer break to complete some writing and enjoy some peace and quiet."

"A bit noisy around here, I take it," Marchand said.

"Sit-ins, teach-ins, demonstrations, and disturbances of every sort and variety. There's too much of everything but teaching and learning taking place on this campus. If this blasted War goes on much longer, I do believe that higher education will cease at this venerable institution.

"But listen to me prattle on about the inconveniences of war as I stand before a real warrior. Do forgive my insensitivity. Please sit down." Steinhardt gestured toward an overstuffed, well-used armchair. "Well now, how are you, Marchand?"

"Alive and well, Professor, and delightedly so."

Steinhardt collected his papers. "I've read that you've become a hero of sorts, shooting down MIG fighters and what not. You were always full of surprises when you were at Elliot House but this is even more of a shock than I would have expected from you."

"Surprised me as much as anyone else."

"We certainly need a few heroes. This damned War seems to have produced very few so far."

"Not so, Professor, you just don't hear about them. What we did was more a matter of luck than anything else. But it makes good press.

Besides, in the short time I've been back, I'm getting the impression that servicemen are more likely to be considered pariahs than heroes."

Steinhardt stood at his lectern and assumed a professorial air as he said, "These are difficult times, Keith. This nation hasn't experienced anything like this since the Civil War. This spring, Martin Luther King was assassinated, this summer, Bobby Kennedy was killed, the nation's universities are in turmoil, and looming over and beneath everything is the War. It's dividing this country in a most frightening way. We must find a way out or I'm afraid the fabric of this nation shall be permanently torn."

"I'm afraid I agree, but tell me one thing, Professor: why do so many people blame servicemen for this fiasco?"

"You're just convenient targets, scapegoats, that's all. Rational people don't blame you but reason is not the code word of our times. However, the public does blame certain senior military officials for being, shall we say, rather disingenuous about the facts of this situation. Since the Tet Offensive, the public has become increasingly aware that the military has lied about so much -- from enemy troop strength, to casualty figures and losses, to the state of American readiness. Unfortunately, individual servicemen are the most accessible targets, not the generals, admirals and cabinet level secretaries with responsibility and authority.

"But the military is not alone in feeling the public's wrath, Keith. Look at Johnson, so despised and disrespected that he won't even seek another term. Nevertheless, the political turmoil is just beginning. I have a feeling that the Democratic Convention in Chicago will turn into a debacle next week. We're in for a long siege, I'm afraid."

Marchand almost raised his hand like a student before he responded. "Don't you think that the next president will take the opportunity to negotiate a settlement?"

"It's clear that Nixon will win this election, and if he does, he'll try to win the War at all costs, no matter what he says now about having a 'secret plan' to end the War. He'll try different tactics, but he'll go for the military victory. Perhaps, he'll try to use more air power and fewer ground troops to disguise his real and aggressive strategy. What do you think?"

"Complete reliance on air power would certainly reduce our casualty figures and remove some of the political heat, but it won't win the War unless he pulls out all the stops and tries to annihilate North Vietnam. But, he couldn't do that without risking direct Soviet or Chinese intervention. And, I don't think that American or world opinion would stand for that," Marchand answered.

"What about more intense application of present air tactics?"

"If you mean interdiction of supplies, forget it. Trying to bomb the supplies heading south from Hanoi and Haiphong is about as effective as trying to empty the Charles River with a bucket brigade. Most of the supplies come south on bicycles pushed by tens of thousands of North Vietnamese Army regulars who move by night along muddy footpaths. There's no way to stop them unless we destroy their entire country."

"Hmmm," Steinhardt nodded.

"Interdiction and all the other tactics we use are effective against sophisticated, industrialized war machines, not Uncle Ho's guerrilla army. We can bomb those trails 'till we level every tree in Southeast Asia but we won't stop the North Vietnamese Army from moving south," Marchand said emphatically.

"What about all the Soviet munitions and trucks coming down from North Vietnam that the Pentagon reports as being destroyed day-in and day-out?" Steinhardt queried as he focused intensely on Marchand from under his huge dark eyebrows.

"Oh sure, we tear up a lot of trucks and destroy a lot of ammunition, but it's only a fraction of the material being transported. Most of it isn't even carried on trucks. It's carried on bicycles, for Pete's sake!"

Steinhardt left his lectern, walked over to the sofa near Marchand and sat down as he asked, "And the Pentagon is fully aware of this?"

Marchand stared intensely at Steinhardt as he replied. "Of course."

"And yet they can do nothing about it?"

"Modern air power is almost ineffective in this type of guerrilla warfare, Professor. The only realistic counterforce would be a strong, viable South Vietnam. And you know better than I that the Republic of South Vietnam is a fiction.

"I often think about the discussions I had with you at Elliot House. Remember how we argued about the importance of an independent South Vietnam? And don't you recall how vigorously you tried to explain that there was no such thing? In fact, now, each time I hear about the ARVN desertions and their lack of fighting spirit, I think about those discussions with you."

Steinhardt was silent for a moment then said quietly, "Yes, I remember those arguments quite well, Keith. I remember how convinced you were that the United States must stand behind its commitments to its allies, including South Vietnam. I couldn't get through to you at all, no matter what approach I used. Your concepts of commitment seemed to block my argument. It's a noble thing to feel commitment as you do. But one must analyze thoroughly the reasons and facts behind one's

453

commitments and stand prepared to question or change those commitments if the supporting facts or logic proves faulty or untrue."

"Yes, I know that now," Marchand replied pensively.

"You simply wouldn't accept the fact that the U. S. is largely responsible for creating South Vietnam and utilizing it as a pawn or a proxy in our cold war against the Soviets and the Chinese. You ignored Ho Chi Minh's nationalism and dedication to the unification of his country and the expulsion of colonial powers from all of Vietnam. You were such a fine scholar in every other respect; I couldn't understand your refusal to think rationally where Vietnam was concerned."

Marchand simply listened without replying.

"But, you know, Keith, I have the same problem trying to comprehend the failure of otherwise rational people in the State Department, the Defense Department, and the current Administration, to analyze the Vietnam situation correctly. These are people I know well, people I've taught here at Harvard, people with extraordinarily fine minds and impeccable credentials. I could name a dozen to you right now.

"Still, I felt strangely defeated in my inability to get through to you. I knew that you, unlike others, would feel compelled to honor your beliefs with action. I still recall my shock when I learned you had volunteered for Navy flight training. I couldn't believe that you would actually do it. You were like a son to me."

Marchand's face flushed when he heard this and he shifted in his chair before responding. "That's a very kind thing for you to say, Professor."

"Enough of the 'Professor' business; just call me Carl."

"Of course, Carl. I suppose I should feel foolish, and I would, except for…"

Steinhardt interrupted, "Oh, don't tell me; I know already. You love flying and chasing pretty women just like every fighter pilot since Von Richthoven."

Marchand laughed then responded. "Not exactly. We've got more than a half-million men in Vietnam, most of whom are in far worse circumstances than I. Every mission I fly that results in a few munitions trucks getting blown up on their way into South Vietnam probably means a few more GI's get to go home in one piece. And, perhaps more importantly, I feel damn certain, despite everything we've said today and years ago when I was your student, that there are millions of South Vietnamese who do not want Communist domination who would do anything to avoid it. Do we simply write them off?

"I'm not so certain, Carl, that Ho Chi Minh is as benevolent as the students on this campus and elsewhere would have us believe. What do we say, what do we do, if the Communists take over South Vietnam and then methodically proceed to liquidate everyone who resisted the takeover in typical Stalin-like fashion? And what can be done if we withdraw from Vietnam and find that the Communists don't stop with their reunification of Vietnam but continue their conquests in Laos, Cambodia and even Thailand? What happens if we find that the Domino Theory really is valid?"

Steinhardt was silent for several moments before speaking. "Those are difficult questions, indeed, and I have no quick nor easy answers. I've often pondered those questions myself and I'm terribly troubled that I don't have comforting solutions. I suppose that occasionally, if not frequently, one must admit that there are no answers, or at least none that one can accept graciously, to the profound questions that confront us." Steinhardt stood, walked slowly to the window overlooking Harvard Yard, and gazed at the familiar oval green lawn crisscrossed by pathways leading to ivy-covered brick buildings, some of which were built before the American Revolution. He seemed to be searching for the accumulated wisdom of those who had studied and taught there during the previous three and a half centuries.

"Perhaps," Steinhardt continued, "it would be better to allow the Vietnamese, and indeed all South East Asians, to settle the question of their own destiny no matter how brutally they may set about doing it. Then the blood, if shed, will be on their own hands - not ours. Strangely enough, in the end, there might be far less blood spilled by the victorious North Vietnamese than will otherwise be the case if America continues this War.

"As for the fate of those neighboring countries, I must admit there is grave risk to them from a militaristic and unified Vietnam. That risk is indeed profoundly disturbing. However, a careful historical review of Southeast Asian history over the last two thousand years reveals that, each time the Kingdom of Annam, or Vietnam as it's now known, threatened the sub-continent with expansionist aggression, China moved to quell the threat. One could reasonably expect such a natural balancing of forces may well be repeated today. The United States may only be interfering in that balancing of power in the region. And, I dare say, at great risk to world peace."

"You're right, Carl, those answers aren't easy to accept, especially if one happens to be a South Vietnamese who has supported the United States and its involvement in his country over the past fourteen years," Marchand shrugged.

"To that comment," Steinhardt changed his tone, "I have no response, so let me change the subject, at least for a moment. Will you apply for a seat in the next class at The Law School?"

"Class of Seventy, I'm afraid not, Carl. I have one more tour of duty in Vietnam. My ship will probably depart early next year, so it will have to be the Class of Seventy-One for me. What do you think my chances are?"

"Well, with your undergraduate record, I'm certain that your chances are excellent, you should know that. But I'm saddened to hear that you must return to Vietnam. What your chances are there is the real question." Steinhardt crossed his arms like a troubled father.

"Wish I had a good answer for you," Marchand said wistfully.

"Actually, your odds of survival will be quite a bit better than they were on your first combat tour."

"How so?" Marchand seemed puzzled by the Professor's almost casual comment.

"I'm informed by very reliable sources in Johnson's Administration that the partial bombing halt in North Vietnam will become a complete bombing halt before Johnson leaves office. That should improve your odds considerably."

"That certainly would be an excellent development. Does your crystal ball indicate whether Nixon or Humphrey would continue this bombing halt?"

"Humphrey would certainly continue it. As for Nixon, the crystal ball becomes somewhat hazy - but I don't think he would cancel it immediately. I think it most likely that Nixon will extend it long enough for you to complete your tour of duty there, however."

"There is one additional question I need to ask you, Carl, now that you've brightened my day so considerably."

Before Marchand could continue, Steinhardt interrupted. "Of course, I'll write your faculty recommendation for The Law School. Just be careful so that the Class of Seventy-One doesn't start without you."

VOLUME ONE: PHANTOM WAR TRILOGY

55.

THANKFUL FOR WHAT?

Winter came early to New England. By mid-October, leaves had colored and fallen, leaving naked branches to accept the season's first snows. Cambridge settled into a solemn gray funk in preparation for the long darkness of winter. Richard M. Nixon was elected thirty-sixth President of the United States on November 5, 1968, plunging the mood of many college campuses into deep depression. Beginning with the shock of the Tet Offensive in Vietnam and continuing through the dual traumas of the King and Kennedy assassinations in April and June, the year 1968 was ending in the worst possible way, as college after college erupted in violence.

As the Thanksgiving holiday approached, Margo Collins avoided the prevailing sour mood on campus by immersing herself into writing her dissertation. On Monday evening, like most others, she settled in an old but comfortable swivel chair from Mitchell Collins' study pulled close to her long campaign desk covered with mountains of books, notes and papers piled on each side of her typewriter. A steadily growing stack of typed pages measured her progress and she was pleased. Snow began falling again and Margo stopped typing long enough to build a fire to break the chill that had crept into the drafty, old Cambridge apartment.

She returned to her writing but was soon interrupted by the telephone. Annoyed, she nearly determined to let it ring, but thinking the caller might be Marchand, she lifted the receiver. The patrician tone of well-spoken Mandarin surprised her. She recognized the voice and replied. *"Nie how mah*, Doctor Li?"

Li replied that he was quite well and then apologized for the delay in contacting her. He requested that the conversation continue in Chinese, explaining again his commitment to caution.

"There is a great struggle taking place in China," Li began solemnly. "It is a struggle that will affect China's future for generations. The outcome of this confrontation is important to the United States, as well. And, you may have the opportunity to influence the direction of the struggle, Miss Collins."

Margo sat up straight. "Aren't you a bit dramatic, Doctor Li?"

"I'll let you decide. You are familiar with the Red Guards, are you not?"

"Certainly." Margo's eyes widened. What next, she wondered?

"The Red Guards were, until their recent dissolution, the clearest example of the great political tension that exists in China today. The Guards reflected not only The Chairman's revolutionary ideals, but more ominously, the influence of four extremely radical individuals who are close to the Chairman. Those radicals, including Mao's wife, Chiang Ching, have exploited the Chairman's desire for ideological purity to enhance their own power. By encouraging revolutionary excesses such as the purges and violence practiced by the Red Guards, they have ingratiated themselves with the Chairman, but tragically, they have largely destroyed China's economy, its educational system, its political stability, and endangered external security. I know that you are aware of all this."

Margo wondered where all this was leading. "Yes, I've seen the effects on China's educational system first hand. In fact, I've written extensively of the Red Guards in my doctoral dissertation," Margo responded in flawless Mandarin, in a tone that revealed none of her doubts.

"These revolutionary excesses have done far more than threaten the educational system. They have weakened China's ability to confront our greatest enemy and yours, the Soviet Union. But there are voices of reason that have almost equal access to our Great Chairman as do the Radicals. The voices of Chou En-lai, Deng Tsou–ping, and others will prevail if they can persuade The Chairman that ideological purity is less important than Soviet imperialism."

"What on earth could I or my father do about that?" Margo was alert and listening quite closely for even the most subtle inflections, terms, and indications of polite extortion. Yet, she was certain that she would have no choice but to try and meet Dr. Li's requests.

"Here it is, Miss Collins. The Chairman must be convinced that China has little to fear from the United States, that the antagonism between China and the U.S. need not continue, and that there is an opportunity for rapprochement. This would solve half of the problem."

"And the other half? What about the Chairman's attitude about the Soviet Union?" Margo asked carefully. "We're all living on the verge of World War III, no matter who aligns with whom."

"The Soviets themselves have shown their true intentions with their recent invasion of Czechoslovakia. And recently the Kremlin has announced the Soviet policy of 'Limited Sovereignty' to justify that invasion. We believe the Kremlin has really announced its intentions and justification for eventually invading China itself. It's really a matter of time before armed conflict takes place on the Sino-Soviet border," Li said solemnly, and then paused.

Margo kept silent a moment, trying to analyze the import of what she had been told. Li was indeed pressuring her, but for reasons that she well understood. "So what message do you wish my father relay to Nixon's staff?" Margo queried, determined to test her role in the game.

"Nixon has already taken some appropriate steps by declaring in his nomination acceptance speech that he wishes to extend the hand of friendship to China. Of course, he was only responding to Hubert Humphrey's campaign rhetoric about China. However, we believe Nixon intends to make good on his promises. He appears to be an astute observer of Chinese politics. But the critical factor is timing. If Nixon waits too long to make a serious overture to The Chairman, this rare window of opportunity will close, perhaps for many years," Li declared.

"How long will this so-called 'window' remain open?" Margo inquired.

"A few months, perhaps a bit longer."

"And what type of overture should be made?"

"That, of course, is the most difficult issue. We understand that for political reasons, Nixon cannot move too quickly regarding China. Yet time is of the essence if the Radicals, which many of us have begun to call 'The Gang of Four', are to be thwarted.

"If Nixon were to make conciliatory statements toward China in his inaugural speech and then follow those statements with concrete steps leading to a lessening of tensions, Chou En-Lai and other moderate forces will gain valuable leverage against The Radicals."

"That will not be easy, Dr. Li."

"Nixon must be persuaded to give evidence of a softening line toward China, or the United States will confront a unified Sino-Soviet monolith dominated by the Soviets, which could overwhelm the U.S. and its allies. For years your government has made many foolish decisions based upon the assumption that a unified Communist superstate actually exists. If the United States does not soon demonstrate its intentions, a unified Communist Bloc might well become reality."

Margo swallowed hard. "I agree." She paused, seeming to think for a moment, "Perhaps my father can be persuaded to make an approach to the Nixon inner circle, if not Nixon himself. However, I would have to convince him that I'm dealing with influential members of the Chinese government and not some fringe element," Margo stated emphatically.

She went on, "As I am sure you realize, at this moment, I still have no proof that what you say is true. In fact, I really don't know who you are or what your position might be. I'm operating on faith, on my unauthorized contacts with unknown Chinese operatives, and my own murky contacts in Hong Kong. And, I'm under some pressure from you regarding my reputation and career as well as my father's. I'm certain you understand that you must present some proof of your credentials and the veracity of your statements before I can act."

"I am prepared to do just that, Miss Collins."

"And just how do you propose to do it?"

"I mentioned that Ricart Sero has spoken favorably of you, have I not?" Professor Li inquired.

"Yes, you did, when we met in Cambridge. I was quite shocked to hear that."

"Sero is also an old and trusted friend of your Father's, is he not?"

"You know that too?" Margo wondered just how much Li knew

about her private life.

"Sero will soon arrive in New York, ostensibly to conduct business for which your father's law firm will be needed. In fact, he is coming expressly to convince Mitchell Collins to listen carefully to his daughter's request and to validate my credentials, so to speak."

"So why do you need me at all? Why can't Sero convince my father to approach Nixon?" Margo asked sincerely.

"As much as your father admires and respects Sero, he would not make such a move without additional persuasion. And who better than his beloved only child for this task? Sero is convinced of that as well as I. We all think that you could be most influential in this matter. Together, you and Sero could, as your saying goes, pull it off."

Margo reflected for a moment, hoping her anxiety was not apparent, before responding. As much as she was intrigued by what she heard, she felt dangerously close to becoming engulfed by extraordinarily powerful forces far beyond her control.

And then there was Marchand. What could Dr. Li's colleagues do to Marchand? They could use him to embarrass the United States by having him accused of consorting with a Communist sympathizer, or perhaps even a spy who has secretly been into the People's Republic of China. Margo felt sick to her stomach as she realized her vulnerability.

She responded slowly, carefully choosing the most precise Mandarin at her command. "I will not risk damaging my father's career or reputation unless there is some credible offer on your part to respond to an American overture."

Dr. Li had presumed Margo's caution and had already prepared his response. "As you are undoubtedly aware, the People's Republic has announced the postponement of the Warsaw Talks with the United States regarding normalization of relations unless the U.S. announces its willingness to negotiate military withdrawal from Taiwan. If the American response to this question becomes favorable, and if the future president, Mr. Nixon, announces that he is open to negotiations on this issue, we will assist the U.S. in solving a most embarrassing problem."

"And what problem might that be, Dr. Li?"

"We are prepared to assist the United States in obtaining the release of the captain and crew of the *U.S.S. Pueblo* which North Korea has steadfastly refused to do for nearly a year. This could possibly happen as soon as your Christmas holiday."

Margo was nearly speechless for a few moments. The capture of the American spy ship *Pueblo* and its crew by the North Koreans had indeed become one of the longest running military and political embarrassments that America faced since the Bay of Pigs fiasco. Negotiations for the release of the crew had dragged on for nearly a year without success and the situation seemed likely to embroil the United States in another Asian conflict which it could ill afford.

"If that could be accomplished, it would indeed set the stage for a rapprochement of enormous consequence. But," she added, "how could I, or even my father, convince Nixon's staff or the departing Johnson foreign policy staff that you could deliver?"

Li replied without hesitation. "You underestimate your father's influence, Miss Collins. Additionally, Mr. Sero is prepared to assist you. His influence with your State Department is not inconsequential. The stakes of this game are quite high, but I believe that you can ably assist us in this great task. There are few who are as well positioned as you and no one else who possesses the linguistic ability as well as the diplomatic and family connections." Li paused, then asked, "So what is your decision, Miss Collins?"

Margo answered firmly in a voice that betrayed none of the

anxiety she felt. "I cannot decline your request, but I may have certain conditions or stipulations of my own in order to proceed. Perhaps you can call me in two days to discuss this matter in greater detail."

"Mr. Sero will address those matters with you when he arrives. Pending the resolution of your concerns, do I have your commitment to proceed?"

Margo answered resolutely. "You do, yes, you do. And do I have your solemn word that all you have said is true, especially with regard to the crew of the *Pueblo?*"

"Most certainly, Miss Collins. Now, I must end our conversation. You have my best wishes for success with this undertaking and your doctoral dissertation as well."

Margo started to ask how Dr. Li knew that she was writing her dissertation, but Li had already hung up. She looked around her room. The fire had gone out.

56.

A LESSON TO REMEMBER

An unfamiliar prison guard roughly shook Commander Lord awake and led him toward the small unlit closet where prisoners were infrequently permitted to shower. Lord stripped bare and trained the cold water from an old garden hose over his face and hair which were still caked with residual dried blood from his beatings. The water shocked Lord into a state of heightened awareness and apprehension, as he still had no idea what fate was about to befall him. After drying himself, Lord was given a nearly new set of striped pajamas and rubber sandals, then told to move out.

Lord stumbled into a large interrogation room where Major Dung sat behind a bare wooden desk. Lord began to shake uncontrollably and his knees seemed to buckle noticeably. He asked himself, "My God, why have they cleaned me up for another beating?" Then he noticed that there was no one else in the room except Major Dung and himself. No guards were there to bind him, kick or beat him. Just Lord and Dung.

Lord stood motionless, waiting for Dung to speak or begin this novel form of interrogation. But Dung said nothing for several minutes while he completed a cigarette. Suddenly, Dung looked up from the desk and motioned Lord to take a seat on the straight-backed wooden chair in front of the desk. Lord surveyed the room, which had been freshly white washed, the floor recently hosed down and mopped. The walls were bare, save for a picture of the ubiquitous Chairman Ho and a calendar curiously printed in French. Lord waited patiently for Dung to speak.

After an uncomfortable silence and a dark, baleful stare at Lord, Dung spoke. "You filthy Yankee dog! I should have killed you when I had the opportunity. A few more kicks, one more shove of your foul head into the concrete floor and you would no longer be here."

Sensing a dramatic change for the better, Lord replied, "So, why didn't you kill me, Major?"

"It is not considered particularly professional for an interrogating officer to preside over his prisoner's death. But still, it happens from time to time. In your case, it should have happened. You have greatly embarrassed the People's Republic of Vietnam with your obscene American gesture. You, like all Americans, are a loathsome dog." Dung ended his epithet with a vicious wad of spit to the floor next to Lord's chair.

Somewhat emboldened, Lord replied, "Would you not have done the same given the chance?"

"Vietnamese do not deal in obscenity. We are an ancient and cultured people. We only wish to rid ourselves of yet another western colonial power and its running dog lackeys such as you."

Lord decided that something rather dramatic had taken place, and concluded that he would speak freely to Major Dung. To hell with the Uniform Code of Military Justice and its commandment to provide only name, rank and serial number if captured by enemy forces, he thought.

Lord spoke slowly and deliberately. "Neither I nor any American serviceman has come here to colonize your country, Major. We are here to follow orders and protect the sovereignty of South Vietnam."

Dung glared raw hatred toward Lord before responding. "I do not have the time or the inclination to educate you, Commander Lord. But I will tell you this much. For more than two hundred years, we have fought against the colonial tyranny of the French, the Japanese and then the French again only to have you Americans take their places. We will destroy you just as we destroyed the French and even the Chinese invaders before them. We will prevail, we will crush you and your damnable airplanes because we have the will, we have the power, and we will never surrender. This is our land, our country, our people and our history. You do not belong here and soon you will leave."

Lord sensed something in Dung's soliloquy that he had never before considered and it sent a cold chill through him. If the average North Vietnamese soldier feels as Major Dung, we are in for the fight of our lives. Then he spoke with determination. "Our commitment to protect the democratically elected government of South Vietnam is as strong or stronger than your will to defeat us, Major."

"The government of Saigon is no more democratically elected than is Chairman Ho but there is a difference, Commander Lord. We belong here; this is our land. You do not belong here. You are not wanted either by us in the North or by our comrades in the South. Do you think that by bombing our villages, in the North and the South, that we will come to love you? Do you not realize that every air raid you send against us here in the North makes our resolve even stronger? Do you not understand that every village your soldiers destroy in the South makes all of us hate you even more? With every bombing of a village, you Americans only sow the seeds of Dragon teeth. You Americans are great fools, all of you!"

Lord had not expected Dung's verbal ferocity or articulation. Still, he clung to the American party line and responded. "We, Americans, wish you in the North no ill will, we only fight to protect an independent and freely elected government in South Vietnam that does not wish to be overrun by your army."

Dung's face turned red with rage. He could barely control his anger but finally he replied with unconcealed loathing. "Listen to me, Commander Lord, and never forget my words as you are returned to your beloved United States. American bombers, and you personally, have rained death upon the Vietnamese people. Your bombs have killed and maimed hundreds of thousands of my countrymen including my mother and father. And just ten months ago, American bombs killed my wife and young son. If I have but one wish, it is to destroy you and all the ignorant fools like you so that we may finally live in peace.

"So now, Commander, take your leave before I shoot you and the hell with the consequences for me and my career. My assistants will take you from the prison and deliver you to Swedish diplomats who will escort you to Paris and your freedom. Never forget what I have said today. Never forget that the people of the Democratic Republic of Vietnam will crush you and your puppet government in Saigon. Never forget how powerful is our resolve to rid ourselves of you. Never forget how much I desire to kill you at this very moment."

Major Dung stood, glowered piercingly at Lord one last time, then left the room.

Lord sat in amazement at both the prospect of his freedom and the intensity of Dung's hatred toward him and all Americans.

57.

HUNGARIAN RHAPSODY

Sero arrived in Manhattan the day before Thanksgiving. He hadn't been in New York for nearly five years and he thought it particularly *apropos* to be in the United States on the most American of all holidays. He was quite pleased at the prospect of spending time with his old friend, Mitchell Collins, and his friend's most unusual and intellectually precocious daughter. But most of all, Sero was delighted to play a role in the clandestine diplomacy developing between the United States and the People's Republic of China. Sero, for years a deeply placed agent of the PRC, could barely contain his excitement as he planned his initial conversation with Collins.

By this time, Sero reasoned, Margo will certainly have described her meetings with Dr. Li to her father. Most importantly, she should have relayed Li's message regarding a diplomatic overture towards China and China's offer of assistance in procuring the release of the *Pueblo* crew. If so, the stage will be set for my part in the play, he thought. Clearly relishing his role in the diplomatic drama, he anticipated a Thanksgiving dinner like no other. Sero's face reflected his eager anticipation as the Plaza Hotel doorman opened the door of his limousine.

Margo had been in New York for several days when Sero arrived. She had already persuaded her father to set a very private Thanksgiving dinner for three instead of the large and festive affair that he normally hosted. "Some of our conversation will require absolute privacy," Margo said solemnly to her father. "Besides, we can have a great dinner party on Saturday when no one has anything better to do." Collins was delighted with the prospect of an intimate dinner with his daughter and Sero, and with it, the promise of intriguing conversation.

When Mitch Collins opened the door for Sero, years of friendship and affection overwhelmed the two in a prolonged handshake and bear hug. International commerce as well as occasional affairs of state had forged powerful bonds of trust and confidence between them. When they stepped back from one another, Collins exclaimed, "Rick, you seem ageless. How do you manage to remain so timelessly elegant?"

Sero laughed heartily and replied, "I have told you may times, Mitch, the key to eternal grace and style is to surround oneself with beauty and drink only the finest wine."

"You have succeeded admirably on both counts, Rick. Please come in; we've been eagerly awaiting your arrival for days."

Sero crossed the foyer and entered the Collins living room where Margo somewhat anxiously awaited him. He embraced her and kissed her forehead with a combination of staged and genuine avuncular affection. Margo responded with kisses to both of his ample cheeks and a tug towards an enormous leather sofa facing a picture window overlooking Central Park. "How was your flight, Rick? You must be exhausted after such a long trip."

Sero denied fatigue, claiming that a good night's rest and adequate pampering from the Plaza's staff had restored his vigor, not to mention his appetite. Margo assured him that he would not be disappointed with her Thanksgiving dinner. "Father and I have never been terribly fond of turkey, so we have peculiar Collins family tradition for this holiday. We serve rack of lamb flown in from a Sonoma ranch run by a retired investment banker from San Francisco. But just in case you might have anticipated more traditional fare, we do have a turkey which Maxine prepared just for you."

Collins presented Sero with an extremely dry Boodles martini and two enormous olives. Sero waited until his hosts had glasses in hand to propose a toast, which he did with his customary grace. "To my two most favorite Americans: may you have more each year for which to be truly thankful. And may this Thanksgiving be filled with affection, excellent food and wine, and perhaps a little intrigue."

Margo winced visibly, but her father didn't notice.

Mitchell Collins replied, "I can guaranty the food, wine and affection; but the intrigue is most probably up to you, Rick. So, let's attend to our more immediate needs and leave whatever more serious matters there are for discussion later this evening. By the way, you should know that tonight is a particularly special occasion."

Collins paused for a moment then said with obvious delight, "My lovely daughter cooks for me once a year if I'm on my best behavior. So tonight, Margo has prepared everything but the obligatory turkey as a special treat to her old dad."

Margo displayed a well-developed set of culinary skills during the meal, which her guest thoroughly enjoyed. Chateau Montelena Chardonnay complemented the most delicious pheasant that Sero had enjoyed in years. Several exquisite Bordeaux including a '61 Chateau Margaux and a '55 Chateau Latour balanced the lamb and marinated asparagus to perfection. Sero was duly impressed and complimented Margo sincerely, "As a restaurateur of some note, please accept my compliments on your splendid culinary efforts. If you ever decide to become an executive chef, I offer you the position at Rick's in advance."

Margo, still nervous about the conversation ahead, made herself smile and replied, "I'm flattered, Rick, but I don't think we'd have much chance of success since I only manage to do this once or twice a year."

"Excellent point, my dear," replied Sero, "So let's talk about your more serious interests in the academic universe. How goes your dissertation?"

Margo somewhat stiffly described her progress, her hopes to complete the first draft in the early spring, and her plan to defend her dissertation in time for June commencement.

"And what then, my dear?" Sero asked.

"I'm talking to a few universities and the State Department," Margo replied.

"The State Department being your first choice?" Sero queried.

Margo nodded as she felt the conversation shifting.

Collins interjected, "Speaking of affairs of state, I understand from Margo that you may have certain information or perhaps confirmation for me regarding a diplomatic mission of sorts. Although the notion of this unknown Chinese gentleman contacting me through my daughter feels implicitly threatening and somewhat manipulative, I must admit that I am interested."

"You refer to Dr. Li, I assume?" Sero responded.

"Presumably that's not his actual name, but Dr. Li is the gentleman," Collins replied.

"Let me begin by telling you that I have known Dr. Li for more than thirty years. Li is his *nom de guerre* and he would rather that I not divulge his true name. In any event, Li speaks directly to and occasionally for the Chinese Politburo. He is a colleague and confidant of Chou En-lai. It is said that he sometimes communicates directly to Chairman Mao.

"What he has suggested to your daughter comes from a very high level within the Chinese government, you can be certain. And, as Margo has undoubtedly explained, Li represents the more moderate forces within the inner circle of the Politburo including Chou himself. A truly significant gesture made by the new American Administration could well influence the direction of Chinese foreign policy for years to come. Who knows where it could all lead?"

Margo responded as Sero expected, "And timing is absolutely critical, Father. Chairman Mao is aging rapidly. As you know, his health is reputed to be quite poor. There are factions that might use his age and condition as an excuse or shield to mask their own agendas which could be much more militaristic and hostile to the West."

Collins listened attentively as Sero and his daughter presented the case for action. Clearly, Margo had given the proposal deep thought and elected to support the effort. Collins assumed this to be true, although it occurred to him that she might have been pressured to do so. With this in mind, Collins questioned Sero at length about Dr. Li's credentials and *bona fides*. He explained that his contacts with Nixon's staff and Secretary of State Designate William Rogers were somewhat tenuous, at best, and that there were many in Nixon's inner circle who would oppose any move toward normalization of relations with the PRC. Collins also stated that he would require clearance from the outgoing Secretary of State, since he did not wish to damage his long-standing rapport with the old guard Democratic Party leadership.

After lengthy discussion among the three, Collins finally accepted Sero's validation of Dr. Li. The opportunity to have a measurable impact on Chinese foreign policy deserved serious consideration and possibly the expenditure of significant political capital on his part. Finally, Collins determined that the risk/reward balance appeared to tip in favor of action.

Collins agreed that Li's carefully delivered offer of assistance in the *Pueblo* matter could well convince the hardliners in Nixon's kitchen cabinet that such action may be worth the risk. Few other options short of war for obtaining the crew's release seemed available anyway.

"Can you imagine the enormous political mileage that Nixon would claim if his office negotiated the *Pueblo* crew's release shortly after his inauguration?" Collins asked.

"That's precisely what Dr. Li is suggesting," Sero replied.

Mitchell Collins watched a wave of relief wash over his daughter's face. He chose not to question further the history between Margo and Dr. Li that had resulted in her involvement in this bizarre proposal. Some things were better left unsaid and unknown.

So, Collins determined to do all that he could to bring this effort to fruition and then to lead Margo away from a career in clandestine international intelligence matters.

No child of his would be a covert agent, especially since he had only one.

PART SIX

December 20, 1968 – March 31, 1969

VOLUME ONE: PHANTOM WAR TRILOGY

58.

FIGHTERTOWN USA

Marchand exited Route 395 onto the main surface street leading to La Jolla, California. The Corvette's top was down and warm southern California breezes filled his senses with a mixture of floral fragrance and ocean salt. He was returning to his rented home just north of San Diego and only five miles south of Naval Air Station Miramar. Miramar was well known as "Fightertown USA" as the ten-foot lettering atop one of the Base's enormous hangers proclaimed. It was home to all the Pacific Fleet's fighter squadrons. If there was a finer place for a young naval aviator to be stationed, Marchand couldn't imagine where it might be. To him and his brethren, Miramar was fighter pilot Valhalla.

Marchand's housemate, Phil Winslow, was Fighter Squadron Twenty One's duty officer for the day, so Marchand had the run of the small house on La Jolla Boulevard to himself. With just a few days left before Christmas, he bought a very small tree that he managed to squeeze into the rider's side of his navy blue Corvette. Once at home, he placed the tree in the middle of the picture window overlooking the Pacific Ocean. He had to laugh at the incongruity of the tiny Christmas tree and San Diego's pitiful excuse for winter weather. "Oh well," he said aloud, "it's the thought that counts."

Marchand took off his khaki uniform, showered and dressed in a clean pair of shorts and a golf shirt in preparation for his one and only bout of Christmas shopping. Before engaging in his least favorite seasonal endeavor, he poured himself a generous Bombay Gin and tonic. "Ah, fortification against the rigors of holiday shopping," he mumbled while flipping on the TV. "Might as well watch the evening news while preparing for this dreadful mission," he said to no one in particular. With visions of half-crazed shoppers pushing and shoving each other along aisles spilling over with Christmas merchandise, he took a long sip of his gin.

A network news anchorman began the coverage of the daily news from Vietnam with the usual casualty statistics. Then he shifted to a story that he told with great animation. "Today, a North Vietnamese spokesman announced the release of U.S. Navy Commander Errol Lord from the POW camp known as the Hanoi Hilton as a good will gesture before the Christmas cease fire begins. "Lord, a senior attack pilot flying from the carrier *Constellation,* was shot down over Haiphong Harbor in January 1968, just one month before the Tet Offensive began.

"You may remember," intoned the famous baritone newscaster, "that Commander Lord was the subject of considerable controversy last summer after a film of Lord signing a confession of his alleged war crimes was released by the French press. Lord's apparent physical condition and his overall demeanor during the North Vietnamese sponsored press conference sparked a furious debate in Congress, and indeed throughout America, concerning treatment of American POW's by their Vietnamese captors."

While a rerun of the confession-signing ceremony played on the screen, the anchorman judiciously avoided mention of Lord's scornful middle digit salute. But anyone who observed the grainy film clearly remembered Lord's courageously defiant "up yours" signal. Lord's hostile gesture told not only the American military but also the general public that captured pilots continued to struggle whenever and however they could. "Lord should be home in time to spend Christmas with his family at Naval Air Station Le Moore, in California," the newsman stated.

Marchand roared with approval as Commander Lord's official Navy photograph faded from the TV screen. "Hot damn, Lord's beaten the bastards at their own game." Exaltation soon gave way to reflection, then to anger as Marchand recalled the flame-spitting surface to air missile that quickly flashed over his left shoulder, then exploded spectacularly alongside Lord's A-4 Skyhawk. "My God," he murmured, "I thought that SAM had my name written all over it. If that had been me, not Lord, I wonder whether I could have survived his ordeal?"

Marchand was about to turn off the television and leave for the nearest shopping center when the evening news report was interrupted by a special announcement. The reporter stated in a strangely somber tone that "Reliable sources within the U. S. State Department indicated that North Korea would soon announce the release of Commander Lloyd Bucher and the crew of the U.S.S. Pueblo who have been held as prisoners of war since their capture last January 24th.

"The release, said to have been negotiated with the North Korean government by officials of the Chinese Communist government in Beijing, would permit all one hundred eight crewmen of the Pueblo to return before the end of the year," the reporter stated in conclusion.

The Pueblo crew's release would provide San Diego a most unexpected but joyous Christmas present, especially for family members of the Pueblo crew, most of whom resided in the San Diego area.

"Damn, the Chinese are full of surprises," he mumbled. "Wonder if Margo has heard about this yet. Hell, she probably wishes she had engineered it," he laughed to himself. But quickly his thoughts turned to Christmas shopping.

Margo's flight arrived in the early afternoon of Christmas Eve. Marchand waited by the exit ramp with a dozen roses and a face lit with anticipation. "Keith," Margo cried as she spotted him, losing all of the composure she had rehearsed before landing. She ran to his arms and he dropped the roses as she passionately kissed him.

On the freeway from the airport north toward La Jolla, Marchand began to enjoy his most exquisite Christmas gift. He stroked Margo's hand, kissed her cheek and ran his fingers through her hair, knowing that Christmas would never again be complete without her. She made him feel at peace and totally content. Indeed, Margo brought him joy.

Margo asked him, "Do you know how much I want you?"

Marchand grinned as he nodded and replied. "I think so." Then he asked, "Do you know how much I need you?"

Margo laughed and said, "Yes, yes, I really do."

"So how do you know?"

"Because you're going ninety in a sixty mile-per-hour zone and because of a few other hints that are popping up here and there," she giggled.

"It shows?"

"Yes, darling, it shows if you know where to look. But if you don't slow this rocket ship down, we won't get to enjoy the show we're anticipating."

Marchand slowed the Corvette to a respectable speed and Margo asked him, "How's your housemate, Phil? I'm looking forward to meeting him."

"He's home in Seattle for Christmas. I'm sorry but we have the place all to ourselves."

"Just the two of us?"

"'Fraid so."

"I'm soooo disappointed. In that case, may I prepare dinner for us tonight?"

"Absolutely not. Unless you're too tired, I have other plans for us tonight."

"Does that include dinner, too?" she laughed.

"Of course, in due time. We've been invited to my Commanding Officer's home for Christmas Eve dinner. I really want you to meet him. You can demonstrate your culinary skills some other day of your visit."

"Are you sure I'll like all that ceremony and military stuff?"

"What's not to like? The Skipper is a delightful entertainer and his wife is quite charming, not at all military."

"I don't know. There isn't much I wouldn't do for you but 'fighter jock girlfriend' is pushing my limit," she replied with mock seriousness. "Of course I'd love to meet your Commanding Officer. I want to see what the Navy really thinks about my beau."

"Well, don't worry about it now, we're home," he announced as they pulled into the driveway.

Margo and Keith arrived at Commander Jack McGruder's residence precisely at 7:00 PM. In the foyer, Marchand dropped his gold embossed officer's calling card into a sterling silver plate resting upon an antique Japanese *tonsu* by the door. He also retrieved his Commanding

Officer's card from a matching silver plate in the time-honored tradition passed down from the British Royal Navy. As he did so, McGruder welcomed the couple. Then, having noticed Margo's fascination with the ritual, he commented, "The Brits taught us manners a couple hundred years ago and believe it or not, some of it actually stuck."

Marchand laughed then took Margo's hand and said, "Skipper, I'd like to introduce Ms. Marguerite Collins of New York and Cambridge Massachusetts."

"Delighted to meet you, Miss Collins," McGruder replied in his deep baritone voice with a mild Southern accent.

"Please call me Margo, Commander."

"Margo, this is my Commanding Officer, Jack McGruder, Commander United States Navy and fighter pilot extraordinaire," Marchand said with a slight bow and full smile.

"I've heard so much about you, Commander. I feel I've known you for a long while."

McGruder smiled, showing white teeth and boyish dimples. "Well, I don't know what tall tales young Marchand has told you but I assure you that the best is only half true and for the rest, I offer my apology." McGruder extended an arm to Margo then led her and Marchand into his large, traditionally furnished living room where his wife conversed with her guests.

Courtney McGruder was a very attractive, slender, black haired woman, nearly as tall as her husband. She was elegant in a straight black after-five gown and her green eyes shone with intelligence and warmth. She turned toward her husband as he and Margo approached. After introductions, she remarked, "Well, Margo, Keith can't seem to talk about anyone but you and now we understand why."

"Courtney, you and Keith are too kind," Margo replied. "But, I thank you and Jack for inviting me to share a part of your Christmas."

"I want you to feel a part of our family, Margo. We like to welcome guests as graciously as possible. Let me introduce you to the other officers and their wives, dear," Courtney said warmly as she guided Margo around the living room furnished in silk covered French colonial furniture, accented with tasteful Japanese flourishes.

The McGruders had invited three couples to share Christmas Eve dinner with them. The squadron's Executive Officer, Joe Garvey, and his wife were the most senior. Garvey was a short, compact man with heavily muscled forearms and penetrating dark eyes that Margo thought were almost capable of piercing solid objects. Garvey's wife, Patricia, was almost five months pregnant. Her sensitive face and large doe-like brown eyes made for quite a contrast next to her husband's ferocious gaze.

When Mrs. McGruder started to introduce her other guests, Margo began to smile broadly. "Courtney, I believe I've met Dr. Davis almost a year ago aboard the *Constellation.*

"Chris, what a wonderful surprise to see you," Margo continued, clearly pleased. "And this is Mrs. Davis?"

"Margo, I'm delighted to see you again. No, she's not Mrs. Davis yet but this is my fiancée, Stephanie Parker. We were engaged in September. Courtney introduced us a few months before the *Connie* left for West Pac last year."

"Well, it certainly appears that everyone has had quite a homecoming," Margo laughed. "So, Courtney, may I assume that you double as the squadron's matchmaker?"

"This time, I'm afraid that I'm guilty," she replied.

Jack McGruder interrupted, "We extend our sincere welcome to you, Margo. And a most gracious welcome to our collective family, the

United States Navy."

Later at the dinner table, Margo leaned toward Marchand and said; "I'm beginning to understand a feeling I had when you brought me aboard the *Constellation* for dinner in Hong Kong. Something you've tried to explain several times since then."

"What's that?" Marchand asked.

"There's a special closeness in your squadron life that outsiders seldom see or understand. Seeing it and feeling it up close makes me a bit jealous."

Marchand smiled knowingly and was about to respond when Jack McGruder inquired, "So what are you two conspiring about? There are no secret conversations permitted at the commander's table," he joked.

"Well, Skipper," Marchand intoned solemnly as he reached for his wine glass, "not wishing to betray a confidence but being under direct orders from my C.O., let me simply propose a toast. Here's to Commander Jack McGruder, Commanding Officer of Fighter Squadron Twenty One and his lovely wife, Courtney, the most gracious hosts at Miramar."

"Here, here!" the guests joined the toast. McGruder smiled and said, "Well done, Marchand, you're off the hook – for now."

The next day, Margo gazed out the dining room window at the breaking surf. She marveled at the ornate Christmas decorations lavishly draped throughout the enormous and splendid *fin de ciecle* dining room. Every mahogany panel gleamed and each oaken spar shone with fresh varnish throughout the hundred-foot domed ceiling, constructed entirely of wood. The warmth of the deeply burnished wood so carefully decorated for Christmas permeated the spirit of the magnificent Hotel Del Coronado formal dining room.

"No wonder you wouldn't let me cook Christmas dinner," Margo commented as she admired the view.

"You've been working so hard on your dissertation; I felt you needed a break, not kitchen duty," Marchand replied.

"But I would love to have cooked Christmas dinner for you. Before I leave, I promise you a taste of my culinary skills."

"Margo, let's not talk about your leaving just yet. There're so many things I want you to see, places to take you, people to meet. You can't leave without coming up to Redondo Beach to meet my folks. They'd never forgive me if you left before meeting them. I want to teach you to surf at the Cove. Next weekend, I want to take you to San Francisco for New Year's Eve with my brother and his wife. And, of course, I want to show you Fightertown and ...."

"Wait a minute, slow down, sailor. This isn't a real vacation. I came just to spend Christmas with you. I need to get back to Cambridge next week for a faculty advisor's meeting. You know I want to stay and enjoy all the plans you've made but if I don't get back soon I'll miss all my dissertation date requirements. I don't want to disappoint you, but duty calls. You of all people understand that."

"OK, OK, you're right. I'm getting a bit nervous now that you're here. I just don't want to let you go," Marchand replied. "But still, I want you to experience as much as you can of my world for whatever time you have left. Won't you at least stay until New Year's?"

"I'll try, darling. Perhaps, I can write a bit while I'm here and you're at the Base. But let's not dwell on that now. Let's just enjoy each other and this wonderful Christmas dinner together. And, Keith, thank you again for this gorgeous gold necklace you gave me for Christmas. I had no idea you would do something so extravagant."

"You're so welcome, but really I had no choice. I simply had to make that one of your Christmas gifts," Marchand said somewhat nervously.

"What do you mean, no choice?" Margo asked.

Marchand reached in his coat pocket and retrieved a small blue velvet box that he carefully placed on the gilt-edged plate before her. "Well, the necklace seemed to match this ring so beautifully, I just had to have it for you." Then he proceeded more slowly and deliberately.

"And I wanted you to have this ring more than any Christmas present I could think of because I love you more than anyone in my world, Margo. You are the center of my universe, the essence of everything I want and need. You're more precious to me than all my plans and dreams. And even if I accomplish them all, they'd mean nothing without you in my world. I want you in my life forever. And, if there is anything or any meaning beyond this life, then I want to be with you for all eternity. My dearest Margo, please say that you will be my wife. Make me the happiest man alive."

Slowly, she opened the crushed velvet ring box to reveal an oval shaped diamond set in a white and yellow gold ring surrounded by diamond baguettes. The solitaire weighed more than two carats and was perfectly clear; its facets sprayed a prism of color in all directions. Margo's face reflected its brilliance and the wide range of emotions she felt as she admired the magnificent engagement ring.

"Oh my God, I don't know what to say. I didn't anticipate your proposal at all. I didn't think you really loved me like this, Keith. Lately, I've felt so melancholy thinking that I'd fallen so completely in love with you against my better judgment. I've been frightened that you might leave me just as suddenly as you appeared in my life.

"I've always been so careful with my feelings. I've always controlled my life and my emotions. But now, my life and my emotions belong to you. I'm yours completely. Keith, I want to be your wife forever. I want that more than tenure at Harvard or a position with the State Department. My love for you simply overwhelms me at times. I love you so deeply that I ache for you whenever we're apart. I'd be so happy and so proud to be your wife. Yes, Keith, of course, I'll marry you. You've given me so much joy tonight."

Marchand reached across the table, removed the ring from its box and placed it carefully on Margo's left ring finger; then stood bringing her to her feet and kissed her long and deeply.

"I give you love," he whispered.

"I give you joy," she answered.

Nearby dinner patrons smiled and stared at the striking couple and when Margo held up her newly burdened ring finger, they burst into applause.

After their waiter opened a bottle of vintage *Veuve Cliquot* and poured the fine amber liquid, the couple drank to their happiness and future together. Then Marchand said, "Should we talk about a date?"

"Sweetheart," Margo replied, "I would marry you tomorrow if you wished but I think it might be better for us to wait until you're home from this last tour of duty. If we married before you finished this cruise, I'd never complete this dissertation. I'd sit around moping, and pine for you each day. I'd be hopeless until you returned. As it is, I don't know how I will cope with your absence."

"That's exactly what I don't want, Margo. I don't want anxiety in our lives. I have all the respect in the world for Courtney McGruder and Pat Garvey but I don't want that for you."

Margo thought a few moments then replied, "Honestly, I don't know whether or why it should make any difference if we're engaged or married while you're on this next cruise. But somehow, I think marriage might make the next year more difficult for you. I want your mind to be as clear as possible when you're dodging SAM missiles and cannon fire. I don't want you worried about what I'm doing or how. You've got to concentrate on what you're doing, not on me or anything else."

"Then we agree. But please say that you'll stay with me through the holidays. I want you to meet your future in-laws before you go. And there's something special happening at Miramar this week that I really want you to attend with me," Marchand said as he took her hand and kissed it tenderly.

"What's going on at Miramar?"

"It's an awards ceremony and it would be great to have you there to share it with me."

"Well, in that case, I wouldn't miss it for anything."

"Splendid." Marchand paused then said, "I wonder what your father will say when he hears about our engagement."

59.

WINNERS AND LOSERS

Margo sat next to Courtney McGruder, wife of Squadron Commander Jack McGruder, in the first row of guest chairs placed in perfectly straight lines inside the cavernous Hanger Number Two at Naval Air Station Miramar. In front of them was a reviewing stand on which nearly a dozen senior naval officers stood. Behind the reviewing stand, two F-4J Phantom II fighter-bombers were parked. Each had been washed and waxed until they reflected light like enormous gray jewels, canopies open and squadron insignia freshly painted on their tail surfaces.

The senior officer present was Rear Admiral Ignatius B. Carter who had just been relieved as Operations Officer of Task Force 77. Also in attendance was Captain John Townsend, Commanding Officer of the *U.S.S. Constellation* CVA-64, Captain Wayne Harrison, Commanding Officer of NAS Miramar and Captain Brian Nelson, the Commander of Air Wing Fourteen who would lead the awards ceremony.

Between the reviewing stand and the seated guests, the officers and men of Fighter Squadron Twenty One and her sister squadron, Fighter Squadron One Hundred Thirteen stood at attention. Each officer had carefully prepared his dress blue uniform complete with large medals and ceremonial swords. Golden-striped sleeves denoting rank, campaign medals and swords gleamed in the hanger's bright overhead lights.

After ordering the personnel of the two squadrons to the parade rest position and delivering welcoming remarks to wives, families and guests in attendance, Captain Nelson introduced Admiral Carter who returned Nelson's salute then took the microphone. Carter, a short, powerfully built officer in his early forties looked out at the assembled officers, men and guests with obvious pride.

"Ladies and gentlemen, officers and men of Fighter Squadrons Twenty One and One Hundred Thirteen, as the most recent Operations Officer of Task Force 77, the naval task force assigned to combat operations in the Gulf of Tonkin and waters off North and South Vietnam, and on behalf of the Commander, Seventh Fleet and the Commander in Chief of the Pacific, I have been directed to attend this awards ceremony and to extend to these men the gratitude and appreciation of the United States Navy for a job extremely well done.

"I have the great pleasure to celebrate the dedication and heroic service of the men of Fighter Squadrons Twenty One and One Hundred Thirteen on their return from a highly successful combat tour of duty to the waters off Vietnam. The Navy also recognizes and salutes the support, sacrifices and commitment of the wives, families and loved ones of these men. Without this support, these men who have served with distinction for over ten months in hostile conditions would have found it immeasurably more difficult to carry out their mission."

Margo looked at the faces of the airmen standing at parade rest. Each man's pride was reflected in the gleam of his sword hilt, the glow of Navy Wings of Gold accentuated by rows of combat medals and officer's gold stripes. She smiled with approval as Admiral Carter continued, "The aviators of these two fighter squadrons supported by their professional enlisted ground crews represent the finest the fleet can offer. They continue the great traditions of the Naval Service begun almost two hundred years ago."

Margo's gaze turned to the rows of enlisted men whose dedication and skill kept the squadron's planes flying safely during the grueling combat routine just completed. Spit shined shoes, brilliantly shined buckles and brass, and impeccably pressed uniforms bore witness to their jobs well done. Her eyes shone with appreciation for their heroic efforts during the squadron's combat cruise, efforts that insured her fiancée had only the best aircraft with which to face his enemies day after day. Then she focused intensely on Admiral Carter as he recounted the Squadrons' combat record.

"During this combat cruise, the pilots and flight officers of Fighter Squadrons Twenty One and One Hundred Thirteen have flown more than four thousand combat sorties, including over fifteen hundred close air support missions in South Vietnam and twenty five hundred combat flights over North Vietnam and surrounding waters. They have destroyed thousands of military targets while carefully avoiding civilian population centers.

"In aerial combat, their extraordinary airmanship has resulted in downing a total of six enemy aircraft while suffering no losses during air combat. Most importantly, they scored the first double MIG-21 kills by a single American fighter aircraft during the Vietnamese conflict."

At this point, Margo stared hard at the two Phantoms on display. Although the fighters were oddly beautiful and impeccably washed, waxed and shined, she knew that their curious beauty masked a deadly purpose, a purpose that Admiral Carter began to describe in great detail. She began to shiver as the Admiral made the whole ceremony very up front and personal to her.

"To you officers and men of VF-21 and VF-113, as a fellow aviator, it gives me the greatest pleasure and honor to present the following awards for gallantry and extraordinary airmanship during combat operations from November 17, 1967 to July 15, 1968 while a part of Air Wing Fourteen embarked in *U.S.S. Constellation, CVA-64.* Lieutenant Commander Kelly Drummond, USN, and Lieutenant Keith Marchand, USNR, step forward."

As Drummond and Marchand marched to the front of the squadron, Courtney McGruder turned slightly towards Margo and noticed her eyes welling with tears. Gently, she pressed a handkerchief into Margo's hand then grasped her free hand gently and with great tenderness. Almost imperceptibly, she leaned toward Margo and whispered, "Remember what I told you earlier today." Margo nodded but continued to look directly at Marchand as Admiral Carter read the technical wording of Kelly Drummond's citations which she barely heard as she recalled her conversation with Courtney.

Before the award ceremony began, Courtney had sought Margo in the crowd. She sincerely congratulated Margo on her engagement and admired her ring. While giving her a warm embrace, she said, "I know that you're nervous about all this; I know because I felt the same way. Marrying a fighter pilot is as exciting and stressful as it gets. It's equal part love and anxiety. I think you've made a great decision though and I can tell you that Jack has given me more happiness than I could ever have imagined; more than a few sleepless nights, too.

"When Jack is on a cruise, I feel incomplete but still I know he's with me somehow. Even the pain of long separations, the fear of losing him and the difficulty of raising a family without a father haven't outweighed the happiness we've had together. It's been stressful; I can't deny that. But the love we share is so special, so intense; I wouldn't trade it for anything. I really want you to know this, Margo. I want you to hear it from someone who's been there."

Margo listened carefully then replied, "Thanks so much Courtney, for sharing such intimate feelings with me. I really appreciate your honesty and candor. But I think my situation is a bit different. Keith and I have decided to postpone out wedding date until he returns from his next cruise, then he plans to leave the Navy to attend law school. I don't know if I could bear the pressure that you and the other wives endure cruise after cruise."

"I know all that, Margo. Jack has told me that Keith plans, at least for now, to leave the Navy when the next cruise ends. You probably think that not being married to Keith will lessen the anxiety and fear of the cruise and you may be right. You certainly won't have a family to worry about. But I can see that you love Keith as deeply as I love Jack and that puts us in the same boat, or ship, as Jack would say. And of course, we wives all know how important everything we say and do is to our husband's careers, to the Navy, and even to the welfare of the nation. I'm sure you've already come to see and understand this, Margo."

Margo withheld her internal struggle with this concept and merely answered charmingly, "Well yes, certainly."

"Just remember, Navy wives have a very strong sisterhood; we've bonded at a very deep level. If you ever need anything, Margo, I mean anything, you call me. I don't care if you're in Cambridge, New York or Hong Kong or wherever, you just call. No one will understand what you're going through like I will. Will you promise me that?" Margo nodded and sniffed as Courtney took her hand and led her to the guest seats just behind the long white braided hawser that cordoned off the guests from the ranks of officers and men of the assembled squadrons.

Margo was startled out of her reverie as she heard Admiral Carter address Marchand. "Lieutenant Keith Marchand, the Secretary of the Navy is proud to award you the Silver Star, our nation's third highest military honor, the Distinguished Flying Cross with oak leaf cluster, and the seventh Air Medal for bravery and extraordinary airmanship in shooting down two MIG-21 fighters in aerial combat over North Vietnam on April 23, 1968." As Carter read the precise wording of the citations, then pinned the Navy Silver Star and Distinguished Flying Cross on Marchand's uniform, Margo felt her heart swell with pride and her eyes tear all over again.

This is just too much emotion for one day, she thought. And what the hell am I doing here in the middle of a military ceremony awarding medals for killing Vietnamese people in a war that is unjust, immoral, irrational and just plain stupid? How in the world did I get here? She asked herself. If I'm not careful I'll wind up as conflicted as my poor sweet Keith.

Then without realizing what she was doing, Margo spontaneously squeezed Courtney's hand firmly and said. "My God, he's beautiful and I do love him so much."

"I know, Dear. I know."

As they drove from NAS Miramar back to La Jolla after the awards ceremony, Marchand was still glowing with pride and savoring just how sweet his life had become. Margo had purged her mind of all anxieties and apprehension for the moment, and snuggled as close to Marchand as she could in the tight Corvette cockpit. She purred in his ear. "I love you so much, my sweet hero." Margo thought a moment then continued. "You really are some kinda' hero. It's really still settling in that you've done something really heroic. It's not just some fighter pilot bravado."

"Thanks Sweetheart, but I don't feel any different, really. Aerial combat happens so quickly you don't think about it. You just do your best; you follow your training and the rest just happens. One guy wins one guy loses. Just like that."

"Except you won, the other guys didn't, and now they're dead, I assume. You never told me."

"They didn't eject from their aircraft."

"Meaning they're dead, right?"

"Right."

They were both silent a moment then Margo surprised Marchand. "You know I'm scheduled to fly home the day after New Year's."

"Yeah, but I'm trying not to think about it."

"Well, would you object to my staying a few more days?"

"Object, are you kidding? I'd be delighted. But what's the catch? You told me last week that you had to return to Cambridge immediately for a meeting with your faculty advisor."

"That's right but I called yesterday to postpone it and let me tell you why. Do you remember the news this morning on the way to Miramar about the *Pueblo* crew?" Margo asked.

"I do recall hearing it but truthfully I wasn't paying too much attention this morning."

"Well, did you hear that the *Pueblo* crew would be returning on January 5th right here at Naval Air Station Miramar?"

"Hey, that's great. I guess I didn't pay attention to that part. Of course, I'm delighted to hear the news, but, tell me, why are you so interested? Did you know one of the crew? Some old boyfriend or something like that?"

"No Silly, I have no personal connections to the crew but ..." Margo paused.

"But what?"

"I'd like to be at Miramar when the *Pueblo* crew returns, if you would take me."

"You would!" Marchand said incredulously. "And why, might I ask?"

She paused for several long moments without answering, trying to compose a reasonable answer. Finally, having thought as carefully as she could, she replied. "Keith, I've told you that my father has connections at the State Department and with the new Nixon administration, haven't I?"

"Yes, you did."

"Well, Dad was somewhat involved in negotiating the *Pueblo* crew's release."

"He was?!" Marchand was astounded.

"And I may have helped a little."

"Well, I'll be damned; you can't be serious! But you are serious."

"I'm afraid so but I really can't say more. I've pledged confidentiality, something you well understand. I can say that I'm proud to have played a part in a true diplomatic success."

Marchand was not entirely certain he understood. "OK. Just tell me one thing, will you?"

"If I can," Margo answered hesitantly.

"Is Rick Sero involved in this *Pueblo* scenario as well?"

Margo was surprised that Marchand would connect Sero to the

release. She deftly tried to change the subject. "Keith, we're driving by the Cove; let's stop here for a few minutes."

Deciding not to press further, Marchand parked the car and took Margo's hand to walk to his favorite viewpoint overlooking La Jolla's most famous beachfront. They stood looking out to the sparkling sea, his arm lovingly around her waist, her head on his shoulder, their love palpably surrounding them. Minutes passed before Marchand could not help but ask about Sero - again.

Margo rolled her eyes as if to indicate that the entire topic was silly. "Alright, for what it's worth, Sero played a small part in the release. But not such an important one, really. It's far more complicated than that.... Look, I want so much to tell you more, but I simply cannot. I just cannot say anything that might place you or my father in danger. I'm tempted to tell you more, but I can't. I just can't do it. Please don't ask me to. I promise you will be proud of me, though.

"You should also be pleased that I've remained so composed about all that's going on. You just don't know sometimes how much I want to snivel and whine about your going back to Vietnam but I've avoided the temptation. So, be the sweetheart you are and promise you won't ask again until you're on your way home and out of the Navy. Promise me, won't you?"

Marchand felt her anxiety, backed off his questions, and sighed deeply. "Margo, I'll always be with you, always." He embraced her tightly, as if to hold her forever.

Margo shuddered just a little, then was still.

VOLUME ONE: PHANTOM WAR TRILOGY

60.

TOP GUN SQUADRON

Drummond and Marchand walked slowly from the VF-21 flight line at NAS Miramar where they had just parked their Phantom, still sizzling hot after an intense air combat training flight. Both were soaked through with perspiration and physically exhausted. But they were ecstatic. Every muscle, sinew and nerve ending pulsed with excitement known only to those who have experienced the explosive thrill of aerial combat in a mach two fighter aircraft. Such was their state of exhilaration.

The strain of high G loading exceeding six, seven, even eight times the force of gravity had drained them of physical energy and replaced it with raw adrenaline, traces of which still raced through their blood. But the sensual joy of pursuing and being pursued through complete three-dimensional freedom in a clear blue sky had easily overcome the stress. They were experiencing a high unique to the world of gladiators, matadors and fighter pilots. While they had only flown a training mission, nothing could mask the intensity of engaging in one of the few remaining true blood sports.

Just minutes earlier, Drummond roared, "Fox 2, Fox 2, break it off, break it off," over the UHF radio to inform their hapless opponents that, had the combat been in earnest, the unfortunate crew would be spiraling toward earth in a miasma of exploding fuel and vaporized aluminum. The rush was indescribable. The successful pursuit reminded them of their Sparrow and Sidewinder missiles slamming into one of the doomed MiG-21's that they had downed just a few months previously in the skies over North Vietnam.

Marchand easily visualized the sleek silver Russian-built fighters disintegrating in orange yellow fireballs. The sight had been terrible but exhilarating. It had been ultimately thrilling and macabre. It had produced the surge of emotion that envelopes a matador as he guides his blade skillfully between the cervical vertebrae of a charging bull then watches the massive, powerful creature crumple at his feet. Death defeated, life exalted and raised to incredible heights.

No other pilot and weapons officer team at Miramar flew air combat training with the energy and intensity that Drummond and Marchand injected into each flight. They weren't just unbelievably good. They had become one with the timeless class of samurai masters that flourish in times of war and practice their deadly skills endlessly in times of peace. Their brilliant tactical maneuvering awed and intimidated other crews that flew against them. Drummond's masterful touch with stick and rudder perfectly complemented Marchand's control over the aircraft's sophisticated weapons system. Together they enjoyed an almost surreal communication with each other. They were practically invincible among the West Coast based-fighter squadrons.

Earthbound, they joked casually with each other on the way to the squadron ready room in mammoth Hanger Two. The bond between them that had been forged in the white heat of actual combat became easy and playful when they dismounted. Drummond walked tall like the Texan he was. He moved as smoothly on the ground as in the sky. His clear gray eyes that were almost telescopic and absolutely formidable to an opponent framed a warm, friendly face on the ground. His voice, which remained sternly controlled no matter how intense the hostile fire, assumed a reassuring quality out of the cockpit. Drummond's manner was as unflappable as John Wayne's in a classic Western film. Marchand often thought of Drummond as the quintessential Navy fighter pilot. He was all that most men wished they could be but rarely ever became.

As they reached the squadron's spaces, Marchand said sincerely, "Damn, I enjoyed that hop, Kelly. I can't wait to see the gun camera films."

"It was a real pleasure, Keith. You've become a real tiger in the air. It's good to hear your voice when we're flying. Calms my nerves. Has in many a tough situation," Drummond said sincerely.

"You really mean that?"

"Bet your sweet ass, I do. When my first weapons officer was injured early in the cruise, I couldn't wait for his return because he was good, really good. And though I truly regret that his injuries were too severe for him to fly again, it's given you and me an opportunity to create the best pilot/weapons officer team at Miramar. Best luck I've had since I started flying Phantoms."

Normally a man of few words, Kelly had just given Marchand the greatest compliment he could have imagined. Marchand replied just as candidly, "Kelly, I know I've talked to you about the accident I had in the training command that knocked me out of the pilot training program and how devastated I was."

"Yeah, I remember what you told me about that experience. It took guts to come back after that accident and finish Weapons Officer training. I think I might have quit under those circumstances."

"Well, I just want you to know that flying in the seat behind you is almost as good as having the stick and throttle in my own hands. I really mean that, Kelly."

Just as they reached the locker room and could no longer talk privately, Drummond put his hand on Marchand's shoulder and said, "We've done some superb flying together and that means a lot to me, no matter what happens. I want you to remember that."

Marchand smiled and nodded in agreement, then walked to his locker to remove his flight gear. He had just unzipped his torso harness and G-suit and hung them in his locker when Phil Winslow tapped him on the shoulder. "Hey Rocketman," Winslow said, "the Skipper wants to see you in his office as soon as your flight debriefing is completed."

"You mean I've fucked up again, huh?" Marchand quipped.

"No more than usual," Winslow laughed. "Seriously, the old man didn't seem to be in a bad mood at all. Just the opposite, really."

After debriefing the flight and enjoying a quick shower, Marchand knocked on Commander Jack McGruder's door, then poked his head in.

"Enter," McGruder barked without looking up from the stack of papers on his desk.

"Lieutenant Marchand reporting as requested, Sir."

"Oh, Keith, come in. You and Kelly have a good hop today?"

"Yes, Sir. We flew a two on one against VF-113's top two crews and came away with five kills and two stand-offs out of five engagements."

"That's pretty damn good flying. They didn't splash you even once?" McGruder inquired.

"Well, once, but the air controller said that we were out of max range when they called missiles away."

"Too bad controllers aren't on the scene all the time," McGruder quipped. He paused a moment before continuing, "You two are the hottest team at Miramar right now, the best of the best and that brings me to the reason I called for you." At that Marchand braced for the bad news he was certain would follow.

McGruder noticed Marchand stiffen and said, "At ease, Marchand."

"Yes, Sir," Marchand said as he relaxed.

"Keith, you know that my year as commanding officer of VF-21 is rapidly drawing to a close and that Joe Garvey is due to relieve me in just a few weeks."

"I'm well aware of that, Sir, and I hope that you know how much the guys, myself included, will miss you as Skipper. I hope that I'm not out of line saying that."

"Not at all, I appreciate your comment and I want to tell you something in the very strictest of confidence. Is that clear?"

"Absolutely, Sir."

"I've received my new orders. They are not at all what I expected."

"I'm really sorry to hear that, Sir. You didn't get a desk job or something like that, I hope?"

"On the contrary, the orders are rather special. I'm to report for duty as the first commanding officer of the Navy's Fighter Weapons School here at Miramar."

"That sounds pretty exciting, Sir. But I haven't heard anything about it around the squadron. What does the school actually do?"

"You haven't heard anything about it yet because it's still top secret. The school is actually a new squadron created to teach the best fighter pilots and weapons officers from each operational squadron the latest tactics and techniques developed for air-to-air combat. The squadron will be manned exclusively by combat-seasoned aircrews who've been highly recommended by their squadron commanders. All others will be students on temporary duty. After formation and development of the training syllabus, we will give each class the most intense aerial combat training the U.S. military has ever known."

"Skipper, that's absolutely fantastic."

"The training will be as realistic as possible, complete with flights against a full time aggressor squadron flying captured or defected MIG-21's and 17's. Our mission will be to train Navy and Marine crews and initially even Air Force crews, until they can operate their own program."

"That's incredible, Skipper. What an honor to be selected as the first CO of the new squadron. How did this all come about, may I ask?"

"Well, as you know, our air-to-air kill ratio in Vietnam is the worst the U.S. has ever experienced in any war or conflict."

"Yes, Sir; the ratio is running just about even, slightly better than one-to-one."

"Precisely, and because it's so poor, the Secretary of the Navy and the Joint Chiefs have authorized this program. The Air Force's record in Vietnam is even worse, so the Navy was selected to create the program."

"What a splendid opportunity, Skipper. You have my sincerest congratulations, Sir."

"Well, thank you. Now let me come straight to the point. I have the opportunity not only to command this new squadron but also to hand pick the first instructor pilots and weapons officers. For the most part, I'm told that my selections will be rubber stamped by BUPERS. So, I've decided that I want Kelly and you to become one of my first instructor teams."

Marchand was dumbstruck. McGruder's information was spectacular in itself but his offer to include Kelly Drummond and himself was simply off the scale as surprise and compliment. He had a difficult time determining how to answer.

"Well, Marchand, say something; speak up, don't just stand there. You've never been at a loss for words since I've known you."

"Skipper, I'm speechless. Of course, I'd be honored and delighted to join you and become one of your flight instructors at the new squadron. But I've still got another cruise to complete before I can rotate to shore duty. What can I do about that?"

"I'll handle that if you're interested, Marchand. I've already checked and you have about twenty months of active duty remaining of your initial active duty requirement. You'd have to extend your active duty obligation long enough to give me a full two year commitment, but I know that you've wanted an early release after the next cruise in order to attend law school. Are you willing to extend your active duty and miss your next law school class?"

Marchand thought for a moment. "Skipper, this a remarkable opportunity and I'm deeply honored that you've asked me to join your new squadron. But since this entails a major change of plans and my fiancée's plans as well, I respectfully request a day or two to make a firm decision and give my commitment."

"That's fair enough; you've got forty-eight hours. And give that lovely fiancée of yours my best regards, Courtney's too. I've never seen my wife take a liking to someone as much as she has to Margo. Anyway, report back to me by Friday at 1600 hours."

"Yes, Sir. And my sincerest thanks, Skipper."

"You deserve it, Marchand. And, remember this is all Top Secret. You can talk to Kelly who's already accepted the new assignment and you can tell Margo that you've been selected for a special assignment Stateside but no more and no one else. Is that understood?"

"Yes, Sir."

"One more thing, you should know that the new squadron will be called 'Top Gun' or something like that. You'll be hearing about it before long."

"Sounds damn exciting, Sir."

"Very well. Dismissed."

Marchand saluted, did a smart about face, and tried to exit the office gracefully, but he was so stunned he nearly tripped while leaving McGruder's office.

61.

FRIENDLY ADVICE

Marchand gunned his Corvette south on Route 395 past the Miramar military reservation, his pulse beating like a drum in his head. He was past excitement, so high he didn't need a Phantom to reach the stratosphere. He couldn't wait to call Margo with the news. He knew that she would share his excitement....

Assignment to the Top Gun squadron, no second combat tour, a wedding just as soon as Margo completed her Ph.D. What more could they want or ask for?

Marchand dialed Margo's number in Cambridge as soon as he arrived home thinking that she would be at her apartment working on her dissertation by eight-thirty P.M. Eastern Standard Time. But by eleven o'clock, he had made three additional calls without success. By then it was too late to call New York so he decided to call the following morning at five o'clock when he arose for an early flight schedule. However, even at that time, there was still no answer in Cambridge, so he dialed the Collins residence in Manhattan.

"Good morning, Maxine, this is Keith Marchand calling for Margo. I hope I'm not calling too early."

"Oh heavens no, Lieutenant Marchand, we've all been up for hours; Mr. Collins has already left for his office but I'm afraid Miss Margo isn't here."

"Oh, well, I've been trying to reach her for a while and thought she might have come home unexpectedly."

Sensing Marchand's deep disappointment, Maxine said soothingly. "Now don't you worry, honey. Miss Margo will call you soon." She thought a moment then added, "Lieutenant, I heard Mr. Collins talking to Margo on the phone yesterday. I think that he said something about her going down to Washington for an interview. So don't fret. She will call you today, I'm sure."

"Thanks, Maxine, you're such a sweetheart." Marchand felt somewhat relieved but was still frustrated as he left for Miramar. I really need to talk to her today, he mumbled to himself. I don't want to accept this assignment without Margo's knowledge. What a foul time for her to have an interview, he thought. And, I hope she's not up to anything but that. I've enough of this secret Chinese communication stuff.

Four o'clock Friday afternoon came and went, but still Margo had not called nor had Marchand been able to reach her. Top Gun decision time had arrived, so Marchand walked smartly from the squadron ready room down the corridor to Commander McGruder's office and knocked on his door.

"Enter," McGruder barked.

"Lieutenant Marchand reporting as requested, Sir."

"So, Marchand, what's your decision? Are you coming with me or not?"

"Yes, Sir. I would be honored to be a member of your Top Gun Squadron. In fact, I wouldn't miss it for anything."

"Glad to hear it, Marchand. I'm delighted to have you and Kelly

510

in the Squadron. Both of you will be instrumental to the program's success. Oh yeah, what's your 'handle'?"

"My handle? The guys call me 'Rocketman'".

"Oh yeah, I remember it now. I like the sound of it, 'Rocketman'." McGruder repeated the nickname several times. "We'll all have handles at Top Gun, gives the operation a little bravado. Good for the ego. Makes you want to kick some ass. I want to see you teaching these guys how to get some attitude, how to kick some serious butt. You can't overdo it or they'll get reckless on you and that's as bad as complacency, if not worse. Balance is the key. I think you can teach it, Rocketman. What do you think?"

"I'm certain of it, Sir."

Marchand left the squadron offices and headed for La Jolla. He was somewhat apprehensive about acceptance of his orders to Top Gun without any discussion with Margo but he felt good about his decision. He could only hope that his fiancée would feel the same.

Within minutes after arriving home, Marchand's phone rang and he was delighted to hear Margo's voice. She apologized for being so difficult to find but explained that she had been in constant interviews for almost two days at the State Department headquarters in Foggy Bottom, Virginia. She was elated because she had been offered a senior analyst position with the recently expanded Bureau of Chinese Affairs Desk, effective as soon as she received her Ph.D.

Upon hearing about Marchand's reassignment to a shore-based squadron, Margo was so excited that she hardly commented about his extension of active duty for an additional eight months. She could easily live with such a brief addition to his naval service if it meant no more sea duty, no more combat, no more Vietnam. Perhaps now they could actually make some definitive plans for their future, she hinted. She even seemed pleased about his assignment to the Top Gun Squadron, the name of which Marchand had not revealed. She far preferred that Marchand teach his deadly skills to others than practice them himself. By the time they had completed their phone conversation, both were nearly ecstatic about their good fortune and promising futures, individually and together.

That evening, Marchand and Phil Winslow left their rented house in La Jolla, committed to visit every officers club in San Diego, from 32nd Street to the Marine Corps Recruit Depot, from North Island to Miramar. Notwithstanding Commander McGruder's instructions to keep quiet about his anticipated assignment to Top Gun, Marchand could not keep the news to himself and Margo alone so he had shared it with his best friend. Winslow was nearly as excited as he as they celebrated all over San Diego, a dedicated Navy town.

Winslow's only regret was losing his roommate during the next cruise, but he was sincerely pleased for his friend whom he knew would have agonized throughout another tour of duty in Vietnam. Although he was not sanguine about fighting in Vietnam, Winslow didn't feel as conflicted as Marchand. Winslow had often worried about his friend during the previous cruise, worried that Marchand's internal conflicts might have disastrous results. He knew that it wasn't fear of combat that consumed Marchand. It was the fear of not doing the honorable thing, whatever the hell that was. Now Marchand could put at least a part of his dilemma to rest.

Still there was something that troubled Winslow. As they sipped their final Irish coffee before heading back to La Jolla, he said, "Keith, you know you're my best friend, don't you?"

"Well, yes, I think I do."

"Then take what I'm going to say as coming from your best

friend, 'cause it does."

"OK, but this sounds rather serious."

"It is, Keith. Let me just say that I'm a bit worried about you."

"Worried, worried about what? Everything is coming up roses, Phil."

"That's just it. It's all the goddamn roses coming up that bothers me. There's too much good shit happening. First, we both make it through a really tough cruise, we both splash a MIG or two. You're engaged to a smashing blond who's brainy as well. And now you get selected to become a Top Gun instructor. That's just too much good shit.... You know how sometimes things get so goddamn bad that you know they will soon get better just because they can't get any worse. Well, the same is true about too much good shit. When it gets that good, it can't last."

"That's some heavy philosophy, ol' boy," Marchand chuckled.

"Not real pretty, I'll grant you, but tell me if your experience doesn't bear it out."

"I guess it does but what the hell can anyone do about it?"

"Only one thing, Keith. Just watch your ass. Be extra careful. Don't let anyone get behind you in the dark. That kind of thing."

"That's pretty generalized stuff, Phil. Can you be more specific?"

"OK, I'll try. Let's say you're all set up at Top Gun and everything is going hunky-fucking dory. You're the stud-king Weapons Officer around Miramar, you and Margo get married and life couldn't get much better. Then you're up with some wanna' be, hotshot pilot fresh from a cruise who's going to show everyone at Top Gun just how good he is. So he pushes the envelope too far during air combat training and you let him do it just to show him that he ain't so good after all. But he really pushes it, pushes it past a deep stall and into a spin, a flat spin that you can't get out of, and you've busted the ten thousand foot practice minimum, so if you punch out you ride the seat into the dirt at five hundred knots. That's what I mean."

Marchand tried not to laugh as Winslow continued.

"Or, you're at sea for a short exercise aboard the boat and one dark, gloomy-ass night the young hotshot you're flying with decides he just wants to go home to his stateroom where it's nice and cozy. Fuck the bolters and hook skips; he's going to land this puppy now. So you ignore that little feeling at the back of your neck and the SOB dives for the deck before you can say 'Jesus Christ'. But the deck is moving up in a swell just as the asshole goes for it so you plaster your butt all over the fantail in a nice orange fireball. That's what I mean."

"Well, goddamn, that's a pretty fuckin' lousy forecast," Marchand said choking over his coffee.

"It's no fucking forecast. It's just a heads up for my best buddy, know what I mean?"

"I guess I do, Phil. I get nervous about that kind of shit, too. I don't know what to do about it, still don't, but it helps to talk about it. That's the problem with aviators; we don't talk about a damn thing. We just keep it inside. So, thanks for the words as off the wall as they are. I'll keep them in mind, buddy."

"Just don't forget, Keith. We've both lost many friends who we can't talk to anymore."

62.

CHANGE OF COMMAND

The change of command ceremony for Commander McGruder took place at 0800 hours on February 5, 1969. Loud applause rang out during the balmy Southern California morning for one of the most respected and revered squadron commanders at NAS Miramar. Every member of the squadron was saddened by his departure, except Commander Joe Garvey. At the end of the ceremony, Garvey had become the official new commanding officer of Fighter Squadron Twenty-One and he was eager to prepare his squadron for deployment aboard the *Constellation* in less than sixty days.

It wasn't that Garvey had any dislike for McGruder, far from it. It was simply the pressure of great responsibility. Now the responsibility was all his, all thirteen brand new F-4J Phantoms, all seventeen pilot/weapons-officer crews, all two hundred fifty officers and enlisted support personnel. But most of all, Garvey felt grave responsibility for getting the squadron to Vietnam as well-trained and ready as possible, and then getting as many of them home again as he could manage. Garvey never fully anticipated how awesome the responsibility was until that day. He was proud that he had been awarded the opportunity and not a little bit anxious about how well he might do.

Marchand approached Commander McGruder to offer his best wishes as McGruder said his final farewells. "It's been a great honor serving under your command, Sir. I look forward to serving in your next squadron as soon as my orders arrive."

"I'm looking forward to your joining me at Top Gun, Marchand. I would have thought your orders would have arrived by now. Give me a call in a week if you haven't heard anything from BUPERS."

"Thanks, Skipper. Best of luck to you, Sir."

"Careful, Marchand, I'm not your Skipper now."

"Aye, aye, Sir."

Marchand looked for Drummond in the crowd and saw him talking to Joe Garvey. As he approached, he overheard their conversation. Drummond had just received his orders to Top Gun and therefore was telling Garvey that he would be leaving the squadron the following Monday.

"Sorry to see you go, Kelly. You're one of the best fighter pilots at Miramar. But you've certainly got a plum assignment at Top Gun and that will damn sure earn you a squadron of your own when you leave."

"Thanks, Joe. When do your senior replacement pilots report on board?"

"Hopefully, next week when you leave. Otherwise my turnaround-training period will be terribly short. I'm also losing two other Weapons Officers next week, not including Marchand. I tell you I wish to hell I could hang onto him. We're really short of experienced Weapons Officers next cruise and I was seriously counting on him. Wish like hell I could do something about those orders of his to Top Gun."

"He's earned those orders, Joe."

"That's not the point. As Naval officers, we go where we're

most needed, not where we most want to go. Right now, he's needed in the fleet a lot more than he is at Top Gun."

"You might say that about me too. You said as much a few minutes ago. Should I request reassignment?"

"Look, Kelly, I don't think that your situation and Marchand's are quite the same. You're a senior Lieutenant Commander; you've had your share of sea tours including combat. Marchand is still a youngster. He should by all rights still be a part of this squadron heading for sea. Not to mention the fact that I need him."

"Well, neither you nor I can tell BUPERS what to do and I think it's up to them, not us. In any event, he's headed this way so let's just drop it, Joe."

Marchand felt the tension and limited his comments to Commander Garvey to sincere congratulations for assuming command of Fighter Squadron Twenty-One.

"Thanks, Marchand. I wish you were going with us but it looks like you're destined for bigger and better things." Garvey replied with an edge of sarcasm.

"I don't know about that, Sir. But I am looking forward to the new assignment."

Drummond intercepted Garvey's next comment by cheerfully stating, "Hell, BUPERS had to let Marchand come with me, I'm getting old now and couldn't see shit if it weren't for his pointing me in the right direction. Isn't that right, Keith?"

Marchand was definitely uncomfortable and decided to exit, so he replied, "I think the water's getting pretty deep for a junior lieutenant. So if you and the Skipper will excuse me, my sword belt is coming loose." Marchand saluted and moved on.

Marchand caught up with Drummond later that morning and

asked what Garvey meant by his earlier comments. Reverting to type, Drummond simply stated that Marchand should check frequently with his detailer at the Bureau of Personnel in order to follow the progress of his orders as closely as possible. "Don't let any grass grow around those orders," were his final words on the subject.

More than a little concerned after his conversation with Drummond, Marchand decided to call his personal detailer in Washington later that afternoon. Each Naval officer has his own detailer who is himself a Naval Officer attached to the central office of the Navy Bureau of Personnel (BUPERS) with whom any officer, no matter how junior or senior, could call and discuss his next assignment. Since his orders to Top Gun seemed to be on hold, Marchand concluded that, at the very least, he must determine what circumstances were holding them up and possibly create some movement. His detailer, Lt. Commander Dick Scott, was direct in his responses to Marchand's questions.

"The problem is simply this, Lieutenant: we are short of F-4 qualified and experienced weapons officers. We've had combat losses, training losses and very few weapons officers extending beyond their initial active duty obligations. Your squadron, as you know, is now two WOs short of the normal crew level. I'm doing my best to bring in a couple of experienced guys from the East Coast and the Mediterranean, so far without success. I can't write your orders to leave VF-21 until I get at least one more WO assigned to your squadron. And that guy should be an experienced WO like you. My boss won't let me send another nugget WO fresh out of training to your squadron."

"So what happens two months from now when the squadron is due to leave on another WestPac cruise and this problem hasn't been solved?"

"Marchand, you've been in the Navy long enough to know the

answer to that question."

"I know, I know, the needs of the Navy always prevail. So I may be on my way back to 'Nam is what you're telling me."

"Look, Marchand, I'll do my best to get those orders for you. But you gotta' know that as much as they want you in that new Fighter Weapons Squadron, there are others who think that you should be going back for your second sea tour like everyone else. The fact that there are serious shortages of experienced combat crews makes the situation even more intense. Right now, I think I can find a replacement for you but I can't promise and I certainly can't tell you when. Call me next week and I'll give you the best update I can, OK?"

"Just tell me one more thing. Should I prepare to go on the upcoming two-week cruise with the squadron aboard the *Enterprise*?"

"I would if I were you."

Marchand hung up the phone in a complete funk. Even a two-week training cruise on the *Enterprise* seemed like an impending ordeal. The thought that he might be headed back to Vietnam was almost too much to bear. He eventually decided to simply ignore the issue with the hopes that it might just go away. Marchand was getting hot and uncomfortable in his high neck white dress uniform and he decided to go back to La Jolla for the rest of the day and just hit the beach. He had high hopes that the sand and water would improve his mood and clear his mind.

63.

SO CLOSE BUT NO CIGAR

Two weeks passed and Marchand still had not received his orders to Top Gun. He had spoken to Commander McGruder who told Marchand that he had done all he could. Lieutenant Commander Scott, Marchand's Detailer, tried to be encouraging but had not found a replacement yet for Marchand in VF-21. Consequently, Marchand was aboard the *U.S.S. Enterprise* sailing out of San Francisco Bay for two weeks of intense sea duty in preparation for deployment to Southeast Asia. Marchand was on the deck as the enormous warship slipped silently under the Golden Gate Bridge with barely fifteen feet to spare.

He looked wistfully at the San Francisco skyline framed by its famed hills and thought it was the most beautiful city he had ever seen. The sun had just risen over the East Bay hills and the low morning sun made many of the City's buildings glow with a pastel warmth that seemed like a postcard. I'm going to return here to live one of these days, he thought. That is, if I live long enough. Thirty minutes later the San Francisco peninsula had disappeared in the mist.

Marchand was assigned to fly with a new pilot fresh from training in the F-4 Replacement Air Group, VF-121, at Miramar.

Lieutenant, junior grade, Mike Cathcart had earned excellent flight grades throughout the training command and the F-4 RAG. He was an Annapolis graduate who had finished in the top five percent of his class, and he was the son of an active duty admiral. Six foot four and movie star handsome, Cathcart seemed to have everything going for him. BUPERS clearly wished to pair Cathcart with an experienced weapons officer who would give him the best chances of survival in combat. When Commander Garvey had informed Marchand of the assignment, he conveyed the impression that the assignment was a real compliment to Marchand's skills and experience.

Marchand, however, detected a degree of arrogance and bravado in Cathcart that seemed somewhat excessive for even seasoned fighter pilots. "He's likable enough and seems quite aggressive in aerial combat training but he's got some rough edges that need trimming," Marchand explained to Winslow in their stateroom later that evening.

"Yeah, like what?"

"For instance, he manhandles the airplane. He doesn't just fly it, he forces it. He's rough on the stick and throttles, if you know what I mean."

"Keith, you can't expect the kid to be as smooth and silky as Kelly Drummond. You sure you're not expecting too much from him too soon?"

"No, I don't expect him to be in the same league with Kelly, few pilots ever are and I've flown with every pilot in the squadron. But there's something rough about his technique. That's what I'm trying to explain. You know that I made it almost all the way through the pilot training program before I was grounded. Well, I just know how a pilot develops a feel for his aircraft and the smoother he is, the better he is. A herky-jerky touch on the stick just means that you're not getting the most out of your bird and may be working against yourself. And, as you know, the smallest advantage or disadvantage may prove critical in combat.

"The other thing I wonder about is his carrier work. I admit Kelly spoiled me. We had a great routine around the carrier. I helped him in every way I could and he never surprised me. He never made a dangerous play for the deck or took any chances. If we were high in the groove, he'd never dive for the deck. If we got a little low, he would always respond with power right on time. He was sweet as honey around the boat. It's gonna' be interesting to see how the kid works the boat."

"Well, like I told you a couple weeks ago, keep your eyes open. If you feel that Cathcart is hot-dogging or getting dangerous around the boat, let him know. Tell him you'll kick his ass or rip his wings off or some damn thing. Just don't let him bust your ass."

"I'll drink to that. Here, let me fill your glass. Must have been a hole in the bottom or something, I thought I just poured it."

"Guess you're right. I practically inhaled that scotch. I've got to tell you something, Keith. I've been experiencing a lot of pain in my bad arm lately. The scotch helps."

"How come you never mentioned that to me back in San Diego? That's serious business, Phil. Have you told a flight surgeon about it?"

"No, not yet. I don't want to raise a problem that might ground me. Hell, we're already short two weapons officers in the squadron. If I'm grounded for any significant time, the squadron is in real trouble and you, my friend, won't be going anywhere near Top Gun."

"For Christ sakes, Phil! You're lucky to still have a working arm after what you went through last cruise. I often wonder how you manage to get back in the plane after that ordeal. Hell, you're fortunate just to be alive. Now you're worried about how short the squadron is on manpower. Or worse yet, worried about me and Top Gun. Get a grip, man; you gotta' look out for number one. If something's wrong with the way that your arm was set, you need to see the flight surgeon immediately. You could be risking your arm and your life. I can't believe you could be so stoic."

"OK, OK. I'll see the flight surgeon as soon as we finish this training cruise."

"Negative, my friend, you're going to see Doc Davis first thing tomorrow morning or I'll haul your ass down to the sick bay to see him and I mean that."

The following morning, Flight Surgeon Chris Davis x-rayed and examined Winslow's right arm extensively. He determined that the humorous, which had suffered compound fractures when he ejected from his burning aircraft last year, had not knitted properly. The orthopedic expertise required to correct the problem was not available aboard ship, so Winslow was flown back to the San Diego Naval Hospital for treatment that almost certainly would require surgical implantation of steel reinforcing rods. Such surgery would require months of rehabilitation work before Winslow could be returned to flight status, if at all.

With the training cruise half over, Marchand and Cathcart still struggled to find a comfortable rapport in the cockpit. Eventually, Cathcart began to listen to and follow Marchand's directions during practice air combat so that their air-to-air combat performance results were steadily improving. Toward the end of the training period, Marchand and Cathcart were winning nearly half of their practice engagements. Around the ship, however, there was still friction between them.

On the next to last night of the short cruise, Cathcart ruined a perfectly good approach to the carrier that might have resulted in a slightly high but perfectly safe landing with their hook catching the number four wire. But, Cathcart was extremely fatigued and desperately wanted to be on the deck. Without warning, he suddenly pulled back on the throttles and pushed the control stick forward in a classic dive for the deck. Worse yet, he almost completely ignored the LSO and Marchand who were both screaming for power. At the very last second, Cathcart shoved the throttles forward and pulled back on the stick. The extremely dangerous maneuver came within a dozen feet of killing them both.

Marchand was furious that Cathcart would attempt such a stupid, junior pilot trick. He was angrier still that Cathcart failed to respond to his and even the Landing Signal Officer's last second calls for more power. After landing, Marchand stayed on hot mike and roared over the intercom. "Cathcart, that's the second time you've dived for the deck since we've been flying together and that's the last fucking time you'll get away with it. The next time you even think about going for the one wire when we're a little high in the groove, I'm calling a wave off over the radio, and we'll fly back to Miramar. You understand me?"

"Fuck you, Marchand, I'm flying this goddamn airplane, I'm the pilot not you. I'll take my comments from the LSO about my carrier landing technique and nobody else, you got that?"

"Look, you arrogant SOB, I don't give a flying fuck what you do when I'm not in your back seat but as long as I am flying with you, you will listen to me about carrier landings and every other damn thing we do together. Either we're a team or we're not, and if we're not, I want out of your back seat right now. You don't seem to understand that if you bust your arrogant ass, I'll be about a microsecond behind you and I don't intend to let that happen."

Marchand turned off his intercom and unplugged his helmet so he wouldn't be tempted to say more or start a fistfight as soon as the engines were shut down.

When they entered the ready room to debrief, the LSO had already arrived and was talking to Commander Garvey. Garvey motioned for both to join him with the LSO. Garvey glared at Cathcart for a moment then said, "Listen well to your grade for that landing."

The LSO was also an F-4 pilot from Checkmate's sister squadron who had made the last cruise and was extremely well regarded. Looking directly at Cathcart, the LSO said, "Mister Cathcart, that was one of the all-time worst landings I've seen since I started waving airplanes aboard carriers. If you had pulled that power back just a little bit longer or failed to shove your throttles into afterburner at the last second, we'd be scraping your charred ass off the fantail. You listened to me all the way down the groove and just because you got a little high at the end, you dove for the deck. You did it so quick I couldn't believe my eyes. What's worse, you ignored my calls for power until it was almost too late and you ignored my call to wave off the landing. But, you were just butt-lucky tonight. It's a wonder you didn't bust your ass completely. You ever do that to me again, Mister Cathcart, I will personally see that you're grounded for good!"

Garvey then looked at Marchand and said, "And what the fuck were you doing, Marchand? Letting this young sonofabitch nearly kill himself and you too. Why the hell didn't you say something to him, wake him up, scream at him or some damn thing? That's why we put experienced Weapons Officers with nugget pilots, to keep them from killing themselves and everyone standing on the deck."

"Skipper, I was as surprised as the LSO. I won't let it happen again," Marchand replied in a thoroughly disgusted voice.

"See that you don't, Marchand. You're not flying with Kelly Drummond any longer. See me in my stateroom as soon as your flight debriefs."

"Aye aye, Sir."

Marchand looked at Cathcart who appeared as though he had been called to the gallows. After Garvey had walked away, he said sheepishly, "I'm sorry, Marchand."

Marchand nodded and walked away; there simply wasn't more to be said. But as he walked to the locker room, he thought of Winslow's warning so recently given. Damn if he didn't peg this one, Marchand thought.

After the debrief, Marchand found his way to Garvey's stateroom and waited for permission to enter. It seemed that Garvey kept him waiting in the passageway for an inappropriately long time but when he was called in, Garvey was still on the phone responding to a difficult phone call. When he finally ended the conversation, Marchand could see beads of nervous perspiration formed on Garvey's forehead. "That was the Air Wing Commander, he wanted to know about that dangerous pass he saw on the flight deck monitor this evening. Seems like everyone has put their two cents in at this point."

"It seems to be a pretty hot topic tonight," Marchand replied still at attention.

"At ease, Marchand, and sit down. I didn't bring you down to my room to chew your ass again. I frankly didn't intend to jump on you earlier but I wanted to spread the grief around a bit so as not to completely humiliate Cathcart in the ready room. Now what I want is your honest assessment of what went on in the cockpit and whether we have a continuing problem."

"OK, Skipper. I'll give it to you as straight as I can. Tactically, Cathcart is an above average pilot who needs a lot of seasoning but has potential if he can keep his ego under control. But his carrier skills are inconsistent, especially at night. One night he flies a perfect approach, gets in the groove and is steady as a rock to an OK three-wire landing.

"Then tonight, we get a bit of a bad hand off from Carrier Control Approach to the LSO. We were high from the beginning and about twenty degrees off heading. Nothing that unusual. Cathcart seemed like he had it under control, he responded well to all of the LSO's correction calls and believe me I was glued to the ball the entire approach. At a quarter mile, the LSO called for another small power reduction that would have given us a four wire or possibly a bolter. I told Cathcart to hold it steady, that he was looking good. Then suddenly, he pulls off the power big time and nudges the nose over. It's a classic dive for the deck. I yelled at him to add power at the same time the LSO called for power.

"On Paddles' third call for power, I saw the ball go into the red. Both Paddles and I were yelling for power and Cathcart finally shoved the throttles into afterburner. By then Paddles is calling for a wave-off and I'm a millisecond from ejecting from the bird. An instant later, we land hard and catch a one wire."

"You're lucky as hell, Marchand. Your bird landed not more than ten feet from the ramp. All the LSOs dived for the net. They thought you guys had bought the farm."

"Skipper, I thought I had bought the farm too. I was so pissed off when I got out of the cockpit; I almost punched the SOB out. I've never had any pilot pull a stunt like that on me. I've gone through too much for a smart-ass from the boat academy to bust my ass on the blunt end of my own ship."

"So what's your recommendation? Yank his wings, ground him for good, send him back to the RAG for more training?"

"Well, Sir, if you really want my opinion, I'd say send him back to the RAG for additional carrier training. He's not ready for the fleet. I will say that without hesitation. I will not fly with him at night off the ship and I wouldn't want to fly with him during a real combat cruise. There are too many things to worry about without having to watch out that my pilot doesn't bust his ass and mine at the same time."

"Put that in formal letter to me, Marchand, because that's what I intend to do, but I've gotta build a full file on this matter. You know that Cathcart's old man is Admiral Cathcart, the Second Fleet Operations Officer. Every detail must be covered. Even then, I'm certain to get a blast from above. You may get some residual heat as well. But I agree with you and I think you did your best.

"You see why I want you on this cruise, Marchand. A less experienced WO with Cathcart tonight might not have stayed on the Ball the way you did, might not have yelled for power like you and the LSO did. My feeling is that you probably saved both of your lives tonight."

The Skipper looked Marchand in the eye and paused. Marchand swallowed hard. He knew what was coming. His fate was twisting in the wind.

"I hate for you to miss the chance to join McGruder and his hotshots at Top Gun but I really need you here for this cruise."

Without flinching visibly, Marchand clipped. "Thanks, Skipper. I'll have that letter ready for you tomorrow afternoon. When will you send Cathcart back to Miramar?"

"On the first C-2 off this ship...."

"One more thing, Keith. I received orders for two weapons officers to report on board as soon as we return from this training exercise. The confidential memorandum arrived from BUPERS just after you launched this evening. So, the truth is, as much as I want to keep you in the squadron, and think it's a serious mistake to let you go, I've got to sign your orders to Top Gun along with McGruder."

Marchand couldn't believe his ears. Fate had intervened again. He was wildly ecstatic but answered calmly, "You've made my day, Skipper."

"Dismissed." Garvey said with a sad smile.

The last day of the two-week deployment was nearly over. Only one launch and recovery of the formal training exercise remained, after which the *Enterprise* would steam back to San Francisco from the waters off San Clemente Island and the Air Wing would launch for their home bases. As the squadron's Line Division Officer, Marchand spent most of the day on the flight deck observing the Division's enlisted men carry out their dangerous and exhausting responsibilities in seemingly controlled confusion.

Men of the Line Division fueled, oiled and pre-flighted the squadron's aircraft, checked their pneumatic and hydraulic systems, started their engines, assisted the flight crews in strapping in the cockpits, conducted final inspections before launch and assisted in the recovery of each plane after landing. All of their efforts took place in the most inhospitable work environment on earth. Although Marchand was a seasoned combat aviator, he never felt safe on the flight deck during operations, so he stayed as close as possible to the Division Chief Petty Officer who always kept an eye out for him.

Marchand was standing next to the Chief during the last recovery. The day was perfectly clear, no clouds, excellent visibility, the kind of weather pilots love. It was an absolutely splendid day to wind up the exercise. They stood near the catwalk behind the ship's island where each landing could be most easily observed along with the work of the Division's men. One of Checkmate's Phantoms was in the groove only seconds from touchdown. Marchand watched closely as the massive jet slammed onto the deck and its engines went to full power. Suddenly, the aircraft began to swerve violently to the left in a shower of sparks.

The landing shock of the thirty-five thousand-pound aircraft traveling more than one hundred fifty miles per hour sheared its left main landing gear axle from the strut. The strut was reduced to little more than a milled titanium spike that dug into the steel flight deck like a jammed asymmetrical brake. The Phantom careened off the flight deck still attached to the arresting gear cable that kept the plane from falling into the ocean.

Just as the plane began to veer off the side of the flight deck, the Weapons Officer initiated the command ejection sequence that fired both ejection seats. But, at the moment the WO's ejection seat fired, the aircraft had begun to roll over the side of the carrier, causing his seat to fire almost horizontally out over the water. With that trajectory, the parachute had no altitude to deploy. Consequently, the ejection seat hit the water head first traveling more than a hundred miles per hour. The heavy metal ejection seat with the Weapons Officer still strapped tightly into it sank immediately.

Milliseconds later, the pilot's seat fired but by that time, the plane had rolled back toward the upright position so that his ejection was normal. The pilot's parachute deployed as designed and he had two full swings in the parachute before hitting the water. He was recovered within two minutes. Helicopters and launches, joined by Navy divers, scoured the area for hours in hopes of finding or at least recovering the Weapons Officer's body but to no avail. The Weapons Officer's quick action had saved the pilot's life but not his own.

Marchand and every man on deck were stunned as the odd spectacle developed. Death had struck again, out of the clear blue, without warning, without quarter. That carrier aviation is a dangerous business seemed to be the only message of the day, as if anyone needed reminding. At the very instant when the Weapon's Officer had disappeared beneath the waves, Marchand realized that the tragic accident effectively ended his hopes of becoming one of Top Gun's newest instructors. He would be leaving on the next combat cruise to the Tonkin Gulf with the *Constellation*. That much was perfectly clear.

64.

GOOD NEWS, BAD NEWS

On March 9, 1969, Marchand returned home after the Weapons Training Exercise aboard the *Enterprise* and found several letters from Margo awaiting him. He greedily read them all several times. He paused the longest on the first letter that she had written just after learning that Marchand had finally received confirmation of his orders to the Top Gun Squadron. She was thrilled that Marchand was not going to have a second tour of duty in Vietnam.

> *March 5, 1969*
> *My Darling Keith,*
>
> *I am so excited about the wonderful news regarding your assignment to the Top Gun Squadron. You most certainly earned it and I congratulate you. You must be ecstatic.*
>
> *Now I can complete our wedding plans and we can begin to plan our lives together. I'm so elated that my feet are barely touching the ground. I've made reservations to fly out to San Diego as soon as you return from the training cruise. We have so much to do and plan that I think it will be better, not to mention more fun, if I'm there with you.*
>
> *I hope that this short cruise was successful and that everyone has returned safely. I'm beginning to realize that no one assumes*

anything about carrier operations, especially the absence of accidents. I worry so much about your safety. Not an hour passes without my praying for you and your squadron mates. Please be careful, my Love.

My dissertation was well received and may be published. So I can now focus on my career plans. I have several additional interviews scheduled with senior State Department officers next week. It appears that I will be offered a serious position in a policy planning or development capacity involving Far Eastern/China operations. Don't worry, we will decide as a team where to make our home base, I promise.

It's almost embarrassing but I haven't met anyone yet whose Mandarin or Cantonese is quite as good as mine. It appears that all the time I've spent developing language skills is about to pay off. I've also dropped some enticing tidbits about my Chinese contacts and my project for initiating Sino-American rapprochement. At times, it appears that my interviewers are more frightened by these communications than anything else. Too close to the real thing for many of them, I think.

Father asked me to send you his best regards and wishes for a quick and safe at sea exercise. Maxine also sends her love. It seems that you have won the hearts and minds of the entire Collins household. My arms ache for you, not to mention the other parts of my anatomy. I miss you and love you with all my heart.

Yours forever,
Margo

Marchand read the letter several times, inhaled Margo's fragrance, then agonized over how to answer it. There was no easy way to tell her that all their plans would be delayed for months now that he would be leaving in four weeks on his next combat cruise to Vietnam. He knew that she would be devastated and he didn't know how to break the news to her. After debating the situation for several hours, he determined that he would ask for several days leave and fly to Cambridge to tell her in person. Nothing else would do and he knew it.

Margo was at the gate at Boston Logan Airport to meet Marchand as he stepped off the flight from San Diego. She was delighted to see him again so soon and so unexpectedly, but she was puzzled about the reason for his trip. She had felt a vague sense of unease when Marchand told her he was coming to see her, but he had reassured her and simply said that he missed her. She was not completely satisfied but longed to be with him anyway. She tried with limited success to contain her excitement prior to the flight's arrival but lost most of her composure as she sighted him walking up the ramp to the Gate.

Marchand wore his dress blue uniform in order to utilize the ticket discount accorded to military personnel in uniform. The sleeves of his double-breasted blue uniform jacket were trimmed with two gold stripes indicating his rank and on its left breast were pinned four rows of medals and his Navy Wings of Gold. He carried his white bridge cap under his right arm and walked with military precision, searching the crowd for his lady.

Margo thought his suntanned face was so handsome and so out of place in Boston's harsh winter climate. Margo looked at him with pride and love. But she knew when she studied his face that something was amiss. She ran to his arms with equal measure relief and alarm. They embraced so intensely that the crowd parted for them and gave them a measure of peace amid the turmoil of deplaning passengers. By the time Margo caught her breath and pulled back from Marchand's lips, she had correctly anticipated the reason for his trip. She looked at him in a most solemn and piercing way and said, "You're going back, aren't you?"

His heart beat an uncontrollable thunderous tattoo but he managed to look directly into Margo's eyes and say, "My Darling, I'll come back to you. I promise with every atom of my being that I will come back to you."

Margo placed her head on his chest and began to tremble softly and sob quietly. "I know," she said, "I know."

At 0900 hours on the morning of March 21, 1969, Marchand stood at parade rest on the deck of the *Constellation* and gazed intensely at his fiancée, Marguerite Marie Collins. She stood just as resolutely at the edge of the carrier pier, her eyes focused on him like a laser. She wore a navy blue wool suit, tailored by St. John, with gold piping that strikingly complemented Marchand's dress blue uniform. As powerful tugboats slowly nudged the massive, thousand-foot long carrier away from the pier, Marchand snapped a multitude of mental photographs of Margo for safe keeping during the long cruise ahead. Her long hair blew softly in the morning breeze, framing her face in gold. Her cheeks momentarily glistened in the sun as her tears fell. She smiled and waved and put on a brave show while her heart was breaking.

Marchand tried to appear dignified and poised but his lower lip would not remain stiff, no matter how he tried. It quivered uncontrollably while the lump in his throat grew to tennis ball proportions and his eyes continued to fill despite heroic efforts to keep them dry. When the Navy band began to play "Anchors Away," wives, sweethearts and lovers hugged each other all along the quay. Officers and men lining the deck of the *Connie* gave way to emotion and dabbed their eyes with sleeves and handkerchiefs. On board and on shore, it was common knowledge that a number of the men embarking on this glorious spring morning would not return home nine or ten months later. The pilots and aircrew members took long melancholy looks at their loved ones realizing it could well be their last.

Short of an Irish wake, the departure of an aircraft carrier on a wartime cruise is one of the grandest, saddest and most memorable spectacles anyone could hope to witness.

As the Ship neared the deep water channel leading away from the carrier pier at North Island Naval Station, Courtney McGruder put her arm around Margo's shoulder and pulled her close as she would her own sister. Margo accepted the gesture then placed her face against Courtney's shoulder and began to shudder and sob softly. Courtney stroked her hair and whispered soft gentling words to her just the way the wife of Jack McGruder's first commanding officer had calmed her almost fifteen years ago when Ensign McGruder's ship departed for the North China Sea and the War in Korea.

Marchand continued to watch the pier until the *Constellation* began to move under her own power and the North Island quay faded from view. He still had difficulty believing that he was embarking on his second combat tour to Vietnam. Even though he had known the moment the accident occurred on the *Enterprise* that BUPERS would not be able to locate another replacement for him before the *Connie's* deployment, he had hoped and prayed for a miracle. But the miracle was not to be, for the War was consuming pilots and weapons officers faster than the Navy could mint and train them.

65.

HE'S LEAVING HOME

Marchand remained on deck as the carrier picked up speed and glided past Point Loma heading toward the mouth of San Diego Harbor and the open ocean. He thought about his dilemma in determining whether to turn in his wings or accept his duty and return to fight a war he had come to loathe. In the end, duty had overcome all his other concerns and misgivings. Duty prevailed over his disdain for a war, the origins of which he now understood with clarity. Duty had even overcome fears for his own survival. Duty had somehow subsumed the tearful, intense pleas of his beloved Margo who had begged him not to return to Vietnam.

His only unresolved problem was Margo. No matter how he tried, Marchand could not justify leaving her. He could not justify her tears, her anxiety, her fears. He could not forgive himself for winning her heart, giving her his ring, then leaving her. He just could not do it.

But it was indeed a strange, almost quixotic sense of duty that compelled him to return to the turbulent Southeast Asian subcontinent. It was not a sense of patriotic duty like that which initially motivated him to join the Navy. Surely, the United States would survive whether it won the war in Vietnam, whatever that sort of winning meant. Perhaps the nation would even be better off if it didn't win the War, he thought. Nor was it duty to the Naval Service that he felt, although he deeply respected and admired the United States Navy with its rich, two hundred-year tradition of valor steeped in dedication. Not even his sworn duty as a commissioned Naval Officer mattered much any longer, although he still accepted that oath as binding and sacred.

The sense of duty that surpassed all of Marchand's doubts, fears, misgivings and reservations found its source in something much more personal and fundamental. Simply put, he felt most deeply, now more than ever, responsibility to his squadron mates who relied upon him, his skill and experience. He was committed to the shiny new junior pilot, Larry Wolfe, with whom he was now paired and whose survival was in no small measure in his hands. He was obligated to Joe Garvey, his new commanding officer who struggled to reconstruct the squadron around a handful of experienced aviators like Marchand, even as they departed for West Pac. He felt a duty to the airmen and sailors manning Checkmate Squadron and the *Constellation*. Most importantly, he felt a responsibility to the American troops fighting and dying by the hour on the ground, in a foreign and hostile jungle filled with confusion and death.

The collective voice of thousands of nameless and faceless soldiers, infantrymen, grunts and ground pounders slogging through the ferocious jungles of Vietnam called to him. Career soldiers and hapless draftees who by chance and by choice struggled mightily to survive in the horrific Vietnamese jungles depended upon the Marchands, McGruders, Winslows and Drummonds of the Navy and Air Force. Aviators alone could provide the massive air power that would keep them alive, or at least enhance their chances of returning home reasonably sound and sane. Marchand knew, understood and accepted the terrible logic of this undeniable duty.

He knew that each strike mission he flew might mean that at least one American soldier or Marine would come home alive, that one less body bag would be delivered to Travis Air Force Base bearing the remains of a soldier's body and a family's future. Each mission meant that a Casualty Calls Officer might make one less visit to an unsuspecting wife, mother or father bringing the dreaded news of a husband or son that would not be coming home.

Marchand knew that his return to Vietnam was inevitable, unavoidable and just, regardless of the underlying morality or amorality of the War itself. With this perspective, he could justify the personal costs, no matter how great. When he balanced his own interests against those who depended upon him, his duty was clear. He would trust his own survival to skill and fate and the God he believed in. He recalled the powerful, soul stirring words of the Navy Hymn, "Oh hear us when we lift our prayer for those in peril in the air."

PART SEVEN

April 2, 1969 – September 10, 1969

66.

ONCE AGAIN
WITH FEELING

As the *Constellation* sailed out of San Diego's great harbor and came to her course to Hawaii, she increased speed to make a steady twenty knots. Ship's speed added to the stiff breeze from the west brought the wind on deck to gale force. Resolute, Marchand went below to his stateroom. His roommate for the cruise, Lieutenant Art Fisher had left their stateroom for the squadron ready room, leaving Marchand with blessed privacy. He poured straight Chivas Regal over ice from the small refrigerator, started a tape recording of Miles Davis playing an intensely melancholy composition entitled "It Never Entered My Mind," then he sat at his desk to write a letter to his fiancée. With Davis' uniquely cool trumpet playing in the background, he sipped the mellow scotch whiskey and began to write.

March 1, 1969
My Darling Margo,

I close my eyes and see your lovely face while your sweet fragrance lingers on my hands and uniform. I can still taste your lips. Most and best of all, I feel your heart and spirit with me as mine is with you during this final separation. When this cruise ends, I shall never leave your side again. And the hell with planning, I want to marry you just as soon as we can arrange it – on a beach, in a forest, in a chapel or cathedral, I don't care; I just want to be your husband.

And I want to thank you for your patience during the last two months. The uncertainties and reversals have been terribly difficult for you, especially at a time when your attention should have been focused on completing your oral exams and interviewing at the State Department. But believe me, my Angel Face, there were many efforts expended on my behalf, including Jack McGruder's and my detailer at Bureau of Personnel (BUPERS). Even Joe Garvey, my new skipper, eventually tried to get my new orders to Top Gun issued. But the accident on the Enterprise was simply too much bad luck to overcome. BUPERS had no other Weapons Officer with even a modicum of experience to make this cruise in my place. So, my number has been called and there was no changing it.

I know how strongly you wished me to turn in my wings and take my chances for an early release from active duty or a shore based assignment. Believe me, Margo; I tried desperately to accept that approach. But that just is not me. I could not make that choice and maintain a shred of self-worth or dignity. You would not want me that way. You couldn't love or respect me nor could I respect myself. This is the way it must be done and we shall pray for my safe return.

You will never know how much I appreciated your coming to San Diego to see us off, especially with your schedule. Sharing the past few days with you has given me the strength and resolve to carry, on even though the path is not the one you or I would choose. Watching you, seeing your lovely face as we slowly pulled away from the pier was the most soul searing experience I've ever known, but your face will remain my most cherished memory until I return to your arms.

My Angel Face, I must close quickly in order to get this letter onto the last transport flight leaving the ship before we reach

Pearl Harbor. You know how very much I love you. Stay strong and beautiful as always.

All my love,
Keith

As Marchand sealed his letter, Art Fisher entered the stateroom. Fisher had joined the squadron just one month before the *Constellation* sailed. He was the squadron's newest landing signal officer and by unanimous opinion, a superb fighter pilot, though one would never know it by appearance's sake alone. His face seemed frozen in a perpetual scowl and he sported a buzz cut on top of his perfectly round head. He was the squadron's first black pilot but he looked more like a short order cook dressed in a naval officer's uniform.

"Miles Davis, huh? You got pretty good musical tastes, Marchand, or maybe that's just a lucky shot."

"Hey, Art, you're a Miles fan too?"

"Man, I brought six hours of Miles on tape. You a serious jazz fan or just a dilettante?"

"Tell you what; you let me know when you want to hear some heavy-weight jazz. I brought some Monk, Coltrane, Bill Evans, Red Garland, Lester Young, Dexter Gordon – you name it, I got some for you," Marchand replied.

"OK, Roomie, I'm impressed. Something told me you weren't just an ordinary, square assed honkey dude."

"Well, I suppose that's a compliment. So thanks. At least we'll enjoy each other's music during this cruise."

"I'll drink to that, Keith. As a matter of fact, how about another stiff one with me?"

"Give me a rain check. I gotta run up to the ready room to mail this letter before that last mail bag goes onto the C.O.D."

Speed reached into his top desk drawer and pulled out a letter he handed to Marchand. "Drop this in for me, will you?"

"Sure, when did you have time to write it? We've only been gone an hour."

"Last night. I couldn't sleep."

"You too, huh?"

Armed with everything from machine guns to nuclear weapons and ready for almost any threat, the floating fortress city *U.S.S. Constellation* headed back to the War, half a world away. Leaving the States yet again was brutally difficult for the crew. Sailors held their goodbye tears in check for one of their rare private moments aboard ship and heartaches were stowed away one more time. It was time to return to fight a foreign people in a far-off land, once again.

Unspoken yet palpable melancholy was visible in the faces of the crew as they began the long sail across the vast Pacific Ocean, away from the beloved streets of home, a home increasingly beset with turmoil and unrest caused by the very War they were returning to fight. Crewmembers felt but did not speak of the invisible but pressing paradox of the times.

Since Lieutenant, junior grade Larry Wolfe was the most junior unmarried officer of Fighter Squadron Twenty One, he was the assigned Squadron Duty Officer on the *Constellation's* departure day. This had allowed married and more senior officers to spend the final moments before casting off with their wives and family members. Now that the Ship was underway, Wolfe relaxed as they embarked upon the five-day sail to Pearl Harbor. He knew that little of any consequence would occur while in transit. To pass the time, Wolfe had read every classified message at least twice, made each required log entry meticulously and begun to tidy up the ready room when Marchand entered.

"Hey, Wolfman, what's goin' on?" he asked.

"Pretty damn boring here, Keith. Almost everyone has gone to hit the rack."

"Yeah, it'll be that way till we get to Pearl. Lotsa' time to read, write letters and study your NATOPS Manual," Marchand replied, referring to the two-inch thick technical specifications and flight manual for the McDonnell-Douglas F-4J Phantom II, the workhorse fighter-bomber of the Vietnam War. The Phantom was a classic warplane unequaled in reputation or results since the glory days of the legendary P-51 Mustang of World War Two.

"Christ, I can already recite it chapter and verse – backwards. What more do you want?"

"From my personal 'Stick Man', I expect nothing less than perfection."

"So, go ahead and ask me something, anything about the bird."

"OK, how many cigarette butts are there beneath the pilot's seat in Number 205?"

Wolfe thought for a moment, then without cracking a smile, he said, "Four."

"Most impressive, Wolfman; how did you know the answer?"

"I counted them a few days ago when we pulled some negative G's. They all flew up on the canopy and lined up at attention. But, is there a lesson here, Rocketman?"

"Of course, there is. Today's lesson is that you can't learn everything about flying from the book. Almost everything but not quite,"

Marchand replied with a laugh.

"Lesson duly noted. Say, are you coming to the movie tonight? It's a spaghetti Western with Clint Eastwood."

"I don't think so. My roomie and I are gonna drink Jack Daniels and listen to jazz until we both pass out."

"Really, so how do you and the Night Fighter get along anyway? He always seems to be in a foul mood to me."

Marchand thought about his new roommate for a moment. "Well, it's too early to say for sure but we seem pretty compatible so far. That scowl of his is just for effect, I think. It's just his way of saying, 'Don't fuck with me.'"

"Is all that bullshit really necessary?" Wolfe inquired.

"Think about it this way, Larry. It's not a piece of cake being a black officer in this man's Navy and a fighter pilot at that. Hell, there aren't two hundred black officers on active duty in the entire Navy to begin with, and there's only a half dozen of them flying fighters. Can you imagine the shit he had to put up with down in Pensacola, not to mention at Naval Air Station Meridian Mississippi? And at every level in the Training Command, there was some peckerwood flight instructor who was an ROTC graduate from Ol' Miss or Southern Methodist University, just waiting to bust his ass out of the program."

"Yeah, guess I might have a perpetual scowl too if I had to deal with all the crap he must have experienced."

"Roger that. You know the Navy has never rolled out a welcome mat for blacks so I would cut him a bit of extra room for attitude. But frankly, I really haven't needed to do that yet," Marchand said. "He's quite a guy."

"Have you flown with him yet?"

"Yeah, I flew with Art two or three times at Miramar before you and I were teamed up, and once during our weapons training exercise on the *Enterprise* when you were Squadron Duty Officer, remember?"

"Oh yeah. Well, I hear he's pretty good and really aggressive. You agree?"

"Let me put it this way; Art's a real tiger in the air. He's got incredible vision and spatial orientation. He can wrap eight Gs on the airplane in a millisecond and he's got killer instincts. He could bust the ass of three quarters of the pilots in this squadron anytime. On his good days, there's only two or three pilots in the Air Wing who can beat him."

"That good, huh? So, who do you think can whip his ass?"

"The Skipper and Deacon." Marchand paused momentarily before finishing. "And you."

"The Skipper and our Ops Officer, that's pretty elite company you're matching me with. I'm not sure I qualify but thanks for your confidence. If you're right, and I'm not convinced you are, it's probably because I've got the best goddamn Weapons Officer in the squadron flying with me. After all, nobody else on the ship has bagged a MIG."

"Atta' boy, Wolfman. And now that you and I are a team, we're gonna' get us at least one more MIG before this cruise is over," Marchand said as a paradoxical feeling of aggression and revulsion swept over him.

67.

APRIL FOOLS' DAY

Four hundred year old institutions by their very nature change their rules and procedures quite slowly, if at all. Harvard University is certainly no exception in this regard. So it was with understandable reluctance that Harvard agreed to confer its prestigious Doctor of Philosophy degree upon Marguerite W. Collins a full two months prior to its 1969 Spring Commencement. The United States Department of State exerted its considerable influence to bring about this rare accommodation by the venerable University, the oldest continuously operating institution in North America.

Of course, Harvard did not and would not waive or amend any of its material requirements for the degree. In fact, Dr. Collins graduated summa cum laude and the political science department was seriously considering publishing her dissertation. Her doctoral thesis, *"The Chinese Educational System During the Cultural Revolution"* was well received not only by scholars at Harvard but also by several organs of the federal government.

The State Department and the Central Intelligence Agency had both developed a keen interest in Margo's family background as well as her first hand insights and research into the arcane workings of Chairman Mao's notorious revolutionary manipulations of the Chinese people. How Margo had acquired specific knowledge about Mao's regime had certainly been a major question in more than a few State Department minds, but the questions were officially overlooked.

In fact, only one person in the West knew that Margo had obtained that knowledge during a brief romantic liaison with a grandson of Chou En-lai the previous year in Hong Kong. That grandson happened to be an undercover agent in Mao's most secret organization dedicated to Chinese hegemony in the entire South East Asian subcontinent. And the person who knew of the affair was Rick Sero. Now that Keith Marchand was deeply involved in her life, Margo's priorities and allegiances had definitely shifted.

After months of extensive interviews with State Department officials including the Under Secretary for Asian Affairs and eventually the Secretary himself, Margo received an offer to join State at an extraordinarily senior level, especially for someone at her career level. Unknown to Margo at the time, several of her interviews had been conducted by senior White House foreign affairs advisors as well as representatives of the CIA's Director's Office. The unusual attention directly reflected newly elected President Nixon's serious intent in forging a breakthrough relationship with the People's Republic of China after years of diplomatic vacuum.

Although Nixon's tactics and ruthless personality were widely scorned both during and even prior to his Administration, few questioned his Machiavellian talents in the international arena. Notwithstanding Nixon's Red baiting background during the fifties, he had developed a serious, almost scholarly interest in Sino-American relations. He clearly wished to base his historical legacy, in major part, on his role in creating a rapprochement between the United States and the People's Republic. It was in this context that Margo Collins' seminal research in Hong Kong, the New Territories of the Kowloon Peninsula, and in Shanghai, came to the attention of the New Administration.

Of particular interest to Nixon's White House were Margo's contacts and relationship with Dr. Tsing and Professor Li. CIA research had revealed that Dr. Tsing was an adviser to and senior member of Chou En-lai's personal staff. As the second most powerful figure in the Chinese Politburo and Chairman Mao's most trusted confidante, Chou was The Chairman's most senior official who remained open to relationships with the West. Chou was also critically important to Nixon's China strategy. Nixon's senior foreign policy advisors thought that Dr. Tsing could provide the ideal, back channel communication link to Premier Chou that they were seeking.

Margo's primary assignment after joining the State Department was to establish frequent semi-official communications with Dr. Tsing on behalf of State with special liaison to the White House. This secret relationship avoided public scrutiny and operated outside of standard diplomatic communications. It became the precise mechanism that the Administration wished to establish with the PRC and Margo provided the conduit that made these communications possible.

Dr. Collins first official day at State was April 1, 1969, April Fools Day. She was met and welcomed by a platoon of State Department officials including the Under Secretary. She had been scheduled for a brief meeting with Secretary Rogers himself but, unexpectedly, the Secretary had departed for Paris the previous evening for an appearance at the Peace Talks. After lunch, she began to settle into her office and organize her desk. She had just begun to transfer some of her personal files into a cabinet when her phone rang. Her secretary announced.

"Your father is on the line for you, Dr. Collins."

"Thanks, Sarah, please put him on, and, one more thing, please call me Margo. I'm not strong on formality."

Mitchell Collins III was calling his daughter from his Wall Street law office to congratulate her on her first day as a State Department officer. "You are the Collins family's first diplomat and I'm terribly proud of you, Sweetheart. Your papa's vest buttons are popping off like firecrackers on the Fourth of July. How goes your first day?"

"Thanks, I'm delighted to be here. Everyone has been most gracious and cordial so far. The swearing in ceremony was really impressive. I only wish you could have been here," Margo said with a trace of disappointment in her voice.

"Honey, I deeply regret missing your swearing in ceremony but my meeting with the Securities Exchange Commission Secretary took forever to arrange and would have been even more impossible to reschedule. But I do have a pleasant surprise for you as partial compensation."

"OK, so what's the payoff for disappointing your one and only daughter?"

"I'll be in Washington for several days next week and we'll have some time to together if your schedule permits."

"That's wonderful, Dad," Margo replied wondering what he really wanted.

"Just hold on, daughter, that's not the surprise. I want to invite you to a dinner party next Friday evening."

"That's nice," Margo said with little animation, "but I'm really busy with appointments next week."

"You don't sound too enthusiastic, Margo. Perhaps, I might peak your interest by identifying the host."

"Just tell me it's not a senior partner from some stuffy old D.C. law firm. Those dinners are sooooo boring."

"No, my Sweetheart; you couldn't be further from the mark this time. This dinner will be hosted by the National Security Advisor himself. How does that strike you?"

Margo was quite surprised. What was her father up to now, she wondered. "You mean Dr. Kissinger? You've got to be kidding. You really don't mean Dr. 'K' himself? Wait a minute. I know; it's April Fool's Day. Very funny."

"Funny or not, just be ready by six o'clock. I understand that he's a stickler for punctuality."

"You're serious, aren't you? That's great! It's the hottest dinner ticket in town."

"And be prepared to discuss your China project with him. I'm told he's anxious to meet you."

"You're amazing, Dad. You've got more contacts than a transistor radio. You really know how to atone for your sins, don't you?" Margo said getting her little dig in sweetly, as she was still smarting from his meddling in her China affairs.

"Well, it's high time that the Collins family makes its presence felt inside the Beltway. It should be a fascinating evening. But I do have one word of caution, my dear."

"What's that?"

"Dr. 'K' is quite a lady's man as I'm sure you know, so be quick on your feet. You don't want your young lieutenant to read about you and the good Doctor in *Newsweek* or *Time*."

"Oh, Dad, stop it; you know all those stories about Kissinger are grossly exaggerated," Margo replied forcefully. She was, however, more than a little concerned that Marchand would someday learn about her affair with Chou's grandson.

"I'm not so sure, but, anyway, we should have a most interesting evening. And, you can be certain that the Doctor will discuss your ideas with his boss if he thinks they have merit."

"That's fine with me as long as he credits the source."

"Now that's a Collins attitude. Chip off the old block, aren't you?"

Margo rolled her eyes and shook her head as she laughed, "Yeah, sure Dad."

After the phone call, Margo rubbed her temples, as if to erase the host of tensions besieging her as she assumed her new post. The job of re-routing her life was at hand. Being a high achiever was one thing. Being a high achiever with a secret was another.

68.

TOO MUCH POWER

White House Chief of Staff Harry Robbins ("Bob") Haldeman and Domestic Affairs Advisor John Ehrlichman entered the Oval Office in lockstep. Although Richard Milhaus Nixon had held office for only three months, his two chief lieutenants had assumed almost military control over White House operations. No one and nothing happened at 1600 Pennsylvania Avenue without the express knowledge and consent of either Haldeman or Ehrlichman or both. And both answered exclusively to Nixon.

April 2nd had brought yet another in a series of late winter storms to Washington so that Nixon looked out on deep snow blanketing the White House lawn. Nixon found the scene exquisitely beautiful and serene but he was feeling anything but serene. He whirled around in the high backed leather swivel chair as the "Germans," as Haldeman and Ehrlichman were known rather derisively among the White House press corps, walked crisply into the Oval office.

"What took you two so long? I called for you both almost ten minutes ago. Goddamn it, you know how much I hate to be kept waiting," Nixon said angrily, his face severe, his eyes sunken and ski slope nose seeming longer and more pointed than usual.

"I'm sorry, Mr. President, but Senator Fulbright and Senator McGovern were here for their appointment and it took a bit longer to see them on their way than we had estimated," Haldeman replied nervously.

Nixon banged his fist on the mahogany desk and bellowed, "What the hell were those two wind bags doing over here?" Nixon demanded to know.

"Sir, they had an appointment to see you, but you were, ahem, 'too busy', if you'll remember, Sir." Ehrlichman replied.

Nixon got up from the desk and walked over to the stereo console near the fireplace. He fiddled with the controls and finally turned the volume down so that his recording of "Montovani's Greatest Hits" was barely audible. "Yes, well, I was indeed much too busy to meet with those sorry 'peacenik' excuses for United States Senators. So, thanks for getting rid of them for me. What the hell did they want to talk about, anyway?"

Haldeman methodically adjusted his tie before answering the President. "Well, Mr. President, they wanted to discuss with you, not us, the timing and scheduling of troop withdrawals from Vietnam."

"The hell I will!" Nixon blustered. "No way am I going to tell those two fools about my plans for Vietnamizing the War. The next thing you know, every word I said to them would be all over tomorrow's *New York Times* and *Washington Post*. And that's just what they are, a couple of Democrat fools. They'll find out what my plans are when everyone else is told and not a minute sooner."

Ehrlichman smiled. This was delicious. He loved hearing Nixon speak when his back was arched like an alley cat confronting a local bulldog. "Yes Sir, Mr. President, that's pretty much what we thought your reaction might be and that's pretty much what we told them."

"Good!" Nixon beamed. "Did they leave in a huff?"

"Yes Sir, I think you could safely say that," Haldeman replied, standing at a slightly modified military parade rest position.

Nixon returned to his desk and sat down stiffly, almost as if he were a cardboard cutout. He looked directly into the eyes of both men, letting them know without uttering a word that what he was about to say was of the utmost importance. Nixon's piercing stare could only be described as extraordinarily cold and equally intense. Then he began, his diction clipped, his words precise and carefully chosen. "As both of you know, my overall plan for Vietnam is to gradually withdraw American ground forces while turning the land war over to the South Vietnamese. Of course, the U.S. will supply all the weapons and supplies needed by the ARVN troops and all the graft that those little generals will need to maintain the party line. This is the core of the concept I call the "Vietnamization of the War."

Both Nixon operatives nodded affirmatively.

"But, in order to carry out my plan for Vietnamization and the eventual withdrawal of nearly all American ground forces, the Republic of Vietnam's Army will require cover and lots of it. Supplying that cover will be American air power provided by Air Force and Navy aircraft flying out of our bases in South Vietnam and Thailand and from our carriers in the Tonkin Gulf."

Daring to interrupt, Haldeman asked, "So, do we resume bombing North Vietnam?"

Nixon's face formed the cold, reptilian smile that signified trouble to those who knew him. "Oh yes, we will resume bombing North Vietnam, as soon as the Viet Cong or North Vietnamese Army commits some atrocity in the South so that we can blame them for the escalation. But when we start bombing the North again, the intensity of our air strikes will be much heavier than ever before. In fact, I plan to increase the number of B-52 strikes in Laos and South Vietnam immediately. And as soon as that bastard, Ho, gives me an excuse, I will send the B-52's all the way north to Hanoi and Haiphong."

Haldeman and Ehrlichman smiled as they listened to Nixon speak. Much of what he said they had heard before but some details were new or different. Sensing that there was more to come, Haldeman tried to anticipate his Commander-in-Chief.

"So, we withdraw American troops in order to pacify the American public while we turn over the ground war and all the attendant casualties to the South Vietnamese Army. Meanwhile, our air power maintains the status quo," Haldeman commented.

"You're partly correct, Bob. But I don't intend to maintain the status quo for very long and let General Giap and Ho Chi Minh call the shots. Oh no! Not only will I not be the first American president to lose a war, I fully intend to win this War."

Ehrlichman nodded assent but couldn't refrain from asking, "Do you intend to use South Vietnamese troops to invade the North? Or do you bomb the dykes and flood the North?"

Nixon frowned. "Absolutely not. American public opinion would never allow for that, any more than it would support the use of nuclear weapons in the North, not to mention against the Soviets or the Chinese. No, none of that 'nuke 'em back to the Stone Age bullshit' that idiot Air Force General Curtis Lemay is constantly spouting.

"My plan is elegantly simple. First, we implement Vietnamization in the South. Second, as soon as there is any excuse or justification, we begin to bomb North Vietnam again; this time in earnest. Not the namby-pamby, let me pick each target so that no one gets hurt bullshit that got Lyndon Johnson booted and hooted out of this office. What I plan to do is to use massive air strikes, including B-52 carpet-bombing, to destroy and I mean destroy North Vietnamese cities, one by one, until Ho cries 'Uncle'. Ha, ha, ha. Uncle Ho, indeed." Nixon laughed so heartily at his own macabre joke that he had to sit down.

"And, gentlemen, if a lot of little brown people in North Vietnam are killed, well that's just too damn bad. When they've had enough of our application of serious air power, Ho Chi Minh will beg for peace. Just you watch."

Haldeman and Ehrlichman stood mesmerized as Nixon described his plan to win the War, a plan that he would never describe to the American public, except to say that he had a plan to win the War, a plan that helped him win the election. Small beads of sweat appeared on Haldeman's forehead as he listened and envisioned wave after wave of fighter-bombers and formations of B-52's laying waste to Hanoi, Haiphong, Vinh and Than Hoa. When Nixon stopped speaking, Haldeman responded, "Yes, Mr. President, I believe that your plan will work, Sir. There's no way that Ho Chi Minh can survive the kind of destruction you envision."

Nixon suddenly stood up and walked to the window overlooking the White House lawn. Neither Ehrlichman nor Haldeman said a word. After a long silence, Nixon turned to face the two senior staffers. "There is just one interim problem, Gentlemen. Until there is a justification to start Phase Two of my plan, we must maintain the status quo, even as I begin troop withdrawals. And I can't do that while General Giap is sending half of his re-supply line from North Vietnam through Cambodia and then into the South.

"Cambodia is Giap's sanctuary. His men stop there to rest and recuperate before continuing into South Vietnam where they're kicking the shit out of the do-nothing ARVN troops and giving our boys hell. We must stop the North Vietnamese from using Cambodia as a staging point on their way to the South. It is imperative that we stop this."

Ehrlichman ventured a reply. "But Mr. President, we can't go into Cambodia. Congress has specifically prohibited us from sending troops or flying combat sorties into Cambodia."

Nixon's face hardened again, his jaw rigid and his eyes becoming mere slits. "What Congress doesn't know won't hurt it," he said in a steely voice. "I won't have Giap taking his troops into Cambodia and laughing at us. I'm going to nail him there and Congress just doesn't have to know about it. I'm going to send air strikes into Cambodia and that's that."

"But Mr. President," Haldeman stammered, "how can you issue a plainly illegal order to the Secretary of Defense, the Air Force Chief, or the Chief of Naval Operations?" We would have hell to pay from every quarter."

"Not if no one knows about the order whether it's illegal or not. Then, there simply isn't problem, Bob. Look, this is the reason I called both of you in here. I intend to bomb those North Vietnamese troops in Cambodia. And, I'm going to do it. I will do it secretly so that no one outside the Defense Department, Air Force and Navy will ever know. And if there are questions from the Defense Secretary Mel Laird or any one else about the bombing, we will develop a story to provide us with cover. And that's where you two come into play."

Haldeman and Ehrlichman both shifted in their seats, uneasily but nevertheless eagerly, like hungry wolves waiting for their share of fresh red meat.

"I want both of you to meet with the Joint Chief Chairman, the Air Force and Navy Secretaries, the Chief of Naval Operations, and the Air Force Chief of Staff. I want you to meet with them individually, not as a group, and tell each one that the White House has a top secret arrangement with Congressional leaders of both parties that allows us to carry out this mission in Cambodia and that it's imperative that this information does not leak outside the Defense establishment and the White House. Tell them that anyone, and I do mean anyone, who passes on any information about this mission outside of the chain of command will be court-martialed and given the stiffest sentence possible at Leavenworth Federal Prison.

"I want them each to believe that we do, in fact, have authorization to bomb Cambodia but that it's completely secret. I don't even want them to discuss it among themselves. Tell them that they should be ready to give a report to the Senate Majority Leader and the Speaker of the House in person, no documents or records of any kind to be allowed. That's our deal with the Congress. The presentation must be made orally. Tell them I will give them forty-eight hours notice of the presentation."

Ehrlichman ventured a question. "Mr. President, after a brief period, won't they eventually inquire or become concerned that no report has been requested or given?"

"Of course, John, of course they'll become anxious, even nervous about their reports. And I'll just let 'em get as anxious as they wish. But I won't say a word to them. Eventually, each one of them will get the message that whatever took place, took place with their full knowledge and apparent consent, and that no one would ever believe that they were under any illusions about secret Congressional authorization."

Ehrlichman nodded in approval. "In other words, they will be trapped."

"Precisely," Nixon answered. "Precisely. Now, you and Bob get your heads together and develop a plan to pull the military brass hats into the loop. I will take care of Melvin personally."

Haldeman, knowing that Nixon had made up his mind on this strategy and that he had to follow suit or leave the White House, then inquired, "Mr., President, what about the pilots and crewmen who will be flying into Cambodia? What will they be told?"

Nixon didn't hesitate for a moment before spitting out his reply. "We tell them that this is a top secret mission with clearance from the White House and other branches of government, on a need-to-know basis. They're all used to that kind of crap. And, we tell each and every one of them that they will suffer the direst of consequences if they dare spill one word of this mission to anyone, family included. I mean it. The pilots are to tell no one, not wives, mothers, fathers, not anyone, about the Cambodia flights. If there is any security breach, that pilot will see Leavenworth before he can change his flight suit. Is that perfectly clear?"

Both men nodded and voiced their concurrence. "Yes Sir, we understand very clearly what needs to be done."

Nixon was visibly pleased. "You know, Boys, by the time any of this has a chance to get out, which all secrets eventually do, we will have established our plan firmly in Vietnam, it will be working and it simply won't be news any longer."

Haldeman smiled knowingly. He had seen this act before. "Yes Sir. We will put the ball into play immediately."

"Good. I want a full report on your progress in forty-eight hours. And, I want air strikes in Cambodia within thirty days," Nixon said with cold finality. Bombs will drop, men will die, but victory shall wear my name, he thought smugly.

69.

DOMINOES

The *Constellation's* Air Intelligence briefing room was crammed to capacity with more than two hundred combat aviators there to hear a special Top Secret presentation directly from the Department of Defense. The Air Wing Commander introduced a senior intelligence officer who had just flown aboard the carrier specifically for the briefing at 0700 hours on the morning of April 15, 1969. The aviators were quite curious about the briefing, guessing that the U.S. bombing halt above the 19th parallel was about to be rescinded and that they would soon be bombing Hanoi and Haiphong.

The intelligence officer began, "Gentlemen, may I have your attention please. I am Captain Justin Rice, Naval Air Intelligence, assigned to the staff of the Joint Chiefs. Everything that you hear at this briefing today is classified Top Secret: Need-to-Know. Nothing I say is to be repeated, written, transmitted, or communicated by any means to anyone outside this group. This means that your letters home to your families, wives, children, friends or anyone else shall not mention the information disseminated here today. Violation of any type or nature of the classified information presented during this briefing will be dealt with most severely, including but not limited to courts martial. Now, with that behind us, let me turn to the briefing itself.

"Commencing tomorrow morning at 0800, you will begin flying strike missions over certain areas of Cambodia. As with our Operation Steel Tiger in Laos, the purpose of these missions is to interdict the flow of North Vietnamese Army regulars and munitions moving south from North Vietnam through Laos and/or Cambodia to South Vietnam. The North Vietnamese government has increasingly taken advantage of Cambodia's neutrality, avoiding our air strikes along Route 1A, using Cambodia for sanctuary and the rerouting of supply lines.

"We will no longer permit the North Vietnamese to utilize this option and will, starting tomorrow morning, pursue the enemy into Cambodia with air power. We will deny sanctuary wherever they move not only in Vietnam and Laos, but now in Cambodia as well. The United States has negotiated the right to conduct these strikes with representatives of the Cambodian government at the highest level. However, the Cambodian government wishes to maintain the image of neutrality because of its sensitive relations with both China and the Soviet Union. We will therefore, maintain strict confidentiality about our efforts inside Cambodia."

Captain Rice continued the brief by specifically identifying those regions of Cambodia, shown on overhead projections, where air operations would be conducted, and where anticipated air defenses would be encountered. When Rice paused for questions, the briefing room was as quiet as an empty church. The aircrews were clearly stunned. Bombing Hanoi and Haiphong was one thing, secretly bombing an avowedly neutral country was quite another.

Eventually, the commanding officer of one of the Wing attack squadrons cleared his throat, stood up and asked, "Captain Rice, you're telling us that we will be flying secret strike ops in a neutral country against heavily armed NVA regulars and no one will know? Are you serious? How long do you think the North Vietnamese will be quiet about this?"

"Well, Commander, one can hardly expect the North Vietnamese government to complain about air strikes against troops which they deny are there in the first place. The Cambodians, who strongly object to North Vietnamese Army troops on their soil, have pledged secrecy in this matter. We will simply play by the same rules used by the North Vietnamese. We refer to it as 'plausible deniability.'"

Commander Jay Kirkland, commanding officer of VF-21's sister Phantom squadron, then rose to ask another question, his voice tinged with sarcasm. "Captain, with all due respect, what happens when one of us is shot down and captured while flying an imaginary mission against an allegedly non-existent enemy in a neutral country? Does he become a plausibly deniable POW?"

As the audience snickered, Captain Rice stiffened, shifted somewhat nervously on his feet and responded. "Of course the Defense Department has considered this possibility and has planned accordingly. First of all, we will conduct full and extensive search and rescue operations to recover any downed aviator just as we always have. Secondly, we are prepared to introduce Special Forces search and recovery teams to retrieve any airman not recovered by SAR methods. And, lastly, we shall issue to each aviator today a specially designed 'Blood Chit' written in ten languages and dialects that offers a large reward in gold bullion to anyone who assists a downed American aviator to escape and evade capture."

Commander Kirkland remained standing and followed with another question delivered in a particularly sardonic tone. "Do I take it from your answer, Captain, or from what you didn't say in response to my previous question, that the United States Government will deny that an aviator downed in Cambodia was flying a mission ordered by his superior officers and sanctioned by the Department of Defense? Did I understand that such an unfortunate aviator would not be acknowledged by his own government?"

Rice answered, "Commander, as I stated previously, the U.S. Government will not acknowledge any combat activity which violates Cambodian neutrality. We will, however, conduct extensive, if not extraordinary, search and rescue operations to recover any aviator shot down during this air campaign. The 'Blood Chits' will add a level of protection that will further enhance the chances of successful recovery."

Not satisfied with Rice's answer, Commander Kirkland continued, "Captain, I don't have immediate access to statistics regarding the literacy rate of Cambodian peasantry. But, if it's anything close to similarly situated Vietnamese peasants, then it approaches zero. A Cambodian peasant who has just watched his rice paddy being turned into a shrapnel-lined mud puddle by our air strikes would, first, turn a downed pilot over to the nearest NVA regular he could find, then use these so-called 'Blood Chits' to wipe his arse. But I do have one final question. Was this air campaign ordered or approved by the Commander-In-Chief?"

"The President is fully aware of this decision," Rice responded with a cold stare.

Marchand then stood and asked, "Captain, I'm Lieutenant Keith Marchand, Fighter Squadron Twenty-One. How will a downed aviator's family be notified? How will he be listed or reported?"

"If the aviator is not recovered quickly, he will be listed as missing-in-action. His family will be notified accordingly."

"Missing-in-action, where?" Marchand queried.

"Simply MIA, Lieutenant," Rice replied sharply. He clearly did not want to hear another hostile and thinly-veiled sarcastic follow-up question.

"So, the family of a downed crewman will not be told the circumstances, is that correct?"

"I've answered your question, Lieutenant. Are there other questions before we pass out the 'Blood Chits?' If not, let's distribute them now. I should also mention that you will be required to sign for these chits and you will be held accountable for them.

"Finally, each crewmember flying into Cambodian airspace will be required to remove all means of identification, including dog tags, military I.D., civilian identification such as driver's licenses, letters, rings, including wedding rings, and any other item which could serve to identify or connect you with the United States Department of Defense."

The room buzzed with softly worded conversation among the combat aviators who clearly were unsettled and displeased with the latest development in the Air War. As the Blood Chits were passed out and signed for by each aviator, Rice flashed a full-sized reproduction of the Chit from an overhead projector onto a screen behind him. He read the English version of the wording on the towel sized ransom document printed in bright red ink on white silk cloth.

Each Blood Chit was carefully folded to the size of a dinner napkin and encased in heavy transparent waterproof plastic. The entire package was designed to fit easily into one of the zippered pockets of a flight suit. The ransom Chit was written in French, Vietnamese, Laotian, Chinese, Thai, and Cambodian and several dialects. The Chit promised payment in gold bullion equal to about ten thousand U.S. dollars, more than any peasant would make in several lifetimes if only he could read it, then find the temerity to hide and transport a downed American flyer.

At the conclusion of the briefing as the pilots and flight officers filed out of the room, Marchand leaned toward Wolfe and asked, "Well, do you hear that clicking sound?"

"What clicking sound is that?" Wolfe asked.

"The sound of dominoes falling all over Southeast Asia. You remember the old 'Domino Theory' don't you? The political theory which predicted that one country after another throughout Southeast Asia would fall to Communism if Vietnam should fall."

"Oh yeah, how could anyone forget that old LBJ bullshit. But wasn't South Vietnam supposed to be the first domino to go?"

"It was, but then again, it wasn't supposed to be the U.S. that pushed the dominoes over to begin with. No, it wasn't clear how this clear and present danger was defined at all," Marchand tried to conclude with a laugh but couldn't.

Marchand returned to his stateroom to read his latest letter from Margo in which she described her first ten days at the State Department and as much of a Kissinger dinner party as she dared without placing Marchand at risk. She was always careful not to disclose too many details of her work or research in China that would create additional problems for Marchand if he were shot down and captured.

The most exciting portion of her letter she saved for last. She told him that she would be traveling to Tokyo and Hong Kong on State Department business in June and that she desperately wanted to rendezvous with him at any port in the Far East where the *Constellation* might weigh anchor during the month of June. Marchand was ecstatic since he had just learned that the ship's port of call during June was scheduled to be Naval Station Yokosuka, Japan.

Marchand decided to return her correspondence right away since he was not scheduled to fly until later that evening and his roommate,

Art Speed, was standing the Squadron Duty Officer watch. Enjoying the peace and privacy of his stateroom, he started a tape of Eric Sati's solo piano compositions then settled at his desk to write.

April 15, 1969
Dearest Margo,

I received your letter this morning and was delighted to learn that your initiation at the State Department has gone so well. Of course, who would expect otherwise, Dr. Collins? By the way, I'm still amazed that Harvard granted your doctorate prior to June commencement. Someone with enormous clout and/or a huge contribution to the endowment must have pulled out all the stops on your behalf. I'll wager that Ol' John Harvard himself rolled over a time or two.

Your description of Kissinger's dinner party was most entertaining. I would have given a month's pay to have attended with you. Oh well, next time. You didn't mention the name of Henry's date. Was it Maria Callas? You are certainly traveling in tall cotton. But then again, eagles fly with eagles, right?

I am absolutely ecstatic about your trip to the Far East in June. It just so happens that the Constellation *will arrive in Yokosuka mid-June and we will be in port for seven or eight days. Let's meet in Tokyo, then take the Bullet Train to Kyoto for a few days, then finish our trip with a few days at Lake Hakone. I'm so excited about seeing you in less than two months I can barely sit still. I miss you terribly. I long to touch you, hold you and make love to you. My entire body aches for you. When this cruise is over, I swear I'll never leave your side for more than a day. I never dreamed that I could miss anyone as much as I miss you.*

As soon as you confirm your travel dates, I will contact a friend in Yokosuka who will make our reservations; so Darling, don't wait to reply. I want to plan a bit of paradise for us. And, Sweet Face, when our trip to Japan ends, there will only be another three months until the cruise is over and I return home for good.

Perhaps we can begin to make some wedding plans during our stay in Japan. After all, we've been engaged for four months. I'd say it's high time to set a date, wouldn't you?

Before I close, there is one matter I want to mention about which I want your input. I want you to send me anything you can regarding our current foreign policy, including military alliances or commitments, vis a vis Cambodia. Let me know whatever you can consistent with your security requirements.

Well, My Darling, that's all for today. Please write soon and know how much I love you. Oh yes, watch out for Dr. K; I hear he's pretty fast on his feet, especially around beautiful women.

Once again, I love you, Sweet Face.

Yours always,
Keith

Later that day, after Marchand and Wolfe returned from a routine Barrier Combat Air Patrol flight and completed their debriefing, Marchand noticed several of his squadron mates having an animated conversation in rather hushed voices. After hanging his flight gear, he joined the group in the ready room. "What's got you guys so fired up?" he asked no one in particular.

Bart "The Greek" Andros replied, "Well, the rumor mill has it that the Black Tiger squadron commanding officer may have turned in his wings."

Marchand was stunned. "You mean Commander Kirkland! You can't be serious," he protested.

"Serious as a SAM at your six o'clock," Andros replied.

"Why on earth would he do that?" Marchand inquired.

"You know the Tigers are flying bomber during this part of the line period. So they were the first to be scheduled for that Cambodian shit. Apparently, Kirkland was so pissed off after that Air Intelligence briefing that he and the Air Intelligence Captain, what's his name – Rice, got into a heated argument. Kirkland told him he thought bombing Cambodia would be a violation of a Congressional prohibition."

"In other words, an illegal order direct from the White House?"

"That's what I understand Kirkland was telling this Captain Rice."

"So he threatened to turn in his wings?"

"The word is that he didn't threaten, he did turn 'em in," Andros said.

"Holy shit, that took some real brass balls. He could be court-martialed!" Marchand said.

"Not likely, you ever see how many medals that guy has on his chest? He'd blow a court martial panel out of their skivvies."

"Yeah, you're right. Besides, Nixon couldn't afford any notoriety about this situation or there goes his 'plausible deniability' bullshit," Marchand said as he walked away considering his own limited options.

Marchand recognized something terribly wrong about these secret orders to bomb Cambodia. He felt a strong need to resist but there was no respectable exit from the situation that didn't entail serious risk. The reality was that morality and honor had become additional casualties of the War. The first commandment of military service, which is to follow orders, was being violated by orders to engage in non-existent combat in a non-existent battle zone. This briefing had created a monumental dilemma for flight crews.

As Marchand walked the long corridor toward his stateroom, he felt the start of an epic headache to match the conflict with which he struggled.

VOLUME ONE: PHANTOM WAR TRILOGY

70.

HAIKU

Margo arrived in Tokyo and took a room at the Hilton, not because she liked it but rather for its ease of location in central Tokyo near the Palace. She would have preferred a smaller Japanese style hotel or inn in another prefecture but she feared that Marchand would have difficulty finding it or directing a taxi to its location. Moreover, the Hilton was closer to the American Embassy where she had several meetings prior to the arrival of the *Constellation* in Yokosuka.

The *Constellation* steamed into the Naval Station at Yokosuka in time to be completely tied up by 0800 on the morning of June 16, 1969. The deep water harbor at Yokosuka, one of the finest in the world, is one of only two in the Orient where an American super carrier could tie up directly at a pier rather than anchor far out in the deep water shipping channel. By the time the officer's forward brow was secured to the dock, Marchand had showered, dressed in civilian clothes and checked out of his squadron on one week's leave. He was one of the first junior officers to salute the Ship's ensign and request permission to go ashore. He was eager to get away from the ship, the Navy, and the War.

He boarded a train for the short hour and a half trip around

Tokyo Bay through Yokohama and into Tokyo. He left the train once along the way, to visit the Buddhist monastery at Kamakura where the largest carved granite statue of the Buddha sat imposingly on a hillside protecting the village of Kiti Kamakura. He had visited the monastery once before during his first tour of duty and had found the monastery serenely beautiful, particularly its small lake, the perimeter of which was lined with cherry trees still in blossom because of a late spring.

Marchand found Kamakura to be among the most tranquil and spiritually uplifting religious sites he had ever visited. He could not pass close by without stopping to meditate, reflect and spiritually center himself.

He arrived in Tokyo early in the afternoon and headed directly for the Hilton. Margo and he held each other for minutes without uttering a word. They luxuriated in their embrace reassuring each other physically and emotionally that they had survived another separation. He held her face tenderly in his hands and kissed the joyful tears from her cheeks.

Then they made love. Passionate and urgent at first, slow and tender as their cravings were satiated, then they clung to one another. Marchand kissed and caressed every inch of Margo's lean supple body, savoring the skin around her breasts, teasing her erect nipples with his tongue. He stroked her deliciously long legs and caressed the soft skin of her beautifully muscled thighs. He nuzzled, stroked and kissed the essence of her womanhood. He buried himself deep inside her, memorizing every second of the experience. Margo wrapped her legs around him so tightly their bodies seemed to fuse. They gave each other joy.

The next morning they took the famous Bullet Train to Kyoto, the ancient capital of Japan renowned for its beauty, elegance and grace.

Marchand's friend at Yokosuka Naval Base had made reservations for the couple at an exquisite Japanese style inn simply known as Yamata Cho. It was located on a short street near the famous Kiyomizu Temple in the Higashiyama district. Kiy Omizu-zaka is one of the main streets in Higashiyama that has been the principle site of Kyoto's world renowned Geishas for more than three hundred years. It was quite difficult for even well placed Japanese to obtain reservations at Yamata Cho, much less American *gaijin*.

Margo's Japanese fluency coupled with her diplomatic skills smoothed their way. She handled their arrival as would a native Japanese, with minimum fuss concerning their ethnicity. After removing their shoes, they were shown to their room. She was most pleased when she first saw the room was decorated in traditional style. The floor was covered with pristine tatami mats and the finest Shoji panels adorned the room and entry. The Shoji were made with delicate rice paper window inserts and lacquered wood. Magnificent rosewood tonsu cabinetry provided color and traditional style. Their bed was a futon placed on especially thick tatami. The room was spotless and smelled of delicate incense. The couple had the blessings of a western style bathroom all to themselves, a truly unique luxury in a Japanese inn. The feel and ambiance of the room might have looked the same for centuries were it not for the electric lights.

Time seemed frozen in place for two precious days as Margo and Marchand enjoyed Kyoto's famous temples including Kiyomizu, the flower gardens, rock gardens and ancient imperial palaces. Kyoto embodied the ideals of Shinto elegance and simplicity and the couple immersed themselves in its beauty. Marchand was especially fond of the flower gardens where each plant and flower had been carefully placed and nurtured. Every rock and pebble contributed to the design while the fountains, ponds and streams balanced stillness with movement and life. Each branch, stone, leaf and flower seemed in perfect harmony with its neighbor. He could easily see that master gardeners had spent many years designing, creating and nurturing these living masterpieces of Shinto philosophy and artistic expression. The rest of the world, and its tensions, politics and chaos seemed far, far away.

Margo introduced Marchand to the beauty of Haiku; seventeen syllable triplets expressing a thought or vision in poetic style for presentation to a friend or lover. Each morning during their brief odyssey, Margo read to him a Haiku poem in both Japanese and English that she had composed while he slept. On their last day in Kyoto, she read to him her composition for the day as he awoke from deep and restful sleep. Each day she had awakened long before Marchand, bathed, combed her hair upward in Geisha style, and with the assistance of the staff of the inn donned a kimono complete with formal Obi, short white socks that covered her feet and ankles and high formal sandals.

As Marchand awoke on the second day of their journey, Margo knelt before him and bowed, then began reading to him in a soft melodic voice first in Japanese then in English:

> *Your smile brings me warmth*
> *Each day, like the Rising Sun*
> *Brings life to the world.*

Then again she bowed her lovely head. After a brief moment she began to perform the ancient and elegant Tea Ceremony for Marchand with nearly the same grace and mastery as a true Geisha. Obviously, Margo had studied the delicately choreographed movements perfected over the centuries by the courtesans of the Imperial Court known to the world as Geisha. Each movement of the cup, saucer and teapot was made with precision and exact timing. Every motion of hand, finger and arm reflected generations of dedication to art in motion. When she finished the ceremony, she again bowed, then knelt Geisha style and gazed upon Marchand with complete devotion.

Marchand had never witnessed anything so completely graceful or felt so loved as he did at that moment. He could not speak, his voice too filled with emotion. His eyes brimmed with tears of joy and love for this incredible woman kneeling before him. He rose silently, grasped her shoulders tenderly and brought her up to him, folded her in his arms, savoring the moment, preserving the memory and the moment for a lifetime, loving her more than he ever thought possible.

Later that morning, as they paused and prepared to leave for Lake Hakone, Margo surprised him by asking, "Would you mind terribly if we altered our itinerary a bit?"

"Sweetface, I'll go anywhere in the world with you just so long as I don't miss ship's movement."

She laughed and said, "I don't think that will be a problem because I would like to go to Yokosuka."

"Yokosuka?" he exclaimed. "Why in the world would you want to go there, to a Navy town, of all places?" he inquired in disbelief.

"I want to see your ship one more time, perhaps the last time. I want to see Chris Davis, your flight surgeon and meet your new roommate, Art, the 'Night Fighter' and the guy you fly with, the 'Wolfman', and talk to your new commanding officer, Commander Garvey. Remember when you took me on board the *Connie* last year in Hong Kong, I enjoyed that enormously. I want to have dinner in the senior officers' wardroom again and meet the ship's Captain. I want to sit in your airplane, the Phantom fighter in the picture you sent me with your name written on the cockpit. I want all these scenes fresh in my mind before you go back to war this one last time."

"What a strange idea, Margo."

"And, I have a surprise for you. A friend of mine from Harvard Business School is on assignment to a shipyard that builds supertankers. It's in Yokohama, of all places. He's offered me the use of his apartment there for the next ten days while he's back in San Francisco. We could snuggle up and play house until the *Connie* sails. Isn't it just a thirty minute train ride from Yokosuka to Yokohama?" Margo thought that this was enough of an explanation. Whose apartment it was really did not matter.

"Well, yes it is. You seem quite serious about this. And, frankly, I don't care where we are as long as we're together. So, what the hell, Yokohama it is."

The next day, Margo walked briskly up the long "L" shaped forward brow leading to the quarterdeck of the *Constellation*. Marchand followed several steps behind chuckling to himself. Here I am on leave, with my woman, and returning to the ship for fun. Fancy that!

Margo's hair, pulled straight back in a simple ponytail rode softly on a summer breeze. She wore tan gabardine slacks and a white blouse with just a trace of make-up. Marchand wore his tropical white uniform making it quick and easy for them to come aboard.

At the head of the brow, Marchand came to attention, saluted the National Ensign then the Officer of the Deck. "Lieutenant Marchand, Fighter Squadron Twenty One and guest request permission to come aboard, Sir."

The puzzled O.O.D. returned Marchand's salute and said, "Permission granted and welcome aboard Ma'am."

The couple proceeded through a passageway to a long up escalator to the O-2 level then forward through another long passageway for nearly an eighth of a mile to Marchand's stateroom. He unlocked the door and led her inside where she saw two bunks, lockers, cabinets, and two desks with combination safes, all in battleship gray. She noticed two massive audio tape decks, amplifiers, tuners and enormous speakers, one setup for each of the room's occupants. On one desktop sat a framed picture of Margo, on the other a picture of an attractive black woman holding a young child.

"Here we are, Margo."

"Supremely functional and a bit austere; that's the only description that comes to mind."

"Yeah. Whenever I'm tempted to complain about the size of the room, I remind myself of the guys living in foxholes, in the jungle or bunkers, if they're lucky. Then I feel fortunate."

"I'm the fortunate one," she said, "my lover, fiancée, soon to be husband, is the most wonderful man I've ever known, the only man to whom I've given my heart completely and without reservation." She reached for him, pulled him close and kissed him, a deep soulful kiss that reflected the intensity of her emotion. Marchand walked to the door and locked it securely.

Later, Marchand led Margo to the hanger bay where twenty aircraft were lashed to the deck with heavy steel chains. He found the Phantom that bore his name on the rear cockpit, "Lt. Keith 'Rocketman' Marchand," and "Ltjg. Larry 'Wolfman' Wolfe" on the front cockpit. He helped her climb up and into Wolfe's cockpit and then his own just behind. He took pictures of his "Bird" in his "bird" as he put it. He then led her to the Checkmate Squadron ready room where to his surprise he found the "Wolfman" himself standing the Squadron Duty Officer watch. After introductions, Larry Wolfe gave her a bear hug and said, "Marchand, Margo is even prettier than her pictures. Where can I find someone like her?"

"You can't," he laughed, "there's only one original and no copies; and she's mine."

"Well all right, can't argue with that. So, how was your trip to Kyoto and beyond?"

Margo gave Wolfe an affectionate hug as though he were a brother she hadn't seen for years. "In a word, it was splendid. We'll tell you all about it later."

Marchand asked, "How would you like to join us for supper in the senior wardroom?"

"Sign me up, Rocketman. Maybe I can catch your roommate, too. He's down at Ready Room Three attending an LSO meeting. I'm sure he'd like to join us."

Before they left the Ready Room, Margo kissed Wolfe on the cheek warmly and said, "When you come to New York, I'll see that you meet a lady worthy of your company."

"I'll be there, you can count on it," Wolfe replied with a broad grin.

Since many of the more senior ship's company and air wing officers were on leave or overnight liberty during the carrier's last few days in Japan, the senior officer wardroom was nearly two-thirds empty for the evening meal. Even the table reserved for Captain Patrick Townsend, commanding officer of the *U.S.S. Constellation*, CVA-64, was practically empty. Captain Townsend was a gregarious and pleasant man so it was natural for him to invite the Skipper of one of his fighter squadrons and several of its junior officers to join him for supper at the Captain's table. The fact that their group included an exceptionally attractive female guest made Townsend all the more eager for their company.

Not only was Captain Townsend a gracious and charming host in the style of the great warship captains of the day, he was ebullient in the tradition of great British Naval commanders of late eighteenth and early nineteenth century legend. He believed in good food and entertaining companionship in the officers' wardrooms aboard current warships as did Admiral Nelson in his day. So, the prime rib, au jus, that evening was roasted to perfection, carved to order by each officer and guest and served on fine china bearing the ship's logo and name embossed in blue and gold with the ship's own Sterling silverware at each place setting. Yorkshire pudding, baked potatoes, fresh asparagus served slightly crisp with Hollandaise completed the bill of fare.

When Townsend was completely comfortable with the group of officers and the guests at his table, and everyone else had finished their meals and left, Townsend ordered his personal chef to bring out six bottles of 1958 Chateau Margaux, *Grand Cru*. To the surprise and delight of all present who were well aware of the Navy's long standing prohibition against alcohol aboard its ships, he ordered crystal goblets brought to the table and filled as quickly as the magnificent wine could be decanted. As the wine was being poured, Townsend ordered another steward to turn on the power to the stereophonic music system located at the far end of the wardroom and soon the sound of a Mozart string quartet filled the room.

Captain Townsend then looked directly at Marchand and asked him to serve as the unofficial Mr. Vice for the evening. In this capacity, Marchand became the official host or master of ceremonies for the evening as would the most junior officer at an official "Dining In" ceremony that each Navy ship or squadron celebrates at least once a year. The Dining In tradition had been passed down along with many other naval traditions from the British Royal Navy to its American cousin that modeled itself largely after the British. Marchand replied, "Of course, Captain, I'd be delighted to serve as Mr. Vice for the evening."

"Well then, Mr. Vice, begin the toast," Townsend said in a merry tone.

Marchand stood, raised his glass and said, "To the Honorable Richard M. Nixon, President of the United States of America." To which all those present responded with a hearty "Hear, hear." Then Marchand having noticed the presence of a British Royal Navy Officer again raised his glass and toasted, "To Her Royal Majesty, Queen Elizabeth II, Regent Queen of England and the British Commonwealth." Again, all present replied appropriately and drank heartily of the great vintage. Since the dinner was not an official, formal Dining In, Marchand skipped the toasts to the various Defense Secretaries and other officials normally included in the various rounds of salutations but he did raise his glass to the head of the table and said, "to Captain Patrick Townsend, United States Navy, Commanding Officer of *United States Ship Constellation, CVA-64*". To which toast a sincere and rousing cheer was raised and goblets drained.

Captain Townsend then stood and said, "To Mr. Vice, Lieutenant Keith Marchand, Fighter Squadron Twenty One, who has done an admirable job as Mr. Vice on short notice and has graced the Captain's table with his guest and fiancée, Dr. Marguerite Collins." After the toast and obligatory salutation, Margo leaned toward Marchand and asked in a whisper, "How in the world did he know about me?"

Marchand smiled and answered in her ear, "Navy Captains have a way of knowing everything and everyone that goes on and about their ships. It's been that way for two hundred years. I suspect that Townsend had Intelligence run a quick dossier on you when he learned that you were coming to supper this evening."

"Well, I feel so very important," Margo said as she shivered a little. "I must say that I'm impressed. And, also very proud of you. No one noticed Margo clenching his hand in her lap as she tried to hide the inconvenient whirl of tension she was feeling.

The remainder of the meal was relaxed, informal and well oiled. Captain Townsend proved to be an exceptionally skilled and easy conversationalist who made everyone at his table feel comfortable. He genuinely enjoyed talking to Margo and made special efforts to extend the hospitality of the Naval Service to her and even make her feel a part of the Navy's extended family. She responded in kind and invited him to dinner with her and her father whenever he might visit New York or Washington.

When Townsend left the table, all officers stood as Navy protocol dictated. He said his farewells to the group and excused himself and as he walked out of the wardroom, Margo quickly excused herself and slipped beside him to take his arm. She leaned toward him and whispered in his ear. He stepped back, grinned broadly and laughed. Then he extended his arm to Margo and escorted her to the wardroom door, speaking softly to her as they walked.

Commander Garvey looked at Marchand and said, "What's that all about? Looks like your fiancée has charmed the socks off the Old Man."

"I don't have the foggiest idea, Skipper," Marchand replied, quite curious himself.

As everyone was leaving the wardroom and Marchand escorted Margo back to his stateroom, he said, "I'm almost afraid to ask you what was said between you and Captain Townsend but I think you may be just about to tell me."

"Of course, I'm going to tell you, silly boy. I asked him if he would be so kind to marry us before the Ship departs."

Marchand was so shocked he forgot to duck as they passed through a hatchway. He bumped his head on the cold steel and saw stars. He staggered a bit from the blow and Margo cried out, "My God, are you alright? Should I call for help?"

"No, no, of course not. I'm OK. It's just that for a moment I thought I heard you say something about Captain Townsend marrying us." He paused and said, "But that was before I bumped my head."

"Well, that is exactly what I said but --"

"But I thought you said you wanted a Christmas wedding in New York," Marchand interrupted, "when I'm all done with this bloody war."

"I do. That is, I still do. And, of course, we will have a Christmas wedding in New York, a big one for my father and your parents and all our friends and family. But this one will be just for us. We shouldn't have to wait. We can even keep it secret if you want but we're separated by too much time and distance; we just shouldn't wait. It has to be now, it just has to be; I want to be your wife now!" She looked at Marchand eagerly, tenderly, almost desperately, trying to discern any sign of hesitancy. But she did not find it. Instead, Marchand shrugged and began to laugh as he reached for her.

Of course. Right away. How obvious. Why not? What better way to tie oneself to this life than to tie the knot with the love of one's life? He wanted it to hold forever.

71.

CROSSED SWORDS

On Friday, June 25, 1969, Dr. Marguerite Collins and Lt. Keith Marchand, USN, were married in a simple, brief ceremony in Captain Townsend's sea cabin. Unlike the rest of the crewmembers, Captain's Quarters aboard a super carrier were commodious and quite tastefully appointed. The bulkheads were paneled with real mahogany and the deck was carpeted with a rich deep blue woolen weave. The bedroom of the Captain's suite was completely separate from the private dining room and the sitting room where the wedding took place.

Chris Davis, the flight surgeon, gave the bride away. Wolfman served as Marchand's best man and the Night Fighter was the other groomsman. Captain Townsend played a tape of Pacelbel's Canon in "D" followed by a Cellini violin-cello duet while he read the formal vows. Margo was radiant. Her simple white gown, purchased from the Base Exchange, was enhanced by her mother's magnificent diamond necklace that she had brought from home for this very purpose. Marchand thought that as beautiful as she always appeared to him, she had never looked lovelier.

Marchand wore his formal, high neck, dress white uniform with medals and his ceremonial sword. His face glowed with joy as though lit from inside. He thought this had been a wonderful and splendid idea and he had never heard of any other young officer having done it. What an incredible woman Margo is, he beamed. What a life I will have with her beside me, he thought. Marchand smiled broadly as he contemplated their future together.

When the ceremony ended and everyone had kissed the bride and congratulated the groom, Captain Townsend grasped both by their right hands and said, "Take care of each other; there is something rare and special about the two of you together. Oh, and one more thing, Marchand, I've talked to Commander Garvey and persuaded him to give you 'basket leave' for the next three days. I've reserved space for you on the C-2 returning from Naval Air Station Atsugi to Cubi Point in the Philippines where you will rejoin the Ship and your squadron since, as you know, the *Connie* will depart Yokosuka tomorrow morning. Any man fortunate enough to have a bride like Margo deserves at least a three day honeymoon."

Marchand could scarcely mumble a reply he was so shocked. Finally, he managed to say, "I don't know how to thank you, Captain. You've been incredibly generous with your time and consideration. We'll always remember what you've done for us today."

"Just enjoy your honeymoon, Lieutenant and Doctor Marchand," he replied.

"Oh no! I haven't made any plans for a wedding trip," Marchand exclaimed in a near panic.

"Not to worry," Margo said, "we have reservations at the Lodge at Lake Hakone."

They left the Captain's cabin and made their way to the quarterdeck to disembark, but, once there, the O.O.D. stepped in front of

Marchand as he prepared to salute the flag. "This way, Sir. I have orders to escort you and Mrs. Marchand to the flight deck."

"The flight deck, what the heck is going on?" Marchand protested.

"Mrs. Marchand? Margo murmured, surprised at the label.

"Just follow me, Sir," The Officer Of the Deck replied.

As they stepped from the island superstructure onto the flight deck, six officers standing three abreast in dress whites snapped from parade rest to attention. With swords drawn, they saluted and then crossed swords in the traditional officer's wedding style. Marchand and his beaming bride ducked under the crossed swords and were met at the end by the O.O.D. who again took Margo's arm and ushered her with Marchand in trail toward a waiting SH-3 Sea Knight helicopter. The chopper's engines were turning but the rotors were disengaged. Officers and men from Fighter Squadron Twenty One cheered loudly as Margo boarded the helicopter. The O.O.D. turned to Marchand as she stepped aboard and said, "The log helo will take you to NAS Atsugi, compliments of Captain Townsend. Mrs. Marchand will brief you from there. Best of luck to you, Mr. Marchand, you have an extraordinarily lovely wife." Then he stepped back and saluted.

Marchand returned the salute and said, "Kindly thank the Captain again for me and for us. He is simply the best of the best."

"I know that Mr. Marchand, I work for him. I'll give him your respects."

As soon as Marchand was aboard and buckled in, the Logistics helicopter pilot twisted the throttle grip on the collective and pulled up. The helo rose from the deck about forty feet, pitched forward and sped away.

When they were airborne, the pilot gave command to his copilot then turned to face the newly weds both of whom were wearing headsets and boom mikes. "Captain Townsend asked me to step up my departure on this log flight in order to get you two to Atsugi in time to catch a train at 1300 hours. You'll be there in plenty of time. Helluva way to start a honeymoon, Marchand, you lucky SOB. Ohhh, excuse me, Ma'am. But you know what I mean."

"You bet your sweet ass, I do," Margo said in her best rendition of naval aviator jargon. As the crew cracked up, Margo quickly but casually glanced back toward the carrier and the sky behind them. It was void of aircraft and glowed a furtive blue color.

72.

BLOOD LUST

On the first day of September 1969, Marchand was enjoying the peace and quiet of a stand down day on the *Constellation*. After mail call, he took his treasure from home to the strangely still flight deck. He found a Phantom parked on the lee side of the ship and climbed up on the wing to read his letter and snooze in the warm afternoon sun. Marchand opened Margo's letter, sniffed its fragrance and settled back against the fuselage to savor her letter.

August 20, 1969
My Dearest Keith,

Do you have any idea how I miss you? You can't possibly, there's just no way. No one has ever missed you the way I do. No one has ever loved you or anyone like I do. No one has ever longed to hold you, kiss you and make love to anyone the way I do. But I am so ready to show you, My Darling Husband.

Thank God, it won't be long. I know the Ship's schedule by heart. You're off the line by September 30th, steam to Cubi Point in the Philippines for two days (why so long?), then sail directly back to San Diego and arrive home on October 21st. Right? But why won't the Navy fly you and your squadron mates home on a charter flight, the way they did last year?

You know I'll be there when your Ship arrives, waiting for you with aching arms and a racing pulse. Now, I just have to determine what to wear. I'm torn between something outrageously sexy, like a micro-mini skirt, no panties and tight sweater with no bra (latest fashion craze here in the States) or something totally demur and wifely like a blue suit. I guess I won't go the micro-mini direction, though. The Shore Patrol would probably think I'm a flooze trying to make a fast buck when 5,000 horny sailors arrive. Then they wouldn't allow me on base. I'm not too certain about the blue suit either. It just seems too conservative for the occasion. Perhaps the way to go is a blue suit with no panties. Ha! That's it, sounds like the best of both worlds. But there's only one sailor I'm looking for. I love you and need you, my dearest Rocketman.

I'm alternately having a ball and going mad trying to plan our public wedding. The church is in Manhattan, I'm in Washington, your parents are in California and you're somewhere in Southeast Asia. Our friends are spread all over hell's half acre from Cambridge to Kowloon, Berlin to Bombay. Dad has all these lawyer cronies he wants to invite and I don't know how many of your squadron mates will be flying in from the four corners of the known universe. Sometimes I think I'll just rent Madison Square Garden, hire the Rolling Stones (I did meet Mick once; and ooooh is he hot!) and throw a bitchin' party.

Seriously, I've reserved the Episcopal Cathedral in Manhattan for the first Saturday after Christmas. I think it will be large enough! My God, what am I saying? I've picked out my dress; it's smashing and simple and I know you will approve. In fact, you loved it when I wore it in Captain's Quarters aboard the Constellation, *so I decided to wear it again.*

I'm trying desperately to organize my bridesmaids. I don't know what I would do without Maxine; she has been an absolute angel and I love her more than ever. She has truly become my adopted mother. In fact, I asked her to be my matron of honor. I hope you don't mind. It will certainly give some of Dad's legal beagle friends from Wall Street quite a start. Imagine, a black matron of honor. Don't you just love it?

Now, if you would just tell me whom you've chosen as your best man and your groomsmen, we will at least have the wedding party established. I do wish you were here to help with those invitations but since you're not, please, please send me your guest list now! Don't wait another minute or these invitations will never go out in time. By the way, I'm sending an invitation to your old Skipper, Jack McGruder. Do you think he'll take time off from Top Gun to come? And, of course, I'm inviting Captain Townsend. He was so generous and helpful to me (us) in June. Marrying us in Captain's Quarters was so romantic. I do think he might enjoy the sequel in a real church, don't you?

Finally, I haven't forgotten your request for information regarding our Cambodian policy. Other than the standard State Department bull, I'm coming up empty-handed. But something is going on; I can sense it and there is a bad taste to it. I shall try to pry something out of Kissinger if I can catch up with him again soon. I also intend to talk to Dan Ellsberg who seems to be quite well- informed regarding Southeast Asian policy, especially Vietnam, Cambodia and Laos. For now, I keep coming up against "Top Secret – Need to Know" files in answer to all my probes. And I'm not on the "need to know" list. I will pursue this; believe me. I just hope and pray that there isn't some secret war going on there, and please Dear God, that you are not somehow involved in it.

Well, I'm beginning to ramble and it's getting late. I need to sleep soon so that I can dream about someone so very special who is far, far away. Please know how much I love you and how it pains me to be apart from you. Most of all, be careful, not brave, and come home to me just as soon as you can. I pray for you at least every hour of each day. Please be safe. Please. Please. Please.

Your loving wife,
Margo

Marchand read and reread the letter, sniffed Margo's fragrance again and again then fell blissfully to sleep on the still Phantom's wing in the gentle land breeze blowing across the Tonkin Gulf from North Vietnam.

When he awoke, Marchand returned to his stateroom where his roommate, Art Fisher had just finished pouring himself a straight shot of Chivas Regal on the rocks. He quickly poured another for his roommate and said as he handed the golden Scotch whiskey to Marchand, "Here, Keith, then take a look at this, will ya?" It was the squadron commander's final draft of Art's citation awarding him the Silver Star medal for his MIG kill three weeks ago.

Marchand read the formal wording of a draft citation referring to Fisher's professionalism, skill and bravery in aerial combat resulting in the destruction of a formidable enemy aircraft. When Marchand finished reading, Fisher laughed and said, "That's some fancy goddamn language and a lot of official bullshit congratulating me for wastin' a guy I didn't even know. Back in Philly, in the 'hood where I grew up, I'd get twenty-five to life or worse for doing the same thing. Funny world, huh?"

Marchand took a long sip of Scotch and thought a few moments before responding. "Last year when Kelly Drummond and I bagged those MIGs, we were totally jazzed for the first week or so. Then, it hit me just like it seems to be hitting you: We had killed two guys. Not some unknown, faceless NVA grunts on the ground, like we do every day, but two guys that we got to know in a strange way, real up front and personal.

"I wanted to kill them, just the two of them. I wanted to kill them clean and simple. I didn't care if they ejected or not, I didn't care if they were Vietnamese, Chinese or even Russians. I just wanted to kill them, blow their airplanes to kingdom come, vaporize them. I wanted them to know, in the last few seconds before their MIGs became fireballs, that Kelly and I were better than they were, superior in the most terrible way, that we had killed them cold.

"It was training and some skill that paid off. And, it was our mission to be sure. But it was mostly luck. But it was something else as well. It was lust, blood lust. I could almost taste it afterwards. I've never told anyone that I felt like this. It seemed vaguely sinful and uncivilized. I was almost ashamed to feel this way. And, if you weren't a good friend and my roommate, I probably wouldn't admit it to you now. So, is that anything like what you felt?"

Speed took another long drink. "Yeah, pretty close to that. Very much like that, in fact. You know, you and I have probably killed couple hundred, maybe a couple thousand guys on the ground and, in my case at least, I never thought much about it. It was my job to kill them. It was their job to die. But this is different. Like you say, killin' another pilot is kinda' personal. Yeah, I admit it. I really wanted to kill that motherfucker. But then, he really wanted to kill me, too.

"Maybe that's the difference, or at least part of the difference. That SOB was really trying to kill me, trying to fry my black ass, to shoot a missile right up my butt and blow it to atoms. So, yeah, I wanted to kill him and I did and I'm glad as hell that I did kill that fucker." Then Speed stopped abruptly.

"But part of you feels weird because you enjoyed killing him, right? Just like I enjoyed killing those two bastards last year. It's terrible but I enjoyed killing those fuckers," Marchand said.

"You think it's evil to feel that way?" Fisher asked sincerely.

"I don't know. All I know is that you're not alone. And, you know what? I want to do it again," Marchand replied. "I want to fight another MIG pilot. I want to turn and burn with the bastard. I want him to scare me shitless then I want to kill him, watch him disintegrate, see him go up in a glorious fireball right in front of me. And afterwards, I want all the guys on the ship and all the folks back home to cheer and tell me what a great guy I am because I blew that nasty bastard away. I know this is really and truly fucked up, but that's the way it is."

Marchand had intended to write a reply to Margo but after his conversation with Speed, he simply couldn't. He had a strange coppery taste in his mouth and it wasn't the scotch. He didn't feel like sharing this mood or his thoughts with his wife. I wonder if I'm even civilized enough to go home, he asked himself. Will I fit in at Harvard or anywhere else? He mused. I've been taught to kill and to my dismay, now I find I like it. He admitted to himself, somewhat abashed and very silent.

Is there enough humanity left in me to be worthy of Margo when I go home? Marchand asked himself.

73.

THE BIG DANCE

The Air Intelligence Officer enthusiastically moved his pointer along an enlarged navigation chart showing the route that an RA-5C Vigilante and her two fighter escorts would fly later on the morning of September 11, 1969. The photo-reconnaissance mission would begin on the outskirts of Haiphong, North Vietnam and continue south for almost three hundred miles to the De-Militarized Zone. The chart had red and blue pushpins indicating the sites of SAM batteries and radar directed anti-aircraft artillery positions along the route. In many areas of the chart, there were so many pushpins they completely obscured its details. Even a casual observer could see that the area around Haiphong was one of the most heavily defended places on earth.

Notwithstanding the Air Intelligence officer's enthusiasm, the chart was as close as he would ever come to a SAM or a round of AAA fire. Such was not the case for Commander Scott Taylor and his reconnaissance navigator, Lieutenant Matt Menendez who regularly flew some of the most dangerous missions of the air war over Vietnam.

During the years immediately preceding the perfection of satellite photography, high speed aircraft such at the Navy's Vigilante performed this mission admirably but often at high cost. The photographs taken by the enormously expensive, high resolution cameras crammed into the plane's belly were so detailed that the trained observer could almost determine whether a North Vietnamese soldier was having fish with his rice for supper.

When the AI officer concluded his brief the flight leader Commander Taylor, took the podium to begin his portion of the brief. "Good morning, gentlemen, good to see so many familiar faces out there for the Navy's version of 'Candid Camera'. When I'm finished, you can stay and ask questions or return to your respective ready rooms for your specific mission briefs.

"Our mission is to capture as much photo-intelligence as possible, showing the amount, type and rate of flow of munitions and NVA troops south to the DMZ or Laos for subsequent infiltration to South Vietnam. As briefed by the Air Wing meteorologist, we anticipate good clear weather all the way south today. We haven't had such good weather for several weeks and that's why we'll be flying such a long segment of the main highway south from Haiphong Harbor to the city of Vinh then to the DMZ. And, as pointed out by Air Intelligence, we'll be flying along some heavily defended areas from our coast-in point all the way to feet wet again.

"After launch, everyone will proceed independently to their air refueling rendezvous, if that's required for your aircraft. I'll leave that for your specific mission briefs. When you've taken on as much gas as you need, the recon group will rendezvous with me at Flight Level 180. We'll be flying an orbit with a ten-mile radius overhead the ship. You Phantom drivers should really top off the gas, since this will be a long flight over hostile territory and I want you guys to have plenty of fuel to protect my backside if we encounter any bad guys along the way.

"After rendezvous, I'll call the flight to move out and take up the heading to our coast-in point. Along the way, I'll descend to thirteen thousand feet and I'd like my fighter escorts to take up position with about a quarter mile spread on both sides; you can step up or down as you brief later. When we arrive about ten miles from coast-in, you A-6 drivers take your stations and stand by to follow us south. And, please keep your fingers on that Standard Arm trigger. Whale drivers stay as close as you can to the gaggle while remaining off the coast and be ready with the gas if we come out sucking fumes or leaking fuel.

"Deacon, I want you and your wingman to keep a constant three G jink on your birds while we're feet dry. You know from experience that I will. When we arrive at the coast-in point, I'll keep my throttles at military power. That gives me about seven hundred miles per hour and I know that you guys have to goose it with a little afterburner from time to time to stay up with me. That's why you must top off your fuel tanks from the Whale just before we head out.

"If I push over, the Vigilante will go supersonic in a heartbeat so be ready with your superheat, as our British friends say. If I'm still pulling away and you guys are using too much gas, call me and I'll throttle back – briefly. Remember you guys got missiles, I don't. All I've got to get me and my Navigator, Matt, home to mama at the end of this month is my 'Road Runner' routine which I'm getting' pretty good at.

"If we pick up heavy triple A and it's radar guided or if a SAM site goes active, I'll call for you A-6 guys to step in with a Standard Arm or two. That usually calms the gunners down a bit. A few Shrikes now and then from you A-7 drivers will also be appreciated.

"Deacon, if we're jumped by MIGs, the show is all yours. You and Wolfman, go get 'em. My Navigator and I will be high tailing it in full combat power and I'll try to find out if the bird will do 1500 knots per hour like the NATOPS Manual says. Again, remember that Mama Taylor will kick your collective butts if Papa Taylor don't come home this month 'cuz those bandits jumped us. Seriously, Deacon, that's about it for me. Unless you have questions, I'll give the podium to Matt who'll cover navigation, then you fellas wrap up the final briefing in your own ready rooms. Deacon, I'll see you overhead at eighteen thousand feet at 0830."

In Ready Room Two, Mark Tanner "The Deacon," VF-21's Operations Officer and one of the best pilots in the squadron, completed the briefing started by Scottie Taylor. As Tanner spoke, Marchand and Wolfe had time to think and talk about the mission they were about to fly. "You know, Keith, this looks like it's gonna be the granddaddy of recon flights. We got two Phantoms, two A-6 Intruders, four A-7 attack bombers, two A-3 tankers and the E-2 Hawkeye all running support for the Vigilante. That's a helluva mission any way you look at it. Somebody's anticipating some real fireworks, I'd say."

"You're probably right. And I think there's more to it," Marchand replied.

"Yeah, like what?"

"Well, like Scottie said, the weather's been for shit the last couple of weeks until the day before the Stand Down day; low level overcasts day after day so that no recon flights have gone up North at all. On top of that, the last few *Time* and *Newsweek* magazines I've read reported that the Paris Peace Talks have produced a lot of smoke and hot air but no peace and are on the verge of being cancelled altogether. So, I'll bet Uncle Ho has used this weather to send as many men and as much ammunition as possible south in order to launch a new offensive."

"So what's new?" Wolfe replied.

"I think that we know what's going on from other intelligence sources but now we want to prove it."

"Prove it to whom and for what reason?"

"The Administration needs to be able to show the evidence to the world, to anyone who will listen, to whoever cares, so that when Nixon cancels the Peace Talks, he can say it's because North Vietnam has been cheating."

"And then what?"

"Then Nixon would be free to resume bombing the hell out of North Vietnam without much political heat back home. As we pulverize the North from the air, he pulls our troops out of the South to appease nearly everyone who demands that he make good on his campaign promises to end the War. It's a perfect strategy. He sends the troops home to keep his critics at bay while he bombs the fuck out of North Vietnam so that he can eventually win the Unwinnable War, the War the Democrats started but couldn't finish."

"Might explain why we're bombing Cambodia, too." Wolfe commented.

"Sure, as long as nobody knows it. And you and I and all the guys flying missions in Cambodia can't say a word to anyone."

"Yeah, well, they don't call him 'Tricky Dick' for nothing."

74.

THOSE BASTARDS

Bob Haldeman entered the Oval Office at 8:00 a.m. on September 10, 1969 and greeted the President. Nixon wasted no time with small talk but proceeded directly to his most immediate concern. "What's this I hear about Navy and Air Force squadron commanders refusing to fly missions into Cambodia? I've even several reports stating that even some junior officers have questioned my orders. What the hell's going on here?"

"Well, Mr. President, one commanding officer of a Navy fighter squadron on the carrier *Constellation* has turned in his wings rather than fly what he calls an 'illegal and unlawful' order. And yesterday, an Air Force wing commander at the Udorn Base in Thailand refused to fly missions in Cambodia until he was shown proof that the orders came from the Commander-in-Chief himself. Also as I understand it, a number of junior pilots have expressed great concern about the Cambodian campaign."

Nixon exploded, "Goddamn it, Bob, I will not tolerate any more insubordination from those snot-nosed bastards! When I give an order that's the end of it. I will not have my directions questioned by anyone. I want that mutinous Navy commander court-martialed immediately! Get

605

the word out to the Seventh Fleet Commander now," Nixon growled fiercely while pounding his fist on the Presidential desk.

Haldeman reeled backward a step recoiling from the intensity of Nixon's tirade. Regaining his composure, he replied. "Mr. President, I must mention that this Commander is a highly decorated fighter pilot who's flown over two hundred missions and shot down a MIG during the War. A court martial would create an enormous amount of adverse publicity for the Navy and ultimately the White House. Worse yet, the attendant press reports would undoubtedly lead to public awareness of the Cambodian air campaign."

Nixon paused for a moment, asking himself why he hadn't though of that. But given the powers at his disposal, he knew that there was a solution to what he considered gross insubordination. "OK, Bob, you make a good point. But these SOBs won't get away with this."

"Yes sir, I'm sure they won't." Haldeman answered.

"That reminds me," Nixon said with a hiss, "that so-called hero Navy lieutenant who shot down a couple of MIGs last year then married Mitch Collins' daughter isn't involved in this crap, is he? Once these idiots get a little publicity, they can get mighty headstrong... What's his name? You know the one whose name was all over the papers last year."

"You mean the kid who's married to that gorgeous State Department officer working on the China project?"

"Yeah, that one."

"Name is Marchand, Keith Marchand, I believe."

"Right. Navy Intelligence claims that he's pretty outspoken about the War. But if he's gone too far and questioned my authority, I want his mouth shut. If he flies his missions and buttons his lip, that's fine. But I don't need any more hero crap or any challenge to my orders. Just see that he keeps his mouth shut. But do it quietly. I don't want to hear anything else from his father-in-law, Mitch Collins. Collins is much too valuable to us on Wall Street to have any ill will toward the White House. Do what you have to do but be very careful not to leave any Administration footprints about this matter."

Haldeman swallowed hard. "Yes, Mr. President, I'll start on this issue right away."

"And one more thing, absolutely no more Cambodian missions for this Marchand kid. Get my orders sent down the chain of command as quickly and quietly as you can. I'm tired of Collins pestering me."

"Yes sir, Mr. President," Haldeman replied standing almost at military attention.

"Alright, now here's how I want you to handle the larger issue; so listen carefully. I will not cover this in our next meeting with Secretary Laird and the Joint Chiefs. First, I want that insubordinate Navy Commander who turned in his wings packed away to some godforsaken corner of the world, to the Navy's least attractive posting, someplace like Adack Alaska. Same thing with those goddamn Air Force squadron commanders. Have them assigned to duty at a missile silo in Nebraska or something like that. And make sure they know that any comments to anyone about this issue will result in a secret court martial and immediate imprisonment at Leavenworth.

"Second, I want each squadron or wing commander with junior officers who grumble or complain loudly about these Cambodian missions to take each one of these young punks to the woodshed. Threaten them with loss of rank, dishonorable discharges, court martial and Leavenworth. If the warnings don't work, pull their wings and send them to the worst possible far off duty stations and under close watch. That ought to handle those young bastards.

"Third, since the bombing has driven the North Vietnamese

Army even farther into Cambodia where our tactical fighter-bombers are at the limits of their range, I want most of these missions to be flown by B-52's out of Guam. That way, we limit the aviators involved to the smallest number possible. Also, long range bomber pilots don't seem to be as picky as these damn fighter jocks who think they can have a say in what they bomb and who they kill. Bomber pilots are accustomed to destroying entire goddamn cities and having a fuckin' ham sandwich on their way home."

Haldeman laughed uneasily and replied, "Yes sir, I've heard General LeMay talk about making the rubble bounce in Moscow's Red Square if he ever gets turned loose on the Russians."

"Damn right, those arrogant, fighter jock bastards must learn that I'm the only one who makes foreign policy in this government, not the Congress, not the courts, and certainly not those Mickey Mouse pilots. In the meantime, as far as the public is concerned, the Administration will continue to say that US involvement in Southeast Asia is limited to supporting South Vietnamese forces in order to protect US troops. That's what we'll say publicly while we continue our covert operations in Cambodia. I want our air power in there and do not spare the horses. We will not withdraw for domestic reasons but only for military reasons. So go, just do it. Don't come back and ask permission each time.

"And for Christ sakes, do something about this Marchand kid. I don't want another goddamn call from Mitch Collins about this matter."

75.

PURE POWER

Marchand sensed that even the plane captains were aware of this particular mission's importance. Squadron Maintenance had prepared three Phantoms for the escort mission, two for launch, and a spare. All three fighters were spotless. Not a drop of oil, fuel, grease or hydraulic fluid marred either plane's exterior.

Marchand had always admired the Phantom, a strangely beautiful aircraft with a long, drooping nose housing its powerful radar and weapons control system. The Phantom's wings slanted sharply upward at the wing fold but its rear stabilator pointed down at nearly forty-five degrees. The Phantoms' engines gulped enormous quantities of air through gaping intakes just aft of the rear cockpit and exhausted superheated twin blast furnaces from variable engine nozzles pointing down at a slight angle. It was, by all standards, an eye-catching but brutishly powerful aircraft. But above all, it was obvious that the Phantom was designed with one purpose in mind – to kill and kill swiftly.

Marchand completed his pre-flight walk around. Satisfied that the plane was in flawless fighting condition, he quickly climbed the boarding ladder and settled into the rear cockpit. As he fastened his lap belt, leg restraints and shoulder harness, Marchand sensed a certain fraternal affection in the way his plane captain re-checked the shoulder straps, armed the ejection seat, and patted Marchand's shoulder for luck. Just before he donned his helmet, his plane captain leaned over the canopy rail and told Marchand that this was the best bird in the entire squadron. Marchand smiled and gave him a thumbs-up. Marchand felt like a matador preparing to meet a ferocious bull.

Marchand reached into his helmet bag and removed his beloved stuffed dog. He rubbed the little beagle's black nose for luck and laughed at the smudges of oil, grease and dirt that stained the once spotless fake fur. "Just a few more missions, Snoop, and then we go home, boy." Marchand mumbled with a fondness that could have been delivered to a real Beagle. For a fleeting moment, Marchand wished he had answered Margo's last letter but then he told himself he'd be sure to write after the flight.

In the front cockpit, Wolfe completed strapping in, quickly reviewed his pre-start check list, set all engine and system switches for start-up, placed the throttles in the start detent, then gave the hand signal to the starter crew to feed high pressure air to the number one engine. When the RPM reached eight percent, Wolfe hit the engine igniter switch and watched the gauges as the engine rumbled to life. After moving the throttle to idle power, Wolfe repeated the procedure for the number two engine.

With both engines operating, the aircraft was alive, alive with enough power to light a city of fifty thousand people, enough power to send its crew hurling to the edge of space at two and a half times the speed of sound. Enough power to destroy a small city.

Moments after completing the post-start checklist, Wolfe

engaged nose wheel steering, unlocked the parking brake, and gave his throttles a nudge sufficient to start moving the aircraft forward. Following the directions of a yellow-shirted flight deck director, he slowly maneuvered the twenty-five ton fighter-bomber toward the catapult track.

As Wolfe neared the starting position, the catapult crew attached steel cables to the aircraft's launch points near its wing roots and the hold back arm under the plane's fuselage. With another brief shot of power, Wolfe brought the Phantom under tension against the hold back arm. The bird was nearly ready to launch.

Marchand completed final pre-flight checks of the radar, weapons system, inertial navigation platform and electronic countermeasure systems. He had a final few moments to observe the almost choreographed performance of the flight deck crew just prior to launch. Positioned on the Number Two catapult less than three hundred feet from the bow of the carrier, he gazed briefly at the dark blue ocean, sparkling in the clear early morning air.

From the corner of his eye, Marchand watched the Catapult Officer take up position to the right of the aircraft's nose between the two bow catapult tracks. He felt the Phantom's nose rise up as the nose wheel strut was extended in order to give the plane the proper attitude for launch. Getting' close, Marchand thought.

Seconds later, the Cat Officer signaled Wolfe to bring the engines to full basic engine power. Wolfe stroked the throttles all the way forward to set the engines at the full unaugmented power setting, then checked his engine gauges. The Phantom now strained against its holdback, roaring fiercely like an angry, chained beast. When Wolfe looked up from the gauges and gave a thumbs up, signaling that all was well inside the aircraft, the Cat Officer extended his right arm, while pointing at Wolfe with his left. The Cat Officer then opened and closed his left fist rapidly several times. Wolfe immediately pushed the throttles outward to the afterburner detent then all the way forward into the last and most powerful afterburner setting.

With afterburners ignited, the Phantom slammed hard against the holdback bridle, lunging desperately for release. The engines emitted an unearthly howl as two spiked jets of white-hot flame shot out from twin exhaust nozzles. Each engine developed its full combat power, more than eighteen thousand five hundred pounds of thrust, while gulping jet fuel at the incredible rate of one thousand pounds per minute.

Wolfe took one quick and final look at his engine gauges, saw that the engine nozzles were wide open, then he looked up and smartly saluted the Cat Officer.

The Cat Officer returned the salute acknowledging Wolfe's total readiness for launch. Wolfe positioned his control stick for take off. Marchand turned the command ejection switch to the rear cockpit and braced hard against his ejection seat. The Cat Officer touched his knee to the deck and, two seconds later, the catapult fired, sending the Phantom streaking down the track. Moving at more than two hundred miles per hour, the fighter crossed over the bow of the ship and became airborne.

Marchand felt the familiar crush of the steam-powered catapult pin him against his seat and he knew that it was a good clean "cat" shot. Wolfe held the control stick firmly, forearm braced against his right thigh. He felt the nose of the Phantom pitch up at the end of the catapult track and the momentary settling of the aircraft as its wings clawed the air for lift. Automatically, his left hand reached for the landing gear handle and moved it into the retract position.

Wolfe scanned his engine gauges quickly, then watched the airspeed indicator and altimeter increase smoothly as the aircraft gained altitude and speed. He retracted the plane's flaps as it accelerated through three hundred knots and set the throttles to power a climb at three thousand feet per minute. Now that Wolfe could safely eject himself should an emergency arise, Marchand returned the command ejection switch to the off position. Feels good to fly such a sweet bird, Marchand told himself.

Wolfe joined the lead fighter flown by Mark "The Deacon" Tanner and Bart "the Greek" Andros. They had launched first and were orbiting the carrier at two thousand feet waiting for their wingman to join up. The other aircraft participating in this reconnaissance mission had already climbed to the rendezvous altitude of eighteen thousand feet overhead the carrier, and were waiting patiently while the fighters chased the A-3B tanker aircraft, affectionately known as the "Whale," to greedily top off their fuel tanks. Wolfe finally eased his fuel probe out of the Whale's receptacle and the mission was on.

It was only eight o'clock in the morning, but the sun shone brilliantly on the sapphire sea sparkling far below. With his two fighter escorts aboard, Scott Taylor keyed his radio transmitter, "This is Sundowner One, heading out." Marchand checked his navigation computer; it showed their "feet dry" point, the point at which the flight would cross over the North Vietnamese land mass, was one hundred twenty-eight miles west-northwest on a bearing of three hundred ten degrees. Flying at ten miles per minute, they would enter North Vietnam's airspace in less than twelve minutes. That allowed Marchand sufficient time to run a weapons check one more time before the big dance began. One more time...

On the way west, Commander Scott Taylor descended from rendezvous altitude to thirteen thousand feet, the altitude at which he intended to fly the mission. As he descended, he increased power almost

613

to full military setting. The Vigilante accelerated to Mach .95, nearly seven hundred miles per hour with the Phantoms holding their position with the fastest aircraft in the Navy's inventory.

76.

MIG TRAP

Thirty miles from their coast-in point, Marchand saw the North Vietnamese coastline clearly. He keyed his intercom, "Let's go hot mike. We're three minutes to feet dry."

Wolfe replied, "Roger, hot mike. Man, this airplane is fast. No problem keeping up with Scottie so far. I haven't used afterburners since launch."

"Yeah, but nobody's shooting at us yet."

"I still think this bird can keep up with him," Wolfe insisted.

"We'll see."

As Scott Taylor's Vigilante and its two fighter escorts neared the North Vietnamese coast, powerful radar systems began searching for them - an occasional sweep at first, then with steady tracking beams. By the time the flight crossed the coastline, Marchand's electronic countermeasures scope displayed at least a dozen radar sites tracking the flight. One by one, the radar sites switched to firing mode, locking a specific aircraft into its fire control system. Once locked onto a particular airplane, the Russian-made Track-While-Scan fire control system provided a constant firing solution to six rapid-fire anti-aircraft artillery cannons. An ECM scope in each cockpit flashed a red warning light each time a TWS radar locked onto one of them.

Crossing over the North Vietnamese coastline, Larry Wolfe knew that ground fire would be only one of the hazards to be faced as they flew directly over Haiphong and turned south for their three hundred mile sprint to the DMZ. His major responsibility was protecting the Vigilante from enemy fighters that he felt certain would intercept their flight. He knew that the ultimate test of his courage and skill as a fighter pilot lurked somewhere along this flight path and he was determined to meet that challenge.

But there would be more. Many Russian-made surface to air missiles would be fired at the flight as they sped south. During this thirty-minute, high-speed gauntlet, the Vigilante and her escorts would face the triple threat of North Vietnamese air defenses including ground fire, surface to air missiles and enemy fighters all along their flight path.

Wolfe began to breathe faster, his pulse increased, and his eyes began to bulge slightly. Paradoxically, he felt anxious yet calm and controlled. Wolfe was ready for combat. Specifically, he was ready for air-to-air combat, the most demanding form of battle ever devised. He had to react almost instantly to everything he heard, felt and saw. Training would replace thinking and skill would provide the winning edge in his cockpit or his adversary's. Wolfe felt like a well trained athlete at the start of competition. It was the moment every fighter pilot lived or died for. Whatever the outcome, he was ready.

In the rear cockpit, Marchand felt equally prepared for the mission. He cleared his mind of everything save the spatial orientation of each aircraft, the flight path, and the state of the art weapons system he controlled. He had experienced aerial combat before and knew the coppery taste of a kill. But Marchand also knew how quickly everything would happen if the flight encountered enemy aircraft. His radar-directed vision could lead Wolfe and him to certain victory or quick death if he failed to see all that was there to be seen.

Suddenly, it began. Seconds after the flight crossed over the Vietnamese coastline, they met heavy anti-aircraft fire. Marchand saw fifty-seven and eighty-five millimeter rounds blossoming orange and red among countless thirty-seven millimeter shells staining the sky with black smudge marks. For the moment, these shells burst nearby but not so close as to cause concern. To prevent these radar-controlled guns from locking onto his aircraft, Wolfe constantly maintained a smooth but constant three G weaving turn.

But, as the flight reached Haiphong, many radar sites went active and stayed locked onto at least one of the three aircraft long enough to direct more accurate fire. Just as the flight intercepted the road they were to follow south, the intensity and accuracy of the ground fire became increasingly deadly.

Four miles west of Haiphong, Scott Taylor banked the Vigilante into a sharp left turn and began the actual photo-reconnaissance part of the mission. Entering the turn, he pushed his throttles forward to the full military power setting, increasing his airspeed to seven hundred fifty miles per hour, slightly faster than sound. In order to remain in position, the two escort pilots used occasional bursts of afterburner power. In supersonic flight, the Vigilante and its escorts didn't remain in range of any anti-aircraft battery for more than fifteen to twenty seconds.

Marchand and Andros increased power to their ECM jamming transmitters for added protection.

Wolfe worked hard to remain in position about four hundred yards to the right and slightly below the Vigilante as it took detailed, panoramic photographs of the Vietnamese roadways. Rivulets of perspiration streamed down his face and forearms and his flight suit was soaked through to his skin as he quickly moved stick, rudder and throttles against acceleration forces equal to three times that of gravity.

Marchand's electronic counter-measures scope danced with tracking lines representing increasing numbers and types of radar sites scanning them. Suddenly, three missile control radar sites switched to the active mode just prior to launching six SA-2 surface-to-air missiles at the reconnaissance flight. A low frequency warbling sound announced imminent SAM attack. One of Marchand's ECM scopes showed that the radar sites were behind the flight, on the defensive perimeter encircling Haiphong Harbor.

Marchand turned in his seat to scan the rear of the flight for SAMs and enemy fighters. As he did, the flight leader of the A-7 attack bombers flying mission support transmitted over the air, "Sundowner, this is Wrangler One, launching Shrikes from your nine o'clock."

"Wrangler One, Sundowner copies."

Immediately, A-7's launched eight Shrike anti-radiation missiles at the SAM command and control sites south of Haiphong. Marchand, looking past his left shoulder, saw the Shrike missiles' white vapor trails as they homed on their targets from a launch point just off the coast. Seconds later, flashing red SAM warning lights in Marchand's cockpit began to glow as a high frequency warbling tone filled his helmet earphones, warning that one or more SA-2 missiles had been launched at the Sundowner flight.

Marchand spotted the rocket exhausts and contrails of six SA-2 missiles as their booster rocket engines thrust them skyward. He was about to call a SAM break maneuver when he saw a series of bright flashes near the missile launch sites. The SAMs, which had been arcing upward and starting to guide on the Sundowner flight, suddenly veered off in different directions and went ballistic. The SAM radars and command centers had either been destroyed or switched off as the surviving operators turned off power to their radar antennas.

Marchand had no time to feel even fleeting relief as he checked the flight's position, course and speed confirming that the flight was on course and precisely eighteen miles south of Haiphong. Two hundred fifty-eight nautical miles remained before the flight could turn west and head home to the *Constellation*. The twenty-two minutes, thirty-eight seconds remaining promised to be more than memorable.

Marchand momentarily looked away from his weapons system to look out of the cockpit just as Wolfe spoke, "Have you looked at the road lately?"

"I don't fuckin' believe it! There's a goddamn traffic jam down there!"

"It's been that way since we turned south. Uncle Ho has half his army on the road heading south. He's using the "bombing halt" to stage another damned Tet Offensive."

"But we're the skunk at the picnic. General Giap's got to destroy this flight or we'll show his cards to everybody," Marchand growled.

Sundowner flight roared south along Route 1A, encountering similar air defense scenarios repeatedly. North Vietnamese radar sites discovered the Sundowner flight, tracked them for one or two minutes before turning their fire control to active mode. The radars then directed anti-aircraft artillery fire at the reconnaissance flight streaking along Route 1A for as long as possible. Simultaneously, missile crews fired SA-2s at the flight as soon as they could lock onto on of the American aircraft. But, as SAMs were launched, A-7 pilots fired Shrike missiles at the offending radar sites. Occasionally, an A-6E Intruder also accompanying the flight joined the cat and mouse game and fired a

Standard Arm missile. The Standard Arm warhead was powerful enough to destroy not only the radar but also its entire command and control center.

As Sundowner flight reached the one hundred twenty five mile waypoint on the route south to the DMZ, Lt. John Rich, Tactical Aviation Coordination Officer (TACO) aboard an E-2 Hawkeye, who was the air controller for the flight, warned them. "Sundowner, this is Hormel, I have two bogeys bearing zero one zero at one hundred ten miles, angels one point five, over."

Bart Andros, the lead Weapons Officer, flying with Mark "the Deacon" Tanner, responded, "Hormel, Checkmate One, copy your last; say Bogeys' airspeed and heading, over." There were subtle traces of stress in Andros' voice.

"Checkmate, this is Hormel, Bogeys' estimated speed five hundred twenty knots, heading zero one four degrees. No response to IFF interrogation, Bogeys are possible Bandits, over."

"Checkmate One, roger. Keep us advised, Hormel." Andros responded knowing that the Bogeys' failure to respond to the Identification Friend or Foe (IFF) electronic interrogation transmitted by Hormel probably meant that the unidentified aircraft were enemy fighters.

Sundowner flight closed on the unidentified aircraft at more than twelve hundred knots, almost fourteen hundred miles per hour. At this closure rate, Sundowner flight would come under attack in less than seven minutes if the Bogeys proved to be enemy fighters.

Two minutes after Hormel's first warning call, John Rich keyed his radio transmitter, "Sundowner, this is Hormel, I have two additional Bogeys bearing two two zero from you at six-two miles, heading one five zero degrees, airspeed six hundred knots, estimated at Angels one or lower."

"Hormel, this is Checkmate, copy your last. Sounds like an intercept heading. Do you concur, Hormel?" Andros transmitted to the air controller.

"Affirmative, Checkmate, estimate contact in approximately six point five minutes. Still no IFF response."

"Roger, Hormel," Andros responded as the air battle began to unfold.

On the intercom's hot mike, Marchand commented, "Wolfman, I think we're heading into a MIG trap with two Bandits ahead and now two Bandits behind us. We're gonna' earn our flight pay today."

"Yeah, and if those mothers want to vector a few more MIGs our way, pretty soon they'll have a fair fight," Wolfe replied.

"Sounds like you got blood in your eye," Marchand said, but blood lust was what he was thinking. "That's good, we're gonna' need all the killer instinct you got, Wolfie Boy."

"Damn right I do. I've been training for this for three years. I'm ready to kick some ass all over North Vietnam." Wolfe's bravado sounded a touch arrogant to Marchand but he ignored it. "Well then, let's kick ass and take some names, Wolfman."

Seconds later, the TACO John Rich transmitted again, "Sundowner, this is Hormel, Bogeys One and Two are at your one o'clock at six five miles, Angels one point zero, airspeed five hundred fifty knots, heading zero five eight degrees, over."

"Checkmate copies Hormel, any IFF response, over?" Mark Tanner asked.

"That's negative on the IFF, Checkmate," Lt. Rich responded.

"Hormel, this is Checkmate, any friendlies in this area?" Tanner inquired.

"This is Hormel, negative friendlies; I've requested Red Crown's clearance to fire if any Bogey closes to less than fifteen miles," Rich transmitted.

"That's a damn good TACO," Marchand said over the intercom.

"Bet your sweet ass, he is!" Wolfe replied enthusiastically. "I'm checking my missile panel now. I'll arm our Sparrows when we close within twenty miles."

"At fifteen miles, I'll put the spotlight on the SOB and we'll blow his ass to kingdom come," Marchand almost shouted as he tried to harness his mounting adrenalin rush.

In the Vigilante, Matt Mendez, the amped up reconnaissance navigator, queried pilot Scotty Taylor, "Hey, they're setting a MIG trap for us, with about three minutes to go before they spring it! What do you want to do? Complete the run or hightail it outta' here?"

"We'll complete this damn mission if at all possible. When the MIGs jump us, Deacon will take one pair and Wolfe will take the other. If all four MIGs stay to mix it up with our escorts, we'll complete the run. How much of the run is left?"

"When we close on the MIGs, we'll have about fifty-five miles to go," Mendez replied.

"That gives us four and a half minutes with no fighter escort. Well, that's Plan A. If one or more of the MIGs comes after us while the Phantoms are engaged, we run for it. I'll just hang a hard left turn to the coast and we'll see how fast this baby will go. That's Plan B," Taylor said.

"Sounds good, Scotty. Plan A it is. I really want to get these photos back to the Ship. With what we've seen today, this is probably our most important recon run of the entire cruise."

"Yeah, Matt, this is probably the most important run you and I will ever make."

"Roger that, Scotty," Mendez said.

77.

TURNIN' AND BURNIN'

Aboard the E-2A Hawkeye flying fifty miles off the coast of North Vietnam, serving as Sundowner Flight's air controller, Lieutenant John Rich stared at his large radar screen as the impending air battle took final shape. None of the unidentified aircraft, called "Bogeys" by airborne controllers and fighter pilots, had responded to his electronic identification inquiries. Moreover, the Bogeys' flight paths clearly evidenced hostile intent. Lt. Rich called Air Force area controllers and confirmed that no friendly aircraft were within a hundred miles of the Sundowner flight. Rich was excited that Red Crown, the Air Controller for the entire Tonkin Gulf, had finally given him permission to clear the Checkmate fighter escorts to fire on the unidentified aircraft if they continued to display hostile intent.

Red Crown's permission to fire was conditioned upon the Bogeys' high-speed approach to the Sundowner flight on a collision course inside a fifteen-mile perimeter without first identifying themselves or responding to Red Crown's electronic Identification Friend or Foe interrogations. Lt. Rich was unusually successful in that his clearance to fire did not stipulate that the Sundowner escorts must first obtain a visual identification of the target aircraft. Now, Rich could authorize his fighters to fire on the Bogeys at ranges up to fifteen miles, an advantage only the Phantoms possessed. Clearly, the Task Force Commander did not want to risk the mission's success by an exercise of undue caution.

As the Sundowner flight closed on the Bogeys, Rich keyed his transmitter, "Sundowner Leader, this is Hormel, Bogeys One and Two are at your twelve thirty at four two miles, Angels zero point five, airspeed six hundred knots, over."

"Hormel, this is Checkmate One, copy your last, say position of Bogeys Three and Four," Mark Tanner called over the air.

"Roger, Checkmate, Bogeys Three and Four are at your four o'clock at one niner miles, Angels one point zero, airspeed six hundred twenty five knots, over," Rich responded.

"Checkmate One, copy." Then Tanner keyed his radio transmitter again, "Sundowner, this is Checkmate One, we've got to go hunting. State your intention, over."

Scott Taylor replied, "Checkmate, Sundowner will continue its run unless engaged. If a Bandit gets too close, we're outta' here. Good luck, Gentlemen."

"Thanks Sundowner, if any Bandit gets past us, we'll let you know. Checkmate Two, engage Bogeys One and Two. I'm taking Bogeys Three and Four."

"Checkmate Two, Roger," Wolfe responded.

John Rich then gave his final position report. "Checkmate One, this is Hormel, Bogeys Three and Four are at your five o'clock, sixteen miles, over."

"Hormel, this is Checkmate One, am I cleared to fire on Bogeys Three and Four?" Tanner inquired urgently.

John Rich paused for several seconds then transmitted, "Checkmate One, you are cleared to fire on your Bogeys. Bogeys are now confirmed as Bandits Three and Four, over."

"Checkmate One copies, cleared to fire on Bandits Three and Four," Tanner replied and immediately slammed his stick hard to the right. As the Phantom snap-rolled inverted, he pulled back hard on the stick, executing a sharp split "S" to the right. The Phantom dived steeply toward the ground with four Gs of acceleration. As the Phantom's nose pulled through a sixty-degree dive, he called his wingman. "Check Two, go hot on your weapons panel and good luck."

"Checkmate Two, roger. Hormel this is Checkmate Two calling a Judy on Bogeys One and Two," Wolfe transmitted, verifying that he and Marchand had assumed control of the intercept.

Marchand scanned the sky with his radar for any sign of the still unidentified aircraft. Ten seconds later, he found the Bogeys and called the E-2 Hawkeye to report. "Hormel, this is Checkmate Two, contact two Bogeys, twelve thirty at three one miles, angels zero point five."

John Rich responded, "Checkmate Two, this is Hormel, those are your Bogeys. If not identified at fifteen miles, Bogeys are assumed Bandits. You are cleared to fire at fifteen miles. Do you copy?"

"Checkmate Two copies," Marchand answered then said to Wolfe, his voice hoarse with exhilaration, "Wolfman, steady on course; push the nose down hard. Bogeys at your twelve o'clock at two niner miles. Bogeys are on the deck probably less than a thousand feet. They plan to pop up and make a surprise run at us. I won't lock 'em up till they're at twenty miles. If their Electronic Counter-Measure systems work, I don't want to broadcast that we got their ass in the frying pan just yet."

"OK, Rocketman, my missile panel is set for a Sparrow shot as soon as we're in range and we get clearance to fire. How's your weapon?"

"My weapon is sweet, Wolfman, real sweet. Fire two Sparrows when we get clearance, then wait and see if we get a shot at the wingman. Oh, wait a second, wait a second! The flight is splitting up. Bogey One is staying on the deck; Bogey Two is climbing."

"OK, let's take our first shots at Bogey Two. We'll keep the high ground for now. What's the range to Bogey Two?" Wolfe replied, breathing hard and fast as his pulse rate skyrocketed.

"One niner miles, still on the nose, climbing through Angels five, closing at twelve hundred fifty knots. Twenty seconds to go for a max range shot. I'm locking him up now," Marchand roared as he squeezed the trigger on his weapon system joystick fixing the Phantom's fire control radar directly on the rapidly climbing MIG fighter, then he keyed his radio transmitter in a final exercise of caution. "Hormel, Checkmate Two is fifteen miles from Bogey Two. Am I cleared to fire?"

"Checkmate Two, this is Hormel. That is your Bandit. I say again Bogey Two is now Bandit Two. You are cleared to fire. I say again, you cleared to fire at Bandit Two, over."

Marchand shouted over the intercom that was set in the hot mike mode, "Bandit at twelve o'clock, twelve miles; we're in range. My weapon is sweet. Fox One, Fox One."

Wolfe squeezed the trigger on his control stick twice. Explosive charges ejected two radar-guided Sparrow, air-to-air missiles from the bottom of the Phantom's fuselage, sending a thumping sensation through the cockpit. As soon as the eight foot long, four hundred pound missiles were free, their rocket engines ignited, sending them streaking ahead and downward toward their target at two thousand miles per hour.

Wolfe stared at the brilliant rocket exhausts until he could no longer see flame spitting from their engines. But he did see the vapor trails of both missiles long after the missiles were out of sight. Both appeared to be guiding on their intended target.

Twenty seconds later, Wolfe spotted Bandit Two. It was a MIG-21, slightly low and climbing, approximately four miles ahead. Suddenly, he saw a bright flash followed by a large explosion and the MIG broke apart. Marchand's weapon system broke lock on the MIG as the enemy fighter disintegrated.

Wolfe felt a rush of adrenaline more powerful than anything he had ever experienced as he watched his enemy's destruction. He keyed his radio transmitter, "Hormel, this is Checkmate Two, splash Bandit Two. Give me a vector to Bandit One."

"Checkmate Two, this is Hormel, Bandit One is at your one o'clock, three point five miles, Angels three and climbing fast. Copy your splash of Bandit Two."

Wolfe looked down and to the right of the Phantom's nose and saw Bandit One, another MIG-21, in a steep climbing collision course. He keyed his radio transmitter and shouted, "Checkmate Two, Tally Ho Bandit One." As he made the call, he immediately rolled inverted and pulled the Phantom's nose down hard, putting his aircraft in a steep dive directly toward the sleek MIG-21.

Three seconds later, the Phantom and the MIG streaked past each other like silver bullets. Instantly, Wolfe rolled his fighter upright, pulled a hard six Gs to bottom his dive and began climbing again. He anticipated that the MIG pilot would pull his nose through the vertical and into a tight looping maneuver. Wolfe's tactic was designed to put the two aircraft in a weaving, vertical rolling scissors engagement. Wolfe was confident he could win this engagement because the Phantom's enormously powerful engines were an outstanding advantage while fighting in the vertical plane. And, Wolfe felt in his gut that he was the better fighter pilot.

By using the Phantom's superior power and climbing ability, Wolfe planned to run the MIG out of airspeed at the top of a climb so that the MIG pilot would be forced to dive to gain airspeed and avoid stalling. Wolfe would then continue climbing for several seconds then execute a quick rudder reversal that would place the Phantom at the MIG's six o'clock position where Wolfe could fire a Sidewinder heat-seeking missile up the MIG's tail.

But the pilot of Bandit One had other ideas. For the moment, he had no intention of engaging the Phantom in a vertical dogfight known to American fighter pilots as a "high speed yo-yo". He was an experienced fighter pilot who knew that he would lose the fight if he allowed the Phantom pilot to engage him in a vertical fight.

Instead, the MIG pilot continued to climb through fifteen thousand feet before rolling his MIG inverted then pulling his nose down from the top of a tight half looping turn, known as an Immelman, toward the Sundowner Vigilante. Scott Taylor was nearly four miles ahead of the MIG and speeding south. When the Russian major rolled out of the inverted position, he hoped to be at the Vigilante's six o'clock position and close to firing position. From there, Bandit One planned a quick burst of afterburner power to bring him within range of his heat-seeking ATOLL missiles or perhaps within range of his lethal thirty-millimeter cannon.

Three miles behind and to the north of Checkmate Two, Mark Tanner was engaged in a furious rolling dogfight with a MIG-21 that TACO John Rich had dubbed Bandit Three. Tanner initially fired two Sparrow missiles at Bandit Three during his steep dive from thirteen thousand feet. But the pilot of Bandit Three executed a maximum-rate-climb directly at Tanner's Phantom as it began its dive while firing chaff bundles to confuse the Phantom's radar.

Tanner's first Sparrow failed to guide even though Bart Andros had aimed his weapon system perfectly and had locked on the climbing MIG well within the Sparrow's firing parameters. The second Sparrow was fired slightly inside the missile's minimum range for a head-on shot so that it fused just milliseconds too late. As a result, the Sparrow missile exploded three hundred feet behind the speeding MIG-21, causing no damage.

With his flight leader engaged in a deadly duel against the lead Phantom, the pilot of the fourth MIG-21 also began a steep climb from treetop level directly toward Wolfe and Marchand in Checkmate Two. As he pulled back sharply on his control stick, the MIG pilot shoved his throttle into full afterburner. The small, extremely agile MIG with its rugged and powerful engine accelerated quickly to nearly eight hundred miles per hour. The pilot of Bandit Four saw Checkmate Two still climbing, presenting him with a perfect shot for his heat seeking ATOLL missiles or deadly thirty-millimeter canon.

But, just two miles ahead of the Phantom, the MIG pilot eyed the prize that he and his squadron mates were sent to destroy – the Vigilante. Bandit Four's pilot was, in fact, an experienced and gifted North Vietnamese fighter pilot who had recently shot down two Air Force F-105 Thunderchief fighter-bombers over Hanoi. As much as he wanted to kill the Vigilante, first he had to destroy the Phantom just ahead. He also knew that the lead pilot of the other MIG-21 section was probably making a dash toward the Vigilante at that moment.

In the E-2 Hawkeye flying fifty miles off the coast almost due west of the city of Vinh, TACO John Rich watched the air battle unfold on his primary radarscope. Despite Checkmate Two's quick victory over

Bandit Two, Rich was more than worried about the direction that the engagement seemed to be taking but there was little he could do about it at this point. The three remaining enemy fighters were, at worst, holding their own. But, in fact, with luck and skill, Bandits One and Four were in position to shoot down two American aircraft in short order. Lieutenant Rich suddenly realized that neither Checkmate Two nor Sundowner recognized the extreme danger of their respective situations.

Rich keyed his radio transmitter, "Checkmate Two, this is Hormel, Bandit Four is at your five o'clock, low, at two point five miles, airspeed seven hundred fifty knots and closing fast. Bandit will be in range for an ATOLL shot at any second; do you copy?"

When Marchand heard Hormel's warning, he turned in his ejection seat to look past the right rear of his Phantom. Looking rearward and down, he saw every fighter pilot's worst nightmare, an enemy fighter closing fast on his exposed six o'clock position. "Holy fuck, Wolfman; there's a fuckin' MIG-21 on our ass! **BREAK RIGHT, BREAK RIGHT!**"

Without looking, Wolfe immediately rolled the Phantom inverted and pulled back hard on the control stick in a desperate attempt to turn into his adversary. Marchand's vision darkened to a narrow tunnel as Wolfe's maneuver produced seven, then eight Gs of acceleration. Wolfe, knowing that the next few seconds would mean life or death for Marchand and himself, pulled even harder on the control stick as death's terrible scythe was poised to strike their existence from the living.

The MIG pilot saw his target suddenly roll and begin a steep diving turn toward him. He had intended to wait a few more seconds to fire his missiles at the Phantom in order to insure a clean kill, but he decided to wait no longer. He pulled his control stick trigger twice sending two ATOLL missiles streaking toward his victim. In a few quick seconds, he expected to see the Phantom blow to smithereens before his eyes.

With the last bit of vision remaining, Marchand saw the two missiles launch from the attacking MIG. With what little air remaining in his compressed lungs, he bellowed as loudly as he could, "**Missiles airborne, missiles airborne!**" Then as the G forces increased, Marchand fired multiple decoy flares as rapidly as he could.

Wolfe's vision was also fading rapidly and his breath came in short gasps and grunts, but he pulled still harder on the stick until his tunnel vision closed up completely and he could no longer see. The Phantom shuddered and buffeted in the grasp of acceleration forces equal to nine times gravity tearing at its very structural integrity. Marchand's vision was completely blacked out but he was still conscious. Both Wolfe and Marchand prayed short simple "Oh Lord, please help me" prayers. They had done everything they could. Only luck or a deity could help them now. And their luck was waning at the speed of light.

Observing the scene on his large radarscope, John Rich was raggedly distraught when he received no reply to his warning transmission. The battle looked bad for Wolfe and Marchand, yet the screen still showed Checkmate Two fighting desperately to survive. But now he had to turn his attention to the other American aircraft in mortal danger. "Sundowner, this is Hormel, Bandit One is at your six o'clock at four miles, angels thirteen, airspeed eight hundred fifty knots and accelerating; do you copy?" he called in a strained monotone.

"Hormel, Sundowner, copy your last. Terminating photo run at this time. Over," Scotty Taylor responded while shoving his throttles into full afterburner and turning west toward the Gulf of Tonkin. Taylor recognized that he was in a race for his and Matt Mendez' lives. With no armament aboard his aircraft, and no Phantoms available for protection, Taylor knew that their only safety was the Vigilante's speed. He looked at his airspeed indicator. It read seven hundred knots, Mach 1.1, supersonic and the big reconnaissance aircraft was still accelerating.

Although the Vigilante was flying at nearly eight hundred miles per hour, Bandit One was still closing in at the rate of three miles per minute. The MIG pilot would need only thirty seconds to pull within range of his heat seeking missiles if he could just maintain his one hundred fifty knot closure rate. Scotty Taylor was fairly certain that he would win the race to the coast that was only twelve miles to the east. But he wasn't certain that he would win by two and a half miles, the distance required to keep him out of Bandit One's missile and cannon range.

Six miles to the north, Mark Tanner strained hard to pull the nose of his Phantom inside the three o'clock position of Bandit Three. He was inverted and pulling through a rudder reversal when he heard the growl of the Sidewinder's heat-seeking guidance system announce that he was within the missile's allowable firing parameters. "What's the range?" he bellowed over his hot mike to Bart Andros.

"Half a mile, Deacon; go for it," Andros yelled back.

Tanner squeezed his trigger twice and two Sidewinder heat-seeking missiles blazed away from the launch rails in a blast of orange-white exhaust. At the extremely close range of the engagement, Tanner was amazed to see both Sidewinders veer sharply to the right toward the MIG. Incredibly, both missiles were guiding toward their target despite the ninety-degree deflection angle from which they had been fired. But the first Sidewinder simply flew past the MIG without exploding. There had been insufficient time for the missile's warhead to fuse and arm itself before reaching the MIG.

But Tanner's second Sidewinder not only guided but flew right up the MIG's exhaust and exploded. The detonation ripped the MIG to small fragments inside a large orange fireball as its fuel also exploded. Tanner instantly rolled the Phantom ninety degrees and pulled away to avoid the debris. He wanted to give a victory cheer but knew from listening to recent radio transmissions that his wingmen, Wolfe and Marchand, were in the fight of their lives. Worst yet, the Vigilante was in serious trouble as well. Tanner's fighter pilot instincts told him to go to his wingman's aid but his primary duty was to protect the Vigilante. He keyed his transmitter, "Hormel, Checkmate One, splash Bandit Three. Give me a steer to Sundowner. Over."

"Checkmate One, this is Hormel, Sundowner is at your ten o'clock at five miles, Angels fifteen, airspeed nine hundred knots. Be advised, Bandit One is at your eleven o'clock at three miles, Angels thirteen, airspeed nine hundred fifty knots over."

"Roger, Hormel; say distance between Sundowner and Bandit One," Tanner inquired.

"Bandit One is trailing Sundowner two point five miles; over," Lieutenant Rich transmitted as he watched Bandit Four close within kill range of Checkmate Two. He choked back a yell, as he was certain that Marchand and Wolfe were about to die.

Tanner had both the Vigilante and now the MIG in sight. He called over the radio, "Checkmate One, Tally Ho Bandit One."

At that moment, Bart Andros roared over the intercom, "Goddamn it, Deacon; the MIG is almost in range for an ATOLL shot at the Viggie. We've gotta' do something quick."

Tanner thought for a second then said, "Do you have both Sundowner and the Bandit on your weapon?"

"Affirmative," Andros replied.

"Bart, lock up the MIG for a Sparrow shot. If you lock up the wrong bird, we'll get a court martial instead of a Silver Star. Can you do it with near one hundred percent certainty?"

"Deacon, fuck the Silver Star. We got one chance to save Scotty and Matt. I can do it!"

"It's your show now, Bart, shoot the MIG!!!" Tanner said, praying under his breath.

Andros moved his weapon control joystick like a surgeon's scalpel. He positioned the intensely focused beam of his radar on the MIG-21 that had closed within two and a quarter miles of the Vigilante. He squeezed the trigger and locked up the MIG in the pencil-thin beam of his weapon system and roared, "**Fox One, Fox One!**" Instantly, Tanner pulled his trigger twice.

The pilot flying Bandit One was waiting until he was exactly two miles astern the Vigilante before firing his heat seeking missiles. He knew that at two miles, the ATOLL missiles would be at their maximum effective range. Bandit One's pilot thought he could not miss the kill. He had only to wait another five seconds and then fire. He knew that this kill would be more important than either of his previous combat victories and would surely bring him a promotion to major, perhaps even squadron commander. He checked his armament panel one final time to insure that all firing switches were properly set.

Suddenly, the MIG pilot's world became white fire, and then wild tumbling, spinning, bone-crushing oblivion, as the first of Checkmate One's Sparrow missiles tore into the MIG's engine bay. Even if Bandit One's pilot had the time and opportunity to eject from his exploding aircraft, it would have been pointless since the MIG was moving faster than the pilot's ejection seat operating limits. The shock of the air blast at over eight hundred miles per hour would have killed him just as surely as the fire and exploding metal inside the disintegrating fighter.

When Tanner saw his first Sparrow destroy the MIG-21, he transmitted in a voice chocked with emotion, "Hormel, this is Checkmate One, splash Bandit One. Sundowner, your six is clear. Take it home, Scotty."

"Checkmate One, this is Sundowner, thanks for saving my bacon. We're headed for the darkroom at twelve hundred knots. See you on deck, over."

"Checkmate, roger. Hormel, where's my wingman? Give me a steer."

"Check Leader, your wingman is at your five o'clock at seven miles, Angels fifteen engaged with Bandit Four. He's in trouble, Checkmate One. Serious trouble."

Tanner whipped his control stick hard to the right. At eighty degrees bank, he hauled back on the stick to commence a maximum rate turn back toward his wingman, Checkmate Two. As he turned the Phantom back north, Tanner asked Andros, "Where's Checkmate Two?"

"Three o'clock, slightly low at eight miles. Bandit Four is at four o'clock, nine miles, and climbing. We can't shoot from here, Deacon; they're too close to each other," Andros answered.

"We gotta' get closer to help," Tanner said as he pushed his throttles into afterburner.

The pilot of Bandit Four watched his first heat-seeking ATOLL missile go ballistic as it attempted to follow the lead programmed by its warhead and it went streaking past Checkmate Two in a straight-line trajectory. But he smiled as his second missile continued to guide despite the enormous G forces imposed by the extremely sharp turn required to intercept the Phantom. The missile was within fifteen degrees of its final tracking solution when the heat-seeking guidance system broke its lock from the American fighter to one of the decoy flares that Marchand had fired in a desperate bid to escape.

Wolfe saw the explosion as the missile detonated not more than two hundred yards from his canopy. Seconds later he watched Bandit Four streak past him, still in a high-speed climb. The MIG was moving so fast that there was no way the pilot could quickly slow his climb and turn back to engage the Phantom. Now, the MIG pilot's excess speed worked against him since it allowed Wolfe to extend his speed brakes, turn inside him and fall into a trailing position.

Bandit Four's pilot realized that the hunter had now become the hunted. By using the MIG pilot's speed and momentum against him, the way that a Judo expert uses his opponent's rushing attack to throw him to the mat, the American fighter had now gained the advantage. Now Bandit Four had no choice but to run. The Phantom was directly behind him, at his six o'clock position, where it could deal death his way.

As Wolfe completed a climbing turn toward the retreating MIG, the distance between the Phantom and the MIG opened quickly. He shouted into his face mask, "Keith, lock him up, lock him up! Twelve o'clock high, two and a half miles. He's out of Sidewinder range."

Marchand's vision returned but he had to shake his head to cage his eyeballs. On his radar screen, he searched for the MIG and found him where Wolfe had indicated and locked his weapons system on the enemy fighter. "I've got him! I've got him! **Fox One, Fox One!!!**"

Wolfe fired his last two Sparrow missiles at the fleeing MIG fighter. The MIG was still accelerating at nearly nine hundred miles per hour, adding precious distance between him and the Phantom. In twelve seconds, he would be out of range of even the deadly Sparrow missiles. But Bandit Four didn't have twelve seconds. He had run out of time and most importantly he had run out of luck. Just five seconds later, a Sparrow missile exploded alongside his cockpit. The explosion's shock wave rocked the MIG, as if it had hit a solid wall.

Microseconds later, red hot twelve-inch segments of continuously wound steel wire that wrapped the Sparrow missile's warhead sliced into the MIG in at least a hundred places including its fuel tanks. The superheated hot steel ripped the MIG's fuselage open like dozens of ravenous can openers, detonating its fuel and remaining armament. The pilot, were he still alive, had no chance to eject before the MIG exploded violently in an ugly orange fireball.

Wolfe watched his erstwhile enemy meet with destiny. Then he keyed his radio, "Hormel, this is Checkmate Two, Splash Bandit Four. Deacon, let's go home!"

Marchand whispered under his labored breath, "Yeah right, home. God take me home."

Wolfe and Marchand raced back toward the *Constellation*, virtually speechless, in the secret, invisible, almost unknown zone where life and death, victory and defeat fuse like Siamese twins, inextricably bound to each other.

78.

THE DEVIL'S HAND

Larry Wolfe was physically and emotionally exhausted. His flight suit was drenched with perspiration, his breath ragged and sharp. He was too fatigued to feel the exhilaration he thought would follow his second MIG kill of the day. His right hand was shaking so much he took his left hand from the throttles to steady it. He was thirstier than he could ever remember and he had an overwhelming urge to urinate. "I'm a fucking wreck," he muttered to himself in a barely audible voice but loud enough to be picked up by his intercom that was still in the hot position.

"Me too," Marchand said, "and we ain't exactly out of the woods yet." In fact, Marchand could barely hold his head upright because of the intense pain in his back and neck which had been severely sprained when Wolfe pulled nine and a half Gs escaping from Bandit Four's nearly fatal attack. His flight suit was wet and cold from perspiration and he would have given a month's pay for a cup of cold water.

"How far to the coast?" Wolfe asked as he peered at the ocean through his gun sight.

"Twelve miles. Just twelve fuckin' miles; we go feet wet in a minute, ten seconds."

"I wonder where the hell The Deacon is. He should have joined us by now."

At that moment, the radio crackled, "Checkmate Two, this is Checkmate Leader, we're at your five o'clock, low, two miles. I'll join on your port side. Let's keep a combat spread until we're feet wet. Say your fuel state."

"Check Two, Roger. Fuel state is two point zero."

Mark Tanner keyed his transmitter, "Hormel, Checkmate One and Two are joined and headed for the coast. We're very low fuel state. Vector the Whale as close as he can get to the coast for a quick rendezvous and tanking."

"Hormel copies your fuel state, Checkmate. The Whale will be waiting for you ten miles off the coast. Steer zero eight five for rendezvous. Do you want to stay at Angels one three?"

"Affirmative, Hormel, I don't want to attract any more SAM fire by going higher and I sure as hell don't want more triple AAA right now. And, Hormel, get some Shrike birds down here, too, in case we need 'em on the way out," Tanner replied.

"Checkmate One, Hormel copies. Shrike and Standard Arm support will be on station in less than one minute to cover your egress," John Rich answered. He was concerned but not surprised that the two Phantoms had only two thousand pounds of fuel remaining. At military power settings, that much fuel would give them fifteen to twenty minutes flight time before their engines flamed out from fuel starvation. Given the intensity of the air battle, Rich was somewhat relieved to learn that the Checkmate Phantoms had even that much fuel. He quickly plotted the rendezvous course heading for the A-3 tanker.

Rich called the tanker pilot. "Whale One, this is Hormel, Steer two four zero for two one miles, set up an orbit on the two four zero degree radial niner five miles from Red Crown at Angels thirteen. Checkmate will rendezvous with you on station. Both are extremely low fuel state. How copy, over?"

"Hormel, Whale copies. We'll be there with all the gas Checkmate needs."

"Whale One, this is Checkmate, thanks for coming in so close to the beach. We'll be sucking fumes by the time we plug in."

"Glad to help any way we can, Checkmate. I'd drive the gas truck closer but we aren't too good at dodging SAMs."

Mark Tanner peered over the Phantom's long drooping nose toward the brown-blue coastline ahead. Safety was so close he could taste it.

Suddenly, gray puffs began to dot the horizon in front of the aircraft. Soon, larger, more deadly black smudges of eighty-five millimeter shells bursting nearby mixed with the grayish explosions of fifty-seven millimeter anti-aircraft artillery. Tanner called his wingman, "Check Two, keep your jink going, we're almost home."

"Check Two, roger, looks like Act Four of the MIG Follies has started," Wolfe responded with a slight hint of dejection.

"Hormel, this is Check One, is Sundowner feet wet, over?"

"Affirmative, Checkmate, Sundowner crossed the beach three minutes ago at damn near Mach two point four. Checkmate flight is all we're waiting for," Rich answered. "That's just you, Babe."

Wolfe scanned the horizon and was surprised at the intensity of the anti-aircraft fire. A mile ahead of him, the sky was filled with gray and black puffs. "Barrage fire, Keith."

Marchand swallowed hard. "Affirmative, Wolfman. We might as well close our eyes and make a dash for the coast, jinking won't help us

643

now."

North Vietnamese gunners were no longer aiming at the two Phantoms as individual targets and no longer required radar to direct their fire. Instead, all the anti-aircraft sites in the area beneath the Phantoms' flight path simply saturated assigned segment of the sky with concentrated fire fused to explode at varying altitudes. In effect, the artillerymen presented a barrage of exploding steel through which the Phantoms had to fly in order to reach the coastline.

Suddenly, a large-caliber eighty-five millimeter shell exploded forty feet beneath Checkmate Two. The shell had proximity-fused to detonate at its closest point of approach to the aircraft. The explosion nearly flipped the Phantom inverted, bouncing Wolfe and Marchand against the sides of the cockpit. Shrapnel ripped into the fighter's engine bays inflicting major damage. Hot metal fragments destroyed the gas generators and turbine section of Engine Number One. Jagged metal shards punctured oil lines and one hydraulic line to engine number two. As the turbine blades and wheels of the Number One engine flew apart violently, they punctured hundreds of holes in the rear of the fuselage and setting the engine bay afire.

Wolfe fought to regain control of the aircraft. Miraculously, he was able to stabilize its flight although that stability was extremely fragile. One hydraulic system still functioned and the control surfaces of the aircraft were still intact. When Wolfe regained control, the Phantom was in a steep dive and vibrating badly. Responding to the fire warning light, Wolfe closed the throttle to the Number One Engine and punched the large red fire extinguishing system button. He hauled back on the stick to bring the Phantom out of its dive and was extremely relieved to feel the stabilator and wing bite into the air stream.

Wolfe yelled over the intercom, "Keith, Keith, you OK?"

"Wolfman," Marchand replied as stoically as he could, "I got a piece of shrapnel through my left thigh, but I think I'm OK; no major damage." Marchand's thigh was blood-soaked and very painful, but he could detect no broken bone or spurting jets of blood that would indicate a severed artery. "I'll handle communications, you just fly this SOB as long as you can."

Marchand keyed his transmitter, "Mayday, Mayday, Mayday; this is Checkmate Two. We've been hit ten miles from the coast five miles north of Vinh. Aircraft on fire. We're going down! Trying to make feet wet before we eject."

Mark Tanner immediately closed with the stricken fighter. He called, "Checkmate Two, this is Check One, your fire appears to be out. Can you stay with it another minute till we make the coast?" Then he joined more closely in order to make a visual inspection.

Wolfe transmitted, "Roger, Check One, we might make it another thirty seconds or so, max. I've shut down Number One Engine and I'm having a hard time controlling pitch and roll. Number Two's oil pressure is dropping fast," Wolfe responded wearily.

John Rich listened to the radio transmissions and felt wretchedly heartsick. He had bonded closely with the two aviators in the stricken plane and couldn't bear the thought of losing them after their incredible MIG kills, and especially now that they were so close to home. "Checkmate Two, this is Hormel; Jolly Green is on the way from Da Nang and SAR helos from Red Crown and South SAR also. RESCAP has been launched from the *Connie* and *Enterprise.* I show you just four point five miles from feet wet."

Wolfe wrestled with the controls of the stricken fighter with all his might and skill. His control stick was increasingly non-responsive, making it nearly impossible to maintain the wings in level flight. He used his rudder pedals to compensate for the loss of effective aileron and spoiler response. With one engine out, he rapidly traded altitude to keep his airspeed as high as he dared.

Wolfe knew the Phantom was dying but he desperately wanted to make the coastline before ejecting from the crippled fighter. He wanted to minimize their parachute hang time in case they ejected just as they reached the water so he descended below two thousand feet. He knew that Vietnamese gunners at the coast would delight in killing the hapless aviators as they hung in their parachutes.

Air defense gunners were still firing, but not as heavily as the concentrated barrage fire that had already proven so deadly. As the wounded Phantom lost altitude, smaller caliber weapons including heavy machine guns posed an increasingly greater threat.

Mark Tanner inspected the badly damaged Phantom and reported, "Check Two, your engine bay is all shot to hell; port side ailerons and spoilers are badly damaged. Looks like your fire is out for the moment. You might be good for a half minute or so. Can you make the beach?"

"Check One, oil pressure on Number Two is almost zero. I'll have to shut it down soon or risk another fire. We'll just take it as far as possible and punch out."

"Roger that, Wolfman, I'll stay with you 'till help comes."

"Just don't flame out while you're sticking around, Deacon. We'll be OK."

Wolfe then spoke gravely over the intercom. "Keith, you and I have talked about this many times and it looks like the worst is happening. We gotta' eject soon. I've got no oil pressure left so I have to shut this sonofabitch down. Get ready to punch out."

"Wolfman, put your RAT out, it'll give us hydraulic and

electrical power after you shut down the engine. Let's stay with this fucker and glide it as far as we can."

"Good idea, we're only a mile from the water now," Wolfe said as he deployed the emergency Ram Air Turbine that quickly spun up while the Number Two engine wound down.

An odd peace engulfed them as the Number Two Engine shut down. The Phantom became strangely quiet as it neared the beach at only five hundred feet altitude. The aircraft vibrated and bucked as it rapidly descended, its flight control surfaces so badly damaged that they chewed the air in ragged uneven bites. As the dying fighter passed over the last spit of land, Wolfe said, "Well, ol' buddy, it's time to go our separate ways. How you doing? Can you pull the face curtain? Should I command eject?"

"No, Wolfman, I got enough juice to pull the handle on the seat. I gotta' tell you two things real quick. I really enjoyed flying with you during this cruise and you were just fuckin' great today. Second, if anything happens to me, you go see Margo for me, go see her personally. You tell her how much I love her. Will ya' do that for me?"

"Sure, Keith, I promise you that. But don't fuckin' sweat it. We're both gonna' have dinner on the *Connie* tonight. But I promise to take care of Margo for you no matter what. And, Keith, you're the best damned Weapons Officer in the Seventh Fleet. You were great today yourself. Thanks, Buddy. Thanks for everything. Have a safe ride, OK?"

"You too, Wolfman," Marchand said. He then focused through his physical pain and braced himself tightly against the back of his eject seat, tightened his shoulder harness, reached up with both hands, and grasped the yellow and black handles on both sides of his helmet. He pulled down sharply on the two handles.

Explosive charges blew the canopy off Marchand's cockpit.

Several milliseconds later, a much larger explosive charge detonated beneath his ejection seat hurling him out of the aircraft. When he was barely six feet from the cockpit floor, rocket engines affixed to the ejection seat fired, thrusting Marchand almost two hundred feet above the falling fighter. As soon as Wolfe heard and felt the blast of Marchand's seat, he took one last look down and saw water beneath him. He pulled the ejection seat handles and followed Marchand out of the dead Phantom. The abandoned and lifeless bird that had performed so magnificently in aerial combat flew on for a quarter mile before crashing into the sea and disintegrating.

Marchand blacked out from the enormous acceleration forces of the ejection. Although he couldn't see, he was fully conscious and felt the shock of the airstream as the three hundred fifty mile per hour windblast slammed into him like a concrete wall. When the rocket engines beneath his seat stopped firing, he felt the seat begin to tumble and then the opening shock of the drogue chute as it stabilized his ejection seat. Seconds later, the main parachute deployed, slowing his descent to less than twenty feet per second. Marchand recovered his vision in time to see blue water beneath him. Before entering the water, he saw the shoreline only five hundred yards away. He winced as tracer rounds whizzed past his parachute canopy, then pulled the toggles on both sides of his Mark 3C life preserver and prepared to enter the water.

Marchand plunged beneath the water and his entire body throbbed with searing pain. Salt water burned the ragged entrance and exit wounds in his thigh. His sprained neck and shoulder muscles were further damaged by the ejection sequence so that each movement was excruciating. When he surfaced, he was shocked to hear the sound of bubbling gas escaping from his Mark 3C. "Goddamn it, my fuckin' life preserver's got a hole in it," he yelled to no one but himself. "What the hell else can go wrong?" He couldn't see the pea-sized holes in one of the two inflation bladders of his life preserver, created by the same piece of shrapnel that had drilled through his left quadriceps. He realized that he was riding quite low in the water. "At least half of this thing must be working," he exclaimed aloud.

Then Marchand made a serious mistake, one that greatly exacerbated the problems he grappled with. Thinking that whatever happened to half of his Mark 3C might soon affect the other half, he decided to inflate his personal life raft as quickly as possible. It seemed like a perfectly logical step since the fifty pounds of flight and survival gear he wore coupled with the loss of half of his floatation gear now threatened to drown him. He reached down to find the eight-foot nylon lanyard that attached his lap belt to the uninflated one-man life raft swinging below him. The raft was compressed to the size and shape of a seat cushion and stored inside the seat pan of the ejection seat. He pulled it up as quickly as possible since the added weight of the raft was actually dragging him below the surface.

With the raft in his hands, Marchand kicked to the surface for a breath, expecting to pull the lanyard sharply away from the tightly packed raft in order to fire the CO_2 inflation device. He ignored the AK-47 slugs sizzling overhead and zipping into the water nearby leaving trails of bubbles behind. But he couldn't ignore the fiery stabbing pain each time he kicked to stay above water. He was positioned to give the inflation lanyard a good pull when a large wave broke behind him driving him six feet below the surface.

Choking, he fought for the surface and, as he did, three North Vietnamese fishing boats shoved off from the shore. Capturing an American airman would bring a reward of money and food to the small fishing village greater than the earnings from a complete fishing season.

Since the downed flier was worth more alive than dead, the pot shots from shore stopped abruptly. The local village chief, a small but powerful man nearly sixty years old, steered his ancient outboard motor toward the area where he had last seen Marchand's parachute.

Overhead, Mark Tanner orbited his Phantom as slowly as he could while his weapons officer, Bart Andros, scoured the surface for any sign of Marchand. Andros had already located Larry Wolfe and actually talked to him on Wolfe's survival radio. Wolfe was uninjured and had experienced a textbook perfect ejection and water entry. Within a minute after water entry, Wolfe was inside his life raft and guiding Checkmate One to his position.

Tanner watched the fishing boats launch from the beach but was powerless to help Marchand. He had just checked his fuel gauge which read one thousand pounds. Given the system's margin of error, he might have as little as seven minutes of flight time remaining before his engines flamed out from fuel starvation. He was forced to leave the scene immediately or risk joining Marchand and Wolfe in the water. He told Andros to mark the position as well as he could on his navigation computer, then added power to climb out toward the airborne tanker while calling for help. "Hormel, this is Checkmate One, mark my position. We're overhead the crew of Check Two. We've got one crewmember in sight and on guard frequency. No joy for the second crewmember but we did observe two good chutes."

"Roger that, Checkmate. Jolly Green should be in position within sixty seconds."

"Hormel, I just hope that won't be too late. There are fishing boats coming into the area. Where are the RESCAP and SAR helos?"

"Checkmate, this is Hormel, Rescue combat air patrol and Search and Rescue helos should arrive at your position within two minutes."

As Checkmate One made one final pass overhead, Tanner rocked his wings in a salute to his downed wingmen then departed the area.

Larry Wolfe looked up and saluted, then used his survival radio to call the SAR helicopters, "Big Mother, this is Checkmate Two on guard, how do you read, over?"

"Checkmate Two, Big Mother reads you loud and clear. Squawk the emergency beacon."

Wolfe pressed the radio beacon locator button on his survival radio until he heard the whoop, whoop of the hulking Sikorsky H-3 helicopter heading his way. He then returned to the radio mode of his survival transmitter. "Big Mother, Tally Ho. I'm at your one o'clock about half mile. Any contact with my Weapons Officer? Over."

"Checkmate Two, Tally Ho your raft. Negative on your W.O."

"Motha', you gotta hurry, there's a reception committee out here. Tell your door gunner to be ready," Wolfe yelled over the radio.

Half a mile away, Marchand retrieved his life raft but before he could inflate it, he felt a strong pull against his left ankle. "Oh fucking great, just fucking great! Now what?" Marchand yelled aloud. He kicked to free his foot and felt a stabbing pain in his torn thigh muscle. But the pulling sensation remained. He felt himself being drawn under water by what seemed to be a powerful hand gripping his left ankle. He ducked under water to find whatever was dragging him beneath the surface. He found nothing at first then he saw what appeared to be several ropes wrapped around his ankle. Shocked, he suddenly realized what was happening.

Marchand remembered that Navy water survival training emphasized getting rid of the parachute immediately upon entering the water. Over the years, so many unfortunate Navy fliers had gotten tangled in their parachute shroud lines and drowned that the First Commandment of water survival had become: "Thou shalt release the parachute immediately upon water entry." Marchand had broken the Commandment for which punishment was typically death by drowning.

A lethal combination of fatigue, pain and distraction had broken Marchand's survival training; now he realized his potentially fatal error. Nearing absolute exhaustion and the onset of panic, he reached up and pulled the quick release fittings of his parachute. Unfortunately, the damage had already been done. Parachute shroud lines had wrapped around his left ankle and now the parachute was doing precisely what it had been designed to do, fill with water and sink.

As Marchand struggled to free himself from the parachute shroud lines, the Big Mother SAR helicopter arrived overhead Wolfe's raft and quickly dropped a Navy diver into the water to assist bringing him aboard. When the diver surfaced, he swam to the raft, reached up and pulled Wolfe face first into the water to keep him from being shot. With the SAR helicopter on scene and rapidly diminishing chances to capture one of the downed aviators, on shore gunners quickly determined to kill Wolfe and bring down the helicopter if at all possible.

Machine gun and rifle bullets sizzled overhead, raising small geysers of salt spray nearby. Wolfe heard bullets slapping against the helicopter's aluminum hull, but with the water whipped into a froth by the helicopter's main rotor blades, he could barely see what was happening. In short order, the diver had hooked himself and Wolfe onto the rescue sling that the helicopter crew had dropped nearby. The rescue crew switched the winch motor to high speed to raise the two men aboard as the pilot moved the helicopter sideways to avoid shore fire. Wolfe's legs skimmed the wave tops as the massive helicopter skittered away from the spot where Wolfe's raft floated. The helicopter had not moved a hundred feet when the raft was hit by a mortar shell and blown away. But the helo crew had done their job and pulled Wolfe and the diver safely on board.

Unaware of Wolfe's successful rescue and struggling against fierce pain, Marchand realized his situation had become critical. His parachute was steadily pulling him under water again and again. He survived only by using his free leg and arms to kick and pull to the surface, take a few quick breaths, then work furiously to free his leg. To his utter dismay, he could not locate the survival knife stowed in his survival vest nor the specially designed, parachute shroud-cutting knife tucked in the sleeve of his flight suit.

To lighten his burden and gain buoyancy, Marchand discarded every item of flight and survival gear. He unbuckled his survival pistol and let it fall away then removed his helmet and the one steel-toed flight boot he could reach. He hesitated for a moment, then unhooked the lanyard attached to his still uninflated life raft and let it go as well. In its packed state, the raft was just another five-pound weight drawing him down to a watery grave.

Freed of nearly fifteen pounds of gear, Marchand found that he could float with the top of his head barely above water. But to survive until the SAR helicopters arrived and found him, he had to somehow cut free of his parachute. However, he was becoming increasingly fatigued from loss of blood and sheer physical exhaustion.

Suddenly, the thought that he might not survive overwhelmed him. He was so utterly alone and had struggled against such overpowering circumstances that he was tempted to give up the fight and let the sea have him. Marchand felt ready to die. He felt a strange sense of peace and tranquility come over him. "Just let it all go," a soothing disembodied voice seemed to say.

Then he thought of Margo. He saw her face and her tears the last time they said goodbye. He forced himself to come back. Even though he no longer had the strength to fight, he willed himself to continue the struggle. He found a power that filled him as if it came from beyond himself. Marchand would not succumb nor lose hope of seeing Margo again without giving everything and then more to the survival fight. He thought for a moment of Captain Peter Daniels, the FAC pilot who had struggled so valiantly to survive but took his own life in order to escape a horrifying death at the hands of his pursuers. He remembered his vow to visit Captain Daniel's wife. I must keep my promise, he told himself. Got to stay alive to keep my promise.

Inspired, Marchand willed himself to break the Angel of Death's lethal grip on his ankle. In that critical moment, he gulped as much air as his heaving lungs could hold, allowed himself to sink a few feet below the surface, and with one hand ripped the pocket containing his shroud cutter away from his flight suit, freeing it to fall several feet to the end of its restraining line. Marchand grabbed the knife and quickly cut away the thick nylon parachute shroud lines. As they fell away from his ankle, Marchand felt Death's grip slipping away. The Angel of Death had retreated for the moment.

For the first time since ejecting, Marchand had the luxury of catching his breath without a struggle. He tread water, breathed deeply, denying his physical pain and began to formulate a survival plan. He heard helicopter blades, but could not locate the aircraft from his low vantage in the water. He knew that it would be difficult for the SAR team to locate him since he had thrown off his helmet with its reflecting tape and highly visible surface. He had dye markers and a flare pencil in his survival vest but he knew his best chance of being rescued was to retrieve his survival radio and use it to guide the SAR helicopter to him.

The village chief watched from a quarter mile away as the SAR team rescued Wolfe and then he saw the pilot begin a sweeping search for the second airman, the one that the chief had first observed ejecting from the silent, doomed fighter. The chief vowed that this Yankee Air Pirate would be his when the morning ended. He knew exactly where the downed flier was located in the coastal waters where he had fished all his life, and the helicopter pilot obviously did not. The chief's main concern was that an idiot militiaman on shore kept taking pot shots at the helicopter and the bullets were flying everywhere. A few of the errant shots even snapped past his boat. He cursed the stupid soldier and vowed to slit the bastard's throat if he shot one of his fishermen.

Marchand retrieved his radio from his survival vest just as he caught sight of the SAR helicopter only five hundred yards away from him moving in the opposite direction. He keyed the transmit button on the tiny radio and gasped, "Big Motha', this is Checkmate Two in the water. I'm at your six o'clock about one-half click."

The helicopter pilot made a sharp one hundred eighty degree turn and responded, "Checkmate Two, Roger. Press your radio beacon and hang on."

As the helicopter reversed course, the trigger-happy militiaman on shore began firing his AK-47 again. The village chief swore aloud as bullets again zinged past his boat and slapped the water. The SAR pilot cursed as he saw fishing boats approaching the area where Marchand should be. Marchand cursed loudly as one of the AK-47 rounds tore through his right calf muscle. Another bullet punctured the single inflated air bladder of Marchand's life preserver.

Marchand slipped beneath the waves, no longer able to use either leg to swim, having lost buoyancy of the useless life preserver.

Already weak from blood loss and exhaustion, the shock of the bullet's passage through his calf muscle was more than he could withstand. As he drifted downward and his lungs began to fill with seawater, his all-consuming thought was only - Dear God, let her know how much I love her. Keep her safe, Dear God, keep her safe. Margo, I love you. Margo, Margo....

Marchand then slipped into darkness.

He did not see the old chief dive into the clear turquoise water, following his bloody trail through the warm water. He could not feel the village chief's strong hands grab his torso harness and pull him back toward the surface. Marchand did not see the SAR door gunner watching helplessly as the old chief pulled his motionless and apparently lifeless body into the fishing boat. He did not feel himself being dragged over the rickety gunwales into the boat or hear the ancient outboard motor sputter and backfire as it rapidly drove the slender wooden boat back toward the North Vietnamese shoreline. Marchand was beyond all feeling.

THE END.

WHAT FOLLOWS THIS BOOK, PROXY WAR?
LOOK FOR:

VOLUME TWO
of the
PHANTOM WAR TRILOGY:

PHANTOM WAR
Written by E.L. Speed

TO REACH THE AUTHOR
AND FOR
ANNOUNCEMENTS REGARDING
THIS BOOK
AND
OTHER WORKS BY THIS AUTHOR
EMAIL US AT:
info@metaterra.com

AUTHOR'S OBSERVATIONS
ON HISTORICAL FICTION
AND ITS CHARACTERS
(See next page for notes on historical context.)

Telling this complicated story through the lens of historical fiction enables the reader to glimpse the complex historical forces that shaped this protracted and costly war. Writing and narrating this book, *Proxy War*, required dedication to historical facts and personages that I, the author, strove to present carefully and accurately. Thus, historical figures in the person of presidents, politicians and generals were often depicted as engaged in imaginary conversations which nevertheless conveyed the truth of known historical facts. For example, certain fictional scenes in this novel depict President Johnson's well known dictatorial and precise command control over the bombing of North Vietnam and the stealth of President Nixon's secret decision to bomb Cambodia. Thus, dates, places and persons that provide the bedrock of this historical period also provide the framework of this work of fiction. As such, care has been taken to describe the dates and venues accurately. So, battles such as Khe Sanh, general officers such as Vietnamese General Vo Nguyen Giap and American General William Westmoreland are pivotal characters in this book as are American Secretary of Defense McNamara and even the Rev. Martin Luther King.

The central characters of this novel are completely fictional as are the aviators who flew the combat missions described in it. The missions flown by the novel's fictional characters were based upon the experiences of many combat aviators who flew actual missions over North and South Vietnam, Laos and/or Cambodia in one of the greatest combat aircraft ever produced, the F-4 Phantom II. The author meticulously avoided the mention of any specific pilot or flight officer who may have flown combat or served in Vietnam. However, in order to depict realistically the lives and routines of the principal characters in this novel, it was necessary to mention actual American Navy ships and bases involved in combat operations while specific squadrons or aviators are never mentioned. Most importantly, the author emphasizes that any similarity between fictional characters and actual historical persons depicted in this novel is unintentional and purely coincidental.

AUTHOR'S NOTE
REGARDING THE
HISTORICAL CONTEXT FOR
PROXY WAR
(See previous page regarding the Proxy War
historical fiction characters.)

This work of historical fiction is set during the time of America's undeclared war in Vietnam. This War spanned the ten year period between the 1965 Tonkin Gulf Resolution and the final, ignominious departure of American forces from Vietnam in 1975. During those years, two American Presidents, Lyndon Johnson and Richard Nixon, met an intractable foe led by North Vietnamese President Ho Chi Minh. This Vietnam War, as it has been titled, was variously described as a civil war, a war of liberation, a war of Communist aggression, and a war of reunification. In truth, the Vietnam War was to some degree all of these. These several common definitions of this War reflected the range of political perspectives and persuasions of that time. But the War is perhaps best defined as a ***proxy war*** among the three major Cold War protagonists, the United States, the Soviet Union, and the already emerging Eastern giant, the Peoples Republic of China. Especially in retrospect, it is against that Cold War zeitgeist that the notion of the proxy war emerges clearly.

Vietnam provided the three nation state protagonists with a war that was fought in someone else's back yard. It allowed America and the Soviet Union to fight the unresolved conflicts of Berlin, Korea, Cuba and Czechoslovakia without smashing the world into radioactive rubble as certain American and Russian generals would have had it. Indeed, Vietnam provided a crucible for the violent clash of capitalism and communism to be fought without the end it all horror of an actual nuclear war as the Cuban Missile Crisis nearly did. Moreover, the Vietnam War enabled the sleeping Chinese dragon to awaken and exert itself throughout Southeast Asia while keeping the expansionist Vietnamese communists and their Russian ally from controlling the entire Asian subcontinent. All of these conflicts were fought by proxy in the historical kingdom of Annam, now known as Vietnam.

ABOUT THE AUTHOR

The author served as a Navy lieutenant and flight officer during the Vietnam War. He flew more than two hundred combat missions in the War's most famous combat aircraft, the F-4 Phantom II (*pictured on the following page*). The author currently resides in the San Francisco Bay area where he is an avid sailor and lover of fine California wines. *Proxy War* is his debut novel, and the first of several, including *Phantom War,* which is the sequel to *Proxy War* and Volume Two of the Phantom War Trilogy.

The author boarding an
F-4 Phantom in 1968.

ACKNOWLEDGMENT

I wish to acknowledge the outstanding efforts and dedication of my editor and literary advisor, Dr. Angela Browne-Miller. Dr. Browne-Miller's guiding hand and extensive experience were indispensable and invaluable in completing this complex historical novel. Indeed, the final manuscript, which became this book, exceeded my own expectations. Dr. Browne-Miller brought to this project her literary skills, talent and deep experience gained in the writing of nearly forty published works of fiction and non-fiction, and in her editing and ghostwriting of almost one hundred other documents and books. Her extraordinary insight and vision were coupled with equal measures of patience and guidance required by the numerous drafts of *Proxy War*. This author can only hope that *Proxy War* significantly reflects not only Dr. Browne-Miller's awesome literary skills and editorial insight but the tremendous effort she gave to the project. At points where *Proxy War* may deviate somewhat from literary rigueur, I take full responsibility as I may have strayed from the good doctor's literary guidance.

E. L. Speed
February 2012

Books by the Author of the
Foreword to this Book
ANGELA BROWNE-MILLER
http://www.AngelaBrowne-Miller.com

Rewiring Your Self to
Break Addictions and Habits:
Overcoming Problem Patterns
Written by Angela Browne-Miller.

To Have and To Hurt:
Seeing, Changing or Escaping
Patterns of Abuse in Relationships
Written by Angela Browne-Miller.
Foreword by Arun Ghandi.

Will You Still Need Me:
Finding Friends, Love and
Meaning as We Age
Written by Angela Browne-Miller.
Foreword by Evacheska DeAngelis.

Raising Thinking Children and Teens:
Guiding Mental and Moral Development
Written by Angela Browne-Miller.
Foreword by Evacheska DeAngelis.

International Collection on Addictions
Dr. Angela Browne-Miller, Editor.

Violence and Abuse in Society:
Understanding a Global Crisis
Dr. Angela Browne-Miller, Editor.

metaterra®
publications

Metaterra® Publications

Proxy War©, written by E.L. Speed, is published by Metaterra® Publications for general distribution to readers all over the world. Metaterra® Publications is an independent publisher. For other Metaterra® publications, see the website page:

http://www.metaterra.com/novelsbytitle.html

Info@metaterra.com

See also these Metaterra® Publications:

Matumba's Legacy
Written by E.L. Speed.
Afterword by Dr. Angela Browne-Miller.

Still Chattel©
Written by Angela Browne-Miller
Foreword by Angela Browne-Miller.

Project Heartfire©
Volume One: Bloodwin Saga
Written by Alias Skye
Afterword by Angela Browne-Miller.

Maka Shan
Volume One: Maka Shan Saga
Written by Anatarra White Wing
Afterword by Angela Browne-Miller.

The Great Return
Volume Two: Maka Shan Saga
Written by Anatarra White Wing
Afterword by Angela Browne-Miller.

www.ingramcontent.com/pod-product-compliance
Lightning Source LLC
Chambersburg PA
CBHW070342030726
47504CB00001B/39